PEOPLE OF THE SWAMP

People of the Swamp

DARREN KOCH

Angustus Publishing

For my grandchildren's grandchildren

Acknowledgements

I would like to thank Vince Jewell and Anna Demetriou for faithfully reading each chapter of the first draft as it was being written. Your constant encouragement kept me going. You were my first audience and I am deeply grateful.

I also wish to thank Jen Mansfield for proofreading the final draft. You have a critical, academic eye and it greatly improved my work. I rarely appreciate your eyes for being critical. I'm usually too engrossed in their pretty blueness and the little clouds floating in them.

Finally, I'd like to thank everyone who has encouraged and supported me in the writing of this book.

The scientific name for the surviving hominids in this story would be *Homo angustus* (tiny human) but they call themselves *"the people"* In the appendices the scientific term is generally used to denote biological factors and the term, *the people* is used when discussing cultural matters.

 The people don't speak English. I have translated their language into contemporary Australian idiom but some words have no direct translation. See appendices for more information.

Prologue

The old man waved his hand, gesturing beyond the circle of light cast by the flickering fire. Beyond the domes of the burrows, the shadows of huge gum trees were dimly visible. "Long long ago... long before we walked this land there were others. The giants. The ones that called themselves, Sapiens."

The children leaned closer, their eyes shining.

"They were not satisfied with their size. They grew and grew... towering over the bracken. Crushing mice and birds beneath their feet. Cats, Foxes, even dogs feared them. They grew bigger than Kangaroos! We would be no taller than their knees. Soon Sapiens filled every corner of the world.

"But nothing can grow forever. Sapiens grew so big that the whole world was not enough to feed them. Then... They collapsed. Shrinking, starving and shrinking even more. They returned to normal size. Became us... *the people.*"

"What about the rabbits?" One of the little ones asked.

G'pa's face was serious. "They didn't shrink, because they didn't grow too much. They didn't need to shrink."

One of the children looked out into the darkness beyond the hive. The bush seemed full of nameless terrors.

G'ma was carving out the inside of a gum nut to add to the pile of cups beside the fire in the middle of the hive. "But the Rabbits, cats, foxes and birds never forgot," she said. "They never forgave the Sapiens and they'll never forgive us."

"They eat us and we eat them."

PRELUDE

Marked by The Enemy

Fire-in-his-hair

His wife was taken by a cat many years ago. Fire-in-his-hair was never the same after that. He had found her spear, broken and bloody by the edge of the swamp. The damp ground was scuffed and cat tracks littered the area but there was no trace of her body. She was carrying their first litter and he was a young man with bright blue eyes and a hint of auburn in his hair. These were the rare flecks of colour that gave him his name.

Many of the tribe wondered why she had left the safety of the fire that fateful morning. No hunter would wander the bush alone. Some said she was reckless, others said she walked in her sleep, but whatever the immediate cause, everyone agreed she had been marked by the enemy and lured to her death.

Ever since that day, Fire-in-his-hair had not slept well. In his dreams, his wife would be fighting, screaming and calling to him while he would be desperately searching the swamp-lands for her.

Cats did not just kill and eat. They tortured their prey to hone their hunting skills. The more they killed, the better they got at it. Fire-in-his-hair knew that she would not have died easily, but neither would she have sold her life cheaply. She was a fierce woman. Everything she did was fierce. Her fire burned fiercely amongst the furs, she hunted the enemy fiercely. She would have bitten, scratched, punched and kicked long after her spear was taken.

It was Berry season when the cat struck, and the tribe was preparing their new clothes for the coming year. Fire-in-his-hair boiled his furs over and over again in the 'purple flower' leaves. Each boil and soak caused his shirt and leggings to get a deeper shade of green. After several days, Fire-in-his-hair's clothes were nearly black.

Berry changed to Winter and the bereaved young man spent most of his time in his burrow, hardly eating. As the cold weather gave way to Wattle season, the tribe shifted mood but Fire-in-his-hair did not respond like the others.

Wattle is the season when adults become fertile and mate. It's usually a festive occasion, full of laughter, teasing and sexual innuendo as the pheromones fly and the people move into fertility. But Fire-in-his-hair did not return to fertility Instead, some other change occurred within the young man's heart.

When the visiting tribe came for the mating, he picked up his spear and pack, turned his back on the wattle fires and walked into the bush. He was driven by a single goal. To find the cat and kill it.

Cats rarely hunt *the people*. They prefer easier prey; frogs, mice, birds, lizards and of course rabbits. In warmer seasons these form the basis of their diet. But in times of shortage, when food becomes scarce, hunger drives them to risk going after a more dangerous quarry. A straight fight between an armed person and a cat could go either way, and few cats would run that risk. But if a person could be ambushed the odds improve significantly. Of all the enemy, cats were the most cowardly. Fire-in-his-hair was no coward. He would find the cat that killed his wife and face it, spear against claw. He would kill it and bring its carcass back to the tribe. *They eat us, and we eat them.*

He returned to the hive every now and then, making it his base, but he stopped hunting with others and would spend entire nights away from the fire. Many of the tribe whispered that he too had now been 'marked by the enemy' and was destined to sell his life to them soon.

Cursed

The boy was a toddler with no name. Like all the tribe's toddlers, he was forbidden from leaving the fire. To adults, toddlers merged into the amorphous mass called "children" and paid little attention. But this child was different. He was always sitting too far from the fire and staring out into the bush. It was whispered he would soon go the way of those marked by the enemy. All children were told to stay by the safety of the fire and most obeyed. But some were lured beyond the hive by curiosity or sometimes to follow a parent. They would never come back. The enemy marked them, called them and finally devoured them.

After the wattles had bloomed and faded, the weather warmed to Harvest season, the tribe focused their energy on gathering bracken roots. The spears would go out in fists to dig up the roots before the heat dried the soil and made the ground too hard. It was while the spears were out harvesting, that the toddler finally left the fire and set off towards the swamp. No one was surprised. The old G'ma's called and scolded but the child paid no heed. He simply wandered through the twisted tea tree that surrounded the hive and disappeared.

His twin saw him go. She screamed and cried and made to run after him, but a G'ma caught her arm. The little girl squirmed and pulled free. The G'ma's arthritic hand was not strong enough to hold the child and she ran into the bush after her brother.

The boy's mother was called Throws-pretty-well. She and her fist were not far from the hive, harvesting bracken root when they heard the commotion. They all knew which child would be leaving camp. They stopped digging and listened, deciphering the shouts to deduce the story.

When she realised that both her children had left the fire, Throws-pretty-well dropped her digging stick and dashed back towards the hive. Somebody called her back but the mother paid no heed. She ran back to the hive alone. It was taboo to run after a child who left the fire. It was deadly to be away from the hive without your fist at the best of times, but to follow a marked child, was suicide. The enemy would certainly be waiting.

Eventually the other spears gathered themselves into formation and went after her. They followed her trail towards the swamp. When the fist broke cover of the towering tea tree, Throws-pretty-well was at the edge of the swamp about a stone's throw away. She was scolding and struggling with her children as she brought them back.

The spears moved out of cover, called and waved. Throws-pretty-well twitched her mouth in that age old expression of mothers exasperated by their children's poor behaviour. Raising children was hard work.

She didn't see. She only heard...

First the desperate shout, "Enemy above!"

Then the swift swish of wings.

The other spears threw themselves to the ground. They glimpsed the flash of brown feathers and heard a horrified scream. When they looked up, a huge Eagle was flying away, a child in its beak and a woman clutched firmly in its talons. At the edge of the swamp the little boy stood screaming for his mother.

Death was a common event in the tribe's existence but to lose a child and its mother was a double calamity. Many people blamed the strange little boy who wandered away from the fire. It was not uncommon for a child marked by the enemy to sell their life but it was an ominous sign to cause the death of his mother and sister, while staying alive himself. Some around the campfire whispered the toddler may be *cursed*.

Once marked, most people sold their life to the enemy. Spears extracted a heavy price while children cost the enemy very little. But sometimes a person marked by the enemy would not sell their lives at all. They would walk the shadowlands between life and death; the realms of The Great Fire where good and evil struggled. Some shadow walkers became *genius* ... instruments of The Fire, bringing wisdom, life and light into the darkness of the world. Others became instruments of evil, bringing death and destruction to all. These were the *cursed*. It was often difficult to tell who was genius and who was cursed. Young spears were often quick to judge but the old ones would not speak of it until the shadow walker had sold their life to the enemy. Only then could the true value of a life be measured.

As the weather warmed, the child grew thin. Usually, if a mother died before her toddler was weaned, another woman would nurse the child. But no one wanted to nurse a child who could be cursed. He was given enough food from the communal pot but without a nursing mother he was always a little bit hungry. When he moved to the edge of the fire and stared out at the bush, the G'mas and G'pas still called him back, but most of the tribe expected him to wander off again. Some even hoped it would be soon. When night fell, he would sit at the edge of the firelight staring at the tribe with haunted, hungry eyes.

The child wandered off again during Fire season, when the spears were out burning the bush to clear the undergrowth. None of the old ones saw him go but when they eventually noticed, they pursed their lips and shrugged their shoulders sadly.

"Perhaps it was for the best," they said.

Croaks-with-the-frogs

Fire-in-his-hair had been out hunting the cat when his life was saved. During Fire season, cats avoided the hive, prowling the far side of the swamp where there was less competition from *the people*. As the weather warmed, the swamp shrank. Insects would swarm across the rotting vegetation near its edge. The insects attracted lizards and frogs which would call out the cat.

Fire-in-his-hair spent many days following the trail of death left by the cat. Cats hunt at dawn and dusk so those were the best times for Fire-in-his-hair to hunt it. Often he would find himself too far from the hive when darkness fell so he would climb high into a tree and wait out the night. It was dangerous to sleep without a fire but Fire-in-his-hair would not risk alerting the cat to his presence. Fire drives the enemy away, and that was the last thing he wanted to do.

The sun was very low when Fire-in-his-hair returned to the hive. Its last rays tinged the forest with a golden glow. The hive was built a good stone's throw from the winter edge of the swamp and was surrounded on all sides by the tea tree forest. The tea tree was twisted and gnarled near the hive, forming a tangled mass that protected against attacks from the sky. The forest stretched further in the other directions until it gave way to the open grasslands the tribe cleared each year by burning. The grasslands were home to the pair of rabbit warrens which provided the swamp people with most of their meat.

The spears would burn most of the day and stay near the safety of their burns until after the danger of dusk had passed. Only the old and children would be in the hive when Fire-in-his-hair returned from his hunt.

The smell of the campfire stirred conflicting emotions in Fire-in-his-hair as he approached. All his life, that smell had been associated with safety and comfort but now a new feeling had been added to the mix, the bitter scourge of memory. In his mind, his dead wife was laughing by the fire. He could smell her hair and remember her stories. The elders said these memories would become sweet some day but for now, they only brought him pain and rage. He needed another kill. He would bring another enemy back to the hive. He veered to his left and approached the swamp. He could hear the croaking of the frogs in the distance and he decided to gather some.

By the time he had found and killed a large frog, the light was fading. He left the swamp and headed to the hive. At the edge of the tea tree, he heard a deeper croak, longer lasting and clearly belonging to a larger animal. He readied his spear and approached from downwind. Amongst the damp reeds at the edge of the water, Fire-in-his-hair saw him. He was curled in foetal position, sucking his thumb and alternatively whimpering and snoring. It was the marked child.

The hunter felt a surge of annoyance. This boy would not show any resistance to the enemy. For a moment he contemplated walking away and leaving the child to his fate but something about the child's weakness, caused another feeling to stir within him.

That evening, in the dusky gloom, Fire-in-his-hair returned to the hive, his spear in his right hand, the dead frog in his left and the little boy clinging to his neck.

That night, after sharing the frog with the child, Fire-in-his-hair lay in his burrow and listened to the soft snores of the other spears pressed closely against him. As he thought of his dead wife, the cat and the strange, marked child, a plan began to form. The child was marked, no doubt about that but many around the fire whispered he was also cursed. A cursed child would draw predators to him like a carcass draws flies. Was it possible the child would draw the cat?

As the faint morning light stained the eastern sky, Fire-in-his-hair crawled into the children's burrow. Using his hunter's sense of smell to guide him in the dark, he found the child and gently shook him awake. "You wanna come with me?" He asked simply.

The child didn't answer. He simply crawled out from his fur, put his rabbit pelt hat on his head, and pulled on his moccasin like shoes. He silently followed Fire-in-his-hair out of the hive and into the tea tree.

So began the strange relationship. Each dawn til dusk Fire-in-his-hair would take the child with him as he searched for the cat. Neither the child nor the man realised that a bigger fire was smouldering beneath the surface of their simple goals and hopes.

As the seasons changed, Fire-in-his-hair was surprised to find himself enjoying the company of the little boy. He was bright and curious, always asking questions and listening deeply to the short fragmented answers the man discarded.

Gradually a hint of light returned to the eyes of Fire-in-his-hair. The marked child never lost the hungry look but as he grew, his feelings for Fire-in-his-hair developed from trust to hero worship.

Over the years, Fire-in-his-hair continued to take the boy with him as they hunted for the cat but they would light a small camp fire to keep warm overnight. His lost wife still filled his dreams with trauma but the child got used to the cries of the man in the night. Eventually the strange little boy entered into a gangly adolescence and whilst some in the tribe never trusted him, he found his own place on the edge of the community. When the boy was eventually called to the Winter fire to receive his name and spear, G'pa called for a name-giver. Fire-in-his-hair slowly got to his feet.

"His name is Croaks-with-the-frogs," he said quietly.

SCAVENGERS

If G'ma thinks so

It was high summer. The season of Smoke. The air was thick with the detritus of bush fires and the sun was an angry orange ball glowering over the tea tree. Fire-in-his-hair and Croaks-with-the-frogs returned to the hive, with a pair of minor birds hanging from their waists. By now the tribe had learned to accept the comings and goings of the strange pair, and they were grateful for the meat they brought back to the tribe whenever they returned. Fire-in-his-hair nodded silently in response to a few muttered words of appreciation. The rigours of his life had aged him more than most men of his age. Deep vertical lines carved his face, and there was now a heavy dose of grey through his tightly curled beard. A small white scar marked his right cheekbone and another jagged across his chin creating a bald patch in his beard. In spite of the wear and tear on his body, his eyes were still hard and blue.

Croaks-with-the-frogs followed him dutifully as he made his way to where the large bonfire crackled and spat in the centre of the hive. The harsh life seemed to have taken a different toll on the younger man. He was skinny, with a shock of dark hair and luminous brown eyes but there was a feral quality to him that caused many in tribe to keep their distance. His rabbit skin clothes were still smokey and un-died like all spears of his age but they were stained and frayed. After a brief exchange of words with Fire-in-his-hair, the young man handed the older his pair of birds and retreated to a niche between two burrows and curled up. He was asleep almost immediately.

Fire-in-his-hair crouched before a flat rock and began butchering the birds. Once prepared, he would add them to the large pottery cauldrons of stew that permanently simmered on the edge of the fire. The cauldrons were continually replenished by whatever food was brought into the hive. The flavour changed with the seasons as different meats, roots, leaves and fruits were added.

Fire-his-hair was plucking the feathers and didn't see the woman walk over.

"That's a good haul," she said.

He looked up at her silently for a long moment as he struggled to remember her name. She was not much younger than him. Her straight black hair was tied off her face with a simple thong and her brown eyes were bright. But flecks of grey in her hair and tell tale lines around her mouth and eyes betrayed her age. Most names have a childhood story associated with it, but this woman's story simply wouldn't come into his mind.

Seeing his blank expression, the woman smiled and shook her head. *Fire-his-hair is a strange fellow.* Still standing, she lifted a leg and poked her foot towards him. The brown rabbit fur shoe was only a hand span from his face.

"Ah!" said Fire-his-hair, flatly. "No-point-shoe! Shit sorry."

The woman squatted beside him laughing. "Never mind, it's not a very interesting name story," she said. "The little girl who keeps losing her shoe."

Fire-in-his-hair smiled but said nothing.

No-point-shoe gestured towards the birds. "You came back with a good haul," she said.

The older man nodded and returned to his butchering.

"You planning to stay around for long?"

"Might head off tomorrow."

No-point-shoe took a bird and began pulling out its feathers. "I'm taking a fist of spears out to track the dogs tomorrow."

Fire-in-his-hair nodded silently.

"But I'm short a point. I'd like you and the kid to come with us," she said.

Fire-in-his-hair pursed his lips. "Who else are you taking?"

"Finder-of-snails and Me-not-talking."

Fire-in-his-hair counted on his fingers. "Thumb, point, tall...What about Sleeps-in-the-sun?"

No-point-shoe smiled inwardly, amazed at how little Fire-in-his-hair knew about the comings and goings of the tribe. "We might be tracking for a few days. Sleeps-in-the sun and Finder-of-snails have a litter," she said. "She's breastfeeding and can't be away from the babies for so long."

He nodded slowly. "So you'll only need a thumb to replace Sleeps-in-the-sun, won't you? Didn't you have a kid in your fist?"

The jaw muscle of No-point-shoe tightened. "We lost her down the rabbit warren last hunt."

Fire-his-hair screwed up his face. "There's no easy way to die," he said softly. "So you want me and Croaks-with-the-frogs to round out the fist."

"Yeah."

Fire-in-his-hair stared at the ground for a long moment. Then he got up, hoisted a log of wood nearly as big as himself and threw it on the fire. The fire spat and threw sparks. He stood staring at it, a faint smile lingering on his face. "We were going to go after the cat."

No-point-shoe pushed down her annoyance. "Well G'ma suggested I ask you," she said, her voice hardening. "But ..." She left the sentence hanging and went back to butchering the birds.

The smile slowly faded from Fire-in-his-hair's face. He watched her work for a moment, then said, "Well... if G'ma thinks so."

Leaving the hive

The fist were up before dawn. The sky was dark, the stars shining like distant fires but the moon had slipped below the tree line and was beyond sight. The protective ring of burrows where the rest of the tribe slept were pale mounds flickering in the firelight. Beyond them the tea tree forest loomed, black and foreboding.

No-point-shoe stood by the fire in the middle of the hive eating a cold cake from last night. Finder-of-snails and Me-not-talking were warming their cakes on the rocks around the fire's edge. No-point-shoe's practiced eye could see the hint of brightness revealing where the sun would soon rise. The dogs would be running soon. The spears had to be ready.

Near the opening of the hive, Fire-in-his-hair checked the coal carrier Croaks-with-the-frogs had made. As the youngest spear, Croaks-with-the-frogs would be responsible for carrying the fire. It was a crucial task and the survival of the fist depended on it.

"Only the Fire protects us." No-point-shoe intoned softly.

She would have preferred to have given the coal to any of the other spears but Croaks-with-the-frogs was too young to risk in the front line. He was too slow a runner to use as a scout and as it was his first scavenge, he would be of no use in the treetops.

Tracking dogs was a dangerous task. She didn't want the strange pair on this trip and neither did Finder-of-snails or

Me-not-talking. But G'ma had insisted that it was time to bring Fire-his-hair back to the fists.

Croaks-with-the-frogs frowned while Fire-in-his-hair checked his coal carrier. For most spears, the carrying of a coal was a specialised task only learned after many seasons of tutoring, but Croaks-with-the-frogs had been carrying the coal for Fire-in-his-hair for as long as he could remember.

"You don't need to check it," Croaks-with-the-frogs said sourly.

Fire-in-his-hair twitched his left eye in a faint semblance of a wink. "I know." He flicked his eyes towards where No-point-shoe and the others sat huddled by the fire. "But they need to see me check it."

Only slightly mollified, Croaks-with-the-frogs slipped into his role. He stared at his coal carrier as if he was waiting for Fire-in-his-hair's approval, a surly expression still on his face.

Fire-in-his-hair made a show of checking the carrier. He moved a bit of the dry grass to check the green grass beneath it. He lifted the corners of the green gum leaves, pretending to check their placement, and the layout of the rabbit skin pouch. Finally, he sat back on his heels. "That's good," he said. "Now just before we leave, I'll grab you a nice coal from the fire and then I'll wrap it for you."

Even in the dim light of the fire, Fire-in-his-hair could see Croaks-with-the-frogs' eyes bulging with frustration. He let the boy stew for a moment before letting his facade slip to reveal a wicked grin. Teasing Croaks-with-the-frogs was always the best way to drag him out of his moods.

It worked. The boy turned to look out into the bush but a smile curled the corners of his mouth.

No-point-shoe finished the last of her cake and pushed herself to her feet. "Rightio! Let's get going," she said.

Me-not-talking looked hungrily at the freshly warmed cakes. "Aw!"

Finder-of-snails laughed. "When she says 'go,' we go," he said. He slung his pack onto his back and picked up his spear. "Come on, girl, carry it in your other hand. We can eat them on the run."

Fire-his-hair and Croaks-with-the-frogs hoisted their packs as well. The coal was warm at Croaks-with-the-frogs' back.

No-point-shoe moved out of the hive into the dark. The fist took shape behind her in single file.

No-point-shoe was in command so she took the most dangerous position. Finder-of-snails followed her as cover. Fire-in-his-hair took the rearguard with Croaks-with-the-frogs in the middle.

Beyond the ring of burrows that formed the hive, the tea tree was stunted and twisted. It curved over the hunters' heads creating a protective canopy, leaving gaps of cleared ground beneath. Long years of coming and going had created several paths through the bush. The main path lead west to the swamp but No-point-shoe turned right and led the fist around the hive and away to the east.

Being surrounded by spears as he walked through the bush was an unusual experience for Croaks-with-the-frogs. In their hunts for the cat, he always went in front. That way Fire-in-his-hair could keep an eye on him. He had become used to the danger and found it normal. Now, protected front and back, Croaks-with-the-frogs felt constrained. He fought down an irrational urge to run away.

"Hey, Kid." Me-not-talking was only a point of years older than Croaks-with-the-frogs, but she still called him kid. She spoke through a mouthful of cake so her words were muffled. "Why haven't you had breakfast?"

Croaks-with-the-frogs kept his eyes front, but half turned his head towards the voice behind him.

"We had some banksia syrup," he said.

"Cha, ya!" said Me-not-talking in an annoyed tone. "But why? Why no breakfast. No cake? It's not good to go out hungry."

Croaks-with-the-frogs swallowed. He wished Fire-in-his-hair would say something but he was silent.

Me-not-talking was still going. "You need food. You should have had breakfast."

Me-not-talking was well suited to her name story. Once she had a thought in her head, it would simply spill out of her mouth. Croaks-with-the-frogs often watched her as she cornered some unfortunate tribe-member and talked at them until their eyes turned to puddles. He wondered how it was possible for a single person to have so much to say. It was clear she was not going to stop until she got an answer.

"The syrup would give us energy," he said. "But it won't fill our bellies. Fire-in-his-hair likes to face the enemy hungry."

Me-not-talking lapsed into a puzzled silence whilst at the rear of the column, Fire-in-his-hair smiled silently.

By the time they had got to the edge of the tea tree the sun was poking through the trees behind them. The freshly burned grassland which stretched before them was sprouting new growth.

No-point-shoe sniffed the air, scoured the sky and listened, a thoughtful expression on her face. "We break for that tree," she said, pointing with her spear. "When I say."

Croaks-with-the-frogs crouched silently and crushed the fear that rose in his guts. The tree was a good sprint from the edge of the cover. They would be in danger the whole way. He had done these runs before, when hunting the cat with Fire-in-his-hair but he never got used to them. Somewhere deep in his memory he vaguely sensed horror swooping from the skies, a terrified scream and the yawning emptiness of being alone.

"Ready? Go!" No-point-shoe broke from the tea tree and dashed out into the opening.

The others ran with her, Fire-in-his-hair searching the sky for threats.

You want an egg?

The fist reached the safety of the tree, blowing hard. The tree, whilst not overly large, gave good cover. The trunk was about as wide as Croaks-with-the-frogs was tall and the canopy towered above them creating a large protected space where they were safe from eagles and hawks.

Finder-of-snails and Me-not-talking threw themselves into a hollow formed between two roots and stared at the sky while No-point-shoe crouched at the drip line and looked out at the grasslands. Croaks-with-the-frogs leaned against the trunk and watched Fire-in-his-hair. The older man was breathing hard between clenched teeth, a wild angry look on his face. He scanned the tree and sniffed the air. A grin crept across his face. "You want an egg?" he said.

Croaks-with-the-frogs was famished. He looked into the tree where the morning sun tinged the canopy. There was movement up there.

"Enemy above!" called Croaks-with-the-frogs.

No-point-shoe threw herself back towards the trunk and rolled expertly into a defensive position, a knee pointed forwards, her back propped against the trunk and her spear pointing out and up. Above her a wattlebird swooped and returned to the nest.

Fire-in-his-hair shot Croaks-with-the-frogs a quick wink. "Come on," he said softly and began to climb.

Croaks-with-the-frogs dropped his coal carrier beside the trunk and followed.

"What are you doing? What are you doing!?" called Me-not-talking.

No-point-shoe ignored her. She gestured to Finder-of-snails. "Get the fire lit, *Brudha*," she said and returned to scanning the western horizon.

Fire-in-his-hair and Croaks-with-the-frogs drew all the attention of the wattle birds as they climbed the tree, leaving the other spears relatively safe on the ground below. Wattle birds usually lay their first clutch of eggs in Wattle season and sometimes have another in Fire but for some reason, this pair had nested late. The birds' desperate attempt to defend their nest revealed that eggs were hidden there. They screeched and swooped at the humans as they approached.

Fire-in-his-hair copped the most attention. Both birds hammered him from above. Every few swoops, a bird would try to strike Croaks-with-the-frogs from below as they returned to position on the branch. The humans clung close to the trunk and pushed on, finding handholds in the thick bark.

Fire-in-his-hair reached the fork where the main branch pushed up and out from the trunk. His feet braced against the branch and his back pressed against the trunk, he looked around the canopy. The nest was wedged in a smaller fork at the end of that branch. As Croaks-with-the-frogs reached the bottom of the fork, the older man pointed. A secondary branch hung only a few *lengths* above the nest. Amongst its leaves was a cluster of decent sized gum-nuts. "There," he said.

They had done this before and Croaks-with-the-frogs knew his role.

"Now!" called Fire-in-his-hair and they swung into action.

The older man climbed towards the nest while Croaks-with-the-frogs scrambled into the higher branch and made for the cluster of gum-nuts.

The wattle birds erupted into a frenzy of screeching and swooping. A bird struck Croaks-with-the-frogs hard on the side of his chest. The shock reverberated through his body and he clung to the branch to avoid falling. His rabbit pelt shirt tore and warm blood seeped beneath his arm. He pushed on desperately. He had to get to the gum-nuts.

With both hunters receiving the same number of attacks, Fire-in-his-hair was able to make better time as he crawled across the branch, but it soon became apparent to the birds that he was by far the greatest threat and they focussed all their attention on him.

By the time Croaks-with-the-frogs had reached the cluster of gum-nuts, Fire-in-his-hair was still a few *lengths* from the nest. A bird had latched itself onto his back, a claw digging into each of his shoulders. It was pecking fiercely at the back of his head. The other bird was swooping at his legs, trying to dislodge him from the branch.

Croaks-with-the-frogs pulled off a gum-nut, took aim at the bird on his friend's back and threw. The gum-nut struck with impeccable accuracy, hitting the bird at the top of its beak. It screeched and flew off. This brought only a brief respite before the birds renewed their swooping. Croaks-with-the-frogs threw again and again. His throws were less effective against the moving targets but they kept the birds off balance and gave Fire-in-his-hair room to move.

As a bird swooped close once more, Fire-in-his-hair thrust up with his spear. The momentum of the bird was enough for his spear to pierce the wing and lodge there. It was wrenched from his hand and both bird and spear tumbled to the ground below.

"Point spear! Point spear," he called.

Croaks-with-the-frogs reacted instantly, throwing his spear across the gap. Fire-in-his-hair caught and swung it into the path of the remaining bird. The point slammed into its breast and the last bird screeched. Both bird and spear plummeted out of the tree.

Fire-in-his-hair reached the nest and looked in. "Tall," he called. "Tall, eggs." He slipped an egg into the pouch at the back of his shirt and grabbed another in his hand and scurried down.

Croaks-with-the-frogs crawled across to the nest, grabbed the last egg and slipped it into his pouch. He followed Fire-in-his-hair to the ground.

No-point-shoe

The others were kneeling around the fire, staring into the flames, when Croak-with-the-frogs got to the bottom of the tree. The birds were laid aside with the eggs Fire-his-hair had brought down. Croaks-with-the-frogs added his egg to the pile and took his place in the circle.

No-point-shoe held her hands palm out towards the fire. "Return to the Fire," she began.

"Return to the Fire," the others replied.

"We come from the Fire."

"Return to the Fire," they repeated.

"Only the Fire protects us."

"Return to the Fire," they said.

"The Fire burns within us."

"Return to the Fire."

"And when our time comes," No-point-shoe paused and the whole fist said together.

"We will return to the Fire."

When Croaks-with-the-frogs would go bush with Fire-in-his-hair alone, they never bothered with the Fire litany but Fire-in-his-hair prepared him last night. The young boy looked across at his mentor who gave him a sly smile and an affirming nod. Croaks-with-the-frogs beamed.

As soon as the litany was over, the spears moved into action. Finder-of-snails continued working on the fire, gathering fallen twigs from the tree where they sheltered and chopping larger branches so the fire would last. Me-not-talking pulled the feathers off the wattle birds and prepared them for cooking.

No-point-shoe opened her pack and brought out a gum nut filled with a waxy amber paste. She approached Fire-in-his-hair with a determined look. "You're an *ashen* mess," she said cheerfully.

It was true. Fire-in-his-hair had scratches all over his neck and deep cuts above his right eye and at the back of his head. Blood was running down the side of his face and the back of his neck, soaking into his rabbit fur shirt. He recoiled as she approached him. "What are you doing?"

No-point-shoe's manner changed from cheerful to firm. "Can't let those cuts be," she said as she crouched beside him. "Your fire will run wild and you'll be dead."

"It'll be alright." He moved his head away.

"It will not be alright!" No-point-shoe spoke through gritted teeth. A hidden rage seeped to the surface and Fire-in-his hair stopped resisting.

"What is that stuff?" he asked.

"Pine resin and tea tree oil."

The old hunter laughed nervously. "You trying to turn me into glue?"

"Shut up!" she said.

Finder-of-snails didn't look up from the fire. "Best just to let her do it, Fire-in-his-hair."

Me-not-talking had stopped working on the birds and was watching the exchange. "Her husband died when his fire ran wild. He died in his burrow. You don't want to die in the burrow!"

No-point-shoe gave her a withering look.

Finder-of-snails snarled at her. "Tsh! That's not your story to tell, you dumb bunny!"

Me-not-talking seemed to shrink a little. Her eyes went wide and she fell silent.

For a moment the atmosphere around the fire was strained, then as if some inner tension had been released, No-point-shoe exhaled slowly, her shoulders sagged.

She continued to smear the paste on Fire-in-his-hair's cuts but she spoke in a low voice. "It's my story. It's his story. But I suppose you might as well hear about it from me. If you guys had stayed around the hive more, you'd already know."

Croaks-with-the-frogs leaned forward to hear better. He didn't regret his hunting days with Fire-in-his-hair but he had missed a lot of campfire time and part of him yearned for it. He wrapped his arm around himself and used his hand to squeeze the cut under his armpit closed. He didn't know why, but he was afraid to tell the others he too had been wounded.

No-point-shoe was still talking. "My husband was Jumps-a-branch. He died last Berry when his fire ran wild. We were hunting rabbits and he was bitten and scratched. That thing must have had poison in it. We thought nothing of it. Just brought the kill back to the hive. The bite was on his shoulder, hidden beneath the top of his shirt. No one saw it, and we didn't mention it."

She finished closing the cuts. The orange paste made clumps over the wounds in Fire-in-his-hair's head. She got up, went back to her side of the fire and sat crossed legged, staring into the flames.

"The next night, Jumps-a-branch was hot. He thrashed around and kicked the covers off. The following morning, he was covered in sweat and barely able to speak. I called G'ma and she saw the bite." No-point-shoe's voice broke and she paused, fighting to regain control. "G'ma was furious. 'Stupid foxheaded thing,' she said. She said we should have told her. She said..."

The morning sun was high now, shining through the smoke haze and warming the land. The plains were brightly lit but No-point-shoe shivered. "She said my stupidity killed him."

The others sat staring, dumbfounded.

"That's a terrible thing to say," Fire-in-his-hair said bitterly.

"She apologised. Straight away, she said she was sorry, and hugged me. But... The fact was. It was true. I killed him." No-point-shoe's tears flowed freely. "He died in the burrow. He had no chance to sell his life to the enemy. They got him for free."

"*Pargronts*," muttered Fire-in-his-hair.

No-point-shoe looked up from the flames. Her eyes were red and streaks of dirt marked the tracks of her tears. Her face was feral. "So when they scratch you or bite you, you bloody well put resin on it. Nobody wants to die in the burrow."

"Nobody wants to die in the burrow," Me-not-talking echoed softly.

This was Croaks-with-the-frogs last chance to mention the cut under his arm. He knew he should speak. He even opened his mouth.

"Right!" No-point-shoe pushed herself to her feet. "Let's get these birds cooked."

The rest of the fist started moving. The fire was pushed slightly to the side, exposing a warm bed of ash. Finder-of-snails poked a hole in the top of the eggs with the tip of his spear and buried them in the ashes. Me-not-talking finished plucking the feathers while No-point-shoe set up a spit across the fire using sticks. Within a few moments, the birds were roasting and a gentle calm had settled over the camp site.

Dying in the burrow

Croaks-with-the-frogs squeezed his side harder and hoped no one would see the blood stain. The others had settled into their own routines. Finder-of-snails was focussed on watching the food and the fire. Me-not-talking was sitting beside him talking about the how good they smelt and how much she was looking forward to eating them.

No-point-shoe had returned to the edge of the tree line scanning the horizon and the sky. Fire-in-his-hair sat with his back propped against the trunk of the tree. He had pulled off some dried sap and was chewing it thoughtfully, his eyes staring blankly into the canopy. Croaks-with-the-frogs sat beside him. "What now?"

Fire-in-his-hair kept his eyes on the branches above. "We eat, and we wait until the dogs howl."

Finder-of-snails looked up from the campfire. He was keen to disengage from Me-not-talking. "They'll be tracking the roos now," he said. "But they'll be doing it silently. Once they start the chase, we'll hear them barking. Then we run."

Croaks-with-the-frogs nodded. He tried to think of something else to say to make the conversation go on. That way they wouldn't have to listen to Me-not-talking for a while, but nothing came to him.

Me-not-talking said, "I hope there's still some nice meat on the bones by the time we get there. I remember once we got almost an entire tail. Have you ever eaten kangaroo? I like it. It's rich..."

Croaks-with-the-frogs closed his eyes.

Me-not-talking laughed. "Are you tired already?" She turned her attention back to Finder-of-snails and went on talking about kangaroo meat.

Kangaroos were the largest herbivore in the land. Sometimes eagles would take their joeys and had even been known to hunt adult kangaroos in teams but on the ground, only dogs could hunt them. Tracking the dogs and scavenging was the only way for the tribe to get kangaroo. It was dangerous, but the benefits were great.

Dogs were the largest and most dangerous predator. A fully grown man would be no taller than a dog's shoulder. Dogs were fast, strong and deadly. A single dog could tear a fist of spears apart and dogs hunted in packs. If it weren't for the Fire, people would have no defence against them. Fortunately, dogs rarely bothered with humans. They usually preferred larger prey.

Croaks-with-the-frogs leaned in and whispered. "Fire-in-his-hair, why is it so bad to die in the burrow?"

The older man sat silently for such a long time that Croaks-with-the-frogs wondered if he hadn't heard the question. Finally Fire-in-his-hair looked away from the branches and stared at him. "You don't want to give your life away for free," he said. "Everyone loses their life eventually but when the enemy takes it, you want them to fight for it. Maybe you can scratch an eye or even a bone could get stuck in their throat. If you die in the burrow, it costs the enemy nothing."

No-point-shoe had been moving around the edge of the tree line, she caught the tail end of the conversation. "Also," she said. "When you sell your life to the enemy, you return to the fire naturally. If you die in the burrow, the tribe has to take you out and return you to the fire."

Croaks-with-the-frogs remembered the funeral pyres, large platforms of wood raised above the great bonfire in the centre of the hive. He remembered the terrible sadness that overwhelmed the tribe. No one could cook or boil water until the dead person had returned to the fire and left only ashes. He rarely stayed around for long on those days. Fire-in-his-hair would get angry and take him away hunting the cat.

The chase

After their meal, the hunters took it in turns to climb the tree and scan the plain for signs of roo. The sun was a crimson orb sinking into the smoke haze when Finder-of-snails called out. "Movement! Movement over there." His arm pointed to the north. "Heading west."

The fist leapt into action. Croaks-with-the-frogs grabbed a suitable coal from the fire and wrapped it in a new fire carrier and the others hoisted their packs and spears. No-point-shoe moved out beyond the tree line. "That tuft of grass looks reasonable cover," she said. "Let's go."

Finder-of-snails, Croaks-with-the-frogs and Me-not-talking sprinted after her while Fire-in-his-hair kicked the fire apart and threw dirt on the flames. Then he took up his usual position at the rear. Eyes scanning the sky for threats.

By nightfall, the fist was only a few sprints from the Kangaroos. The mob had finished their dusk feed and had entered a thicket of tea tree. From the top of a large gum, No-point-shoe could see the open space where they sheltered. Rather than risk a full fire, Croaks-with-the-frogs used the coal to set a small blaze on the other side of the tree trunk.

"I'll take this watch," said No-point-shoe as she fed the flames. "Finder-of-snails, I'll wake you next and Fire-in-his-hair can take care of the fire before dawn."

The others climbed into the tree to snatch some sleep.

Croaks-with-the-frogs found a place where a tall of branches splayed out, he lay across them on his stomach staring at the ground.

Below him, Me-not-talking looked up from her place. She was propped on a large branch with her back to the trunk. "You ever slept in a tree before?" she called. "You won't get much sleep tonight." She smiled. The idea that Croaks-with-the-frogs would not sleep well seemed to give her pleasure.

Croaks-with-the-frogs looked at her silently for a moment, then closed his eyes.

"You won't get much rest on your stomach," she called.

"Nobody is going to get any rest if you don't shut up!" said Finder-of-snails, laughing.

Fire-in-his-hair leaned out from his place amongst some mistletoe. "Croaks-with-the-frogs always sleeps on his front when he's in a tree. He likes it."

Me-not-talking let a out a small squeak of disappointment and went silent.

Croaks-with-the-frogs buried his face in the crook of his arm and smiled.

The eastern sky was a pinky grey when the hunters were woken by the dogs barking. They roused themselves as the roos broke from the cover of the tea tree and bounded towards the south east, a point of dogs chasing.

The fist climbed down quickly. Croaks-with-the-frogs took a new coal from the fire and wrapped it. By the time they were ready to go, the kangaroos were over a *scout* away but the barking of the dogs ensured they would not escape.

The fist ran all morning, eating only the flies they could catch on the run. The sounds of the hunt gradually got further away.

When the sun was past its zenith, the energy of the fleeing roos was sapped. The dogs' barking changed to a mournful howl. No-point-shoe crouched in the grass and turned back to the others with a malicious grin. "They've got 'em. They're feeding," she said.

A gum tree towered between them and the howling dogs. She led the fist to it and they rested around the trunk as Finder-of-snails climbed up to scout the area. "I can see them," he said. "A few *scouts* away."

No-point-shoe looked at the sun slowly sinking. "We've gotta move. We've gotta get there before dark."

Croaks-with-the-frogs was hurting. The long run had exhausted him and the wound in his side had opened up again. The blood resumed seeping into his shirt. But there was no time to say anything now. The fist was on the move and he had to keep up.

The grass was long, almost over their heads. They only needed to crouch to ensure they could not be seen. The fist pushed through at a brisk pace in single file. No-point-shoe's uncanny sense of direction lead them straight towards the feeding site.

The battle

No-point-shoe called them to a halt as the sun turned red in the west, painting the scattered clouds with a soft orange tint. She had brought the fist within a good sprint of the feeding dogs. The wind was at their back driving their scent towards the pack. Croaks-with-the-frogs unwrapped his coal and relit the fire in the shelter of a scrubby wattle.

Finder-of-snails climbed up to survey the scene. From his vantage point he could get a clear view of the dogs feeding. This was the most important part of his task. He had to decide when to move on the pack. If he waited too long, the dogs would have eaten all the meat and broken the bones, rendering them useless. If he called the fist in too early, the dogs would still be hungry and they'd fight to keep their kill. If the dogs resisted, the fist would be lucky to get out alive.

He waited until the dominant dogs had finished and were dozing contentedly in the twilight. A few of the pack were gnawing on bones half heartedly but only a single dog was truly feeding. It was time. "They're ready!" he called.

No-point-shoe and Fire-in-his-hair pulled a branch of pine from their packs. Each branch was topped with a large lump of hardened pine sap. They plunged the branches into the fire and the resin tips erupted into flames.

"*Only the fire protects us,*" chanted No-point-shoe.

The others grabbed sticks and leaves from the around the base of the tree, set them on fire and threw them into the dry grass. They smouldered there, giving off thin columns of smoke. The blazing torches were given to Me-not-talking and Croaks-with-the-frogs. As the youngest spears they would be responsible for burning the grass and holding the torches aloft. The others would defend them with their spears.

The fist moved steadily towards the fallen roo. No-point-shoe held the centre, her face contorted in rage. On each flank Fire-in-his-hair and Finder-of-snails crouched and roared defiance. Croaks-with-the-frogs and Me-not-talking moved back and forth across the line setting fires wherever they went.

The first dogs caught the whiff of smoke and snarled. As they saw the approaching humans, more of them left off their feeding and approached. The two groups drew to within a good stone's throw of each other. For an instant, Finder-of-snails feared he had called the fist in too early and the dogs were going to fight. But as the fires grew around them and the smoke increased, the dominant dogs, who had finished feeding, backed away. The other dogs did likewise, snarling and snapping. On their own the humans were no threat, but the smoke in the air and the sight of flames set off instinctive warning signals. The last dog crouched over the carcass of the roo. He was still hungry and reluctant to abandon his meal to the fire. He glanced at his retreating pack and turned, snarling at the approaching fist.

No-point-shoe pointed at the remaining dog. "Let's take him!" she screamed.

With that, the hunters charged, Croaks-with-the-frogs and Me-not-talking carrying their brands high. When they got within a few *lengths* of the dog, Croaks-with-the-frogs threw his blazing torch flush into its face. The dog yelped, and jumped from the carcass and fled snarling towards the rest of his pack.

The humans clambered over their prize, cheering and whooping.

The grass fire was not big but there was enough smoke and flames to deter any attack from the air. The fist had run all day with little food. They fell on the carcass with gusto. The skull was smashed, exposing the brain and the fist shared it amongst themselves, the raw matter smearing their faces.

"They eat us," chanted No-point-shoe.

"And we eat them!" responded the others triumphantly.

Croaks-with-the-frogs looked around the group and smiled. He had never belonged before, but now they were all smiling at him and making eye contact.

Finder-of-snails slapped him on the back. "Sizzling throw, kid," he said. "You planted that resin fair on that dog's muzzle."

The others laughed in agreement and Fire-in-his-hair looked at him with pride.

No-point-shoe didn't glory in the triumph for long, she was soon scanning the surroundings again. "C'mon," she said briskly. "We gotta set camp." She gathered some of the still burning grass into a small pile. "Get some wood."

Using the fading grass fire as tinder, the fist collected wood and leaves and set a proper campfire. They roasted the leftover meat on skewers and sat long into the night, eating and harvesting as much as they could from the carcass.

They slept in shifts, taking it in turns to watch the fire and eat from the carcass. By the time the sun was clear of the tea tree, the last of them were awake and the fist prepared to leave.

The carcass only had meat to feed the tribe for a single meal but that was not the main purpose of the quest. The most valuable things scavenged were the bones, the teeth and the claws. These made excellent tools. Each hunter carried a share of the meat and some bones or claws. No-point-shoe cut off as much the undamaged skin as she could carry and rolled it into her pack. Fire-in-his-hair hoisted the mighty jaws onto his back with all the valuable teeth. No-point-shoe looked at him with admiration but the old hunter did not notice.

The journey home

By mid morning the fist was travelling. Behind them, crows fought over the remains. They moved slowly, burdened by the weight in their packs. Their sprints across open ground had to be shorter. The wound in Croaks-with-the-frogs' side had scabbed overnight but as the day's hard running wore on, he could feel the slow seep of blood at his side.

No-point-shoe had hoped to make the shelter of the tea tree before dark, so they didn't stop for lunch. Their stomachs were full from the night before but the lack of rest began to take its toll on the youngsters.

"Hey!" Me-not-talking said as they caught their breath beneath a copse of blackberry. "Are you OK? You seem to be flagging."

If it had been anybody other than Me-not-talking who had asked, Croaks-with-the-frogs would have admitted to his wound. But something about the young girl's manner annoyed him. She seemed to want him to fail. "I'm alright," he said.

Fire-in-his-hair looked hard at him but Croaks-with-the-frogs didn't make eye contact.

As the sun began to sink, it became clear the fist wasn't going to make it to the tea tree before dark. They were all struggling with their weights and panting. They'd dare not be caught in the open at dusk. That's when foxes, cats and owls would hunt. No-point-shoe led them to a cluster of thin wattles and called a halt for the night. Croaks-with-the-frogs lit the fire again and they cooked some more of the kangaroo. The elation of the previous night had faded after the long, hard run.

"I'm sorry we didn't make the tea tree, *Bruhds.*" No-point-shoe said. She grinned at Fire-in-his-hair. "Running across the plains is harder work than creeping around the swamp, eh?"

The old hunter smiled and nodded.

"Get some rest, I'll tend the fire for the first nap."

Croaks-with-the-frogs rolled himself into his rabbit pelt with relief. He fell asleep almost immediately but his sleep was full of tortured dreams of running across the plains with his stomach torn open.

He woke to a gentle shaking. "C'mon, kid," Finder-of-snails said softly. "We're moving."

Croaks-with-the-frogs shook himself awake. The morning sunlight cast long shadows. "What... What about fire watch?"

Finder-of-snails smiled and nodded his head towards Fire-in-his-hair. "We did it for you. You looked like you needed the rest."

Croaks-with-the-frogs shook himself awake and looked shamefully across at where Me-not-talking was sleeping.

"Don't worry about her," Finder-of-snails laughed. "We let her sleep too. C'mon... get some breakfast."

The fist gathered around the fire, eating some 'roo and dandelion leaves. Croaks-with-the-frogs thought the others looked in much better spirits after the rest.

"I'm going to want a bath when I get back," Fire-in-his-hair said. "I smell."

No-point-shoe laughed. "You'll smell worse after your bath. The swamp water is foul this time of year."

Fire-in-his-hair cocked his head. "I like it."

Finder-of-snails and Me-not-talking laughed.

Croaks-with-the-frogs gently pushed against his side. The bleeding had stopped again but he felt weak and tired. A dull ache pounded in his head. He stared at the flames and chewed on the roasted roo. His stomach resisted the food but he forced it down.

No-point-shoe pushed herself to her feet. "We're only a couple of *scouts* from home. If we get moving now, we should be able to make it before the day gets too hot."

Fire-in-his-hair spat a piece of gristle into the fire. "Sounds good. Let's do it."

"You looking forward to getting home?" Me-not-talking said.

Croaks-with-the-frogs didn't answer. He felt sick and weak and couldn't be bothered making small talk with Me-not-talking. He dragged himself up and rolled his pack.

Me-not-talking gave him a sour look. "Someone's grumpy," she said.

Finder-of-snails smiled at her. "I'm looking forward to getting home," he said. "I want a drink of hot dandy and some of Sleeps-in-the-sun's fresh cakes."

I tore my trousers

The fist broke camp and set off again. No-point-shoe was leading, followed by Finder-of-snails, then Croaks-with-the-frogs, Me-not-talking and finally Fire-in-his-hair as the rear guard. The sun was warm and the hunters continued their short sprints across the scorched grassland. In the distance they could see the thick forest of tea tree that ringed the swamp. Once amongst the tea tree, they would be safe from aerial attack and the journey would be a lot less nerve-wracking.

Croaks-with-the-frogs was not travelling well. The loss of blood had made his exhaustion worse. When he started running, the matted fur under his shirt tore at the scab and the bleeding began again. The sun didn't warm him, it only shone in his eyes, making his headache worse. As the fist entered a patch of grass that had escaped the burn, he tried to keep his eyes focussed on the back of Finder-of-snails ahead of him but for some reason he kept drifting towards the left.

"Hey! Stay in formation," he heard Me-not-talking say.

"Croaks-with-the-frogs! Are you Ok?"

To Croaks-with-the-frogs, everything happened as if he were under water. The grass swayed and the ground rose to meet him. He heard voices.

"No-point-shoe! He's down."

"Why?"

"Finder-of-snails take front."

Croaks-with-the-frogs was rolled onto his back. He looked into the concerned face of No-point-shoe. "What's the matter?" she said.

Croaks-with-the-frogs was too frightened to speak. He stared at her blankly then closed his eyes against the sunlight flickering through the yellow grass. As he lapsed into unconsciousness, he heard a gasp and a scream.

When No-point-shoe turned back to tend the fallen youth, Finder-of-snails crouched into a defensive position guarding the front of the formation. He scanned the sky for hawks or eagles and peered through the grass for land based enemy. Behind him he could hear the others gathered around Croaks-with-the-frogs.

The grass was too high for him to see clearly and he was conscious that the finger of hunters behind him were vulnerable. To his left, a cluster of rocks poked above the grass. He headed for it to gain a better vantage point.

As he climbed the rocks, he checked the sky for signs of hawk. He didn't see the snake sunning itself between the rocks. It struck like lightning, sinking its fangs through his rabbit fur and pumping venom into his thigh.

Fire-in-his-hair heard Finder-of-snails scream and saw him fall from the rocks. He caught a glimpse of the brown scales and knew what it meant. He dashed to the rocks to find Finder-of-snails struggling with a snake nearly as long as he was. The snake was trying to swallow the struggling hunter whole.

Fire-in-his-hair plunged in and drove his spear into the neck of the beast. The snake reared and struck back. The fangs pierced his thick shirt and scratched his skin but they could not get deep enough to pump the poison. Fire-in-his-hair twisted away and plunged his spear in again. The snake coiled its body abound his waist and squeezed. He stared into the yawning, cavernous mouth and grabbed at it, trying to stop it from swallowing him head first.

No-point-shoe drew her hand axe and sprinted towards the rocks. She smashed the axe into the head of the serpent. The snake shuddered and tried to wheel around.

Fire-in-his-hair kept his hands firmly on its mouth, stopping it from changing direction. No-point-shoe struck again and again until her blows penetrated the snake's skull and pierced its brain. Eventually, the snake stopped fighting and lay still, its tail faintly twitching as the blood seeped. No-point-shoe hacked at the neck until the skull came away completely.

She turned towards Fire-in-his-hair. "Are you OK? Did it poison?"

The old hunter pushed himself to his feat. Blood smeared over his face. "I'm fine," he said and dashed to where Finder-of-snails lay amongst the rocks.

Fire-in-his-hair crouched beside the young man. "Can you get up?"

"Yeah sure," Finder-of-snails said easily. He slightly raised his head. "But... I don't think I want to."

Fire-in-his-hair paused. "Where were you bitten?"

"My thigh."

The old hunter tore Finder-of-snails' trousers away and exposed the twin punctures caused by the snake. The bite was red and swelling. The venom had gone deep.

"Did you cut my trousers?" Finder-of-snails said.

"Um... yeah."

"Aw shit! Sleeps-in-the-sun'll be mad."

Fire-in-his-hair lamely covered the tear he had made. "It'll be OK. You can have mine."

"How many pairs of trousers do you have?"

"Um... Are you sure you don't want to get up?"

"Yeah. Let's go home." Finder-of-snails turned his face towards the morning sun. "The sun is nice here... but it's not very warm. Get the kid to light a fire. Warm us up before we get home. I'm looking forward to seeing Sleeps-in-the-sun again. She's a good woman. Where is she?"

Fire-in-his-hair looked around helplessly.

No-point-shoe pushed her way to Finder-of-snails' side and cradled his head in her arms. "She'll be here soon, *Brudha*. Just relax. We'll be home soon."

"Ah. That's good. I could do with a nut of dandy. I'm cold."

No-point-shoe lay beside him and hugged him. "Things will warm up soon. Just relax."

Finder-of-snails lay his head back. "Yeah. I could do with a rest... rest my eyes for a bit."

No-point-shoe stroked the side of his head. "You're a good man, Finder-of-snails," she said.

Finder-of-snails smiled. "Ah, there you are," he said. Then his face went serious. "I'm very sorry but I tore my trousers."

And with that his eyes lost focus and he lay still.

~ 2 ~

SMOKE

By the fire

Croaks-with-the-frogs woke in the darkness of his burrow. Beside him Fire-in-his-hair snored softly. He lay awake, staring at the dome of mud above him. The dim light of the night sky shone through the small air holes. He tried to remember what happened, but nothing came to him. He only knew he was ravenously hungry.

He threw off the rabbit-pelt cover and pulled on his shirt and trousers. His side ached, and he felt with his fingers where a pad of rabbit fur was tied in place by several strips of hide. He took the pelt with him and crawled out of the burrow towards the fire.

The hive consisted of a ring of burrows made of dried mud and coated in ash. There was a burrow for each fist, a couple of burrows for the elders and a single crowded burrow for the children. Each nursing mother shared a burrow with their litter and their husband. There was also a burrow for stored food.

The burrows were circular and wide enough for a tall man to stretch out and sleep. The walls were straight to about waist height but then curved to a roof that rose to about chest height. The burrows abutted each other, forming a solid barrier that protected the hive and each burrow had a single entrance that faced the large fire, blazing in the centre of the hive.

Night time was more quiet than daytime around the hive, but there were always people gathered around the fire. Croaks-with-the-frogs saw G'ma sitting beside No-point-shoe amongst a cluster of other members of the tribe. They were looking at him. He smiled at No-point-shoe but she looked away, as if she hadn't seen him. Feeling a bit foolish, he found a seating log away from the others, drew the rabbit fur around him and stared at the dancing flames. He tried not to stare across the fire, but he could see G'ma and No-point-shoe were arguing. G'ma wagged her finger and No-point-shoe got up and stomped over to where he sat. Her mouth was a tight, straight line.

"So you're up," she said tersely.

Croaks-with-the-frogs nodded.

"You hungry?"

He nodded again.

No-point-shoe went over to where a large pot was simmering by the fire and filled a wooden bowl with stew. She grabbed a cold cake from a pile off to the side and brought them to Croaks-with-the-frogs. She plonked the bowl on the ground before him and dropped the cake into it. The stew slopped over the edge as the cake landed.

Croaks-with-the-frogs leaned back, his eyes wide with fear. She seemed very angry, but he couldn't work out why.

"How does your side feel?" she said, in that same sharp tone.

"It's OK."

Without speaking, No-point-shoe lifted his shirt and checked the bandage. "Hmm... It hasn't started bleeding again." She seemed annoyed the wound had stayed closed. "Eat your stew," she said and got up walked away towards the burrow he shared with Fire-in-his-hair.

Croaks-with-the-frogs dipped his cake into the stew and chewed thoughtfully. He tried to remember the journey home after scavenging the 'roo but the last thing he could recall was lying in the grass while No-point-shoe checked his wound. After that, everything was blank.

From behind him in his burrow he could hear No-point-shoe scolding. It was unusual for anyone to raise their voice at night. Eventually, he saw Fire-in-his-hair come staggering out of the burrow, pulling on his shirt. The old hunter, sat beside Croaks-with-the-frogs and blew out a deep breath.

"How are you feeling?" he said.

"OK."

Fire-in-his-hair reached across and pulled off a piece of Croaks-with-the-frogs' cake, dipped it in the young man's bowl of stew and started eating.

Croaks-with-the-frogs smiled. "You could get your own, you know?"

Fire-in-his-hair shot him a mischievous smile. "What's the fun in that?"

They sat together for a while sharing the stew and cake. When it was finished, Fire-in-his-hair said, "You still hungry?"

Croaks-with-the-frogs nodded.

The old hunter got up, refilled the bowl and grabbed a freshly baked cake from near the fire. He brought it back and the two set about eating again.

"Is this roo?" asked Croaks-with-the-frogs.

"Yeah."

"It's nice."

Fire-in-his-hair didn't respond. He stared thoughtfully at the fire for a while, then said, "Do you know what happened on the way home from the scavenge?"

Croaks-with-the-frogs felt uneasy, as if there was something important he was missing. "Um... Not really. Last thing I remember is falling into the grass."

Fire-in-his-hair kept his eyes on the fire and took a deep breath. Then he plunged in and told the young man about the snake and the death of Finder-of-snails. "You passed out from loss of blood. We couldn't carry you both home... we left Finder-of-snails out there."

Croaks-with-the-frogs' heart hammered in his chest. "I... Is that why No-point-shoe is mad?"

"I suppose... maybe."

"I shouldn't have passed out. I killed him."

Fire-in-his-hair's response was terse. "Finder-of-snails was killed by a snake!"

Croaks-with-the-frogs started to cry. "They all blame me."

"No-point-shoe is shitty because she left him on point. She's mad at you for not telling us about the wound, but you didn't kill him."

"I'm cursed."

Fire-in-his-hair screwed his face in disdain. "Frogshit!"

Croaks-with-the-frogs' voice started to rise. "It's true... I've heard them say it and now I've done it again."

Fire-in-his-hair turned around savagely, spilling the stew on the ground. His face twisted in rage. "Shut up!" he said. "Who are you crying for?"

Croaks-with-the-frogs blinked at him, frightened.

Fire-in-his-hair didn't let up. "Who!? Are you crying for Finder-of-snails? Sleeps-in-the-sun? Or maybe their babies? If that's why you're crying, then that's OK. Those are good tears. But you're not. You're crying for yourself. Finder-of-snails is dead, his wife is alone and you are crying for yourself."

"I'm not crying for myself," Croaks-with-the-frogs lied.

They sat together staring at the fire in sullen silence. Then Fire-in-his-hair said, "You are not cursed. People die all the time while others live. You don't cause their deaths and you can't save them. No one is cursed."

The young man said nothing.

Fire-in-his-hair turned and grabbed his shoulders and forced him to stare into his eyes. "No one is cursed, Croaks-with-the-frogs. Every life matters! Your life matters! Don't you ever let me hear you talking about being cursed again. Your life matters!"

Croaks-with-the-frogs stared into the old hunter's eyes, and nodded miserably. He wanted to believe him. With all his heart he wished it was true.

It's not Berry season

As the Smoke season's heat faded and the days grew shorter, the wound in Croaks-with-the-frogs' side healed and left only a puckered scar. His strength returned steadily but his sense of isolation never left. Even though No-point-shoe's anger faded, she was never really warm towards him. Me-not-talking wouldn't even look at him. He would often overhear her telling anyone who would listen about the dog tracking, and how Croaks-with-the-frogs had caused the death of Finder-of-snails. No-one in the tribe was cruel to him, but they kept their distance and when they looked at him, there was fear in their eyes.

One morning, after Croaks-with-the-frogs had finished his breakfast and was reaching for his spear, G'ma called, "Croaks-with-the-frogs, get me a nut of dandelion, darling?"

The others around the fire paused in their conversation. One of the older spears got up, "I'll get it, G'ma," she said.

"No." G'ma replied, smiling. "I want Croaks-with-the-frogs to get it for me."

Croaks-with-the-frogs felt as if all eyes were boring into his back as he picked up the hollowed out gum-nut, scooped the hot water simmering in the cauldron into it and sprinkled some ground, roasted dandelion root into the brew. He brought the steaming gum-nut to G'ma.

"Thank you, darling." she said. "You didn't get a nut for yourself?"

Croaks-with-the-frogs was a bit thrown. "Um... Fire-in-his-hair and I are about to go hunt the cat, G'ma."

"Oh, that cat won't be going anywhere, dear. Get yourself a nut of dandy and sit with me."

Croaks-with-the-frogs looked across to where Fire-in-his-hair stood with his pack and spear. The hunter rolled his eyes, went back to the fire and began knapping a new point for his weapon.

Croaks-with-the-frogs made himself a nut of dandelion and sat beside G'ma.

G'pa and G'ma were the oldest of the tribe. Not all the tribe were their descendants but they were the last of their generation and even though their usefulness around the tribe was limited, they were respected as the tribal leaders. G'pa was tall and thin and it was said he was once a fierce hunter. His name was Terror-of-Magpies. Now he was simply called G'pa and he sat by the fire paying little attention to the goings on around him. G'ma sat beside him. She was small and her face was wrinkled. Croaks-with-the-frogs had never seen her hair, because she always wore her rabbit fur hat tightly over her head. She was always cold.

As they sipped, G'ma talked. She talked about Berry season and how it was her favourite time of year. She asked Croaks-with-the-frogs what his favourite season was and wanted to know why. As she spoke, she would often reach out her hand to touch him on the arm. When the dandelion was finished, she patted the top of his head. "Thank you, darling," she said. "Now, when you go out to collect the berries, can you please bring us a few? G'pa likes his sweet but I like mine with a bit of zing. Get me a tart one."

"Um... G'ma... we weren't going to collect berries. We were going to try to hunt the cat."

"Oh." Her face fell like that of a little girl.

Croaks-with-the-frogs suddenly felt very protective of her. "Maybe we could get some berries before we go?"

"Oh would you? That would be lovely, darling!"

Croaks-with-the-frogs stood and made to leave.

"Don't get me any berries," G'pa said. "They're not sweet enough yet."

Croaks-with-the-frogs was shocked. He had no idea G'pa was paying any attention.

"Just bring a couple of tart ones for G'ma."

Croaks-with-the-frogs stared at the old couple.

G'ma smiled up at him. "I've had a lovely chat."

"Lovely chat." echoed G'pa nodding as he stared into the fire.

"You must come and sit with me again."

"Come again." G'pa repeated.

Croaks-with-the-frogs collected the used gum-nuts and dropped them into the pile beside the cauldrons. He smiled and waved at G'ma and caught sight of G'pa staring at him, a wry smile on his weathered old face.

"We've gotta get some berries for G'ma before we go hunting."

Fire-in-his-hair looked up from his knapping. "We what?"

Croaks-with-the-frogs shuffled his feet awkwardly. "She wants some berries. She likes them tart. G'pa likes them sweet."

"What?! You wanna go collect berries?"

"Well... no but G'ma..."

"It's not berry season."

"Maybe we can get the berries and then go hunt the cat."

Fire-in-his-hair pushed himself to his feet, a bemused smile on his face. "We can hunt the cat tomorrow. Let's see if we can find G'ma her ashen berries."

Blackberry bushes grew in the grasslands to the west, beyond the tea tree. That's where the tribe burnt during Fire season. The burning stopped the blackberries from taking over but the fire never fully destroyed the bushes. Every year after Smoke, the bushes would burst into fruit.

Blackberries were a crucial part of the tribe's diet. They ate the berries raw, they added them to their cakes and stews, and they squashed them for juice. The juice was drunk with water by children but adults added it to the wattle toddy to ease its bitterness.

Wattle toddy was made by boiling wattle bark and yellow-root to form a mild hallucinogen. Pure toddy was used by the eldest G'ma ritually but watered down toddy was drunk for recreation. After a few nuts of watered down wattle toddy, even the grumpiest adults would find something to laugh at.

Fire-in-his-hair never drank wattle toddy. When the tribe started drinking and laughing, he would either go off to his burrow or leave the hive, taking Croaks-with-the-frogs with him and he had never shown any interest in gathering black-berries.

The worst of the heat had passed but the berry season had not yet arrived. The air was still thick with smoke and the horizon disappeared into a reddish haze. The bushes had only a few small clusters of red berries. They were hard and inedible. The longer they searched for a partially ripe berry, the more annoyed Fire-in-his-hair got.

"Fuck a frog!" he said angrily. " I can't believe you told G'ma we'd get her berries. It's not ashen berry season!"

Croaks-with-the-frogs rubbed his ears in frustration. "I'm sorry. I just couldn't say 'no' to her."

It took them the entire morning to find a pair of small black berries.

Fire-in-his-hair made Croaks-with-the-frogs carry them. "You can give them to her," he said grumpily as they walked back to the hive. "They probably taste like possum piss."

Croaks-with-the-frogs tried to hide his smile. Fire-in-his-hair had different levels of anger. When he was really angry, he was terrifying. He never swore then. But he would swear ferociously when he was only a little bit angry and it always made Croaks-with-the-frogs laugh.

By the time the two hunters had returned to the hive, the word had gotten around about G'ma's quest. There was much laughter and good natured teasing as they dragged them-selves back to the fire.

"Ah! The mighty hunter is back!" called No-point-shoe, smiling. "I'm starving. What did you bring us for lunch?"

Fire-in-his-hair tried to scowl at her but he slipped into a rueful grin instead.

The others joined in. "Didja get any berries, boys?"

G'ma ignored the laughter. She had eyes only for Croaks-with-the-frogs as he held out his hands with a berry in each. "Thank-you, darling," she gushed. It was if she was receiving the greatest gift of her life.

"Thanks, G'ma," he said, blushing and walked awkwardly away.

"What did you thank her for?" Fire-in-his-hair said as the young man plonked himself beside him.

"I don't know. I had to say something!"

The old hunter laughed and ruffled Croaks-with-the-frogs' hair playfully. "Come on. We've still got time before dark. Let's see if we can find something to hunt near the swamp."

A miserable pair of coots

The following morning as Croaks-with-the-frogs and Fire-in-his-hair were preparing to leave, the young man saw G'ma smiling and waving at him.

"Oh shit!" Croaks-with-the-frogs whispered.

"Pretend you can't see her," said Fire-in-his-hair.

"I can't. She's looking right at me." Croaks-with-the-frogs smiled and waved half heartedly.

"A nut of Dandy?" called G'ma.

"Oh for fuck's sake!" said Fire-in-his-hair.

Croaks-with-the-frogs laughed. "I'll just have a nut with her and then we'll go. I promise."

Fire-in-his-hair scowled. "No berries. No fucking berries! It's not Berry season!"

"I get it, I get it." The young man repressed his smile as he turned away. He grabbed a gum-nut and made a new brew of dandelion root. He brought it to G'ma then made another one for himself.

When he returned to where G'ma and G'pa were sitting, he noticed G'ma had moved away from G'pa a bit and was patting the log between them for him to sit. Croaks-with-the-frogs sat between them, feeling even more awkward. Nobody ever sat between G'ma and G'pa.

"Ah!" exhaled G'ma as soon as he sat. "What a lovely nut of dandy!"

G'pa was staring into the fire, seemingly oblivious to his presence.

G'ma smiled and put her hand gently on Croaks-with-the-frogs' fore-arm. "What are you planning to do today, dear?"

"Well... Fire-in-his-hair and I were going out to the far side of the swamp to hunt the cat."

"Pshah!" G'pa exclaimed.

Croaks-with-the-frogs turned but G'pa kept staring into the fire.

"We won't be able gather any berries today, G'ma."

"Of course, dear. It's not yet Berry season."

Croaks-with-the-frogs was a bit lost. He wondered if G'ma had heard Fire-in-his-hair grumbling and he didn't want to offend her. "We want to try and get the cat before the summer ends. We'll probably be away for a few days."

"Ridiculous," snorted G'pa.

G'ma turned on him savagely. "Shh!"

But G'pa was talking now and wouldn't be silenced. "You do realise its not the same cat don't you?"

Croaks-with-the-frogs looked at him. He thought maybe G'pa was talking to himself.

The old man stared at him with rheumy eyes. "The cat that killed Fire-in-his-hair's wife has long gone." G'pa's head wobbled as he spoke.

Croaks-with-the-frogs wondered if his neck was struggling to hold it up. It took a moment for him to realise G'pa was fully aware of what he was saying and speaking directly to him.

"Cat's don't live for more than a few fists of winters," the old man said. "It's dead. You're wasting your time hunting something that doesn't exist."

Croaks-with-the-frogs' mouth fell open. Deep down he knew the original cat was long gone but hunting the cat had become so much a part of him, he couldn't imagine life without it.

G'ma was furious. "Leave him alone. Let them hunt if they want to. If it makes them happy, what harm does it do?"

"Makes them happy?" G'pa scoffed. "I've never seen a more miserable pair of coots in my entire life."

Something cracked within Croaks-with-the-frogs and he felt nervous. He sipped his dandy faster, desperate to escape. On the other side of the fire, Fire-in-his-hair was preparing a coal carrier and sorting out the packs. He was oblivious to what G'pa was saying. In fact, as the young man scanned the people around the fire, he noticed no one was paying any attention at any of them. It was as if Croaks-with-the-frogs had slipped inside a hollow tree and disappeared from sight when he sat between the old couple.

G'ma was still talking, "Don't pay any attention to him," she gestured gently across to G'pa. "He doesn't know what he's saying."

G'pa grumbled. "I bloody know what I'm saying."

"He says things without realising."

"I realise exactly what I'm saying!"

"He doesn't mean it."

"I think these boys are wasting their lives hunting that *ashen* cat and I'm going to say it!"

"He's old now."

"I'm not that old that I don't know..." G'pa's words cut off in frustration. "Where's my fucking dandelion!?" he exploded. "You get yourself one!"

G'ma nodded at Croaks-with-the-frogs sagely. "There. See?"

Croaks-with-the-frogs did not see. He gulped at his dandelion even more and the hot drink scolded his throat.

G'ma kept talking. "This is the problem. He didn't get a nut of dandy."

G'pa stared into the fire and shook his head. He spoke slowly and deliberately, emphasising every word. "You are a stupid woman. Do you know that?"

G'ma pushed her hands forward, dismissing him. "This is what I have to put up with." She said with a strong tone of martyrdom in her voice. "I never thought I'd have to put up with this when I was old."

They sat in silence. Croaks-with-the-frogs was dying to escape but couldn't work out how to get away.

G'ma started talking again. "Nobody knows what he's like. Only me."

G'pa let out a short laugh but said nothing.

"So rude."

Croaks-with-the-frogs could stand it no longer. "Well... thanks for the nut, G'ma and G'pa. I'd better be off now. I think Fire-in-his-hair is ready to go."

"Yes, Yes." G'ma said, forcing herself to be cheerful. "You go. Good luck with your hunt."

G'pa looked at him and shook his head, the same wry smile on his face.

The Cat Trap

Fire-in-his-hair had been working on a new strategy and was keen to put it into practice. "I need another man to help with it," he told Croaks-with-the-frogs as they skirted around the edge of the swamp.

At first, Croaks-with-the-frogs thought Fire-in-his-hair was talking about someone else. When he realised he "the other man," the young hunter felt a surge of pride. "I'm a man!" he thought with a smile.

As they walked, Fire-in-his-hair explained the concept but Croaks-with-the-frogs found it hard to follow. The plan was to build something that would kill the cat without either hunter having to risk contact.

They walked all morning and ate a cake on the way. At midday, Fire-in-his-hair found cat footprints close to the swamp. Croaks-with-the-frogs followed him as he traced the trail deeper into the tea tree until the tracks disappeared across the harder ground.

They found a spot where a pair of strong tea trees were growing just under a *length* apart. "Here," Fire-in-his-hair said, triumphantly. "We'll build it here." The old hunter opened his pack and brought out a pair of newly made hand axes and a few long strips of hide.

"Go back to the swamp, and net us a couple of frogs." Fire-in-his-hair said. "Don't smash 'em. Leave 'em looking healthy."

Croaks-with-the-frogs shrugged and did as he was told. By the time he had returned with the dead frogs, Fire-in-his-hair had cut back the branches of the tee trees leaving a pair of straight, strong trunks parallel to each other. He had also cut a pair of branches, of varying lengths and thickness with notches and grooves in the wood.

A large forked branch had been cut back creating a long length of wood with a wicked spike protruding from its end. "This is the killing stick," Fire-in-his-hair said with a wicked grin.

Croaks-with-the-frogs marvelled. "What are you doing? I'm so confused."

Fire-in-his-hair laughed. "You won't be confused if it works. We'll be bloody heroes!"

"Will it work?" Croaks-with-the-frogs was doubtful.

"I made a few little versions back at the hive while you were sick. They worked. Now we're just doing the same thing only bigger." The old hunter grinned with excitement. "Look," he said and dived into his pack again. He brought out a small contraption about the size of his palm. It was made out of sticks and tied together using hide.

Fire-in-his-hair pushed the contraption into the soft ground. "These two sticks are the trees and this is the cross-piece," he said pointing with a small stick. "We have to tie our hide around that pair of trees in the same way that this hide is. Here is where we put the frog, and this sets the trap." He placed the miniature killing stick between between the loop of hide and wound it back. After several turns, he wedged the last stick into place, propping the killing stick into the air. "Now, imagine the frog is here," he pointed to the end of the smallest stick. "And the cat comes to get a free meal. He tapped the place where the frog would be. The small stick holding the killing stick in place fell away. The killing stick under pressure from the twisted hide, spun wildly until, it flung itself into the air. Fire-in-his-hair laughed. "Dead cat, boy! Dead fucking cat!"

Croaks-with-the-frogs was amazed. He had never seen anything like this little contraption. He stared at the older man in wonder. "What do you call it?"

"I dunno. Doesn't have a name. I've been thinking about this for ages. But I've only just worked out how to set that little stick." He turned towards the large branches lying around the trees. "Now," said Fire-in-his-hair. "Take that hide, and climb onto my shoulders.

Before long a larger version of the cat trap took shape between the pair of trees before them. A frog skewered on small stick hung out as bait and a large killing stick with a wicked spike was poised above it.

For several moments the hunters stood staring in awe and their creation. "That sizzles!" said Croaks-with-the-frogs. "What about the second frog?"

Fire-in-his-hair laughed. "That's our dinner. Come on. Let's get out of here. It will be dusk soon and the cat will be hunting. We don't want to scare it off."

Terror-of-Magpies

The small fire crackled and spat throwing sparks into the night sky. Fire-in-his-hair and Croaks-with-the-frogs huddled close picking at the remains of the roasted frog. They had hiked a couple of good sprints downwind of the trap and made camp in the shelter of a fallen Eucalypt. They kept the fire small to avoid scaring off the cat. Above them, the stars were masked by the smoke haze.

Croaks-with-the-frogs couldn't stop thinking about the trap. Nets were often used to catch small game. Croaks-with-the-frogs used his net to catch their dinner but net hunting always relied on hiding in the bush and throwing the nets. Often the throw was too slow and the faster animals would get away.

"This cat trap could change everything!" Croaks-with-the-frogs enthused.

"Hmm?"

"I think we should call it the winding trap. Because we wind it."

"Winding trap eh? OK... that's not bad."

"We could make them smaller to catch birds or mice. We could get rabbits. We might even be able to make them bigger and catch Roos!"

Fire-in-his-hair laughed. "Why would a roo want to eat a frog?"

Croaks-with-the-frogs was only slightly disheartened. He had forgotten about the frog. Most of their food came from animals that ate grass or seeds. The trap's uses were limited. "Still..." he said stoutly, "We could get magpies... or rats?"

Fire-in-his-hair nodded thoughtfully. "Yes. I suppose we could get rats."

The pair lapsed into silence. Croaks-with-the-frogs was still thinking about the winding trap.

But the mention of magpies had set Fire-in-his-hair thinking about G'pa. "What was G'pa talking about this morning at the fire?"

Croaks-with-the-frogs felt a sinking feeling. "Did you hear him?"

"No. But I saw him. He seemed pretty fired up.... for G'pa."

Croaks-with-the-frogs laughed. "Yeah. I didn't even know G'pa could talk."

Fire-in-his-hair looked at the younger man with a bemused smile.

"Well... I thought... you know... cause he's not all there... um ...you know... in this thinking."

Fire-in-his-hair's smile became a little bid sadder. "Why do you say that?"

"Because... he never talks. He just sits there and... his head shakes. He just seems to go from the fireside to his burrow. It's always been G'ma who does the talking."

Fire-in-his-hair was silent for a long time. Croaks-with-the-frogs though the conversation was over when the old hunter finally spoke. His voice was low. "It's a common mistake people make. They think because you don't talk, you're not thinking. Often it's exactly the opposite. Those who talk, don't know. Those who know," he laughed shortly. "Well they know that words don't work."

Croaks-with-the-frogs stared at him silently. He didn't understand what Fire-in-his-hair was talking about.

Fire-in-his-hair kept talking. "G'pa was one of the best hunters in the tribe. They called him Terror-of-magpies. He was the one who taught me that trick of throwing the gum-nuts at birds when we attacked their nests. He would go first and I had to find a nearby branch and throw the nuts." The old hunter smiled, sadly. "He was absolutely fearless. If it weren't for him..." His words petered out. "The thing is, he never made a big deal of it. He was always like that ...very low key."

They sat in silence for a while watching the fire dance. Then Fire-in-his-hair began talking again. "One day we were out gathering wattle seeds. I wandered away from my fist and came across a Blue-tongue." Fire-in-his-hair twitched his body and raised his hands in a pantomime of fear.

Croaks-with-the-frogs laughed.

Blue-tongue lizards hunted all through the lands around the swamp. They were big, some of them were nearly as long a fully grown man and they could deal a savage bite. A bite from a blue-tongue would often fester and few survived it. In spite of this, the lizards avoided humans. A blue-tongue lizard was no match for a fist of spears but it was a dangerous enemy for a single hunter.

Fire-in-his-hair was still talking. "I had only just received my spear. I was shitting myself. I stared at the lizard. It stared at me." The old hunter waited, letting the tension rise. "Then suddenly, I realised I wasn't alone anymore. Terror-of-magpies was standing just behind my shoulder. I didn't hear him come up. He just appeared there. He didn't say anything. He just stood there beside me." He laughed. "That Blue-tongue saw the two of us facing him and made tracks bloody quick."

Fire-in-his-hair shook his head and smiled at the memory. "After it had gone, the old boy still didn't say anything. He just squeezed my shoulder and then walked back to the others."

Croaks-with-the-frogs found himself lost in the story. He struggled to match the quavering old man by the fire with the legendary hunter, Terror-of-magpies. The way Fire-his-hair described it, Terror-of-magpies then seemed like Fire-in-his-hair now. The way Fire-in-his-hair wandered away from his fist then, reminded Croaks-with-the-frogs of himself. That was the sort of thing he would do. How could Fire-his-hair have been so thoughtless? He wondered wether one day, he would be a strong comforting presence like Fire-in-his-hair and Terror-of-magpies.

"What was the old man going on about anyhow?" Fire-in-his-hair said.

Croaks-with-the-frogs jumped back to the present with a start. He had pushed the morning's uncomfortable conversation to the back of his mind.

"Oh... " The young hunter squirmed. "He and G'ma were fighting."

Fire-in-his-hair laughed. "What about this time?"

Croaks-with-the-frogs sat silently for a long time.

Fire-in-his-hair leaned around the fire to stare at him. "What's the matter?" he said.

"G'pa... said that the cat was dead."

The old hunter sat very still. "Go on."

"He said that cats don't live that long."

Fire-in-his-hair stared into the fire.

Croaks-with-the-frogs' words tumbled out. "He said we were wasting our lives chasing something that doesn't exist.... Said we were a miserable pair of coots. What is a coot?"

Fire-in-his-hair laughed. "I don't know. It's something the old boy used to call us when we were being stupid. Something to do with a bird, I think."

"Well according G'pa, we're a miserable pair of them." Croaks-with-the-frogs scratched at his ear, "G'ma reckons he was grumpy because no one made him a nut of Dandy."

Fire-in-his-hair laughed. "G'ma is nuts."

"I'm not so sure. G'pa said it himself."

Fire-in-his-hair became serious. "What did he say?"

"I dunno... something along the lines of 'nobody made me a nut of dandy.' He was shitty about it too. He said 'Fuck'!"

Fire-in-his-hair laughed shortly then lapsed into silence. After a long while, he said, "You get a nap, Croaks. I'll tend the fire."

As the young man drifted off into sleep, Fire-in-his-hair crouched beside the fire, a dark shape, staring thoughtfully into the flames.

The killing stick smashes down

While Fire-in-his-hair and Croaks-with-the-frogs were settling down by their fire, the cat prowled amongst the tea-tree. It approached the winding trap cautiously. The pungent smell of dead frog was mixed with the stench of human. Freshly hacked wood and turned up soil all combined to set off its warning instincts. It gave the contraption a wide berth and padded silently towards the swamp seeking live prey that had not been tainted by the foulness of humans.

Late that night a Tawny Frogmouth saw the dead frog skewered in the trap. It swept silently out of the trees and without landing, it dug its talons deep into the frog's flesh. The Frog didn't come away easily and as the bird beat its wings, the trigger was dislodged sending the killing stick smashing down. The stick shattered the legs of the flailing owl. It dropped the frog, and flew away.

After repeated attempts to land on its broken legs the owl tired. It struggled to maintain itself in the air and finally, overcome with pain and exhaustion, it collapsed onto the ground amongst the bracken and wattle trees.

On its dawn hunt, the cat found the struggling owl. The feline pounced and scampered away with it's prize. It would not need to hunt again for a good while.

Behind the tea tree, the red sun was wreathed in smoke. Fire-in-his-hair and Croaks-with-the-frogs returned to their trap. The stick was lying on the ground with the frog still attached. There were no tracks, no sign of the cat or any other enemy but the trap had been sprung and caught nothing.

Their shoulders slumped.

"How?" gasped Croaks-with-the-frogs.

Fire-in-his-hair stood staring at his creation in silence.

The younger man crouched closer to the ground, sniffing the leaves and the soil. "There's no sign of cat or fox or anything! Did we not set the stick properly?"

Fire-in-his-hair said nothing.

Croaks-with-the-frogs examined the killing stick closely. He found a faint trace of blood near the spike and a single downy feather on the ground. "An *ashen* bird!" he cursed. "Must have been an owl! *Douse* it!"

Fire-in-his-hair started to laugh softly. "Come on, boy. Let's go back to the hive. Bring the frog."

G'pa's nut of dandy

Croaks-with-the-frogs thought about the winding trap all the way back to the hive. He was sure it would only take a little bit of tweaking for it to work. He tried to discuss it with Fire-in-his-hair a few times but the older man merely responded in monosyllables. After a few attempts, at conversation, Croaks-with-the-frogs gave up and made the journey home in silence.

When they returned to the hive Fire-in-his-hair was even more withdrawn than usual. He sat alone working on his new spear head.

"We needed to hide our scent." Croaks-with-the-frogs said as he sat himself beside him.

"Mmm."

"And we needed to find a way to stop anything taking the bait from the air.... Scatter leaves on the ground."

Fire-in-his-hair said nothing. He kept working at the edge of his stone blade with a kangaroo tooth.

Croaks-with-the-frogs suppressed his frustration. "I still think it can work, Fire-in-his-hair."

The older hunter looked up from his work and smiled but his eyes were sad. "Why don't you take the model, from my pack and see what you can do with it. Let me know how you go."

Croaks-with-the-frogs continued to puzzle over the winding trap for the rest of the day. He also wondered what was wrong with Fire-in-his-hair. It wasn't like him to give up so easily.

Fire-in-his-hair went to his burrow soon after dark. After the first nap of the night, Croaks-with-the-frogs lay awake in the burrow for a long time, waiting for his friend to stir. He was sure Fire-in-his-hair was awake but the older man refused to get up. Eventually Croaks-with-the-frogs left the burrow alone for his wake period. When he returned, Fire-in-his-hair was asleep.

When morning came, Croaks-with-the-frogs left the burrow and saw G'ma waiting by the fire. She waved at him. "A nut of dandy?" she called.

The young man went to the gum-nut pile and made a brew for both G'ma and himself.

G'ma smiled warmly. "There you go, darling," she said as if she had made the dandelion.

Croaks-with-the-frogs smiled at her. There was something about sitting next to G'ma that make him feel special. There were other people who sat with her during the day but the early morning... the first nut of dandy was his time.

G'ma began her usual chatter but Croaks-with-the-frogs stopped listening. From the other side of the fire, he saw Fire-in-his-hair leave the burrow. The old hunter, stood for a while staring at G'ma and G'pa. Then without speaking to anyone, he walked across to where the gum-nuts were piled and made a brew of dandy. He took the brew to G'pa.

The old man looked up into Fire-in-his-hair's face and took the nut without speaking.

The hunter returned to the nut pile and made another brew. He returned to the fire and sat on the far side of Croaks-with-the-frogs beside G'pa. The two men sipped their drinks and stared into the flames.

"It's cold this morning," G'ma said cheerfully.

There was a moment's silence before Croaks-with-the-frogs said, "Yeah."

"Summer is fading. It will rain soon." She sounded like a little child, eager for rains to come.

Croaks-with-the-frogs looked across her to where G'pa and Fire-in-his-hair sat staring silently into the fire. He wondered if they were going to say anything at all.

"I don't like the rain," G'ma said.

Croaks-with-the-frogs laughed. "I thought you sounded like you were looking forward to it."

"It gets cold. I like Berry season."

"It's not Berry season yet, G'ma," Croaks-with-the-frogs shot a nervous glance towards Fire-in-his-hair but the hunter wasn't listening.

"No, no. Not yet." said G'ma. "But we need the rain, even though it's cold. We need to get the bracken roots out."

"Yeah."

"We'll have to put that 'roo hide over the fire to stop it from going out. Sometimes, it rains so hard that you'd think the whole fire would get washed away."

"Yeah. That would be bad."

"We can't live without fire."

"No."

"*Only the Fire protects us.*"

The conversation rolled on like this as they drank their dandelion root. G'ma initiating the talking and Croaks-with-the-frogs doing his best to respond, while G'pa and Fire-in-his-hair sat silently staring at the flames.

When the drinks were finished, the sun was peeking through the tea tree. Croaks-with-the-frogs reached out, took G'ma's nut and stood up.

Fire-in-his-hair arched his back and reached out for G'pa's.

The old man turned to him and they stared into each other's eyes for a brief moment. Then G'pa handed over his empty nut, and briefly rested his hand on Fire-in-his-hair's shoulder.

"Thank-you, Terror-of-magpies," said Fire-in-his-hair softly, and he pushed himself to his feet and walked away.

Motes of dust

When Sleeps-in-the-sun was told about the death of Finder-of-snails, she took to her burrow and refused to come out. No-point-shoe would bring her food and sit with her, listening to her talk.

"He would sing a single line of a tune, over and over again," she said one morning. Sleeps-in-the-sun was sitting with her back propped against one of the posts that supported the mud wall. The babies crawled over her, pulling at her hair and feet then pulling at each other.

This was not the first time, No-point-shoe had heard this story. "Yeah. I never knew what song he was singing."

"He was so tuneless!" Sleeps-in-the-sun laughed, but even in the gloom of the burrow, No-point-shoe saw her eyes glittering with tears.

"Sleeps-in-the-sun, maybe today you and I can collect some wattle seeds?"

The other woman was silent.

"I mean, we can never have too much in storage."

Sleeps-in-the-sun picked at the rabbit pelt that covered the floor of the burrow. "It's strange," she said. "The things about Finder-of-snails that so annoyed me when he was alive, have become the things that I miss the most."

No-point-shoe suppressed her annoyance. "The birds are picking it up. Soon they'll be none left. We've got to do our bit."

"I don't think so," Sleeps-in-the-sun said. "The litter is still too small."

All babies were born in Winter. The new mothers stayed in the warmth of the burrow for the first winter and when wattle season came and the weather warmed, they'd come and go as they please. But they didn't go far. They were always able to return to feed the babies when they got hungry. Babies stayed in the burrow for most of their first few seasons until the end of their first summer when they would start crawling. Then they'd begin exploring the hive and engaging with other people around the fire. They wouldn't go for long before finding their way back. Sleeps-in-the-sun's litter had started crawling soon after the kangaroo scavenge and the death of Finder-of-snails but because Sleeps-in-the-sun had not left the burrow, the babies hadn't either.

No-point-shoe took a deep breath. "It's not good for you to stay in the burrow so long, Sleeps-in-the-sun. Even G'ma is worried about you."

Sleeps-in-the-sun pulled her knees to her chest and rested her chin on them. She stared at her feet, saying nothing.

"We need to collect the last of the wattle seeds." No-point-shoe said. "Smoke is nearly over. I can't go out without a fist... and ..." She hesitated. "We've lost Finder-of-snails."

"The fist won't be the same without Finder-of-snails," Sleeps-in-the-sun said, sadly.

"No. No it won't, but we've still got to go on. We can't stay in the burrow for ever."

Sleeps-in-the-sun looked into her friend's eyes. "Why not?"

No-point-shoe blinked, then laughed, then became deadly serious. "Because we've got to go on. You can't just die in the burrow."

Sleeps-in-the-sun speared her with her eyes. "Why not? What difference does it make? We're all going die. The whole world is trying to kill us. Why should we bother fighting? Don't you see? We're all dying... each in our turn."

No-point-shoe stared at her, unable to find a response. The silence stretched and she remembered her own experience of loss when Jumps-a-branch had died in the burrow.

Sleeps-in-the-sun went back to picking at the fur on the rabbit pelt. One of the babies began to fuss and pull at her shirt. She loosened the laces and allowed the child to latch onto her breast. The other baby saw what was happening and started to cry. Sleeps-in-the-sun lay on her back and allowed the second baby to attach to her other breast.

No-point-shoe lay beside her, staring at the dried mud roof that curved over them. The morning sun sent shafts of light through the ventilation holes. Motes of dust floated through the air in front of her. They danced out of the dark into the light and disappeared into the darkness again. *"We are like that,"* thought No-point-shoe.

The two women lay beside each other for some time before No-point-shoe spoke. Her voice was low and heavy. "Sleeps-in-the-sun, you have spoken a deep truth," she said. "But there is also another truth." She paused, trying to find the words. "Life matters. Everything about life is really, really important. I don't know why. I just know it is." She paused again, wrestling with her idea. "I don't know which truth is deeper. Your truth or mine. Are we insignificant specks of dust or are we... bearers of the fire? Does the fire need us? Does the fire matter? I don't know. But I choose to live as if it does. You have a pair of babies and they are bearers of the fire. They must leave the burrow. So you must leave the burrow. If you decide not to, you can die in here. I won't condemn you for making that choice, but I think it would be a terrible loss."

Sleeps-in-the-sun cried silently as the babies nuzzled.

No-point-shoe pulled herself into a crawling position. "I'm taking Me-not-talking, Fire-in-his-hair and Croaks-with-the-frogs out to harvest wattle seeds today. I'd really like you to come with us." With that, she turned and crawled out of the burrow into the bright morning sunlight.

Sleeps-in-the-sun

No-point-shoe crossed the fire and found Fire-in-his-hair crouched over a flat rock, pounding wattle seeds and dried bracken root into a floury paste. "What are you doing?" she asked, incredulous.

Fire-in-his-hair didn't look up. "I'm helping make the cakes."

No-point-shoe stared at him for a moment. "I've never seen you do that before."

"I used to do it. I used to be a good cook."

No-point-shoe shook her head in confusion. "Anyhow... We need to gather the last of the wattle seeds. They won't last much longer. You wanna come?"

Fire-in-his-hair wiped the flour from his hands and scraped what he had made into the communal pot. "Sure. I'll get the kid."

No-point-shoe's mouth tightened but she said nothing. She knew Croaks-with-the-frogs would come with them but part of her hoped Fire-in-his-hair would suggest someone else. After the kangaroo scavenge, she had told G'ma she didn't want Croaks-with-the-frogs in her fist anymore but the old woman had absolutely forbidden her from excluding him. No-point-shoe had never seen G'ma so adamant and no-one dared oppose G'ma when she had set her mind on something. Croaks-with-the-frogs was now a regular part of her fist.

She watched Fire-in-his-hair dust the flour off his clothes then walked with him towards his burrow. "I've asked Sleeps-in-the-sun to come with us too," she said.

Fire-in-his-hair nodded, "Good. That's good."

"I don't know if she will come."

He stopped walking and turned to look at her, a thoughtful expression on his face. "OK... well, we'll wait and see if she comes."

No-point-shoe smiled. She was terrified Sleeps-in-the-sun would never leave her burrow and the fist would be shuffling around the fire for days. But the fact that Fire-in-his-hair was willing to wait with her, significantly eased her fears. A thought popped, unbidden into her mind. "*If Fire-in-his-hair waits, then all will be well.*"

No-point-shoe went to find Me-not-talking. She was beyond the ring of burrows that encircled the fire. She had pegged out a rabbit's pelt and was smearing the animal's brain matter over the exposed skin.

"We're going out to gather wattle seeds," said No-point-shoe. "You coming?"

Me-not-talking rocked back on her heels and looked up at her. "Who's 'we'?"

No-point-shoe crushed down her annoyance. "Me, you, Fire-in-his-hair, Croaks-with-the-frogs and Sleeps-in-the-sun."

Me-not-talking's eyes widened. "Sleeps-in-the-sun and Croaks-with-the-frogs. Both?"

"Yup."

"Are you crazy? You want to send Sleeps-in-the-sun out in the same fist as the person who caused the death of her husband?"

Several arguments ran through No-point-shoe's mind. From 'G'ma says so' to 'Nobody caused Finder-of snails to die.' But she had had these arguments with Me-not-talking many times before. Even though No-point-shoe wasn't completely convinced of the wisdom of keeping Croaks-with-the-frogs in the fist, the fact Me-not-talking would not accept the situation made her very angry. "That's right, Me-not-talking. The whole fist is going to get wattle seeds. You can come or you can find another fist!" And with that, she walked back to the fire.

Fire-in-his-hair was waiting for her. Beside him sat Croaks-with-the-frogs, fiddling with the strange collection of sticks he had brought back from the their last attempt to hunt the cat. No-point-shoe considered the pair as she approached. Since that last cat hunt, Fire-in-his-hair seemed to have become more normal, even to the extent of helping make cakes. But Croaks-with-the-frogs seemed to have got even weirder. He took that spinning stick thing everywhere he went and was constantly playing with it, tinkering with it or starting into space. It was disturbing.

"You're not bringing that winding thing out when we gather seeds," she ordered as she stood over the two seated men."

Croaks-with-the-frogs looked up at her in fright. He shook his head. "I'm just working on it while we wait," he said.

"Working on it!?" thought No-point-shoe, but she nodded and said nothing.

After a little while, Me-not-talking approached the group. She had her spear in her hand and her basket on her hip. She sat sullenly beside the others and waited.

Time passed.

"Maybe we should eat something," said No-point-shoe.

"I could finish making those cakes?" There was no enthusiasm in Fire-in-his-hair's voice.

"I'm hungry too," said Me-not-talking. "We can do it together."

No-point-shoe nodded and the pair moved off.

Croaks-with-the-frogs was torn. Part of him was relieved Me-not-talking was not waiting with them. Her hostility towards him was barely disguised and when she got sullen, she could cast a pall over the whole group. On the other hand, he didn't really feel much more comfortable alone with No-point-shoe. He wished it was he who volunteered to go make the cakes with Fire-in-his-hair. As he sat twisting the trap, he wished he could get along with other people the way No-point-shoe or Fire-in-his-hair did. They were never lost for words or awkward.

The group was eating the freshly baked cakes when the hide covering Sleeps-in-the-sun's burrow was pulled aside and the young woman crawled out. Croaks-with-the-frogs stopped eating and stared

No-point-shoe pretended to be engrossed in her lunch. She laughed too loud and said, "Fire-in-his-hair, these are good cakes. You should cook more often."

"I can cook for you anytime you like," the old hunter said seriously.

Sleeps-in-the-sun squinted in the midday light. She found her way to where her spear was resting beside the entrance to her burrow, picked it up and walked towards the group. At the mouth of the burrow her babies cried and fussed. She ignored them.

"You want a cake?" asked Fire-in-his-hair.

Sleeps-in-the-sun smiled gently. "Thanks," she said.

The babies continued to whimper for a while but after the fist left the hive and they could no longer see their mother, they pushed past the entrance hide of the burrow and crept out into the day. They were hesitant at first but the sights, sounds and smells of the hive sparked their curiosity. They were soon crawling around the fire exploring everything they could reach. They climbed over G'ma, sucked on cakes and sniffed at the simmering stew.

The fist gathered wattle seeds without incident. They each took turns watching for the enemy while the others gathered. As the day waned, they retuned to the hive each with a basket nearly half full of seeds. When they saw their mother returning, the babies scrambled towards her, whimpering and pulling at her shirt.

Sleeps-in-the-sun picked them up, a worried look on her face.

G'ma laughed. "They haven't shed a tear all day. It was only when they saw you, that they turned on their performance."

One of the older mothers, joined in the laughter. "Babies always try it on when you first leave. They were fine."

Sleeps-in-the-sun smiled gratefully. She fed the pair and took them back into the burrow to sleep.

The others watched, exchanging nervous glances. When the young woman pulled back the hide and returned to the fire, even Croaks-with-the-frogs could sense the palpable feeling of relief and elation.

"Come and have some stew," said Fire-in-his-hair.

No-point-shoe laughed. "Why? It's not like she did much work out there."

Sleeps-in-the-sun laughed. "My basket was just as full as yours."

"That's because No-point-shoe eats more seeds than she gathers," said Fire-in-his-hair.

Everyone laughed. The banter wasn't that funny but the the joy of having Sleeps-in-the-sun back around the fire kept bubbling over into laughter.

The Evening

As the sun set, casting pink and purple hues across the sky, they shared the evening meal. Me-not-talking started to sing. She began with a high lilting call, "Bikani-Balibo Bikani-Balibo."

They were not words. Just a random mixture consonants and vowels. After a few repeated calls, Me-not-talking launched into a longer string of sounds with a undulating melody. Other people joined in, instinctively harmonising either in the higher or the lower register. As Me-not-talking paused to take a breath, some of the men would echo her call in an even lower register. The effect was a joyous cacophony of sound.

After a few moments, Me-not-talking fell silent and a satisfied murmur rolled around the fire. Then one of the men began. "Dolape-Dakuno, Dolape-Dakuno." His voice was deep and his opening call was slower and more somber. When he started his main melody, others began to clap and stomp there feet in a slow, steady rhythm. As before, others joined in, harmonising and adding variations to the sounds.

Croaks-with-the-frogs had heard singing before but never joined in. Usually when the songs began, Fire-in-his-hair would go to his burrow and Croaks-with-the-frogs would tag along behind. As a result, Croaks-with-the-frogs never got the knack of harmonising or creating a melody. He looked across the fire where Fire-in-his-hair was sitting and waited for the older hunter to get up and leave.

But Fire-in-his-hair did not leave. He sat silently staring into the flames, a sad smile on his face. Croaks-with-the-frogs got up and sat beside him. The older man shot him a swift, unreadable glance and went back to staring at the fire. A slow tear trickled down the side of his cheek and disappeared into his beard. Croaks-with-the-frogs did not understand what was happening. He looked around the fire but being engrossed in their singing, no one seemed to be noticing. Finally his eyes fell on G'ma and G'pa sitting in their usual places. The couple were staring intently at Fire-in-his-hair. G'pa's eyes were red, and G'ma was openly crying, dabbing her eyes with her sleeve.

Croaks-with-the-frogs wanted to say something to comfort his friend but he had no idea why he was crying or what he could say to make him feel better. He remembered the story of G'pa putting his hand on Fire-in-his-hair's shoulder. So the young man stood, feeling terribly foolish, and placed his hand on his friend's shoulder. The older man, reached across with his other hand and squeezed it. Croaks-with-the-frogs stood there with his head bowed wondering what to do now. He was uncomfortable and he wanted to go. But Fire-in-his-hair seemed to be grateful for his presence. He may have been doing the right thing by standing there with his hand meaninglessly resting on his friends shoulder.

After what seemed an age, Fire-in-his-hair moved his hand away and looked up into the young man's eyes. "You're a good man, Croaks-with-the-frogs," he said, softly.

Croaks-with-the-frogs smiled and went to his burrow and brought back his winding trap.

Sleeps-in-the-sun's babies woke and crawled out of the burrow. They worked their way around the circle of singing adults until they found their mother. They fed briefly but they weren't very hungry and there was far too much excitement going on around the fire. The singing, the clapping, the flickering flames casting dancing shadows on strange faces all created a heady mix. The babies pulled away and continued to explore.

Mostly they were ignored. Less than half the babies lived to adulthood so being detached from young ones was a kind of defence mechanism for the adults. There was already too much grief in their lives without adding to it. The babies found other children who also paid them little attention. Most people were absorbed in the singing or watching the singers.

When they reached the part of the circle where Fire-in-his-hair and Croaks-with-the-frogs sat, however, things were different. They weren't singing. The large, silent man ignored them and kept staring into the flames but the younger one was winding a stick on a thin piece of hide. The babies didn't understand what they were looking at but the spinning stick was fascinating. They stared at it for a moment then reached out to touch it.

"Wow! Hey!" squawked, Croaks-with-the-frogs.

The babies recoiled in fear.

The young man turned to them and laughed. "You can't touch that, babies. It will hurt you."

The babies reached out again.

"No!" Croaks-with-the-frogs said firmly. "Not for babies. Here... Croaks-with-the-frogs will spin for you." And with that, the young man held the winding trap out of their reach but in clear sight and wound the stick. When he let it go, the babies eyes widened in awe. Croaks-with-the-frogs laughed and wound the stick again.

When the evening had tired and the singing had faded. Sleeps-in-the-sun went to find her babies. She found them asleep, curled up on Croaks-with-the-frogs. The young man was also asleep, lying on his back, his winding thing still in his hand. She stared at them for a long moment. A memory stirred within her of Finder-of-snails, sleeping in the burrow with the babies and she smiled. Trying not to disturb the sleeping young man, she gently picked up the babies and walked quietly away.

Croaks-with-the-frogs snapped awake. He saw Sleeps-in-the-sun carrying the babies back to her burrow and was overcome with shame. *"Of course, she wouldn't want her babies around me. I'm the one who killed their father."*

Early the following morning, Croaks-with-the-frogs was up and ready to hunt the cat. But No-point-shoe took the fist out to collect wood and Fire-his-hair took Croaks-with-the-frogs along. When the young man asked why they weren't hunting the cat anymore, the older man merely shrugged, an unreadable expression on his face.

Fire-in-his-hair never hunted the cat again. He spent the evenings sitting quietly by the communal fire, listening to the songs and smiling at the stories. He and Croaks-with-the-frogs became regular members of No-point-shoe's fist. Croaks-with-the-frogs missed the old days when they would go out alone to hunt the cat. Although nobody in the tribe was rude to him, something deep within the young man felt he didn't belong.

~ 3 ~

BERRY AND WINTER

Oaks-wi-fogs

The long heat of Smoke season broke and the rains came at last. The air cleared and the dry ground opened itself to the quenching waters. The land responded by bursting into life. It was Berry season. Berries were everywhere. Blackberries erupted amongst the thorny bushes, mistletoe berries appeared in the trees. The grass became green and rabbits became plentiful. The ground softened and the bracken roots became easier to dig out. The swamp expanded attracting more tadpoles, insects and birds. The harshest season was over.

The babies born the previous Winter began to eat solid food for the first time. The sweet blackberries supplementing their mother's milk. The abundance of food made life easier for everyone. The toddlers were weaned allowing their mothers greater freedom. The evenings became cooler and longer allowing the tribe to spend more time around the fire, singing, dancing and telling stories.

Sleeps-in-the-sun's litter rapidly caught up with the rest of their generation. They ate blackberries and sucked the juice of stew off soggy bread. They crawled around the camp-fire pulling themselves onto their feet to reach beards and faces. Like most children, they were gently swatted away by the adults. But Croaks-with-the-frogs wouldn't swat the tod-dlers away. The young man was secretly pleased when they would approach him. Their fascination with his winding trap flattered him and unlike most of the other adults, the chil-dren had no idea he was cursed or even unusual.

Croaks-with-the-frogs made a new winding trap. Unlike the original with a sharp killing spike, this one had small pieces of rabbit fur glued to each end of the spinning stick. He had also carved a new notch in the spinning stick and tied it in place. The toddlers could now spin it and let it go without fear of it coming apart or them being hurt. The pair started fighting over the new trap so Croaks-with-the-frogs made another one.

The toddlers carried their "windy things" with them wherever they went and when other children saw the wind-ing things, they became attracted to them as well. Croaks-with-the-frogs made more. The older children, those old enough to understand the whispers and pick up on the un-spoken fears of the adults still avoided him but for all the toddlers and babies in the tribe, he became a favoured play-mate.

When No-point-shoe led her fist back to the hive after a hunt or a forage, it was often Croaks-with-the-frogs who got the most enthusiastic welcome.

"Oaks... Oaks! Oaks-wi-fogs!" the little ones would chorus.

Croaks-with-the-frogs' face would light up and he would share out some blackberries or ruffle a child's hair. His sudden popularity with the little ones had given the young man a new lease on life.

Whilst most of the tribe considered it strange and a little bit unsettling, they turned a blind eye to the developments.

Me-not-talking, however was not so sanguine. "No good will come from this," she said in hushed tones. She had spoken to No-point-shoe and Sleeps-in-the-sun several times but both women would always justify their acceptance of the strange young man claiming orders from G'ma. She decided it was time to press her case.

During the evening meal, after a successful rabbit hunt, Me-not-talking found her way to the seat beside G'ma.

"I love fresh, roasted rabbit," the old lady began.

Me-not-talking was not there for small talk. "G'ma," she said seriously, "I'm very worried about Croaks-with-the-frogs."

"Oh?" The old lady sounded genuinely surprised. "Why is that, darling?"

The young woman collected her thoughts. "I think he is a danger to the tribe."

G'ma said nothing.

Me-not-talking pushed on. "Even if we ignore his part in the death of Finder-of-snails, these winding things are having a bad effect on the babies."

G'ma nodded thoughtfully.

Me-not-talking was encouraged. "They are not natural. They make the little ones selfish and they fight amongst themselves over these things." She paused for a moment, then plunged in. "I think the winding things are cursed."

Me-not-talking watched G'ma's face for a reaction. She knew the old woman would never admit Croaks-with-the-frogs was cursed. Every morning they would share their nut of dandy and the two of them would chat like a pair of old friends. If the truth were told, a part of Me-not-talking was a bit jealous about this. A small part of her wished G'ma would have a morning chat with her, but a larger part knew she couldn't stand G'ma's endless prattle. By pointing her finger at the winding things, Me-not-talking hoped she could limit the damage Croaks-with-the-frogs was doing without challenging G'ma's favourite.

G'ma sat for a long time, staring out across the fire. Beyond the ring of seats around the fire Croaks-with-the-frogs was rolling around in the dirt with a tall of little ones. He had been down on hands and knees, pretending to be a rabbit. A toddler had grabbed him and he had rolled over, Sleeps-in-the-sun's babies had crawled over to the commotion and joined in. Now all of them were growling and rolling and generally making a lot of noise.

G'ma smiled. "Look," she said.

Me-not-talking followed her eyes to the tangle of children wrestling with Croaks-with-the-frogs.

"What do you see?"

Me-not-talking pursed her lips. "They are making a lot of noise. They'd better stop that when people start going off to sleep."

G'ma's voice was sad. "What else do you see?"

Me-not-talking was getting irritated. "He's interfering with the little ones. Nobody does that! It's not normal, G'ma!"

"Look at his face. Can't you see it?"

"See what?"

G'ma took a deep breath. When she spoke, her voice was low and breathy, from her chest, laden with awe. "The fire! The fire is burning there, Me-not-talking."

"What!?"

G'ma's voice returned to normal. She stared at her hands on her lap, speaking softly. "We don't control the fire, darling. We just sit around it and draw warmth and light from it. It flickers and sparks and goes wherever it wants to. We can't restrain it or start it again once it's gone out. We say that we carry the fire, but really... the fire carries us. Croaks-with-the-frogs is being carried by the fire. Sometimes it burns where we don't want it to go."

The young woman leaned her head back and stared at the darkening sky. G'ma was still given great respect even though her mind was slowly fading but it was clear to Me-not-talking that G'ma's mind was decaying more rapidly than she had previously thought.

The Green Team

The weather was starting to cool, and *the people's* clothes were frayed and thin. They needed to be replaced. The tribe made their clothes together at the end of each Berry season to celebrate the beginning of a new year. Children's clothes were the pale, smokey colour of un-dyed rabbit skin, but those who had names and were able to carry spears, dyed their clothes in different colours according to their taste. Croaks-with-the-frogs received his spear last Winter so this was going to be his first experience of dying his clothes.

Nestled amongst the coals around the fire several large pottery cauldrons were placed. Each were part filled with boiling water and a differed type of dyeing agent. Fire-in-his-hair threw both his pants and his shirt into the Green dye vat. The more the clothes were boiled, the stronger and darker the colours would become. As usual, Fire-his-hair intended to leave them until they became almost black.

Croaks-with-the-frogs wanted to do the same. He also threw his clothes into the pot and stood beside the older hunter, an expression of suppressed joy on his face. The clothes hadn't been boiling long when No-point-shoe and Sleeps-in-the-sun approached the pair.

Sleeps-in-the-sun was pulled along by the arm, her new clothes dragging listlessly on the ground. No-point-shoe's beaming smile was in stark contrast to the look of utter misery on the other woman's face.

"Oh so this is the green team is it?" she said cheerfully.

Fire-in-his-hair nodded. "I like mine dark green."

No-point-shoe looked at Croaks-with-the-frogs and the young man blinked.

"Um... I want mine green too," he said nervously.

No-point-shoe threw her head back and laughed. "You can't both be wearing the same clothes. We won't be able to tell you apart."

Fire-in-his-hair looked at Croaks-with-the-frogs thoughtfully but said nothing.

Croaks-with-the-frogs tried to hide his disappointment. He so wanted to be in dark green like Fire-in-his-hair.

No-point-shoe's expression changed from laughter to compassion. "Hey, I've got an idea. Let's be the green fist. Let's all have some green in our clothes!"

Fire-in-his-hair looked at her in surprise. Sleeps-in-the-sun shrugged apathetically.

Croaks-with-the-frogs caught a strange look on No-point-shoe. As she stared at Fire-in-his-hair, her lips tightened and her eyes widened. She flicked her eyes quickly towards where Sleeps-in-the-sun was staring longingly at her burrow. A look of realisation came over Fire-in-his-hair's face. "Ah yes. Great idea," he said with absolutely no conviction. "We can all be different shades of green."

Croaks-with-the-frogs didn't understand what was going on. He really wanted his clothes like Fire-in-his-hair but he had a feeling that something more important was at stake here. "Can I have my trousers dark green?" he asked.

No-point-shoe was bursting with enthusiasm. "That'd be sizzling. Dark green trousers and a pale green shirt. You'll blend right into the bush. Come on Sleeps-in-the-sun, you put your shirt in here too."

Sleeps-in-the-sun handed over her shirt and No-point-shoe added it to the boiling cauldron.

Fire-in-his-hair said, "Take your shirt out, Croaks-with-the-frogs, let No-point-shoe put her trousers in. That way we'll all have some green on us."

As Croaks-with-the-frogs reluctantly did as he was told, the older hunter put his hand gently on his shoulder. "You'll look good, boy," he said gently.

No-point-shoe laughed. "Come on, Sleeps-in-the-sun, what will be our other colours?"

Sleeps-in-the-sun forced a smile. "I don't know, she said. How about red?"

"Yes!" said No-point-shoe. "Red's a great colour... just a hint of it. I might do brown. That way we'll match." And with that, she dragged Sleeps-in-the-sun off towards the other cauldrons.

Croaks-with-the-frogs stared at his pale green shirt. "What was all that about?"

Fire-in-his-hair watched the women leave, a look of deep sadness on his face. "Dyeing day is always tough," he said softly. "You always choose your colours to match your wife's. Today, no matter where Sleeps-in-the-sun goes, Finder-of-snails will not be there."

Croaks-with-the-frogs didn't really understand but he didn't say anything. *Isn't that what it's like every day?*

After a few days, everyone had changed their clothes. Their old clothes were thrown on the fire and the people moved around the tribe admiring each other's choices. No-point-shoe looked good in her pale green pants and dark brown shirt. Sleeps-in-the-sun had left her clothes to boil for only the briefest time. Her red pants and green shirt were both pale. "Still part of the green team," said No-point-shoe.

"What's this green team?" asked Me-not-talking.

No-point-shoe's face fell.

Me-not-talking looked around the rest of the fist. She had pale yellow pants, and a dark red shirt. "How come I'm not part of the green team?"

"Oh. Shit. Sorry," said Fire-in-his-hair with no conviction. He was a little bit sorry for Me-not-talking.

"It's not really a green team," said No-point-shoe. "It was just a joke. Because we all wanted green in our clothes."

Me-not-talking looked from face to face, frowned and walked away.

"I'm really tired, guys," said Sleeps-in-the-sun and she turned towards her burrow.

When she had disappeared behind the entrance hide, No-point-shoe slumped despondently to the ground. "This is bloody hard work!" she said.

Meat in Winter

As Berry turned into Winter, rabbit numbers declined and meat became scarce. Croaks-with-the-frogs began leaving the hive on his own. He still spent some days with his fist or around the fire, but he would often wander off early in the morning, stay out all night and return the following day.

The tribe was sitting around the fire on a cold and rainy afternoon. The morning's hunt had only brought a pair of rabbits and the stew was thin. The kangaroo pelt protected the fire from the rain but the hunters were getting wet. Most people had given up on the stew and taken their cakes into the shelter of their burrows.

"How can we operate as a fist, when he keeps skiving off!?" No-point-shoe complained as she and Fire-his-hair sat in the rain.

The older man shrugged his shoulders. "It's my fault," he said softly.

"Why?"

"He misses our trips, hunting the cat."

No-point-shoe frowned. "Well he's supposed to come hunting with us. We're his fist!"

Fire-in-his-hair stared at a rivulet of water running between his feet. "I think I've damaged that boy," he said, sadly.

The children, were impervious to rain. They were jumping into puddles and throwing mud at each other. Sleeps-in-the-sun's children were no longer toddlers. At the end of Berry, they had moved into the children's burrow and found their proper place. Now they were scuttling around with the other children, playing in the rain. Suddenly, the boy looked up and called, "Oaks! Oaks-wi-fogs!"

The other children joined in and they ran to where the young man was pushing his way through the wet tea tree. "Oaks, Oaks!" mimicked Croaks-with-the-frogs. "Little Oaks!"

As the little boy approached, Croaks-with-the-frogs squatted down and pulled something from his backpack. "Look what I've got," he said grinning.

The children stared in wonder.

"Mouse! Yummy!" Croaks-with-the-frogs said triumphantly.

Me-not-talking was sitting miserably by the fire. She looked up at him suspiciously. "How did you catch a mouse?"

Croaks-with-the-frogs laughed. "I got lucky."

As Winter dragged on, Croaks-with-the-frogs' luck continued to run. Each time he left the hive alone, he would return with fresh meat. Mice, birds, even possums, were provided for the tribe. By the end of Winter, most of the tribe had come to accept his comings and goings. Like Fire-in-his-hair before him, he was strange and clearly marked by the enemy, but he was a good hunter and his steady provision of meat, made most of them overlook his other idiosyncrasies.

G'ma and G'pa in the burrow

The winter sun cast a pale light through the air holes in the roof of the burrow. Small specks of dust floated into the line of light and out again. G'ma watched them flicker as they moved. Beside her she heard the familiar smack of G'pa's lips as he sucked on his tooth. He was awake too. "It will be Wattle season soon," she said.

"Hmm."

"We have a finger of marriageables."

"Mm."

"Are you OK?"

He breathed out sharply. "You drank the toddy again last night."

"Yes." Her voice was small and far away.

"I worry about you."

"I know."

"You need to go easier on the toddy," he said, his voice rising in annoyance.

"I need it." G'ma's voice became clipped, like she'd bitten the words off. They'd argued about this before.

"Yes, but not every night. I understand just before Wattle season or before the new names are given... but you've been taking it every night! It'll destroy you!"

G'ma breathed deeply. "We'll all be dead soon enough."

"Stop it, Throwing-pine-cones," he said harshly. It was rare for him to use her real name. He only did it when they were fighting. "It damages your mind, not your body. You know this!"

"There is too much at stake. I need to *see.*"

"What rubbish! What's at stake? A couple of kids get married, they have babies, they get names. Life goes on."

"Not this time, darling," she said softly, as if she were talking to a small child. "I see twists... swirls in the fire."

G'pa sat up and threw the rabbit pelt off. "Twists and swirls!? What does that mean? You're losing it! You can't take the toddy every night. Every morning you get more and more... strange. It takes most of the day for you to return to normal. One day you won't come back. It'll burn out your mind... and you'll be a living shell."

"Important things are happening. Things will be set in motion this Wattle. We must tread carefully."

"None of your dreams are about Wattle. It's always about Croaks-with-the-frogs. It's like you're obsessed with that boy."

G'ma smiled at him, sadly.

The old man forced himself to frown, resisting his instinct to return her smile. "What are you smiling at?" he said in a surly rumble.

She reached out and touched his cheek. Once his beard was dark and curly but now it was thin and grey. The years were taking their toll. "This will be my last Wattle, darling," she said softly. "We need to bring some extra observers with us this season."

G'pa said nothing as he pulled on his shirt and fumbled with his boots.

"I have *seen* this, Terror-of-magpies."

The old man wouldn't look at her. "If you say so," he said, sadly, and crawled out of the burrow into the bright afternoon light.

~ 4 ~

WATTLE SEASON BEGINS

Making cakes

Wattle trees played an important role in the life of *the people*. The seeds provided crucial protein, the bark was boiled to make toddy, and the wood burned easily and hot. But the most significant time of year was when the wattle trees burst into flower. During Wattle season the bush was dappled in a yellow glow. When the flowers were fully open and the intoxicating scent of the wattles filled the air, *the people* became fertile.

The people of the swamp spent each Wattle season with a neighbouring tribe. To the north, the river people and to the south the people of the lake, took it in turns to share the wattle fire. The children would play together, the adults would sing, dance and tell stories and the young men and women would pair up. By the middle of wattle season, when the pollen was flying and the pheromones were rampant, the young couples would be called to the wattle fire and they would pledge their lives to each other.

Like those before it, the most recent coming of Wattle Season, began with a small shiver of excitement as the days lengthened. When the blue leafed wattles flowered, the tribe was thrown into activity, gathering bracken roots, pounding stored wattle seeds so that there would be enough food for the visitors. Once they arrive, the tribes would hunt together to provide meat and this would increase the bonds between them.

After the death of his wife, Fire-in-his-hair used to find Wattle Season agony. While the visitors were being shown around and gifts were exchanged, Fire-in-his-hair would sit apart, watching the activities with an unreadable expression on his face. When the wattle pollen blew and the sexual excitement rose, Fire-in-his-hair would take Croaks-with-the-frogs out into the swamp to hunt the cat.

This year Fire-in-his-hair involved himself entirely in the preparations. He pounded bracken root and baked cakes as if he had spent his entire life around the fire.

"Are you coming to dig roots?" asked No-point-shoe as she stood beside him, her spear in one hand and her digging stick in the other. It was early morning and the day's activities were beginning. Behind her stood Sleeps-in-the-sun and Me-not-talking.

Fire-in-his-hair leaned back on his heels and wiped the smashed bracken root from his hands. "There are plenty of people out harvesting. We need more hands baking the cakes and pounding the flour."

No-point-shoe looked around the hive. Most of the hunters were getting ready to leave. Only a few of the older people were working by the fire. She screwed up her face. "That's G'pa work."

Fire-in-his-hair laughed. "Well, my pretty young lady, I have bad news for you. We're not far from being a G'pa and G'ma."

"Ha! Speak for yourself!" She looked around again. "Where's that useless friend of yours?"

The old hunter shrugged. "Croaks-with-the-frogs is out wandering the swamp."

Me-not-talking snorted in irritation. She didn't say anything but the look on her face said it all.

The conversation lapsed. "Maybe you guys could join up with another fist," No-point-shoe said.

Me-not-talking tossed her head in derision but Sleeps-in-the-sun rested her hand gently on the younger woman's shoulder. "Sure. There's plenty of fists going out."

After the Sleeps-in-the-sun and Me-not-talking had left, No-point-shoe squatted beside Fire-in-his-hair. "OK, G'pa, how about you show me your baking skills."

Fire-in-his-hair grinned and pushed himself to his feet. He set another large rock beside the one he was using and took a thick stalk of bracken root from the pile that had been harvested the day before. "The most important thing to do is to make sure that all the dirt is wiped off the root. You do that, while I pound this one."

The pair fell to work in a comfortable silence.

After a while, No-point-shoe said, "We are a finger, not a fist, Fire-in-his-hair."

He continued to pound the bracken in silence.

"You know what I'm talking about."

"Croaks-with-the-frogs?"

"I can't hold this fist together. He comes and he goes. Me-not-talking hates him, Sleeps-in-the-sun needs routine. we..." her words trailed off.

Fire-in-his-hair swept the smashed bracken into a large pottery dish, took a hand-full of roasted wattle seeds from the storage pot beside him and began pounding them into a fine flour. "There'll be marriages by the wattle fire soon," he said softly. "New people will come in. Would you like to find a couple to replace me and Croaks-with-the-frogs?"

No-point-shoe's heart broke. "No! I don't want to lose you. And G'ma says Croaks-with-the-frogs is important and we must keep him. I just don't know how to do it and hold the fist together."

As the wattle seeds turned into a fine, dark grey powder, Fire-in-his-hair swept them into the bowl with the smashed bracken root. He said nothing.

No-point-shoe put down the now clean bracken root. "What is wrong with that boy?"

Fire-in-his-hair stopped working. He looked at the large rock in front of him. His words barely audible. "I've damaged him," he said.

"You keep saying that," said No-point-shoe, "but it's not true. You're the only person that has ever had time for him. And you've made him a good hunter. Every time he comes back from his wandering, he brings meat."

Fire-in-his-hair was silent for a while, focussing on pounding the bracken root. Finally, haltingly, he began to speak. "I could have been his father.... if Eyes-are-dancing had lived and we'd had... But the trouble is, I was so wrecked after I lost her. It's like I was in a daze ever since. It's only since I found my feet in your fist that I've begun to feel human again." He looked across to where she sat, "I'm very grateful for that."

No-point-shoe replied without hesitation. "I was glad to have you. I always worry about the young ones. It's so hard to look after them all. It's wonderful to have an experienced hunter to share the burdens."

"How do you think Sleeps-in-the-sun is travelling?"

She took a deep breath. "I don't know. She's sad all the time, but that's to be expected. The good thing is that she is still getting out and about. I'm glad she went digging roots today, but she never does anything with much enthusiasm."

Fire-in-his-hair stopped pounding the bracken root and stared at her. He saw the care lines on her face and read the worry in her eyes. "The fire burns bright in you, No-point-shoe. It is an honour to be part of your fist."

No-point-shoe could not explain why her eyes tingled and her tears welled. "Let's just wait and see how the Wattle season plays out," she said. "Maybe Me-not-talking will take a husband and we can add him to the fist. Then Croaks-with-the-frogs can be... like a..." Her words trailed off.

Fire-in-his-hair laughed, sadly. "Is there such a thing as a fist thumb?"

The Lake tribe arrive

The Lake people arrived as the green leafed wattles began to flower. G'ma and G'pa stood at the entrance to the hive, spears in hand to welcome them.

"I am Swims-like-a-fish from the People of the Lake," their oldest G'pa called. "We seek the shelter of your fire."

"The Fire protects us all," replied G'pa, raising his arms in welcome.

"I am Rolls-in-the-berries from the People of the Lake." Their oldest G'ma called. "We seek the shelter of your fire."

"The Fire protects us all," replied G'ma, and she too raised her arms.

As the travellers from Lake filed in through the hive's entrance, the elders embraced formally. G'ma smiled warmly and gushed with enthusiasm, but beneath her cheerful exterior, her emotions were roiling.

When she was young, Wattle season was a joyous celebration of life, now it was a burden. Marriage negotiations were always difficult and it was not unusual for tensions to run high between the two tribes. The young ones usually chose their own partners but it was the G'mas and G'pas who decided which couples stayed with the Swamp people and which couple returned to the Lake. This often lead to tensions. Some couples were more valuable than others. As she embraced the G'ma from the Lake people, she tried to remind herself that this burden was also a privilege.

"We have brought avocados for you," Rolls-in-the-berries said with a proud smile. She gestured towards those members of her tribe who were carrying the gifts. At that signal they piled the large green fruits at the edge of the fire.

"Oh... lovely!" exclaimed G'ma.

There was a murmur of approval from the people of Swamp. The avocados would be added to the communal pot and enrich the flavour of the stews. The avocados only grew near the lake. The fruits ripened in winter but stayed fresh throughout Wattle. After each Wattle, G'ma would have the large seeds of gifted avocados buried but no tree had ever grown near the swamp. *Maybe this year.*

"You must be very tired after your long trip," she said. "We've prepared a burrow for you."

Rolls-in-the-berries frowned slightly. She wondered if this was a subtle dig at to her tribe's strength. In spite of their cheerful and slightly dotty exterior, the Swamp tribe's G'ma and G'pa were wily and had more years experience than her. Underestimating them would be a fatal mistake. She forced a smile, and followed the old G'pa from the swamp to the prepared burrow. This will be the place where the elders of the Lake tribe would sleep and where marriage negotiations would take place.

As she walked her eyes drank it the sights of the swamp tribe's hive. It was bustling with children and the people seemed healthy and happy. She felt a pang of unease. The Swamp tribe seemed to be flourishing but each year her tribe was diminishing.

The old man stopped at the entrance and motioned for her to lead the way into the burrow. The Swamp people's elders would follow them in and it was customary for there to be some preliminary discussions at this time.

It was dim inside, but the late afternoon sunlight shone through the air holes spaced evenly around the domed roof, creating enough light for the negotiators to see. There was plenty of room for people to sit in a large circle with their feet stretched out towards the centre. Rolls-in-the-berries and Swims-like-a-fish took their places inside, each resting their backs against an upright beam.

As was the custom, they had brought a pair of observers. Observers were those who were waiting in the wings to replace the senior G'ma or G'pa when the oldest ones died. It was their task to watch and listen to the proceedings so they would be able to take up the negotiations seamlessly when that inevitable day came. To the ordinary spears of the tribes, anyone who had out-grown their fertility was called G'ma or G'pa but amongst the seniors of the tribe, there was a definite hierarchy. Observers seldom spoke during negotiations. All the talking was done by the Senior G'ma's and G'pa's of the tribes.

The Swamp tribe's G'ma and G'pa were followed by a finger of observers. They spread out taking up half the uprights in the burrow. Every post-fertile person from the Swamp tribe was present. Rolls-in-the-berries shot a sidelong glance towards Swims-like-a-fish. The significance of this was clear. Extra observers meant the lead negotiators didn't expect to survive until the next Wattle.

Swamp tribe's G'ma offered a wooden platter with small green cakes made out of bracken roots infused with dandelion leaves.

Rolls-in-the-berries took a cake and forced herself to smile. "Thank you, Throwing-pine-cones," she said, stiffly. She always felt defeated in the negotiations with the Swamp folk. She put it down to what she considered the devious manipulations of Throwing-pine-cones. She felt a surge of relief knowing this would be the last Wattle negotiations with her.

Terror-of-magpies didn't wait for the cakes to reach him. "Negotiations shouldn't be too difficult this year," he said, his head wobbling in his usual way. "We each have a boy and a girl."

Rolls-in-the-berries paused, a cake part way to her mouth. "I hope we have more weddings than that," she said. "We also have a fine young man who needs a new wife. And a woman who still has a few years of child bearing ahead of her. We would like to find both of these partners."

"Ah..." the old man mentally kicked himself for forgetting the widows and widowers. "Yes, we have some older ones too. Maybe they will find each other."

Rolls-in-the-berries chewed her cake thoughtfully. "The... strange one... the one in black. He might suit our older woman."

Terror-of-magpies glanced sideways at Throwing-pine-cones but the old woman sat silently, chewing her cake. It looked like he would have to do the talking this afternoon. "Oh... You mean, Fire-in-his-hair? I ... um... not sure he'll return to fertility this season."

Rolls-in-the-berries snorted and on cue, the other members of the lake tribe did likewise.

Throwing-pine-cones frowned, but said nothing.

Swims-like-a-fish put his hand on the knee of his fellow negotiator and leaned forward. "How about our Sleeps-in-the-sun. I believe she is single again?"

G'pa's head wobbled even more. "Well... she's only just lost her husband, she's not likely to come into fertility this year."

Rolls-in-the-berries licked her lips and shook her head in derision.

G'pa's annoyance erupted. "...And she's originally from your tribe. Surely you wouldn't want to breed her back into your own tribe!"

"No... No... of course," Swims-like-a-fish raised his hands in apology.

G'pa was mollified. "We have a young man who might also return to fertility this year. He may suit your older woman."

"He *might* return to fertility?" Rolls-in-the-berries nodded her head towards the entrance of the burrow. What about the woman from the River? She has been widowed for a few years now."

G'pa was hesitant. "If you mean No-point-shoe, I'm not sure. She's older but she may suit your young man.... If she returns to fertility."

Rolls-in-the-berries exploded. "If!... If they return to fertility! This is not a game of bones, Terror-of-magpies. This is the future of our tribes! We have a healthy man and woman in our tribe. They need to breed and we need the children. We can't pander to your moping."

G'pa was nonplussed. "What are you saying?"

"I am saying that you are too soft on your young ones. You allow them to mope and mourn and not breed for years. Each year your young one's grieve, costs our tribe more children. We are losing numbers. And you are more concerned about the wounded hearts of your young ones."

"We can't... force them..."

"No. But you can put pressure on them. You pander to them! Why has that River woman not returned to fertility!? It's been years!"

Throwing-pine-cones' head snapped up and her eyes speared the G'ma from the Lake tribe. Each word fell like a hammer blow. "No-point-shoe will not marry your young man," she said, "She may return to fertility or she may not but that is not the reason. I am a river woman too and I understand how she thinks. She finds your men, dull, cold and heartless. They are not the right stuff to return her to fertility."

Rolls-in-the-berries sputtered.

G'ma drove on relentlessly. "If you want your young men to find mates, I suggest you teach them to be more gentle and caring."

The mouths of the Lake tribe's delegation fell open in shock and horror.

G'pa spread placating palms towards the Lake's delegation. "Thank you for your advice on how we should manage out tribe, Rolls-in-the-berries. We appreciate your wisdom and we will certainly think about what you've said. We know you only want what's best for us." He paused, then, "And please give some thought to our advice on the management of your tribe. I'm sure you understand that we only want what's best for you too."

Swims-like-a-fish was stony faced. "Let's leave it there for now, shall we?"

They all crawled from the burrow in sullen silence.

Listens-for-ducks

Sleeps-in-sun was sitting by the fire when the Lake tribe arrived. She leapt to her feet and grabbed No-point-shoe in excitement. "They're here!" She squealed and dragged her towards the entrance of the hive.

No-point-shoe laughed and allowed herself to be pulled along. But she reached out grabbed Fire-his-hair as she went and he followed too.

"What's the story?" He asked.

"My Tribe," said Sleeps-in-sun excitedly. "That's the story. It's been ... ages!"

There were many people milling near the entrance, welcoming each other with warm hugs. Sleeps-in-sun found a place as close to the entrance as she could get. No-point-shoe and Fire-his-hair stood behind her awkwardly.

Many of the Lake folk were familiar to her and Sleeps-in-sun waved and smiled at each, but her eyes kept searching for the special face. It had been long years since they had parted. Eventually she saw him, a man her own age with a shock of dark hair that matched hers. His spear slung lazily across his back and a laconic smile on his face.

"Ah!" She said as she engulfed the newcomer in a hug, "So you've decided to show up, did ya?"

The Lake man hugged her back, briefly. "I decided to make ya day."

Fire-his-hair scratched under his shirt. "You guys know each other?"

"Litter mates," said Sleeps-in-the-sun.

The man from the Lake tribe pulled away awkwardly and Sleeps-in-sun laughed. "Listens-for-ducks, this is Fire-in-his-hair and No-point-shoe. They're part of my fist."

No-point-shoe smiled. She understood the bond between litter mates. Her brother had wandered away from the fire when they were toddlers and was never seen again but she never forgot that special bond.

"I know No-point-shoe" said Listens-for-ducks as he nodded at her. Then he turned to Fire-in-his-hair. "But I've not seen you around much. You from the river?"

Fire-in-his-hair shook his head. "I'm a Swamp man," he said but would add nothing more.

Listens-for-ducks looked askance at Sleeps-in-the-sun but she widened her eyes and shook her head with a smile.

Listens-for-ducks laughed. "You know my wife, Sniffs-the-wind?"

Fire-in-his-hair was sure he had never met her. He smiled and nodded at her.

No-point-shoe laughed. "He should know her. She's a good swamp woman. But he wouldn't have a clue," she said. "He spent most of his time wandering around the bush looking for cats."

Fire-in-his-hair nodded apologetically. "I'm sorry," he said.

"I remember you, though," said Sniffs-the-wind gently. "I'm very glad to see you've returned to the tribe, Fire-in-his-hair."

"No-point-shoe did it," said Sleeps-in-the-sun. "She's the best fist leader in the tribe." She looked across to No-point-shoe and their eyes met. "She looks after all of us. Without her... well, I'd hate to think what life would be like."

No-point-shoe's eyes misted. She smiled and looked at her feet.

"Come on," said Sleeps-in-sun, her enthusiasm erupting, "Let's get you guys some dandy."

The little party headed towards the cauldrons simmering by the fire.

As they walked Sniffs-the-wind leaned across, "Who else is in your fist, Sleeps-in-the-sun?"

Sleeps-in-the-sun began an animated conversation about the make up of the fist. It soon developed into her sharing about the death of Finder-of-snails while the couple nodded sympathetically.

The Fire

Croaks-with-the-frogs returned to the hive soon after sunset with a point of mice tied to his pack. Sleeps-in-the-sun's little ones were more steady on their feet now having lived through their second winter. They ran to great him calling, "Oaks... 'Oaks!"

Croaks-with-the-frogs laughed as he saw them running. The little boy had a shock of dark curly hair like Finder-of-snails and the girl was fair like Sleeps-in-the-sun. As he got through the entrance of the hive, the children jumped and wiggled their bottoms.

"Oaks, Oaks," mimicked Croaks-with-the-frogs. "My little Oaks!"

The children tried to jump on him, but he gently held them off. "Not now, kids. I need to put these mice into the stew pot and then I'll show you what I've got."

"Mouse! Yummy!" said the boy.

" 'tew pot!" Said the girl and they followed him to the fire.

Fire-in-his-hair saw the commotion and laughed. "Ah! The mighty hunter has returned. With a point of mice."

Croaks-with-the-frogs grinned at him. "I still can't work out how to get a rabbit."

"Ah well... keep trying. You'll get there." The older man, took the mice from him. Let me skin and pot these for you."

"Thanks."

"Do you want the pelts?"

Croaks-with-the-frogs shrugged.

"I reckon Sleeps-in-the-sun could make a nice hat out of them."

"Fair enough."

The children had used up all their patience. "Oak, Ooaaks!" They whined. The little boy held onto his pack and hung off it.

Croaks-with-the-frogs frowned. "Stop it. Wait a moment and then I'll show you what I've got for you."

The little girl picked up on the meaning first. She pulled her hands towards her mouth in a grasping motion and screwed up her face. "Wait. Wait."

Croaks-with-the-frogs laughed. "Yes. That's right. You're a good waiter aren't you? Come on." He walked a short distance from the fire to just outside his burrow and swung his pack down. "I've got something for you but this is not something you can can eat."

" 'tew?" Said the little boy.

"No." Croaks-with-the-frogs suppressed a laugh as he rummaged in his pack. "It's not something you can eat."

"Eat 'tew."

Croaks-with-the-frogs laughter bubbled out. "Yes. We eat stew, but this is not for eating." He pulled out a lump of rich orange resin. It was almost perfectly round and fitted neatly into his hand. It was shiny and smooth and the light danced as it passed through it.

The children stared in wonder.

"Thumb," said Croaks-with-the-frogs giving the lump to the boy. He dove into his pack again. "Point," he said pulling out another lump and gave it to the girl. "And finally..." he plunged his hand in again. "Tall!" He pulled out a larger, less smooth lump.

The children jumped with excitement. "Tum," called the boy thinking that was the name of his gift. "Tum!"

"Now wait," said Croaks-with-the-frogs screwing up his face and making the waiting sign with his hands. "I'm going to show you ... the ... thing."

The little girl mimicked his expression. "Waiting. Waiting."

The boy copied her.

Croaks-with-the-frogs took one of the flat rocks from beside the fire and brought it to where his pack was lying. He put his lump of resin on the rock and struck it with a hammer stone. Soon the resin was smashed into a collection of small crystals and powdery dust.

The little girl's face fell. "Boken.... No Boke it!"

"No. No. It's not broken. It's part of your gift."

The little boy struck his lump of resin on the rock.

Croaks-with-the-frogs caught his hand, quickly. "No! Don't you break yours. You keep yours."

The boy stared at him.

"Just wait." Said Croaks-with-the-frogs making the waiting sign again.

"Wait. Wait." mimicked the girl.

Once Croaks-with-the-frogs was sure the little boy wasn't going to break his lump, the young hunter went back to the fire and collected a small coal on a piece of bark. By the time he had returned to the two waiting children, a small crowd had gathered. Several other children had left off their playing to come and see what was happening. A few of the older ones had run back to their burrows to get their winding things to show the visitors from Lake people. To the little ones in the tribe, Croaks-with-the-frogs was a maker of marvels.

Some of the Lake children, started to play with the winding things and a few of the swamp children regretted their generosity and took them back. They pretended to be showing them how to use them but in reality they were not really interested in sharing the device. They were only showing it off. Even a few adults noticed the commotion outside of Croaks-with-the-frogs' burrow.

"Now," said Croaks-with-the-frogs as he squatted beside the crushed resin on the rock. "Hold your resin towards my crushed one."

The children looked at their resin balls in confusion.

Croaks-with-the-frogs held their hands up so they could see both their lumps of resin and the crushed resin on the rock. He grinned, and with instinctive, theatrical timing, he said, "Ready?" And dropped the small coal into the crushed resin.

The resin burst into flame. It hissed and spat, throwing sparks and casting deep shadows in the fading light. The children gasped.

The adults smiled, in condescension. They all knew what pine resin did when it burned.

"Look at your lumps," Croaks-with-the-frogs pointed at the children's lumps of resin. "There's your gift," he said breathlessly. "There!"

The balls of resin glowed and sparkled as it caught the light of Croaks-with-the-frogs' little blaze. It was as if each child had a pair of fist sized flames in their hand. The children stared in wonder and a hush fell even on those who looked on. Only the hissing and crackling of the resin fire broke the silence.

Croaks-with-the-frogs' eyes were misty. He reached his hands towards Sleeps-in-the-sun's pair of children. "This is my gift," he said softly. He placed a hand on each child's chest. "The Fire."

The children stared into his eyes.

"The fire that burns in my heart, for you."

Some of the adults from the Lake twisted their faces in a mixture of disdain and disgust. Attention seeking behaviour towards children was unseemly. The Swamp people shrugged. It was just another oddity of Croaks-with-the-frogs.

But G'ma had been watching intently from her place by the fire. Now she sat with silent tears running down her face.

"Why are you crying?" asked G'pa.

"I don't know." She replied.

The little mouse girl

Croaks-with-the-frogs saw other children looking with yearning at Sleeps-in-the-sun's children and their fire stones and he felt a pang of shame. Even if he could have brought back enough round lumps of resin for all the children, the little trick wouldn't have been as good if it was aimed at everyone. Sleeps-in-the-sun's children were special to him. He couldn't deny that, but he also knew what it was to feel excluded, and the longing still ached in his heart.

"When I go out again," he said to the other children, "I'll get more fire-stones. I'll get fire-stones for all of you."

The children smiled but beneath their smiles, Croaks-with-the-frogs could see their disappointment. They didn't want to wait.

Their hidden disappointment only intensified the boy's shame. His face, flushed, he pushed himself to his feet and walked to the pile of wooden bowls to get himself some stew.

As he leant to pick up his bowl, he noticed someone standing behind him. The fire was behind them, casting their face into shadow, but in spite of this, Croaks-with-the-frogs knew it wasn't anyone from the Swamp tribe. It must have been one the visitors. They were small. At first he thought it was one of the children, but he could see the deep red of their shirt and the pale trousers. It must be one of their young female spears. She stood with her feet slightly apart and her hands on her hips, staring at him.

Croaks-with-the-frogs looked down, afraid to catch her eye. "Excuse me," he muttered, as he walked around towards the stew pot simmering by the fire.

"No! I don't think I will," the girl said.

Croaks-with-the-frogs stared at her in shocked horror. She had turned now and the firelight flickered and danced on her face. She looked vaguely familiar.

"Well? Aren't you going to say hello?" She said archly, her top lip curled in disdain.

Croaks-with-the-frogs was nonplussed. "Um... Hello."

The look of disdain was replaced by one of outrage. "You've forgotten me!"

Croaks-with-the-frogs looked at the girl again. He only knew one person from the lake tribe, the little mouse girl....

It was the wattle before last. Croaks-with-the-frogs was watching the other children play by the fire when a girl walked up to him and said, "Hey, boy? How come you don't play?" Before children got their names they were all called either, 'boy' or 'girl.'

The boy shrugged. Staring at the girl. She was small. She looked like she was a year younger than him but her voice and manner were confident. She wore the typical smoke tanned rabbit skins of all children and her hair was short and mouse coloured. In fact, everything about the girl reminded him of a mouse. Her size, her hair, even the expression on her slightly pointed face were all mouse like. He didn't know what to say.

The mouse girl stared at him intently. "You just sit here staring. Don't you want to play?"

"I... don't know."

She laughed. "You don't know if you want to play?"

The boy found himself torn. Part of him wished she would say something nasty and leave him alone. But another part of him enjoyed the fact she was talking to him and didn't want it to stop. He glanced past her to where the other children were playing. None of them were paying him the slightest attention.

Without another thought, the boy leapt into honesty. "I don't usually play with the other kids," he said. "I go hunting with Fire-in-his-hair."

The little girl cocked her head, doubtfully. "You're too young to hunt," she said scornfully.

"I know," whispered the boy. "I don't do the hunting. My job is to find the cat. Then Fire-in-his-hair will kill it."

The little girl's scorn evaporated. "How do you find the cat?"

The boy's face fell. "I don't know. I've never found it. We've found its tracks and we've seen where it's killed, but... I've never been able to find it."

She squatted down in front of him, her eyes wide with excitement and fear. "Does a cat hunt near here?"

For the first time, the boy noticed her eyes. They were a pale blue. Almost the colour of the sky. As he looked into them he thought he could even see little clouds floating in the blueness. He shook his head and brought himself back to the conversation. "It hunts down at the swamp."

On a sudden impulse, the boy had leaned across and said, "You wanna go down to the swamp and see if we can find some tracks?"

She chewed her bottom lip thoughtfully. "Children mustn't leave the fire."

The boy looked around the hive. Fire-in-his-hair was no where to be seen. He wondered if he was sleeping in his burrow or maybe he was out hunting on his own. "No one would care if I left the fire." he said, sadly.

The mouse girl misunderstood. "Maybe if we didn't go for long."

"Um.. maybe."

"Just down to the swamp to find some tracks." Her blue eyes sparked.

Nobody around the fire saw them slip away. The boy led her through the tea tree and down to where the land became boggy at the edge of the swamp.

After a while, the boy stopped and pointed at a faint disturbance in the dirt. "There!" He whispered. "There's Cat."

The little girl crouched and stared at the tracks. It didn't look like anything and her disappointment showed clearly on her face.

The boy was suddenly ashamed. He'd thought she would be impressed. "Well... anyway... that's what cat tracks look like," he said helplessly.

The girl screwed up her face and rubbed her hand over the tracks.

"I suppose we should be getting back," he said, but he didn't want to go back. This was a part of his life he only shared with Fire-in-his-hair and he enjoyed sharing it with another person.

"Thank you for taking me to see the cat tracks, boy," she said solemnly. Her head bowed a little as she said it mimicking an adult's formal expression of gratitude.

The boy stared at her in amazement. There was no mockery or judgement in her eyes. She spoke to him... like a respected equal.

When they returned to the hive, the Lake people's G'ma grabbed the girl by the arm and gave her a hard whack on the backside. She was pulled away from his sight and he heard shouting and more smacks.

Fire-his-hair was preparing his pack. "Where have you been?" He asked, a faint smile on his face.

Croaks-with-the-frogs said nothing.

That evening as dusk fell, Fire-in-his-hair took the boy out to hunt the cat.

The-tiny-one

Croaks-with-the-frogs stared at the young woman standing before him. This couldn't be her. There was nothing mousey about this girl. She blocked his path as if she was in complete command of her surroundings. Her hair was thick and it spread from her face in loose curls. She was small, like the mouse girl, but there were faint curves of adolescence in her breasts and hips. She was utterly terrifying.

In spite of his fear, Croaks-with-the-frogs stared into her eyes. In the firelight, all he could tell was they were pale but he remembered the sky blue eyes of the little mouse girl with tiny clouds in it and he hoped with all his heart that her eyes were still the same.

"I remember you," Croaks-with-the-frogs said unconvincingly. "I just didn't recognise you."

"Hmph!" The girl seemed to get even more offended by that. She shifted her weight, pushing her hip out to one side and folded her arms. "My name is The-tiny-one," she declared proudly.

Croaks-with-the-frogs nodded, dumbly.

"So... do you have a name?"

"Croaks-with-the-frogs," he replied miserably. He suddenly felt ashamed of his name.

She laughed. "You always loved frogs and that ashen swamp. You got me thrashed!"

"Ah... yeah... I'm very sorry about that."

"I forgave you for that ages ago." She waved her hand in dismissal, then leaned closer. "I haven't forgiven you for running off the next day and leaving me with no one to play with, and I will never forgive you for forgetting me!"

"I didn't forget you. I just didn't recognise you."

"Same thing!"

"It's not!" Croaks-with-the-frogs found himself quite amazed at how easy it was to argue with this girl. Not only that, arguing with her was such fun, he wished it would go on all night.

The little girl looked at his empty bowl. "Are you gonna put some stew in that?"

"Um... yes."

"And are you going to get any stew for any of the guests? Or are you too important now?"

All the fun went out of the argument. Croaks-with-the-frogs was overwhelmed with shame. She knew how unimportant he was. She could see the way everyone in the tribe thought he was cursed. Her sarcasm bit deeply.

Without speaking, he went to the stew pot and filled his bowl. He took a cake and gave both the bowl and the cake to the girl. Then he got another bowl of stew for himself and settled down away from the fire near the entrance to his burrow.

The-tiny-one stood staring as he walked away. She had been looking forward to meeting the strange swamp boy again all Winter. Following the cat trails by the swamp all those seasons ago, had been the greatest adventure of her childhood. She had been looking forward to more this Wattle season. She had imagined the boy would be waiting for her and they would play together. She had a name and a spear now, so they could go following cat tracks without getting into trouble. But now it had all turned out wrong.

He had been nowhere to be seen when the Lake people arrived, and she feared maybe he had been killed in the years since they met. She thought of asking the dark clothed man who took him hunting the cat, but Fire-in-his-hair was baking cakes around the fire like an old woman. Perhaps, his young partner had been killed and Fire-in-his-hair was now no longer the great hunter. She pushed down her disappointment and mingled with others.

When Croaks-with-the-frogs arrived at the hive, The-tiny-one was overjoyed to find him alive. His looks hadn't changed much, she thought. He was still skinny with the same large, brown eyes, but he carried himself into the hive like a returning hero with a point of mice hanging from his pack and the children squealing in delight.

As he walked past her, she smiled at him, but he looked right through her. When he produced the fire trick for the children, everyone was shocked. But she couldn't explain how the simple trick with the resin moved her so deeply. The fire, the children's awed faces and the heartfelt sincerity in the young man's voice shook her to the core.

Without thinking, The-tiny-one had resolved to confront him. To force the strange swamp boy to recognise her existence, but her nerves had caused her to be loud and silly. To make matters worse, even after he admitted that he didn't remember her, she kept on pushing, trying to eat stew with him. Eventually he had given her his own bowl to get rid of her, and walked away to eat by himself. As she sat by the fire with her face arranged in a welcoming smile, the shame and embarrassment of rejection scoured her heart.

The boy who lost his burrow

A shadow covered Croaks-with-the-frogs as he sat eating his stew. He looked up to find No-point-shoe standing in front of him, blocking out the flickering light from the fire. Behind her Fire-in-his-hair stood awkwardly. Inwardly, the young man cringed. He expected some recrimination from his pine resin thing. No-point-shoe's face was stern but there was a hint of a smile around the corner of her mouth.

"Come on, misery guts," she said shortly. "It's time you were taught to sing."

Croaks-with-the-frogs looked up at her in horror. He had never sung. He was always beside Fire-in-his-hair who sat sullenly when the singing began. He looked at him now, his eyes pleading.

Fire-in-his-hair chewed his lip and nodded. "She's right, Croaks," he said, sadly. "I should have taught you to sing long ago."

Croaks-with-the-frogs was shocked. "You don't sing!"

"I used to."

No-point-shoe reached down and grabbed the young man by the arm. "And now it's time for him to sing again."

There was no resisting No-point-shoe when she had a mind to do something. She gently hustled the two men to where Sleeps-in-the-sun was sitting by the fire with Listens-for-ducks and Sniffs-the-wind. She plonked Croaks-with-the-frogs down between her and Fire-in-his-hair. "Now," she said to Fire-in-his-hair, her eyes dancing. "You can show him how to sing."

"Can I finish my stew?" asked Croaks-with-the-frogs.

"Finish your stew but just listen at first." Fire-in-his-hair took a deep breath as if he was about to start singing, then stopped and said, "It's just one word.... a nonsense word but you change the tune to create a background sound." He sang. "Dip, Dip, Dip, Dip. Dip, Dip, Dip, Dip. Dip, Dip, Dip, Dip. Dip, Dip, Dip, Dip."

Croaks-with-the-frogs stared at him in amazement.

"Can you hear the change in pitch? Medium, Down, Down again, Then Up. Then we start again. When you're ready, join in." Fire-in-his-hair began to sing in earnest and soon other men around the fire joined in. People clapped their hands to the beat and others began to stamp their feet.

Sniffs-the-wind took up the beat and launched into a higher cascade of notes. No-point-shoe joined in with her and soon the air was filled with a cacophony of harmonious sound.

Croaks-with-the-frogs had never seen Fire-in-his-hair immersed in the tribe's singing before. The fact that all this had begun with his rather plain notes was extraordinary.

In a little while, the young spears began to dance, moving gracefully around the fire to the beat of the music. Most of the dancers were those of marriageable age. Croaks-with-the-frogs saw Me-not-talking twirling and singing at the same time.

After a few moments, the singing faded to silence then somebody from the lake people started another beat. "Come on, Croaks-with-the-frogs," said No-point-shoe with a grin. "Join in."

All of them joined the beat of the Lake people and Sleeps-in-the-sun clapped her hands in time.

The tribes continued to take it in turns to sing and after a few rounds, the young men sat and joined in the singing. Only the marriageable women danced around the fire. They danced for a few songs, then they sat down to join the singing and the marriageable men took their turn to dance. This dancing and watching continued well into the night.

A large wooden bowl of wattle toddy was passed around and each person had a sip. Fire-in-his-hair took the bowl in both his hands and drank. Then he smiled at Croaks-with-the-frogs, and passed the bowl across the young man to No-point-shoe. No-point-shoe grinned, drank and passed the bowl on.

As the night wore on, the organised pattern of dancing and singing broke down. Men and women of all ages would dance around the fire. Sometimes they would dance singly, other times in larger groups or in pairs. Even the children joined in the dancing. Listens-for-ducks and Sniffs-the-wind left their seats and joined in, disappearing into the swirling mass of bodies.

Croaks-with-the-frogs felt a pang. He knew this would usually be the time when Fire-in-his-hair would take him away from the tribe. He wished Fire-in-his-hair would do so now. Part of him didn't want to be a part of this. And yet another part of him, wished Fire-in-his-hair had never taken him away. He wished this could have been a regular part of his life like it was for the others.

Suddenly, No-point-shoe was on her feet. "Come on!" she said, laughing. She swayed her hips and moved her hands in a a circular motion.

Croaks-with-the-frogs gaped.

Sleeps-in-the-sun smiled and nodded but she didn't get up. She only clapped harder.

"Is anybody gonna dance with me!?" No-point-shoe said.

As if the night couldn't get any more strange. Fire-in-his-hair pushed himself to his feet, an embarrassed smile on his face. He took No-point-shoe's hand and the pair disappeared into the twirling dancers around the other side of the fire.

Sleeps-in-the-sun leaned in close to the boy's ear. "This is good," she said, her voice shaking with emotion.

Croaks-with-the-frogs had no idea what she was talking about. What was it that was so good? And why did the young woman's voice quake so? He kept his face neutral and stared at her, nodding.

She reached across, put her arm protectively around his shoulder and gave him a motherly squeeze. "It'll be alright," she said. "No one expects me to do anything because this is the first Wattle since I lost Finder-of-snails. So, if you want, you can just sit here and clap with me."

A wave of relief washed over him. Sitting beside Sleeps-in-the-sun, the young man was now able to relax and watch what was happening from a position of safety.

He saw the little mouse girl dancing around the fire. Once he caught sight of her, he couldn't stop staring. It was not just the way she moved that entranced him. It was the way she fitted in so easily. She was surrounded by other young ones. She laughed and threw her head back and others joined in, meeting her eyes. He wished she would come and ask him to join in the dancing but she didn't even look at him. And why would she? He was an outsider.

Sleeps-in-the-sun leaned towards his ear again. "That girl in the red top is a hot dancer isn't she?"

Croaks-with-the-frogs stared at her.

Sleeps-in-the-sun laughed. "I can see you staring at her. I don't blame you. She moves beautifully."

Croaks-with-the-frogs blushed. "Her name is The-tiny-one," he said.

A wicked smile spread across Sleeps-in-the-sun's face and she pushed him, playfully.

Not long after, Fire-in-his-hair and No-point-shoe slumped down beside them. They were breathing heavily and laughing. "These old bones can't handle all this action," said Fire-in-his-hair.

"Your bones aren't old yet," said No-point-shoe with a snort. "But make no mistake, if you can't keep up, I'm going to dump you from the fist."

"I'll outlast you, G'ma," he retorted.

She laughed and cuffed him playfully on the back of his head.

Sleeps-in-the-sun leaned over to No-point-shoe and said something to her. She pointed towards where the The-tiny-one was dancing and both women shot Croaks-with-the-frogs an appraising glance before returning their gaze to watching the young girl.

Croaks-with-the-frogs squirmed. "I might go off to the burrow soon," he said. "I'm getting tired."

"Ah." said Fire-in-his-hair, flatly. "Sorry. I forgot to say. We've given our burrow to the lake people."

"What!?" Croaks-with-the-frogs was appalled.

"They've got to sleep somewhere. And we used to always go hunting the cat so..."

"You mean they always slept in our burrow?"

Fire-in-his-hair shrugged. "You never noticed?"

"You can crowd in with us," said No-point-shoe. She laughed. "I don't think Me-not-talking will be needing her sleeping spot tonight."

Croaks-with-the-frogs sighed and pushed himself to his feet. With an accusing look at Fire-in-his-hair, he dragged himself off to his burrow to fetch his rabbit pelt bedroll. As he bent down to enter, he groaned, as if the weight of the world was on his shoulders.

No-point-shoe watched him leave, then burst into laugher. "Oh the sufferings of youth!" She turned to Fire-in-his-hair. "You are such a beast. How could you impose such grief on that poor boy?"

Fire-in-his-hair looked down and smiled, marvelling at the mystery of it all. "He's a really strange kid. Sometimes he seems like a grown man and other times, he's like a child that can't leave the fire."

"He's gonna make a run for it tomorrow."

Fire-in-his-hair looked up at her. "You think? And miss the rabbit hunt?"

"It's all over his face. He wants out of here."

"Maybe I should take him to hunt the cat."

No-point-shoe repressed a desire to shout. She paused for a moment as if considering the suggestion. "No," she said, slowly. "That's no solution. Next year the boy has to stand before the fire and marry. No-one is going to want to marry him if he runs away from the dancing and he can't hunt a rabbit."

"He's a good hunter," said Fire-in-his-hair defensively.

"He needs to stay."

Sleeps-in-the-sun leaned across to add her bit of information. "He's been staring at that little dancing girl all night."

"Really?" Said Fire-in-his-hair doubtfully.

The women took it in turns to fill in the details.

"Staring at her as if she's a haunch of rabbit and he hasn't eaten for three days," said Sleeps-in-the-sun.

"He's still a male."

"She's a bit too smooth for him."

"We've got to keep him here," said No-point-shoe decisively. "He'll try to run early morning. Someone has to be awake to stop him."

Sleeps-in-the-sun got lazily to her feet. "I'll do it. I'm a bit sick of all the sparkling eyes and wiggling hips. I'll sleep now and be up when he makes his move."

Fire-in-his-hair shook his head. "It's like we're tracking roos."

Sleeps-in-the-sun laughed. "Yeah... but a really sulky roo."

After Sleeps-in-the-sun walked away, Fire-in-his-hair said, "She won't be able to keep him in the hive. Maybe I should get up early too."

No-point-shoe leapt to her feet and pulled him up. "Oh no you don't, G'pa! We're going to find that bowl of toddy and then we're dancing some more."

Your life is not about you

It was still dark when Croaks-with-the-frogs gathered his sleeping pelt and crept out of the burrow. Sleeps-in-the-sun was fast asleep. Only a handful of people were gathered around the fire, sipping hot drinks and speaking in low, intermittent snippets. Only the lilting sounds of birds hinted at the approach of dawn. The young man readied his pack. He collected some wattle seeds from the storage pot, added his tools and a cake. Then he set about preparing a coal carrier for his journey into the bush.

He had just placed the glowing coal on the bed of grass when a shadow fell over him and a gravely voice said, "Where are you going?"

G'pa was standing over him. The old man was still wrapped in his sleeping pelt. He had placed it over his bald head in a vain attempt to keep himself warm in the predawn chill. His feet were bare and his spindly calves were exposed.

Croaks-with-the-frogs opened his mouth to say, I'm going to hunt the cat but he remembered what G'pa thought of that quest so he closed it again. He stared at the old man in stupid silence.

G'pa crouched beside him, allowing his sleeping pelt to fully cover his body. His face was haggard and his eyes had the telltale red rims of someone just awoken from sleep, but the expression on his face was kind. "What's the matter, boy?" He said gently.

Something in the old man's manner opened a pathway in Croaks-with-the-frogs. "I've got to get out of here, G'pa," he said. The words tumbled out. "I don't like all this Wattle season stuff. I can't sing, I can't dance, I can't talk to girls. Nobody wants to be around me. Last night only Sleeps-in-the-sun sat with me. I... " He was about to confess his shame at the encounter with the little mouse girl, but he stopped himself in time.

G'pa sat silently and let the boy talk, but his eyebrows flicked upwards when Croaks-with-the-frogs mentioned his inability to talk to girls. When it was clear that Croaks-with-the-frogs would say no more and he began to wrap the coal for his journey, the old man reached out and put a gentle hand on his forearm. "Are you happy, boy?" He asked.

Croaks-with-the-frogs stopped wrapping his coal. "No," he said miserably.

"Are you happy when you are away from the tribe?"

Croaks-with-the-frogs wanted to say 'yes' but once more something in the old man's presence demanded honesty. "Not really... but I'm happier than I am when I'm here."

The old man nodded.

The rabbit skin used to wrap the coal carrier flopped open, exposing the coal glowing in the darkness. Both men stared at it.

After a moment, G'pa said, "Croaks-with-the-frogs, I have something very important to tell you. Will you listen to me?"

"Yes." The young man looked up and the hunger in his eyes was clear.

"When I was your age, I was unhappy too," G'pa's head wobbled as he spoke. "But I realised something very important. It has taken me a long time. I still haven't fully accepted it, but I began to learn it when I was your age. And the more I understand it, the happier I become."

Croaks-with-the-frogs stared at him in silence, but he wondered how the old man could consider himself happy.

G'pa waited, watching the boy's face closely, waiting for him to digest his words. Then, "Your life is not about you, Croaks-with-the-frogs. That is why you are unhappy. You think your life revolves around you. It does not. You must revolve around life."

Croaks-with-the-frogs blinked. He didn't understand.

G'pa tried again. "You can't make yourself happy, Croaks-with-the-frogs. You have to stop thinking about yourself. You need to start thinking about others. You said Sleeps-in-the-sun was the only person who sat with you at the fire. No." The old man leaned closer to emphasise his words. "You were the only person who sat with Sleeps-in-the-sun. If you weren't there, she would have been on her own."

G'pa paused for a moment to give his words time to sink in. "Soon, G'ma will be up and looking for you, to share her nut of dandy. If you're not there, she drinks her dandy on her own. The Lake people are our guests. They need to be made welcome. Today is the rabbit hunt and they need you to hunt with them. It's not about you. It's about them. Once you turn your attention away from yourself and towards others, you will find yourself happier and you won't need to run away anymore. Do you understand?"

Croaks-with-the-frogs stared at him and nodded.

The old man man smiled, then with a soft groan pushed himself to his feet. "The fire burns brightly in you, Croaks-with-the-frogs. Let it burn." And with that, he shuffled back to his burrow.

G'ma's eyes gleamed in the faint light of the burrow as the old man moved towards his place beside her. "So... was he there?"

"Yes. Ash it was cold out there."

"Was he trying to leave?"

G'pa tugged at her rabbit pelt. "Yes. I'm freezing."

"Did you convince him to stay?"

"I don't know. I did my best. Let me in."

G'ma relaxed her grip on her pelt. "You don't know? Ach! You're freezing! Get your feet off me!"

"Just let me warm them up." He snuggled closer, luxuriating in her warmth.

"Keep them still. How could you not know if he's going to stay?"

"I did what you said. Now let me sleep."

"He has to stay for the rabbit hunt!"

Silence.

"You had to convince him to stay."

More silence.

"Terror-of-magpies.... Are you awake?"

A soft snore.

"Blood and Ash!"

When Sleeps-in-the-sun scrambled out of the burrow, the eastern sky was a pale grey. She had woken to find Croaks-with-the-frogs and his sleeping pelt gone. She threw on her pale green shirt and dashed out, silently cursing herself.

She sighed with relief when she found the young man, fully clothed, sitting on one of the stone seats facing the fire. "Ah... You're up early," she said forcing a cheerful tone into her voice.

"Yeah."

She looked at the partially prepared pack on the ground behind him. Beside it was an unwrapped coal carrier. The coal, lying in its bed of grass, was cold and dead. "Are you going... out?" she asked, hesitantly.

Croaks-with-the-frogs followed her eyes to where his coal carrier lay and smiled sheepishly. "No. I'm not going... I... It's the rabbit hunt and..."

Sleeps-in-the-sun's face broke into a relieved smile. She was glad she didn't fail in the task No-point-shoe had set her.

The young man stared at her. *If you weren't there, she would have been on her own.* His eyes watered. Croaks-with-the-frogs had never been needed before. It was exhilarating. He took a deep breath and hesitated. It was as if he were standing at the edge of a swamp and something was calling him to dive in. He was frightened, and reluctant, but somehow he knew G'pa's words were the truth. The fire was calling to him and he had to respond. "And... tonight, " he said hesitantly. "At the fire... maybe you can show me how to dance?"

Sleeps-in-the-sun crouched in front of the young man and ruffled his hair. "Sure, kid. It would be my pleasure."

~ 5 ~

THE RABBIT HUNT

We don't usually hunt with the tribe

By the time the sun was poking above the tops of the tea tree, the hive was a bustle of activity. Spears were sharpened, tasks were allocated and a hurried breakfast was eaten. Nearly everybody was heading off on the rabbit hunt. Only the G'mas and G'pas were left by the fire with the confined mothers and the children. Every fist was sent out.

The tribes marched in groups. The leading group was made up of the most experienced hunters, Fire-in-his-hair and No-point-shoe were with this group. After them came the younger spears and those of marriageable age. There was pushing and laughing as they set off into the tea tree. Me-not-talking was in this group. The final group were the youngest spears; *flushferts*.

Flushferts would climb down the rabbit holes with spear and brand to chase the rabbits out of their warren into the waiting nets of the older hunters. Only young spears could do this because older spears were too big for the warren's narrow passageways. If a *flushfert* was to get stuck, it would be a terrible death. Croaks-with-the-frogs had never been a *flush-*

137

fert. When he was small enough, he wasn't in a fist and now he was too big to learn.

There was more than a fist of *flushferts* guided by a few experienced hunters from the Swamp tribe. Most of the young spears had only just been given their names last winter and had not dyed their clothes yet. But some of the *flushferts* were young girls with coloured clothes. The-tiny-one from the lake tribe was one of these.

Croaks-with-the-frogs watched them leave and wondered what role The-tiny-one had been given. He was to be the fire lighter, so he had made a pair of carriers each with a glowing coal. He would only carry the coals and his spear into the hunt.

"What are you still doing here?" It was Sleeps-in-the-sun. She was allocating the groups and was going to walk out to the rabbit warren behind the *flushferts.*

Croaks-with-the-frogs froze. "Aren't I supposed to go with the young ones?"

"Blood and ash!" Sleeps-in-the-sun pressed down her annoyance. She remembered the boy had not been on a rabbit hunt before and she cursed Fire-in-his-hair for taking him away so often. "You've got to be with the lead group. The fire must be lit, otherwise they are worms on a rock out there. What were you doing?"

Croaks-with-the-frogs stared at her. He didn't want to tell her he had been watching The-tiny-one get ready to leave. He wanted to go and talk to her and he hoped he might be able to walk out to the warren with her.

Sleeps-in-the-sun didn't wait for an answer. "Go! Run! You've got to catch the lead group or else there'll be trouble."

The young man, hoisted his carriers onto his back, picked up his spear, and dashed through the tea tree. As he pushed past The-tiny-one, he said, "I'm really very sorry. I wanted to walk with you to the Warren." By the time he had finished his sentence, he was behind the group of marriageable spears. He called back over his shoulder, "But I'm supposed to be at the front."

The courting spears around him started laughing.

"Thanks for the update."

"Good to know the fire is well in hand."

"Run, boy. Run!"

Croaks-with-the-frogs felt his face colour as he pushed through the group. He resented the spears of his own age and those a little bit older. He couldn't understand why they disliked him. He knew he'd made a mistake but why did they have to laugh at him and make him feel like a fool?

Then he realised The-tiny-one would have heard them laughing at him and a deep shame replaced his anger. It took all his will power not to turn around and run into the bush. He wanted to be anywhere but there.

By the time he reached the tail end of the leading group, Fire-in-his-hair was looking around nervously. When he saw the young man, his face broke into a relieved grin. He stepped close and put his arm around the boy's shoulder.

"Whew! Sorry. I forgot you were with the lead group," he said.

Croaks-with-the-frogs looked at him in anger about to say something surly but he saw the nervousness in the older man's eyes and he remembered G'pa's words. *Fire-in-his-hair needs me*, he thought. "It's OK," he said. "We don't usually hunt with the tribe."

Fire-in-his-hair nodded and pulled a nervous face.

It was mid morning when they arrived at the rabbit warren. The experienced hunters crouched beneath a large gum tree and scanned the sky for hawks. No-point-shoe sniffed the wind and motioned to Croaks-with-the-frogs and Fire-in-his-hair. "Leave your spears," she said. "Grab some sticks and leaves for the fire." Once they had each gathered a good armful, she said, "On my call, we break cover." After another quick search for danger, she said, "Let's go!" She ran, crouching into the open grassland, spear at the ready.

Fire-in-his-hair and Croaks-with-the-frogs followed, their arms full of twigs.

"Set a fire here." She dug her spear into the soft ground to mark a place and ran on.

Croaks-with-the-frogs dropped his bundle of sticks at the place where she had marked and ran behind her, mimicking her crouching run with his eyes scanning above and below.

At the sight of the humans, several rabbits dashed into the safety of their burrows.

No-point-shoe marked out another pair of places for a fire to be set down wind of the original site and Fire-in-his-hair dropped enough twigs and leaves to mark both places. Then they all dashed back to the protection of the tree.

Croaks-with-the-frogs grabbed his spear and some more kindling and set himself to head out again.

"Do you want me to come with you?" asked No-point-shoe.

"I'll be right," he replied. "No sense risking both of us." And with that he sprinted to the nearest pile of firewood.

This was the most dangerous part of his job. Out in the open with no-one to cover him, he would be exposed and vulnerable until he got the fire lit.

All the spears were now crowded under the spreading branches of the tree. They watched the sky and the horizon in helpless worry. If anything attacked Croaks-with-the-frogs, they would not be able to help him.

Despite his young age, the boy was experienced at laying and lighting fires quickly and his regular expeditions beyond the fire alone meant he was surprisingly confident. Within a few moments, the fire was lit and a thin trail of smoke snaked into the air.

The tribes let out a relieved cheer and ran out into the grassland and gathered around the freshly lit fire.

Croaks-with-the-frogs didn't wait. He ran further out to the next pile of kindling and set another fire. Then he sprinted to the final site and lit that. By the time he lit the last fire, the fire closest to the tree was sputtering and running low on wood. He dashed back to the tree, gathered a few larger logs and returned to blow life into the sputtering blaze.

The fires sent a steady cloud of smoke across the plain giving the tribes protection from arial attack. With the wind at their backs, the older spears moved across the grasslands, finding rabbit holes and caving them in to block the runs. Some runs were not caved in. Several other openings where the wind was blowing away from the hole were left open but large sock shaped nets were pegged over the mouths of the warren. Above each of these sites, a small protective fire was lit and loose groups of hunters gathered around, waiting.

Into the warren

Croaks-with-the-frogs squatted by the fire closest to the tree. He was gasping for breath after his long sprint circuit. Around the crackling blaze stood the *flushferts*. He saw The-tiny-one standing before a large entry to the rabbit warren. She was staring into it, kicking her feet and loosening her neck muscles by moving her head from side to side. The other *flushferts* stood staring into the fire. Fear marked their faces, but The-tiny-one's jaw was set in a determined line. Each *flushfert* had a spear in one hand and another stick with a lump of pine resin on the end of it.

An older woman from the lake people addressed the *flushferts*. "Alright!" she said in a commanding voice. "Do you all remember your turning pattern?"

The young ones nodded.

"Who are the lead *flushferts*?"

The-tiny-one and another girl from the swamp people who was the same age as Croaks-with-the-frogs put up their hands. The-tiny-one kept staring at the rabbit hole, her lips were tightly closed but her mouth twisted into a silent snarl.

The woman nodded. "You turn right, then left, then right, then left."

The other girl in coloured clothes nodded. "Right, left, right, left," she repeated.

The-tiny-one said nothing.

The woman glanced at her then back to the tan clad young ones gathered around the fire. Next?"

A pair of young ones raised their hands nervously.

"You will turn, left, right, left, right."

"Left, right, left, right," they repeated.

"Next?"

Another pair raised their hands.

"Left, left, right, left."

The young ones echoed her dutifully as the other ones continued to repeat the instructions they had been given.

"And the tails?"

The last pair of young ones raised their hands.

The woman pointed towards a young boy from the lake tribe, a quizzical look on her face.

"I follow The-tiny-one and keep turning left," he said in a quavering voice.

The woman nodded and turned to other tail.

"I follow Dirt-on-her-face and keep turning right," he shouted.

The woman smiled briefly, then her face hardened. "OK. So remember, that warren wants you dead. You lead with your fire brand and support it with your spear. When the firebrand goes out, leave it behind and drive with your spear. Once you've taken your last turn, then get the blazes out of there! Look for a glint of light and head for it."

The young ones nodded.

"Remember," She repeated. "That warren wants you dead!" She paused for a moment, then, "Alright! Light 'em up!"

The *flushferts* turned and placed their resin lumps into the fire. Sparks flew as each lump burst into brilliant flame.

The-tiny-one looked around the group, her face twisted in rage. "Come On!" she roared and without a backwards glance, she threw herself headlong into the rabbit warren. Those who were meant to follow, scrambled after her.

The other lead *flushfert* went to a different opening, she hesitated then with a terrified scream, crawled in. As the last young one disappeared into the warren, Croaks-with-the-frogs stared in awe at the hole The-tiny-one had disappeared into. *Is there anything that girl can't do?*

The-tiny-one crawled through piercing light. The blazing brand ahead of her was blinding. She saw nothing except the sputtering flame. She could smell the harsh fumes and taste the acrid smoke in the back of her throat. On her hands and knees she raced through the warren, feeling the walls close around her. "Come on, you *pargronts!*" she roared. The ground grazed her knuckles and knees.

Ahead of her she heard scrabbling and the ground shook as rabbits fled from the fire and fumes. Behind her the *flush-ferts* were shouting. They were struggling to keep up. She turned right. She heard an unearthly shriek and something big slammed against her brand. The fire went out, leaving only a dull red glow in the darkness. She roared defiance and charged on. "Fuck you!"

She turned left. The tunnel dipped and narrowed. She hit her head on something hard protruding from the roof and for a moment, she stopped moving. Then the rage returned. She was forced to lower her upper body and crawled ahead on her elbows. She screamed again and surged into the darkness, her rump scraping the roof, dislodging sand and dirt.

The red glow of her brand soon faded to black. It was now dead but she could tell from the smell that it was still smoking. She continued to carry it as she advanced. The tunnel got smaller. Crouching lower, her chest grazing the hard packed dirt, she pushed on, roaring her defiance into the darkness. There was more movement ahead as rabbits scattered. Behind her was silence. The other *flushferts* had taken their own passages, spreading fear and chaos through the warren.

The smell of smoke began to fade. Only a hint of the smoke blown in from the fire outside remained. She dropped her brand and looked for a way out. Everything was black. She crawled on alone with nothing but her spear. This was the most dangerous part of the journey when a cornered rabbit would be as likely to attack as run away. In the distance she could hear the calls and screams of the other *flushferts* as they pushed through their passageways. The darkness stretched on and she pushed down a rising panic, replacing it with rage. "Come on you *pargronts!*" she screamed. "Come and get me!"

As she turned a corner, she felt the tunnel widen. She returned to her knees and increased her speed. She caught the strong musk of rabbit and her spear pushed something. There was a scrabble and dirt fell from the roof. She roared and thrust her spear forward. The darkness erupted into a shriek and something slammed into her face. "You ash fuckers!" She crawled on.

In the distance she thought she could see a faint shimmering. She raced for it on hands and knees, screaming in desperation and ignoring the fluid pouring from her nose. As she got closer, the shimmering got brighter becoming a pale light patch shining from a passage in the upper left into the darkness of her passage way. She had found a way out. She had only to reach the lit passageway and follow it to the surface.

When she was less than a *length* from the lit passage, she was plunged into darkness again. Something large had blocked the run. It was a rabbit, too frightened to leave the burrow and frozen where the lit passage met the darkened one. If The-tiny-one was to get out, she had to go through that rabbit.

With a desperate scream, she charged, thrusting her spear into the blockage in front of her. The rabbit turned, shrieked and struck back at her with it's claws. A musky smell enveloped her as its fur pressed against her face. Her spear was wedged against the wall. The rabbit pushed her backwards and teeth smashed into her left shoulder. Her shirt tore and the pain exploded down her arm. She wrenched her right arm free and plunged the spear into where she knew the rabbit would be. It howled and pulled away. There was a sharp crack and her spear broke off.

The rabbit turned and moved up the lit run towards daylight. She followed until she reached it frozen again in the run, it's bulk eclipsing the light of the entrance. She pushed her broken spear into its rump and roared. "Get on! Ash it!

Get the fuck out!" The rabbit lurched and bounded from the warren.

The opening was clear and light flooded in. She was blinded again. Outside she could hear screams and human voices. She clambered towards the light.

She screamed. "Hold off! It's me!" She burst out of the run and into the daylight.

It took a few moments for her eyes to adjust. She lay on her back in the long grass listening to the sounds of battle nearby and breathing the fresh air in relief.

Bringing the rabbit down

No-point-shoe and Fire-in-his-hair were crouched around a rabbit hole that emerged from an embankment. They had caved in many of the other entrances to the warren but left this open. They had pegged their net down with a few forked sticks, and now gathered with Listens-for-ducks and Sniffs-the-wind to wait for a rabbit to try to get out. It was traditional during the wattle hunt, for the fists to be scrambled. Me-not-talking, being of courting age, was off with a makeshift fist made up of marriageable spears.

From the entrance closest to the big tree, the woman in charge of the *flushferts* waved a blazing stick in the air. "All in!" She called. "All in!"

Sleeps-in-the-sun scrambled over the crest and joined the other hunters around the net.

"Ah!" said Listens-for-ducks, "So you've decided to show up, did ya?"

Sleeps-in-the-sun shot him a cheerful grin. "I decided to make your day."

"Look lively," called No-point-shoe. "Something's coming."

From inside the warren, they could hear shouts and curses as the *flushferts* worked their way through. Being downwind of the opening, the hunters were able to keep their presence hidden from the rabbits within. Suddenly something rumbled at the opening and a large rabbit bolted straight into the sock shaped net. The pegs were pulled from the ground but the net was tangled around the animal. It couldn't get traction.

The hunters pounced on it, screaming. Their spears plunged from all sides but no one could land a mortal blow. The rabbit kicked fiercely with its back legs and sent No-point-shoe tumbling against the embankment. Sleeps-in-the-sun and Listens-for-ducks stood side by side blocking the rabbit's headlong dash. It tried to veer to the left but the net tripped it. Listens-for-ducks plunged his spear into its shoulder and the rabbit squealed.

Fire-in-his-hair climbed onto the rabbit's back and tried to slam his spear into its neck but the Rabbit bucked and his spear only slipped through the skin. He tumbled onto the ground.

No-point-shoe shook her head clear and grabbed her spear. She threw herself at the beast from behind and drove her spear into its side below its ribs. It let out a piercing scream as the spear struck into its vitals. Blood spurted from the wound and spattered No-point-shoe's face. The rabbit thrashed its back legs several times, and lay still.

"Skewered it!" shouted Listens-for-ducks, triumphantly.

"Great work," said Fire-in-his-hair as he climbed to his feet. "Are you OK? It kicked you pretty hard."

"I'm fine." No-point-shoe laughed, the glint of victory in her eyes. "Smooth move on it's back, *brudha*."

Fire-in-his-hair shook his head in embarrassment. "The back is usually a good place to strike from. If I can get my spear through the shoulder blades..."

"You need to stay up there to do that," teased Sleeps-in-the-sun.

The laughter and banter continued. As they untangled the carcass from the net.

Sleeps-in-the-sun pulled up short. "Hold on," she said holding her hand up for silence. "What's this?"

From within the warren, they heard a high pitched human voice screaming.

No-point-shoe's eyes widened in fear. "What the fuck is that!?"

Listens-for-ducks laughed. "That's The-tiny-one. She's mad as a motherin' maggie."

The group crouched outside the hole and continued to listen.

"There's another rabbit down there," said No-point-shoe, her voice heavy with fear. "It will have smelt the death of this one and it won't come up."

Fire-in-his-hair dropped the net and grabbed for his spear. "The kid's stuck down there." He made towards the entrance but pulled up short, realising the hole was too small for an adult to crawl through.

No-point-shoe picked up her spear and climbed the embankment above the hole. "We can dig her out from the the top."

"Hang on, hang on!" shouted Listens-for-ducks. "She's the best I've ever seen. Give her time, she's not trapped yet... Gather around the entrance." He crouched a *length* away from the hole, his spear poised.

The others took up positions and waited. "Wish we had time to reset the net," said Sniffs-the-wind nervously. "This could be dangerous."

No-point-shoe had jumped off the bank and taken a place in the semi circle. "Don't take any unnecessary risks," she said. "If a rabbit bursts out and you can't hold it, let it go."

Within the warren, they heard The-tiny-one scream and an unearthly screech emanate from the hole. There was a few moments' silence and a rabbit burst out, scrambling and squealing.

The hunters erupted into shouts, "Look out!"

"Get it. Get it!"

"Bring it down!"

The rabbit seemed to be labouring. It didn't make a dash for the scrub or swerve to avoid the spears. It squealed and lashed out with its teeth as it staggered out of the hole. The broken haft of a spear protruded from its chest.

Fire-in-his-hair leapt onto the beast's back and this time he stayed there. Driving his spear down between it's shoulder blades.

The Rabbit let out another howl and collapsed, kicking out one last time with it's back legs.

No-point-shoe turned back to the entrance of the warren. Lying beside the hole was the young girl who danced so beautifully the night before. She looked a mess. Blood was streaming from her nose and a cut high on her forehead. Her left eye was blackening and the side of her face was discoloured. Her hands were grazed and blood oozed from a tear in her shirt near her shoulder. In her right hand was a broken haft of a spear. The head of the spear was embedded in the rabbit's chest.

"What did I tell you?" said Listens-for-ducks.

The-tiny-one opened her eyes and smiled, revealing blood stained teeth.

No-point-shoe smiled back. "That was the best piece of *flushferting*, I've ever seen, girl."

Twists-the-reeds

While No-point-shoe checked The-tiny-one's wounds, the others prepared the rabbits for the journey to the hive. A pair of long straight sticks were found and each carcass was tied to it by its paws. Listens-for-ducks and Sniffs-the-wind hoisted a stick on their shoulders while Fire-in-his-hair and Sleeps-in-the-sun hoisted another. "You guys coming?"

No-point-shoe prodded at the bite on The-tiny-one's shoulder. "Can you walk?"

The young girl nodded and pushed herself, unsteadily to her feet.

No-point-shoe kept a wary eye on her. "Walk with me," she said. "If you need support, you can lean on me."

The-tiny-one smiled. "I'm OK," she said, but she walked close to the older woman.

The band of hunters headed off towards the hive. The fires were mostly out now, but the smoke still hung across the grassland giving them some security from attack. As they approached the large gum tree, they saw Croaks-with-the-frogs standing beside a fire, feeding the flames.

Sleeps-in-the-sun called to him. "Hey, kid. Look what we got!"

Croaks-with-the-frogs' face was red and he was on the verge of tears. "One of the *flushferts* is stuck down there!" he screamed. "I can hear her sobbing!"

The others dashed to Croaks-with-the-frogs' fire.

When the boy saw The-tiny-one, his face broke into a relieved grin. "Oh! I thought it was you down there," he said.

As soon as he said it, Croaks-with-the-frogs cursed himself, but mercifully, The-tiny-one didn't react. She stood at the hole where she had entered with her head cocked, listening. From inside she could hear the definite whimpering of a child. "It's one of boys that followed me down," she said. "Light me a brand."

Croaks-with-the-frogs stared at the blood pouring from her nose. "You're not going in there again?"

"Can you do this, girl?" asked No-point-shoe.

The-tiny-one nodded.

"Do as she says, *brudha*," said Fire-in-his-hair. "We've gotta get that kid out."

Croaks-with-the-frogs lit the end of a stick and handed it to The-tiny-one. "I don't have any more resin," he said. "This fire won't last long at all."

"Then better give me your spear too," she said and without another word, she plunged back intro the rabbit hole.

Croaks-with-the-frogs' warning had proved correct. The fire lasted only a few moments but the stick smouldered and smoked, giving her some security and she crawled through the warren. This foray into the warren was different to the last. There was no rage, and no screaming. Blinded in the darkness by the glowing tip of the brand, The-tiny-one needed to use her ears to find the trapped *flushfert*.

The whimpering sound carried through the warren. She turned right and called out, "It's OK! I'm coming! It's me! The-tiny-one!" She kept her voice calm, but inside she was anything but. Without her protective rage, The-tiny-one was utterly terrified. The darkness closed in and the animal smell assailed her. Her shoulder was aching and her left arm could barely carry her weight.

From further in, a terrified voice bleated, "I'm stuck! I'm stuck! There are rabbits here and I can't get out!"

"It's alright. It's OK. I'm coming. What's you're name?" Her voice quavered.

"If I go forward, they attack me and I can't turn around!" The boy's voice rose in intensity until he finished nearly hysterical with fear.

The-tiny-one desperately got herself under control. "It's OK! I'm The-tiny-one. I can you hear you." She turned right again and the tunnel narrowed. She crawled on, her stomach grinding against the ground.

The whimpering was just ahead of her now. The boy had turned into a passageway to a sleeping quarters. A more experienced *flushfert* would have backed out before they reached the dead end but he had pushed on, obeying his orders unquestioningly. The rabbits had nowhere to run so the brand would have no effect. They would fight to the death and a lone boy was no match for terrified, cornered rabbits.

The-tiny-one took a deep breath. Dust and smoke filled her nostrils. She resisted the urge to cough, and kept her voice calm. "Alright, boy. I'm here now. I'm right behind you."

"I can't get out." The boy was less hysterical now but his control was extremely fragile.

"My name is The-tiny-one. What's your name, *brudha*?"

"It's me, Tiny-one," the boy wept. "Twists-the-reeds."

"Oh, hello Twists-the-reeds." The-tiny-one said forcing a cheerful tone. "It's OK. I can get you out. I'm going to reach out with my hand and touch your foot. Let me know if you can feel it, OK?"

The boy whimpered his assent.

The-tiny-one reached out her right hand and felt the soft touch of the boys clothes. "Can you feel me touching you?"

"You've got my leg." Twists-the-reeds laughed, and his hysteria threatened to burst from beneath the surface.

"OK. OK." The-tiny-one closed her eyes. "I'm going to grab your ankle and then start pulling you out, but you have to crawl backwards with me. Do you understand? I can't pull you out unless you crawl out too."

"I can't turn around." The boy began to cry again.

"No. That's OK. You don't have to turn around. Just wriggle your way backwards."

The-tiny-one hoped the boy wasn't stuck, but that panic had driven him to freeze. If he was genuinely stuck, she would not be strong enough to pull him out with only one arm. She tugged on his leg. "Come on, Twists-the-reeds, wriggle your way backwards."

The boy wiggled and the gentle pull on his leg was enough to get some reverse movement. The more he moved, the more the boy wriggled. Soon he was desperately wriggling back down the passageway. The-tiny-one guided him, back the way they had come. It was a slow crawl but eventually both of them got to the entrance of the warren.

Fire-in-his-hair reached in and grabbed The-tiny-one by the legs and hauled her out.

He dived in again, fumbled around in the darkness for a moment before grabbing Twists-the-reeds and pulling him free.

By now, most of the spears were gathered around the entrance to the warren. They burst into a mighty cheer when the young ones were pulled clear.

Once outside, The-tiny-one's pent up stress and fear erupted to the surface. She began to cry. Silently at first but as the trickle turned into a flood she collapsed on to the ground, her chest heaving. "I want my G'ma," she gasped between sobs.

"G'ma's back at the hive," said one of the lake tribe's spears as she slapped The-tiny-one gently on the back.

No-point-shoe was amazed at the lake tribe's lack of compassion. They expected the youngsters to bounce back as if nothing had happened. When she first married and left the river tribe, No-point-shoe had thought the swamp people were hard and callous, but these Lake people were even worse. She shot a questioning glance at Sleeps-in-the-sun.

The younger woman smiled and shrugged. "Lake people are tough," she said.

No-point-shoe would have none of it. She pushed her way to the side of The-tiny-one and put her arm around her shoulders. "Croaks-with-the-frogs grab my end of the rabbit and follow me," she barked. Then with a soothing coo, she led the young girl back towards the hive. "Come on, dear, I'll take you to your G'ma. She'll be very proud of you. You were so brave! Hold your head up, like this and pinch your nose."

The hunters headed back but No-point-shoe didn't lead The-tiny-one straight to the hive. Instead she led her to the edge of the swamp. By the time they arrived, the girl had stopped crying, but No-point-shoe didn't take her arm away.

"Now before we go back to the hive, I need to check out your wounds," she said.

The-tiny-one nodded. Her nose had stopped bleeding.

"Fire-in-his-hair and Croaks-with-the-frogs keep watch."

The men perched themselves on a low branch and watched the sky for hawks. No-point-shoe dipped some rabbit fur in the swamp water and washed the girl's face. Then she took out her gum-nut of ointment and began smearing it on The-tiny-one's cuts. "I don't like the look of that shoulder," she said. "Don't put any strain on it, but you need to keep moving it or else it will freeze up."

Croaks-with-the-frogs stared at them from his place on the branch. He couldn't for life of him work out why No-point-shoe was being so sweet. "What's with her?" He whispered to Fire-in-his-hair.

The old hunter laughed softly. "It's Wattle season," he said. "Everyone goes crazy in Wattle season."

The cut on The-tiny-one's head had stopped bleeding but the wound was jagged and ugly. On a whim, No-point-shoe broke a small twig of wattle blossom from a nearby tree. She bent it into a curve and tucked it behind each of the girl's ears, so the flowers partially hid the wound. "There," she said. "Now, not only are you brave but you're pretty too."

The-tiny-one's face burst into a radiant smile.

As the pair returned from the banks of the swamp, The-tiny-one was luxuriating in the pampering. She saw Croaks-with-the-frogs staring at her and beamed at him.

Croaks-with-the-frogs stared at her blackened eye, the bruised face and half hidden wound on her forehead and his heart stopped beating. The thought came to him, unbidden. *I have never seen anyone so beautiful in all my life.*

6

FIRES MERGE

Back at the hive

Once back at the hive, No-point-shoe set The-tiny-one down beside the fire. "You just rest here," she said. "I'll get you a nice nut of Banksia 'n toddy."

The-tiny-one smiled, soaking up the attention.

No-point-shoe returned with the toddy and sat beside the young girl, in companionable silence.

The-tiny-one sipped her toddy and wiggled her feet in front of the fire, watching the rest of the tribes as they bustled around her.

The largest rabbit was spitted over the fire to be roasted for dinner, while the remaining rabbits were butchered and set to stew with some of the avocados. The new stew should last for several days.

Sleeps-in-the-sun and Croaks-with-the-frogs were part of the group skinning the rabbits. Once their task was done, they washed the gore off their clothes and returned to sit with No-point-shoe and The-tiny-one. Fire-in-his-hair was part of the group making cakes. He was still pounding the dough on the other side of the fire.

Croaks-with-the-frogs wanted to speak to The-tiny-one but he could think of nothing to say. He sat beside her sipping a nut of Banksia with no toddy added, and stared at the fire, wracking his brain.

By the time The-tiny-one had finished her Banksia and toddy drink, her head was nodding involuntarily.

"How about, we tuck you into bed," No-point-shoe said. "If you have a nice nap this afternoon, you'll feel fit and well tonight for the feast."

The-tiny-one smiled and got to her feet. She handed her empty gum-nut to Croaks-with-the-frogs. As the boy took it, she found herself staring at him. His eyes were big and brown and she thought for a moment she could see her own reflection in them. The reflection changed and fire replaced it. To The-tiny-one it seemed that within Croaks-with-the-frogs' eyes, she had become engulfed in flame. Like the incident with the resin balls and the children, she was suddenly deeply moved and couldn't work out why.

No-point-shoe shot Croaks-with-the-frogs a bemused look as she gently led the girl towards her burrow. "Don't worry, dear," she said. "It's just the Wattle toddy. It often makes you see things differently."

After they had left, Croaks-with-the-frogs asked Sleeps-in-the-sun, "Why did No-point-shoe give her Wattle toddy? I didn't get any last night."

Sleeps-in-the-sun grinned. "You'll have plenty of years to have Wattle toddy, boy. It makes you see things and feel things that you don't need to feel. Some say it's a way of communing with the fire but I'm not convinced of that. It burns out your brain if you drink too much, but it's good for aches and pains. That's why No-point-shoe gave it to the girl. She'll sleep well this afternoon and have wonderful dreams."

Many of the hunters were crawling off to their burrows for a nap. Fire-in-his-hair set his last cake to bake and arched his back. He waved to Sleeps-in-the-sun and Croaks-with-the-frogs as they sat on the other side of the fire and motioned with his hands that he was too.

Sleeps-in-the-sun smiled and waved back. "I think I'll catch some sleep too," she said to Croaks-with-the-frogs. "You wanna come?"

Croaks-with-the-frogs' eyes darted quickly from side to side. "Um... No... No, I'll just sit for a while. There's... not going to be much room in the burrow with... everyone there."

Sleeps-in-the-sun laughed. "It's a tight squeeze but it's not unusual for there to be more than a fist in a burrow during Wattle season."

"Oh... yeah... OK... but I'll be alright."

The older woman shook her head. "You are a strange little fellow, Croaks-with-the-frogs." She pushed herself to her feet and headed for the burrow. After a few steps, she turned back to him with a grin, "But don't forget... we're dancing tonight, you and me."

Croaks-with-the-frogs smiled and waved.

In the darkness of the burrow, The-tiny-one lay on her side facing the wall and slept deeply. Behind her No-point-shoe faced the same way, her arm laid protectively across the young girl's waist. Fire-in-his-hair snuggled in behind and Sleeps-in-the-sun squeezed in behind him.

"Where's the kid?" asked Fire-in-his-hair.

Sleeps-in-the-sun, chuckled softly. "He didn't want to come... said it was too crowded."

No-point-shoe's voice was muffled, she was on the verge of sleep. "He's a weird kid. Maybe you really have ruined him, G'pa."

Fire-in-his-hair could tell from her tone she was smiling, but he didn't smile. Croaks-with-the-frogs' weirdness, echoed his own and Fire-in-his-hair knew it was he who caused most of the boy's wounds.

Sleeps-in-the-sun wriggled close to Fire-in-his-hair's back drawing warmth from him. "I don't think you guys should keep calling each other G'pa and G'ma." She said cheerfully. "You're not that old."

No-point-shoe snorted. "I'm not that old. But Fire-in-his-hair is."

"I've only seen a couple more winters than you, old woman."

No-point-shoe laughed sleepily. She pushed her bottom back into Fire-in-his-hair's loins and wiggled. "G'ma is old, then there's the hills. They're even older than G'ma.... And then finally..." She chuckled. "There's Fire-in-his-hair. Oldest of all!"

Fire-in-his-hair didn't respond. Within a moment, the two women were asleep on either side of him but he lay in the burrow with his eyes staring into the dim light, his emotions whirling. He could feel the soft rounded cheeks pressing against him and the smell of No-point-shoe's hair was full of promise. The last time he felt like this was many years ago. The memories were sweet but they tore at his heart. He reached his arm across the body of No-point-shoe and wept silently.

Croaks-with-the-frogs sat by the fire and looked around the hive. The sun was high and warm. The last of the hunters had disappeared into their burrows and even G'ma and G'pa had gone for a nap. Only the nursing mothers and a few of the older children were still up to feed the fire and keep an eye on the food. The boy picked up his spear and his empty pack and with a final glance towards his burrow, he sprinted out of the hive and into the bush beyond.

A new spear for The-tiny-one

Fire-in-his-hair did not sleep well. He couldn't get comfortable but he didn't want to move and disturb the others. In addition, he wanted to avoid rubbing himself against No-point-shoe. That would make matters even worse. As soon as he heard some extra movement around the fire, he crawled from the furs and went out.

He got himself a nut of dandelion root and took a place by the fire. There were not many people up and about. A few of the old ones were checking the food and the children were playing near their burrows. He sipped his drink and stared into the flames.

Even outside the burrow, he could feel the soft curve of No-point-shoe's rump pressing against him. His blood pulsed in his loins and he felt a surging of desire. Her hair had tickled his nose and the smell of her made his heart pound. Something wild and dangerous was about to erupt from within him and he clutched at his gum-nut in desperate fear. He closed his eyes and tried to think about Eyes-are-dancing. He summoned her broad gentle face and her sparkling black eyes. But the image was nothing more than a pale creation of his own imagination.

He opened his eyes again and stared into the fire, sipping his drink with his mind mercifully blank.

The-tiny-one lay alone in the burrow and stared at the mud caked wall. She was glad the ground felt solid again.

Throughout her nap, the floor was heaving and swirling beneath her. It was like she was surrounded by an entire tribe of eyes, calling to her and pushing her onwards into a land of dreams. The dreams were full of dark passages, rank with the stench of rabbit and the plaintive cries of trapped children. She had crawled through the darkness, expecting attack at any moment. Her brand nothing more than a faint point of red light far in the distance. As is the way with dreams, the light changed to become a fire, crackling and burning in the darkness. The darkness became the sad brown eyes of Croaks-with-the-frogs. For reasons she couldn't explain, the dream was both alluring and terrifying. *I am never going to drink that toddy again.*

She swept the furs away and crawled into the afternoon sunlight. The area around the fire was full of people. Some cooking, others chatting or working on various tasks. Croaks-with-the-frogs was nowhere to be seen and the young girl pushed down a pang of disappointment. She grabbed her broken spear and walked over to where Listens-for-ducks was mending his rabbit net. "Could you please help me make a new haft for my spear?"

Listens-for-ducks looked up from his net and tried to force his face into a frown. "You've broken another one, girl," he said, but his smile betrayed him. He reached his hand out for the broken spear and looked around the fire.

He saw Sleeps-in-the-sun at the entrance. Her hair was wet and the fur that lined her clothes was dripping water into the dry sand at her feet. The young woman smiled and waved as she approached. "Hey, Ducks," she said.

"Where have you been?"

Sleeps-in-the-sun leaned over her brother and shook her head. The water spattered from her hair and landed on her brother's face. "Soaking rabbit pelts," she said.

"Ash off, Sleepy shoes," he said. "I haven't had to put up with that for half a lifetime, don't start it again now." In spite of the harsh words, his eyes twinkled, revealing a nostalgic joy. He turned to The-tiny-one. "She used to wake me up that way when we were kids."

The-tiny-one smiled. She only vaguely remembered Sleeps-in-the-sun when she was part of the Lake tribe.

Listens-for-ducks stood and showed his sister The-tiny-one's broken spear. "We're going to get a new haft. Come with?"

Sleeps-in-the-sun nodded and went over to her burrow to get her spear. The little party left the hive together and headed out into the bush to find a suitable branch. Soon after they returned, Listens-for-ducks set about scraping the branch down to a smooth haft for The-tiny-one's spear, while, Sleeps-in-the-sun and The-tiny-one worked on the point.

They reheated the point of the old spear in the fire until the glue softened and became runny. Then The-tiny-one pulled the stone spear point clear and rinsed it clean. Sleeps-in-the-sun pulled out her stone sharpener made from a rabbit tooth and worked the edge and the point until it was sharp again. After a while, she arched her back and stretched. The light was fading and a faint orange hue tinted the western sky. "We'll have to leave it there, kid," she said. "Tomorrow, we'll head out to find some pine resin to make more glue."

At that moment Croaks-with-the-frogs burst from the tea tree and ran into the entrance of the hive.

"Oaks, Oaks," called Sleeps-in-the-sun's children.

Croaks-with-the-frogs was gasping for breath. He had clearly been running for a significant period of time and was exhausted. He bent over and rested his hands on his knees and sucked deeply.

The children jumped and pulled at his pack. "Oaks Oaks," they chorused.

"Little Oaks," replied the young man between gasps. "What would I do without my welcoming party?"

"Oo hunt? B'ing mouse?"

Still panting, Croaks-with-the-frogs swung his pack off his back and laid it on the ground. "Yes. Only a thumb mouse." He pulled it from his pack and showed it to the children.

They stared at it in wonder. And the young man laughed at their awe-filled expressions. "It's not a very good 'un," he said. "The pelt is damaged. You wanna help me skin it?"

"Me 'kin it.... me 'kin it!" they chanted.

Croaks-with-the-frogs led his little party of admirers away from the entrance to where a large flat boulder was set between a pair of burrows. He set about skinning his mouse while the children generally got in his way and stopped him from finishing his task. The young man laughed and chatted while he worked.

The-tiny-one stared at him in amazement. Fully grown spears who have coloured clothes rarely associate with children. And they certainly don't play with little ones who can barely talk. This was considered unhealthy, and yet something about the compassionate way Croaks-with-the-frogs stared at the children, touched The-tiny-one deeply. Was this part of the reason why she found him so fascinating?

A few of the other children gathered around, standing awkwardly at a distance. The older ones sneered derisively while the toddlers and younger children watched the interaction with undisguised yearning.

Croaks-with-the-frogs looked up from his skinning and grinned at a few of the littlest ones. "Hey, sparks," he said softly. "I've got something for you."

The children's eyes widened and they stepped closer.

Croaks-with-the-frogs dipped into his pack and pulled out a few balls of resin and handed them out to the children.

The children grabbed the balls and stared at the boy with shining eyes.

The-tiny-one wondered how he was able to know which child wanted the resin and which thought the action ridiculous. It was as if he could read their minds just by watching their faces.

Sleeps-in-the-sun watched the interplay and grinned at her young companion. "Well, that's a handy coincidence," she said. "The kid's brought resin for us." And with that Sleeps-in-the-sun stood and crossed the camp. "Hey, Croaks!" She called. Can you spare any resin for our best *flushfert*?"

The-tiny-one's insides froze. Was Sleeps-in-the-sun unaware of what the balls of resin meant? Did she realise what she was asking? She tried to grab the woman's sleeve and stop her but Sleeps-in-the-sun was not slowed. The-tiny-one found herself following clumsily behind.

Croaks-with-the-frogs looked up at his friend with a nervous smiled.

"Glad you showed up, kid," Sleeps-in-the-sun said. "I thought you were going to try to wriggle your way out of dancing tonight."

"I told you I'd dance. I just needed to..." his voice trailed off.

Sleeps-in-the-sun ignored the boys discomfort. "Anyhow... we need to fix The-tiny-one's spear and we wondered if you've got any resin we can use for glue."

Croaks-with-the-frogs wouldn't meet The-tiny-one's eyes. He rummaged in his pack and mumbled. "I don't have much." He extended his hand and showed Sleeps-in-the-sun a few broken slivers resting on his palm. "It's enough to light a fire but not enough for glue."

She laughed and cuffed him playfully across the top of his head. "You gave it all to the babies, ya bunny."

"Um..." Croaks-with-the-frogs looked across at The-tiny-one, a terrified look on his face.

Sleeps-in-the-sun laughed cheerfully. "You seem to have an endless supply." Then, as if she had been struck with a new thought, "Hey, how about you take the kid out tomorrow to show her where you get the resin?"

Croaks-with-the-frogs stared at The-tiny-one.

The-tiny-one stared back. For an instant, she was trapped in her dream again. The faint memories of dark tunnels and a blazing fire. *Douse that toddy,* she thought.

Sleeps-in-the-sun stood watching the pair for a moment, then she started laughing again. "By the blazes, torturing you kids is too easy. It's not even fun." She paused as the pair stared at her in confusion. Then she laughed again. "Naa... it's fun. Great fun." And with that she ruffled Croaks-with-the-frogs' hair and walked back to the fire.

You don't have to sit with me

As evening settled in, the tribes gathered around the fire to eat. The roasted rabbit was carved and placed on fresh cakes. There was laughter, jokes and muted singing as the food was served. The more they ate, louder they became as the sense of celebration increased.

Fire-in-his-hair didn't take his food to eat by the fire. He found a place between the storage burrows and ate on his own.

No-point-shoe saw him withdraw and came over. "Are you OK?"

He pressed his lips together tightly as if trying to stop himself from speaking.

No-point-shoe squeezed in beside him and they ate together in silence.

Their food was almost finished when Fire-his-hair said, "I think I might be getting fertile."

No-point-shoe said nothing. She stared at him for a long moment, then went back to her food.

"You don't have to sit with me," he said without looking up.

"I know," she replied and took another mouthful of cake. The silence descended again.

After a while, Fire-his-hair said, "I'm too old to get fertile."

No-point-shoe laughed, softly. "I don't think so."

They finished their food in silence. No-point-shoe went to the cauldron and got a nut of hot dandy for each of them and they sat wedged between the burrows, pressing against each other as they sipped their drinks.

Gradually, the tribes shifted from eating to singing. Someone started a beat and others joined in harmony. Soon the young marriagables were dancing and eventually they were joined by others. The toddy was passed around and the celebration went into full swing. They had survived another day, another hunt. More enemies had been killed and today, nobody had died. It had been a good day.

Fire-in-his-hair watched the tribes celebrate. Sleeps-in-the-sun was trying to show Croaks-with-the-frogs how to dance and the The-tiny-one was laughing because the boy had no sense of rhythm. He thought back to their days of hunting the cat together. He let the guilt wash over him and wondered what the boy did now when he prowled the bush alone. He remembered his own dark days before he found the child, when he would hunt the cat alone. The anger, the misery, the gnawing sense of futility. "I have not been fertile for a fist-fist of wattles," he said flatly.

No-point-shoe nodded in the darkness. "They whispered about you even when I came to the tribe. They said you were marked and trying to sell your life. Nobody expected you to survive for long."

Fire-in-his-hair said nothing for a long time. When he began to speak his words came slowly, then they tumbled. "I wasn't... trying to sell my life... I was looking for Eyes-are-dancing... my wife. I ... didn't believe she was dead... I thought

I would find her somewhere. I had this crazy idea in the back of my mind that I didn't even admit to myself. But I thought the cat still had her. That if I could find the cat, then I would get her back."

No-point-shoe stared at him.

"Eventually, last summer I admitted to myself that the cat was dead. If the cat was dead, then so was Eyes-are-dancing."

He lapsed into a prolonged silence and No-point-shoe wondered if perhaps he was not going to say any more. Finally he said, "And now... I'm feeling... things."

Deep within No-point-shoe's chest, flames erupted. It warmed and tingled through her body and she shuddered at the thought of it. "I knew Jumps-a-branch was dead. I had to drag his body from the burrow.... I was young and I should have returned to fertility in a few years. But I couldn't. Either I was around my own family from the river people or... I just don't like those coast men. They're... " She paused for a moment then said, "Not like you."

Fire-in-his-hair rubbed his hand across his mouth. "I feel like an awkward kid."

She laughed girlishly, her eyes shining in the firelight.

"Do... don't you think we're too old?" He said.

She dropped her nut of dandelion onto the ground. The dark liquid spilled out and soaked into the sand. "I don't care," she said.

Fire-in-his-hair leaned towards her. The tip of his nose gently touched her cheek. He could smell the fragrance of her skin and he was swept by a wave of emotion. He stopped, and pulled back, embarrassed and afraid. "I feel like a bloody kid," he said again.

In contrast, No-point-shoe laughed. A wanton, womanly laugh that set fire to his flesh. She reached out, pulled him towards her and pressed her lips against his.

Old instincts and long suppressed memories rose to the surface, entangled in smells, and tantalising touches. Like the walls collapsing in an old burrow, emotional barriers were slowly stripped. Their breathing became heavier and more urgent as hands probed and souls expanded.

Fire-in-his-hair left his drink and followed No-point-shoe back to the burrow. In their private sanctuary, No-point-shoe laid bare her wounds. She lay unprotected and exposed with breasts heaving in urgent need.

Fire-in-his-hair paused and stared at her in the darkness, drinking in all her vulnerability and sweetness. For an instant an image of Eyes-are-dancing flitted into his awareness. The memory brought a tang of pain but it no longer had the power to undo him. He focussed on the breathtaking woman who lay before him and the last of his reticence crumbled.

This is No-point-shoe and I am hers.

Dancing

Croaks-with-the-frogs was putting all his energy into trying to dance. The singing was loud and melodious and several men were pounding logs with sticks to keep the beat. The-tiny-one led the way swaying her hips and stepping lightly to the beat as she moved around the fire. Croaks-with-the-frogs followed closely, trying to mimic her actions. Sleeps-in-the-sun followed him, shouting encouragement and criticism between gales of laughter.

"No. No," she said between laughs. "Your hips, swing your hips."

Croaks-with-the-frogs waved his lower body from side to side.

Sleeps-in-the-sun's laughter rose in pitch. "Just your hips. Not your whole body. Watch what she is doing."

The-tiny-one turned her head and looked at him over her shoulder, her eyes sparkling in the firelight. "Like this." She swayed her hips and her hands floated gracefully out to either side.

Croaks-with-the-frogs flapped his arms.

Sleeps-in-the-sun laughed hysterically. "Oh Blaze! Oh Fire! This is hilarious. Bend your knees, kid. Try to feel the music."

Croaks-with-the-frogs bent his knees and waddled.

Sleeps-in-the-sun could take no more. She collapsed onto the ground, holding her stomach. "I can't.... I can't breathe."

Croaks-with-the-frogs stopped dancing and watched her roll. "I've been trying all night," he said, laughing. "I'm doing everything you say." It was true, he was trying to follow Sleeps-in-the-sun's instructions but he knew he looked nothing like The-tiny-one. She seemed to glide around the fire like a swan in flight.

The-tiny-one stopped dancing and joined in the laughter, putting her hands on her knees as she did. "You are the worst dancer, I have ever seen, Croaks-with-the-frogs."

"Thank you!" The boy tried to sound sullen, but his smile betrayed the fact he was enjoying the attention.

Sleeps-in-the-sun rolled over and crawled away from the dancers. The young ones followed her as she found a place to sit near the entrance to a burrow. "I have failed you, Croaks-with-the-frogs," she said with mock solemnity. "I promised I would make you into a dancer to captivate a young woman's heart, but I have only succeeded in turning you into a wombat."

The-tiny-one laughed uproariously. "You dance like a wombat!"

Sleeps-in-the-sun reached out grabbing Croaks-with-the-frogs' hands and fell to her knees. "Can you ever forgive me?" she pleaded.

Croaks-with-the-frogs tried to be offended but couldn't stop himself from laughing. "I will never forgive you for doing this to me," he laughed.

The-tiny-one collapsed onto Sleeps-in-the-sun and they rolled on the floor laughing.

"I can't remember the last time, I've laughed so hard," said Sleeps-in-the-sun.

Croaks-with-the-frogs stood, watching the girls laughing for a moment before looking around the fire. Some people had already retired to their burrows. Some had not bothered to retire, but had curled up in their furs by the fireside. Around them others remained awake, engrossed in their own activities. Laughing, singing, eating or dancing. Some of them had already slept out and their furs were left scattered randomly across the ground. From several burrows, Croaks-with-the-frogs could hear the women crying out their wattle calls as they merged fires. *People get strange during Wattle season.*

Then his eyes fell on G'pa who was sitting in his usual spot and staring straight at him. The old man's face was haggard and gruff as always but something in the tilt of his head and the faint twitch of his mouth signalled the old man's approval. He nodded at Croaks-with-the-frogs and the boy's heart swelled with pride.

Sleeps-in-the-sun slowly regained control of herself and dragged herself to her feet. "I need a drink," she said.

"No more toddy for me," protested The-tiny-one. "I hate that stuff! Gave me nightmares."

Sleeps-in-the-sun shot her a brief questioning glance then led them to the large pottery vat filled with banksia syrup. Beside it the wattle toddy simmered. She poured a large gum-nut of banksia for each of them but did not add any toddy.

"This trip to get the resin," Croaks-with-the-frogs said. "It's a couple of *scouts* away. It's hard to get there and back in one day."

"Is that what you did today?" asked The-tiny-one.

Croaks-with-the-frogs nodded, feeling a rush of embarrassment.

Sleeps-in-the-sun drained her gum-nut and poured herself another one. "Well, you guys'll just have to camp out overnight." She sat in the dirt and crossed her legs. "You're both grown, with names and spears. You can carry a coal." She glanced up at The-tiny-one and added, "I have a spear you can borrow, girl."

Croaks-with-the-frogs opened his mouth but no words came out.

"What!?" she asked laughing. "You camp out all the time."

The boy glanced across at the The-tiny-one.

She bristled. "I'm not afraid!"

"No. It's not that." Croaks-with-the-frogs took a breath. He couldn't work out how to get out of this without telling the truth, so he sank onto the ground, mirroring Sleeps-in-the-sun's pose. "If we're both out all night..."

The-tiny-one sat too and looked at him quizzically.

"I mean..." he turned to Sleeps-in-the-sun. "Then you'll have no one to dance with."

Sleeps-in-the-sun stared at the young man for a long moment, her mind wheeling. Little clues and hints fell into place and the picture became clear. Croaks-with-the-frogs had run back to the hive today because he didn't want her to be alone. Several thoughts and feelings surged to the surface within her. Her first instinct was annoyance. She was not an invalid who needed care. Least of all from some weird little misfit. But then other thoughts emerged. She remembered the laughter and the joy of this night. She looked into the large, frightened eyes of Croaks-with-the-frogs and her heart melted.

"You really are a precious little spark, aren't you?" She reached out and gently squeezed his shoulder. "Thank you, Croaks-with-the-frogs," she said respectfully. "I have not had this much fun since Finder-of-snails was taken. I really enjoyed dancing with you tonight."

The young man blushed furiously and looked down.

"But I'll be fine tomorrow night, *brudha*. Don't worry about me." She waved her hand expansively around the hive. "I have both my tribes here with me. And I'll be waiting for you when you come back."

Wattle call

Croaks-with-the-frogs swallowed the last of his banksia and yawned. "I'm getting tired," he said. "I think I'm gonna hit the burrow."

The-tiny-one stood. "Yeah. Me too," she said. "We'll need a good sleep for tomorrow's trip."

They all headed towards the burrow.

The-tiny-one led the way. She was only a few paces from the entrance when she stopped dead. From within the burrow she could hear a woman screaming. "Oops," she laughed and turned on her heel.

Croaks-with-the-frogs was perplexed. "What's going on? Is that No-point-shoe, screaming?"

Sleeps-in-the-sun had come behind. She was laughing too. "Best leave them to it eh? How about we all have a nap out in front of the fire?"

Still smiling, The-tiny-one headed back to where a few spare furs were left and started laying them out.

Croaks-with-the-frogs was getting distressed. He turned to Sleeps-in-the-sun "You're just leaving her there!? Is she alright?"

The others stopped and stared at him in stunned silence for a moment, then The-tiny-one burst into laughter. "Are you serious? That's her Wattle Call."

"What?"

"You don't know what a Wattle Call is?"

Croaks-with-the-frogs became embarrassed. "Well, I've heard of them... and I've heard a few in the last few days but..."

The-tiny-one stared at him. "You are so weird!" She said shaking her head in amazement.

Sleeps-in-the-sun inserted herself between the young ones. "What has Fire-in-his-hair told you about the Wattle season?" She asked, gently.

Croaks-with-the-frogs looked at The-tiny-one and his face reddened again. "That people go crazy and it's not good to stay around the hive for too long."

The-tiny-one repressed her smile. "Oh burn my burrow! You don't know how people merge fires?"

"I know!" The young man squawked. "It's just this wattle call stuff. Is she in pain?"

The-tiny-one erupted into another gale of laughter.

Sleeps-in-the-sun turned and frowned at her. "Just get some sleep, kid," she said forcefully.

The young girl stopped laughing and laid out the fur she had found. She wrapped herself in it and lay with her back to the fire, staring at Sleeps-in-the-sun with a shamefaced expression on her face.

Sleeps-in-the-sun grabbed a fur and handed it to Croaks-with-the-frogs. She then took another and wrapped herself in it. They sat crossed legged, wrapped in their borrowed furs, staring at each other as the fire crackled.

Croaks-with-the-frogs was swept up in a series of complex emotions. He was ashamed, and angry. But he was also curious. There was something about the way Sleeps-in-the-sun was behaving that made him feel like something of great import was about to happen. He was afraid and excited at the same time.

Sleeps-in-the-sun took a deep breath. Then she said, almost to herself, "OK... where do I begin this?"

Croaks-with-the-frogs stared at her in silence.

"Fire is the heart of the world," she said. "Everything comes from the fire and everything returns to it once its time comes. We are children of the fire and the fire burns within us."

Croaks-with-the-frogs nodded. He knew this. He had heard the old ones talking about this many times. He wondered why Sleeps-in-the-sun would be repeating this now, and why her voice held such emotion. Her cheeks were flushed and her eyes would not meet his. She stared at her feet as they protruded from her fur.

"But in Wattle season, the fire blazes more brightly. Even the trees spark and give off flame."

Croaks-with-the-frogs kept his face neutral but inside he was dubious. Was she talking about the wattle blossoms?

Sleeps-in-the-sun still didn't look up. "The fire inside us burns more brightly during Wattle too. We feel it roaring... and dancing like... it's trying to get out." She looked up briefly and met his eyes, hoping to see some flicker of understanding. There was nothing. Only his usual wide, frightened brown eyes. *He's too young. He has not felt the burn, yet.*

The-tiny-one had drifted off to sleep. She started snoring softly.

Croaks-with-the-frogs glanced at her briefly, felt a surge of relief and returned his attention to Sleeps-in-the-sun.

The young woman looked down again and continued talking. "When your fire is like that, it's searching for another. It's reaching out." She mimicked the reaching with her hands clumsily. "And then, it finds... someone." She scratched her head, struggling for words. "It's like you find this person whose heart is open and they reach out to you." Then her words came thick and fast, tumbling over each other in a cascade. "The fire blazes in both of you and then the flames merge. A point of fires becomes a thumb." She held up both her pointing fingers and then replaced them with a single thumb. "A single mighty blaze, greater than even the fire in the middle of the hive. You each become consumed by it and all you want to do is to have it inside you and around you." Her voice quavered. "You want to get close and you can't get close enough. It's like you want nothing to come between you and the fire in the other. No walls, no distance, no furs. You just want to wrap yourself around him and have him inside you." A slow tear trickled down her cheek.

Croaks-with-the-frogs was swept up in her words. He hardly understood anything she was saying but he felt the force of her emotions. He stayed silent, his mouth open and dry.

She shook her head briefly as if reliving a fond memory. "And then the fire bursts from your..." She gestured towards his loins. "... and into her heart." She pressed her hand against her chest and new tears appeared on her cheeks.

The boy stared back in awe.

"And then we cry out." Her voice quavered. "That's the Wattle Call. We cry out because the fire is so wonderful and you never thought that life could be so good. And you never want that moment to end." She stopped talking and wept silently.

After a moment, Sleeps-in-the-sun lay in her furs and stared towards the fire. "That's what is happening in our burrow. And it's very, very good."

Croaks-with-the-frogs lay beside her, staring at the sky. "Who's in there?"

Sleeps-in-the-sun started to laugh. A slow chuckle at first but it soon bubbled out musically. "How much of what I said, did you understand?"

The boy paused. "Most... A bit... Not much." He turned onto his side and faced her. "But I got most of the ...um idea, I think."

She reached out and touched the boy on his shoulder. "Fire-in-his-hair and No-point-shoe are joining their fires in the burrow. At the end of the Wattle season, they will stand before the tribes and declare themselves married."

"Really!? Fire-in-his-hair! But..."

Sleeps-in-the-sun started laughing again. "Yes. And it's wonderful."

Croaks-with-the-frogs rolled back onto his back and looked at the moonlit clouds drifting across the sky above him. The singing and dancing had dropped to a low murmur now. Thoughts roiled through his mind. "So this is what happens when everyone marries?"

"Yeah."

"When you..."

"Yeah." He heard the faint crack in her voice.

"It must have been awful when you lost him."

"Terrible, boy. Just terrible."

Tears stung Croaks-with-the-frogs' eyes. "I'm really so very sorry, Sleeps-in-the-sun."

She didn't recognise the guilt, she only heard the sympathy. "Thank you, Croaks-with-the-frogs," she said formally as she rolled onto her back. "You're a good man."

They lay together in the darkness, listening to The-tiny-one's soft snores.

Sleeps-in-the-sun started talking again. "After Finder-of-snails was lost, I thought I would never recover. I still don't think I ever will. I felt like a tree that had its branches cut off... I'd lost my right arm and I needed to learn to carry my spear in my left... I can't begin to tell you how much it hurts. I can't explain it to anyone. I feel so alone." She paused and whimpered softly. "G'ma says that it's all part of the glory of the fire. That the pain and the joy are a single thing. But I don't understand what she means. She lost her first husband when she was my age. Did you know that, Croaks-with-the-frogs? That G'ma and G'pa had both been married before?"

Silence.

She sat up and looked across. The boy was fast asleep, his mouth open. By the firelight, Sleeps-in-the-sun could see a faint streak of dirt where his tear had run. He had moved the fur off his chest and his shirt had ridden up, exposing his pale stomach and his small belly button.

Sleeps-in-the-sun smiled, sadly and pulled the shirt down to cover his tummy and placed the fur back over him. Then she rolled over to face the other way and silently cried herself to sleep.

7

THE PINE FOREST

A couple of handfuls of last year's wattle seeds

The first drops of rain began falling in the middle of the night, driving those who slept by the fire back into the burrows. Croaks-with-the-frogs slept badly, unable to move in the overcrowded space as the rain hammered on the hard, mud roof.

As the birds began their morning chorus, Croaks-with-the-frogs lay awake. He had mixed feelings about the trip. Part of him was as excited as The-tiny-one about it and wanted to get going as soon as it was light, but another part of him was filled with terror.

His resin supply came from his secret place. It was always his plan to show Fire-in-his-hair first then reveal it to the rest of the tribe. What if she thought the place was silly? What if she looked at him the way Me-not-talking does... like he was *cursed?* He didn't think he could survive that look from The-tiny-one.

The rain had stopped when Croaks-with-the-frogs crawled from the burrow, but it was still overcast and windy. The tea tree provided some shelter from the wind but the air was cold. G'ma and G'pa were huddled by the fire. G'ma was wrapped in her sleeping fur to try to keep out the chill. The fire flickered and danced in the gusty wind. She looked up at Croaks-with-the-frogs and he waved at her but she did not respond. He pointed to the pot of simmering Dandelion root and raised his eyes in query. G'ma stared blankly. "Her eyesight must be fading," he thought. The boy went over to the pot, filled a pair of gum-nuts and brought them to G'ma.

She stared at him.

"Nut of dandy, G'ma?" he said.

G'ma smiled. "Oh, that's alright dear. Croaks-with-the-frogs will get me one."

The boy stared at her, a bemused smile on his face. "Um... It's me, G'ma. Croaks-with-the-frogs."

G'ma frowned then her eyes widened in surprise. "Ah, there you are! I was wondering when you were going to crawl out of the burrow."

Croaks-with-the-frogs sat beside her and gave her the drink. "It's cold this morning, isn't it."

"Oh yes," said G'ma, "Very cold! Are you going to hunt rabbits today?"

"No, G'ma. The rabbit hunt was yesterday, remember?"

She showed no sign of remembering. He glanced across to G'pa but the old man merely scowled into the fire.

"We're going to get The-tiny-one some resin for her spear."

G'ma stared at him for a long time. It was as if she was trying to remember something then she said, in a oddly resigned tone, "Oh that's a good idea, dear. Get some resin."

G'pa looked across at him. "You going with your fist?"

"Ah... no... I'm just taking The-tiny-one."

The old man frowned thoughtfully but he turned back to the fire and said nothing more.

G'ma said. "There was a lovely pine tree up... there. We would always get resin from it. Then one day, there was a storm and it got hit by..." She faded into silence.

"Lightning?" guessed Croaks-with-the-frogs.

"Now they get resin from another tree." And with that, she was off, chatting about the weather, the fire, the wattles and whatever else came into her head.

When their drinks were finished, Croaks-with-the-frogs stood and collected the gum-nuts.

G'ma smiled as she handed hers over. "That was a lovely chat, darling. Thank you for coming over."

"Lovely chat," G'pa grumbled.

"You must come again soon."

"Come again soon," G'pa echoed. The old man looked up from the fire to meet the boy's eyes. He had a stricken look on his face. He shook his head, sadly and returned to staring at the flames.

The-tiny-one was spending the morning with Listens-for-ducks and Sniffs-the-wind. They had formed an impromptu fist with Sleeps-in-the-sun, No-point-shoe and Fire-in-his-hair. The-tiny-one was a little bit annoyed she had been so easily replaced. "What if I had wanted to come?" she said to Listens-for-ducks.

The young man laughed. "You still could have. It's not like you've been replaced."

Sniffs-the-wind smiled at her gently. "You've got a job. You're going to get the resin. I thought you were excited about getting the resin?"

"I am. I am. I just..." The-tiny-one lost a bit of confidence. "I don't want to miss out on..."

Listens-for-ducks laughed harder. "Digging for bracken is hardly an adventure, ya dumb bunny. D'you want us to sit around the fire all day waiting for you?"

The girl was silent. She liked Listens-for-ducks but sometimes he could be a bit harsh. Like the other people of the swamp, Sniffs-the-wind was a gentler soul. *I prefer swamp people to lake people.*

After a solid breakfast of stew and cake, Croaks-with-the-frogs and The-tiny-one set off. Croaks-with-the-frogs carried his tools and a coal, but other than that, his pack was empty. The-tiny-one didn't have many tools. She'd only had a small hammer stone and a sharp stone shard. She had wanted to bring several cakes as well as her tools but Croaks-with-the-frogs had shaken his head. "You won't need it," he said. "There's food on the way. Best if we travel light."

As the pair walked past the storage burrow, Croaks-with-the-frogs shot a quick glance around the hive, before ducking inside.

"What are you doing?" The-tiny-one asked.

"Shh." Croaks-with-the-frogs lifted the lid off one of the pottery jars and took a couple of handfuls of last year's wattle seeds. He slipped them into a small pocket sewn into his pack and crawled out again.

There was nothing wrong with a hunter taking food from the common store, but something about the way Croaks-with-the-frogs did it, made The-tiny-one feel uncomfortable.

"Why do you do that?" she asked as they left the hive.

Croaks-with-the-frogs' voice was low. "I'll show you later."

Beneath the twisted trunks of the tea tree

The sun was over the tea tree now but heavy clouds in the east blocked it. In the west, the clouds were thinner and faint patches of pale blue were visible through the tops of the trees. Above them, the vault was grey.

The tea tree surrounding the hive was on a small promontory of solid ground to the east of the swamp. The swamp curved around giving partial protection from north and south as well. Long years of travel had created paths through the tea tree.

From the entrance of the hive a path headed towards the swamp. Another path curved around the hive and headed east to where the bracken ferns grew and beyond that, the open plains of the rabbit warrens. Less worn paths headed north and south. These were only used during Wattle Season. North was the route taken to reach the river people whilst south was the path the lake folk used when they arrived.

Croaks-with-the-frogs led The-tiny-one south. The path was familiar and it skirted the edge of the swamp. The trunks of the tea trees were thick and tortured, bending over the path and covering the sky in a canopy of brown and olive green. Walking in single file beneath the twisted trunks of the tea tree, they were nearly as safe as being by a fire.

"This is the way to my hive," she said. "It's a long way. We had to camp out overnight. Have you ever gone on the Wattle journey?"

"Croaks-with-the-frogs' face reddened. "No. Fire-in-his-hair hated Wattle season. When the tribe went visiting, he'd take me out hunting the cat."

The-tiny-one laughed. "Hunting the cat. Boy, did I get a hiding after we went hunting the cat. Someone even wanted to name me 'Hunts-the-cat' but G'ma wouldn't hear of it."

"Yeah. I'm sorry about that."

"Gee you say sorry a lot."

Croaks-with-the-frogs paused. "Um... do I? Sorry, I didn't realise..."

The-tiny-one started laughing.

"What?"

"You just said sorry again. You're sorry for saying sorry too much."

Croaks-with-the-frogs blushed and stared ahead at the path. He wished he could make conversation smoothly. He wished he could make his words flow, the way No-point-shoe or Sleeps-in-the-sun did. If he couldn't speak well, then he wished he would be quiet like Fire-in-his-hair who only spoke when he absolutely had to. Instead, he was always talking and always saying the wrong thing. *I'm like Me-not-talking,* he thought miserably.

The-tiny-one was still talking. "I think you say 'sorry' so often because you get into trouble so much. People in your tribe are always getting mad at you."

"They don't like me very much," Croaks-with-the-frogs said sadly.

"I think your fist likes you."

The boy smiled. "Yeah. They're good people. Even No-point-shoe is alright."

The-tiny-one was shocked. "Alright!? Just alright? She's the best!"

"Well she likes you because you're a sizzling *flushfert*. But she gets annoyed when things... muck up."

"She's the leader of the fist. She's gotta do that. It doesn't mean she doesn't like you."

"I suppose."

The-tiny-one pushed on. "No. I mean the other people in your tribe. Not the ones in your fist."

Croaks-with-the-frogs snorted.

"Some of them looked at you like you had done something wrong when you gave those kids the resin balls."

Croaks-with-the-frogs cringed inwardly. He wished she would stop talking about this. He was ashamed.

But The-tiny-one was oblivious to his discomfort. She kept talking. "I think it's crazy. That resin thing you did for the kids was the most amazing thing I've ever seen."

Croaks-with-the-frogs stopped walking and turned around to face her. "Really?"

The-tiny-one's face was was alight. "It was wonderful!" She clutched her hand to her chest. "I felt... like... the fire was burning in me too."

Croaks-with-the-frogs's eyes stung. He turned away quickly and pushed on along the path. "Gee," he said but couldn't think of anything else to say. After a while he said, "Thank you Tiny-one," and bowed his head, formally.

The young girl laughed merrily and switched conversation. "I really like this part of the bush. Your tea tree is so twisty. It makes me feel like I'm in a burrow made of tea tree."

Croaks-with-the-frogs looked around. "Yeah," he said. "It does feel a bit like a burrow. Around the other side of the swamp, the tea tree is taller and straight. It's only near the swamp that the tea tree twists like this."

"I wonder why that is?"

Croaks-with-the-frogs looked back over his shoulder. Behind him The-tiny-one looked around at the tea tree, her face pensive. Something in her expression moved him.

They walked on in silence and Croaks-with-the-frogs puzzled over his reaction. Most people he knew didn't ask questions unless they expected an answer. And if he asked a question and someone didn't know the answer, they would usually either make something up that was silly or else they would get annoyed. Fire-in-his-hair wouldn't get annoyed. He'd just shrug his shoulders when he didn't know the answer to one of Croaks-with-the-frogs questions, but he wouldn't puzzle over it. He either knew it or he didn't. The-tiny-one was enjoying the question without needing the answer. He liked that.

After they had walked for a while, Croaks-with-the-frogs turned off the path and headed west.

The-tiny-one stopped, staring towards the south.

"This way," said Croaks-with-the-frogs. "We have to go around to the other side of the swamp."

The-tiny-one kept looking down the path. "This is the way to my hive," she repeated.

Croaks-with-the-frogs grinned. "Yeah. You said."

"I know, but it's a bit... I don't know. I'd like to show you my hive." She turned and followed him towards the west. As they walked she kept talking about the path to her hive. "It's a great journey. The path follows a valley and then climbs a hill. At the top of the hill is a big gum. We send a hunter to climb right up to the top branches. From there, he can see the lake. Our hive is on the western side of the lake."

"Maybe you can take me there one day," Croaks-with-the-frogs said absently.

"I'd like that."

The path was well worn and it turned north, skirting the swamp. After they had walked well over *a scout*, the bush began to thin. Through the tea tree on their left, They could catch glimpses of the swamp. "Keep sharp now," said Croaks-with-the-frogs. "There's less coverage here." He crouched and slowed his walk, scanning the sky and their surroundings with more care.

"Is this where cats hunt?" The-tiny-one asked, trying to keep the fear from her voice.

"Yeah," said Croaks-with-the-frogs. "But it's unlikely to be hunting at this time of day. Even at dawn or dusk, when it does hunt, it would avoid us if it could."

The-tiny-one cocked her head. "Why? Wouldn't they try to hunt us? *They eat us and we eat them.*"

The boy was silent for a while, then he sighed and started talking. "I don't think it really wants to hunt us. I think it's scared. Fire-in-his-hair never got close to it in spite of all his trips and searches."

"But... Everyone knows that cats are dangerous, Croaks-with-the-frogs. What about Fire-in-his-hair's wife? A cat took her didn't it?"

The boy shrugged. "Ye-es. But I think there might have been something wrong with that cat. It wasn't winter but maybe it was starving. Otherwise, it wouldn't have tried to take on an adult with a spear. That's why Fire-in-his-hair needed me. When I was a kid, the cat wasn't afraid of me. Fire-in-his-hair would let me me walk ahead, hoping that I would lure the cat."

The-tiny-one sucked in a disapproving breath.

Croaks-with-the-frogs laughed shortly. "But it never worked." He paused. "Once... Once it nearly worked. The cat came close and I saw him through the trees. I stopped. I was shitting myself."

"When was this?"

"Years ago. Before I got my name."

"I remember the way its tail twitched as it watched me... just stared at me. But then, it saw Fire-in-his-hair creeping up behind me and it turned and ran. Fire-in-his-hair chased after it, screaming, but we weren't fast enough to keep up. It was gone."

They walked on in silence for a time then The-tiny-one said, "You know? You always talk about cats as if there is only a single cat?"

Croaks-with-the-frogs half turned. "What?"

"You don't say, 'cats' or 'them.' It's always, 'it' or 'the cat.' I think that's strange. Have you noticed that?"

He hadn't noticed. Croaks-with-the-frogs thought for a while then, "Fire-in-his-hair always talked like there was a single cat. The cat that took his wife."

They walked on.

The clouds became thinner and white patches glowed amongst the grey. "Are you getting hungry?" The-tiny-one asked.

"Yes," he replied. "But we're not there yet. Just a little bit further on."

She scrunched her nose curiously and walked on in silence.

Digging for bracken

The sun was high in the cloudy sky and several fists were spread out amongst the fields of bracken that bordered the rabbit warrens. Sleeps-in-the-sun was on lookout duty while Fire-in-his-hair, No-point-shoe, Listens-for-ducks and Sniffs-the-wind dug for roots.

When undisturbed, the bracken gave reasonable cover but the act of digging the roots caused the fronds to wave and eventually fall. It was a clear sign to predators that something was there. Sleeps-in-the-sun scanned the horizon. The enemy was everywhere.

Sleeps-in-the-sun scanned the sky most of all. Eagles, hawks, and even magpies or minors could be serious threats to the digging humans. There were always birds in the tree tops and flying across the sky but her job was to keep watch in case they took an interest in the people below.

"So... how did everybody sleep?" she asked brightly.

Listens-for-ducks picked up the cue straight away. "I slept like a log," he said between grunts. The hole he was digging was already knee deep but he was still only half way to the edible root. "It was a bit noisy last night though."

"Yes! Strange animals were out in the bush, I think."

Sniffs-the-wind started laughing. "You guys are terrible."

Listens-for-ducks stopped his digging and looked innocently. "Who me? I just thought maybe others heard something." He turned to Fire-in-his-hair. "Did you hear anything last night?"

Fire-in-his-hair's smile was a mixture of pride and embarrassment. "I don't know about you. I heard some sweet music."

No-point-shoe threw down her digging stick. "OK. That's enough!" She was trying to be angry but the smile on her face simply wouldn't go away.

The others laughed.

"We're only joking," said Sniffs-the-wind. "I think Listens-for-ducks is just jealous."

Sleeps-in-the-sun laughed. "Ew."

Her brother caught her meaning before the others did. "I think it's Sniffs-the-wind who's jealous. But I'm not sure she can sing as well as No-point-shoe."

"Well you'll have to find out tonight," his wife said with a saucy flounce.

"We'll all find out tonight," said Fire-in-his-hair.

And they burst into laughter again.

Sleeps-in-the-sun watched them as they dug and laughed and teased. There was a bittersweet tang to not being fertile during Wattle season. Usually people's conversations were focussed on food, shelter or even deeper philosophical things like the nature of Fire but during Wattle, the dominant conversation was sex. Everything reminded people of sex and every thought carried a titillating frisson.

Not being fertile, Sleeps-in-the-sun did not share the preoccupation but she remembered when she did. She could play the role, and join in the jokes, but she felt removed from it. She enjoyed the happiness of her *brudhas* but it also caused her pain because it reminded her she was not the same. *Will I always be a stranger in my own tribe now?*

It was someone else who made the call. A voice further into the bracken field called, "Enemy above!" Other voices joined in, "Hawk! Hawk!"

It was not a hawk. But it was easier to call Hawk than eagle. The diggers scrambled for their spears. The lookouts dropped to a knee their spears pointing towards the sky. Sleeps-in-the-sun looked around desperately. "Where is it? I can't see it!"

Someone called, "coming out of the sun."

And the shouts rose in intensity. "Diving!"

"Get down! Get Down!"

Sleeps-in-the-sun whirled towards the sun just in time to see the flash of brown and black as the giant bird swept past. It threaded its way between the upright spears of the lookouts. It's target was the exposed backs of the diggers. In one fluent movement, the eagle entered the bracken, grabbed Listens-for-ducks by the shoulders and few away.

As if she were under water, everything became silent and slow. She threw her spear. It struck the eagle but it bounced off harmlessly. She saw her brother twitch as the bird flew into the grey sky. Far away she could hear somebody screaming. There were other voices too. People were trying to talk to her, telling her something. She wished they would be quiet. She wanted to listen to the screaming. Someone was screaming in agony. She knew that voice. It was her own.

The rain camp

The The-tiny-one followed along as the path slowly curved towards the west. They entered a region of denser bush. Wattles and gums were mixed amongst the tea tree, increasing the forest protection. The youngsters walked easier. "There!" said Croaks-with-the-frogs, pointing. In the distance, a mighty gum tree had fallen onto the forest floor, its roots had torn a large hole in the ground.

The-tiny-one followed him to where the base of the long dead trunk was propped above the ground by the gnarled roots. Beside the tree a small circle of rocks had been laid around the unmistakable black stain of a fire pit. Croaks-with-the-frogs gathered some dried leaves and twigs from beneath the dead branches and unwrapped his coal. "Can you blow this into a fire?" he asked.

The girl nodded and set to work.

Beneath the trunk, sheltered from the wether, a few small stacks of wood were piled. Croaks-with-the-frogs hauled out a stack then dug closer to the roots. He soon brought up a package wrapped in a rabbit hide. The young man unwrapped the hide and brought out several dry cakes. He dipped them in the water which had collected in the hole caused by the uprooted tree then lay them on the rocks around the fire.

By now, The-tiny-one had a cheerful blaze going. The fallen tree shielded the little fire from the prevailing wind and the dry wood from beneath the trunk crackled and spat as the cakes warmed.

Croaks-with-the-frogs smiled at her, nervously. "We'd always keep a stash here for when it rains."

The-tiny-one fed the fire with another piece of wood. "This is great! It's like a mini hive."

The boy's face beamed with pride.

They sat in comfortable silence watching the fire burn as The-tiny-one fed the flames.

Croaks-with-the-frogs cocked his head towards the other piles of wood nestled beneath the fallen trunk. "If you're tired, we can rest here and burn another pile of wood."

The-tiny-one smiled but shook her head. "I'm not tired. Just hungry."

The boy took the hint and handed her a cake. It was only slightly warm and the water had not dried off completely, but The-tiny-one was keen to put something in her belly. Croaks-with-the-frogs looked at her nervously as she ate. The cake was stale, but The-tiny-one could tell it had been well made. The bracken had been pounded smooth and it was laced with dandelion leaves and insects.

"Did you make these?" she asked around a mouthful.

"Yeah. They taste better when they're warm."

The-tiny-one laughed and gestured towards the other cakes warming by the fire. "This is OK. My next one will be warm."

In a little while, Croaks-with-the-frogs took a cake for himself and began to eat. The-tiny-one looked around the little clearing caused by the fallen tree. "So how often do you camp here?"

"Only after a rain. Fire-in-his-hair used to have us camping all over this side of the swamp when we'd hunt the cat, but we'd only come here after a rain... for the dry wood."

She stared at him intently and the young man shifted awkwardly, a nervous smile on his face.

"You really miss hunting the cat, don't you?"

Croaks-with-the-frogs stared into the fire and nodded as he chewed. "Fire-in-his-hair stopped coming last Smoke. It's not as much fun out here when you're on your own."

"But you hunt with your fist? No-point-shoe, Sleeps-in-the-sun? They're great. I'd love to go out with them."

The boy shrugged. "It's not the same... I liked it when it was just me and Fire-in-his-hair."

"Then why do you keep coming out alone?"

He shrugged again, but said nothing.

They finished the rest of the cakes in silence. The-tiny-one found they tasted much better once they were fully warm. By the time the last cake was eaten, the fire had dwindled to coals. Croaks-with-the-frogs set up a new coal carrier and placed a large smouldering coal within it. Then they hoisted their packs, threw sand on the fire and set off again.

The hazy purple mass

They headed west. The-tiny-one stayed close as Croaks-with-the-frogs led her away from the swamp. The day wore on and the clouds thinned even more. Small patches of blue became visible amongst the grey and white. The bush was dense, a mixture of gums, wattles and tea tree. Thick grasses grew in small clearings but the youngsters avoided them. Everywhere was dangerous, but the open areas were the most dangerous.

They had walked nearly a scout when she sensed the land was rising. The path wound and twisted and the further they walked, the steeper the path became. The trees became scarce but they crouched through a large patch of bracken which gave them good cover.

Further up the hill, in the distance, The-tiny-one saw a huge pine tree. It towered over the surrounding bush, its deep green foliage contrasting with the olive of the gums, wattles and tea tree. "There!" she said, pointing. "We can get resin from that."

Croaks-with-the-frogs looked back over his shoulder at her. "We could, but I don't use that tree."

She laughed. "Why not? It's a beauty."

The boy stopped and stared at it in the distance. "Yeah," he said and his voice carried a strange almost sad tone. "That's... part of the reason why I don't... It's so old and... I can't bring myself to wound it."

The-tiny-one stared closely at the hungry eyes of her companion. "You are a very odd fish, Croaks-with-the-frogs," she said seriously.

The boy blushed and set off again through the bracken. He cursed himself for his stupidity. What was it about that girl? No matter how hard he tried, he seemed unable to stop talking to her. It was like all she had to do was look at him, and he would blurt out his most secret thoughts. Even the ones that made no sense.

The bracken gave way to grass and leaf litter as the path grew more steep. Smaller pine trees were dotted amongst the tea tree and a few struggling gums. The-tiny-one thought any of those pines could have been suitable for resin, but she didn't suggest it. The boy clearly had something specific in mind and she followed him. He was a weird kid, but his weirdness fascinated her.

The path curved towards the north as they climbed and the ground became sandy and loose. A few small weeds struggled to survive in the infertile soil, and the trees became thinner. Climbing became harder and The-tiny-one had to use her hands to keep up. *Where is he taking me?*

Croaks-with-the-frogs stopped. "Here," he said, softly.

The-tiny-one scrambled up the last few *lengths* of the dune and stood beside him. Her mouth fell open in awe. Before her was a sweeping vista of land. The hillside was sheer as if part of the hill had fallen away leaving a view to the north and the east. She had never seen anything like it. At the base of the hill, patches of sunlight flickered on the water of the the swamp. To the east, the land seemed to stretch on forever. All the way to the horizon the bush stretched in a myriad of different shades of green. Patches of sunlight highlighted some places whilst other regions were in shadow. The shadows moved over the land, driven by the wind and for an instant the whole world seemed like a single huge beast, sleeping beneath the sun.

After a moment, Croaks-with-the-frogs gently touched her arm and pointed to the north. A hazy purple mass spread across the horizon in that direction. The-tiny-one squinted at it. "What is that?"

"I dunno." he said. "It never moves. It only changes colour. Sometimes it's green, other times blue or grey. I think it's land."

The-tiny-one stared at it in amazement. "Land?"

"Yeah... but piled up on itself like... I think it's a long line of hills. Like this one but bigger. Much, much bigger."

She continued to stare at it. "It reminds me of burrows. A lot of giant burrows." She looked at him in a mixture of horror and doubt. "You don't think there are giant people who live there?"

Croaks-with-the-frogs laughed. "No. If those things were burrows, we'd be able to see the people walking around. And there's no fire."

The-tiny-one was only slightly comforted by this. The purple shapes on the horizon were still unfamiliar and frightening. "And they never move?"

"Never... they only seem to change colour depending on the time of day and the weather."

"They make me feel... small," she said finally.

"Yeah. This whole place makes me feel small. I think it's great." Croaks-with-the-frogs turned to head further along the path.

The-tiny-one didn't move. She remained frozen, staring out at the land. "I feel like I want to cry," she said.

He stopped and stared her. Her eyes were filling with tears and a crimson glow tinted her cheeks. "Why do you want to cry? Are you sad?"

The-tiny-one didn't look at him. She clutched at her chest with her hand. "No... I don't know. Sometimes, things make me want to cry. When I see something beautiful, or I hear a lovely song. It's not sad... it's ... I don't know."

Croaks-with-the-frogs watched her in silence. Inside he was bursting to ask her questions but he pressed his lips tightly together and said nothing.

After a long time, she turned to him, her eyes glistening. "Thank you from bringing me here, Croaks-with-the-frogs," she said, solemnly.

The boy stared at his feet in embarrassment, then turned and the led the way further up hill.

The pine forest

The path curved and they reached the highest point of the hill after walking only *a stone's throw*. The top of the hill was actually the beginning of a ridge. The crest ran directly east. To its left, the slope they had climbed with its scattered tea tree and bracken fern seemed thick and impenetrable. But to the right of the crest, the land was profoundly different. Large, dark pine trees stretched away down the hill. Croaks-with-the-frogs stopped, his voice hushed. "Here it is," he said.

He crouched, holding his spear at the ready and led the way down into the pine forest.

The trees were huge, towering over them and plunged the land into a permanent twilight. The floor of the forest was covered in a thick coat of orange needles. Near the top of the ridge a few spindly gums and wattles had struggled for survival but as they headed further down hill, these disappeared completely and they entered a land more exotic than The-tiny-one had ever seen before. In some places, patches of blackberries survived in the gloom, their new leaves just beginning to bud. In other places, where the trees were fewer, a few dandelions and other grasses defied the stifling blanket of pine needles. The air was thick and the silence heavy.

The silence crept into The-tiny-one's soul. She lowered her voice instinctively, as if she didn't want to wake whatever was sleeping in this alien land. "Does anything live here?"

Croaks-with-the-frogs matched her whisper. "Oh yeah! And things hunt here too. I've seen signs of cat, and foxes."

"It all seems so... lifeless. Are there birds?"

"Yeah. Some things live here. Be careful."

He led her steadily down the side of the hill. Eventually they came to an open place where long ago a large pine had crashed to the ground. In the hole caused by the up-rooted tree a shallow puddle had formed. Beside the rotting trunk, a few rocks had been arranged loosely around a fire pit. Croaks-with-the-frogs gestured at them. "Hard to find rocks here," he said.

He swept away the pine needles beside the rocks and brought out a pile of small twigs, pine needles and resin wrapped in a hide. With practised efficiency, he arranged them into a small pile and used his coal to light the fire.

The-tiny-one broke off dead branches from the the fallen tree and added the wood. Soon the fire was crackling and spitting in the gloom. The sight of the fire lifted her spirits and she found herself breathing easier. "What is this place?" she asked.

Croaks-with-the-frogs propped himself on a pine branch that had been laid beside the fire pit. "I dunno," he said, his voice filled with wonder.

"I've never seen so many pine trees."

"Yeah," he said opening his eyes wide. It was a signal that when he had first found the place, he too had been amazed and slightly overwhelmed by the experience. "You hungry?"

The-tiny-one laughed shortly. "Yeah. Don't tell me, you've got another stash of cakes here?"

Croaks-with-the-frogs grinned and raised his eyebrows. Then he turned and began scrabbling beneath the fallen trunk.

The-tiny-one watched his bottom wiggling as he dug through the needles and it made her want to laugh.

Croaks-with-the-frogs pulled the hide wrapped cakes out and laid them around the fire, then he pushed himself to his feet and grabbed his spear. "Let the fire burn down to coals." he said. "I'll be back soon."

She sat by the fire and watched him creep off deeper into the forest. It was deep into the afternoon now and the sun was sinking through the pines. All around her the forest gloom thickened. She huddled closer to the fire and wished Croaks-with-the-frogs would come back soon. She didn't like being alone here.

Plenty to eat

Croaks-with-the-frogs wasn't gone long. He returned, grinning proudly with his pack bulging. "Plenty of food here," he said slinging his pack onto the ground by the fire. "Weird stuff... but good eating."

He pulled out from his pack the largest snail The-tiny-one had ever seen. It was as big as a large gum-nut and it filled the boy's palm. Its massive foot protruded from it's shell. In the bush near her hive, there were snails to be found, but these were usually small, no more than a snack but this monster would be meal. Her mouth fell open in amazement.

"Heaps of 'em here," Croaks-with-the-frogs said, his voice a whisper. Wherever the wood rots, these things grow."

"Are they safe to eat?"

The boy laughed merrily. "Oh yeah. Good eating."

He took out a few more snails from his pack and threw them shell down on the hot coals. They sizzled and spat. The fading light and the smell of food made The-tiny-one feel ready for sleep. "I suppose we can get the resin tomorrow, she said. "It's getting dark now."

Croaks-with-the-frogs twitched nervously, looking around and shifting position.

"Are you alright?" she asked.

"I've um... got to get things ready for breakfast tomor-row."

"What?"

He chewed his bottom lip and lowered his voice. "Can I show you something?"

"Um... yeah."

He reached into his pack and brought out the wattle seeds he had brought from the hive.

He crushed the seeds into a dark powder with his hammer stone and turned the seeds into a thick sticky paste by adding the slime from one of the snails. He glanced at her, an unmistakable look of fear in his eyes. "I've never shown anyone this before," he said. He breathed heavily and pushed himself to his feet. "Best take a brand, Foxes and cats will be out hunting."

Croaks-with-the-frogs led her further into the forest. He carried his spear and a piece of bark with the wattle seeds smeared thickly over it. The-tiny-one held a burning stick of pine in her left hand and a spear in her right. The flame cast flickering shadows on the trunks of the trees.

A short distance from their camp, a pair of logs lay parallel to each other, forming a small passageway. At the end of the passage, sticks and mud had been piled to form a rough wall but in front of the wall was a strangely familiar structure It was a pair of upright posts affixed to a horizontal beam. A strip of hide formed a loop between the uprights. "This... looks like..."

"A windy thing."

"The things you make for the kids to play with?"

"It's not for kids." Croaks-with-the-frogs' voice was heavy. "It was never meant for kids. This is a trap. Fire-in-his-hair thought of it, to try to catch the cat, but he couldn't get it to work." He stared at the contraption and a hint of pride bubbled up to cover his fear. "I got it to work."

"Really?" The-tiny-one couldn't for the life of her see how that thing could catch anything, let alone a cat. "Isn't it a bit small?" It was no higher than her knee.

Croaks-with-the-frogs laughed. "This isn't for cats. It catches mice." And with that, he plunged into action. At the side of the contraption, a flat sheet of woven bark covered a pair of well crafted sticks. The first was smaller, with a thin branch forming a fork. He smeared the sticky wattle seeds over the smaller branch and rested it against an upright. The other stick had a vicious spike on it's end. He threaded it through the loop of hide and wound the stick again and again until the tension in the hide was nearly too great for him to hold. He propped the wound stick against the forked one so the wattle seed mixture was facing away from the trap. Then he placed the sheet of bark across the top of the logs.

He stood back and once more she saw the fear and pride mingling in his face. "The bark and the logs stop the mice from getting to the trap. The only way they can get to the wattle seeds is along the passage. They try to eat the seeds, and the windy thing spins. It's taken me ages to fix all the mistakes, but now... it works. It always works."

The-tiny-one stared at it. No matter how hard she tried, she simply couldn't see how it could work.

The boy waved his hands, his voice a fierce whisper. "I've got heaps of these, all over the forest. Most are small. They catch mice, but I've even built a bigger one over on the other side of the ridge. It caught a possum. Do you see?"

She stared at him, blankly.

"This changes everything!" he said. "We don't have to crawl down burrows and fight hand to claw... risking death for every meal. We just build these traps and the food comes to us."

The-tiny-one didn't say anything. She feared the poor boy might have lost his mind.

Croaks-with-the-frogs picked up his spear and the bark with the wattle seeds and headed off in a different direction. The-tiny-one followed him silently and watched as he set another pair of traps. By the time he had finished, the brand was a smouldering red dot in the dark.

She was relieved when they got back to the camp site. Croaks-with-the-frogs seemed to become more normal then. The snails were cooked, and he served her a pair on a warmed cake. He blew the fire back into flames and they sat eating in silence. The boy focussed intently on his food. She didn't know what to say to him. She had always known he was a bit odd and many in her tribe had teased her about the weird kid who led her off to hunt the cat. But this was the first time she had felt Croaks-with-the-frogs' weirdness was actually dangerous. She couldn't put her finger on why she felt this. She only knew something about his intensity disturbed her. She wished she was back in the safety of the hive and not trapped in this alien place with this strange boy.

Croaks-with-the-frogs stared at his food or at the fire. He couldn't bear to look at The-tiny-one. The girl had said nothing but her whole demeanour displayed her rejection. She didn't understand. This was the reason he hadn't told the rest of the tribe about his traps. He knew they would find them disturbing and reject him. People were wedded to their old habits. He even doubted Fire-in-his-hair would accept his idea. The boy chewed his snails and cursed himself for his stupidity. Now he had blabbed to The-tiny-one and she was looking at him like he was a crazy person.

Once they'd finished their meal, Croaks-with-the-frogs threw a few more branches on the fire. "You can take the first nap," he said without meeting her eyes. "I'll look after the fire."

"Thanks." The-tiny-one curled herself between the fallen tree and the fire and closed her eyes. She heard him moving around the camp, gathering wood and pine cones and bringing them back to the fire. As she drifted off to sleep she saw again the blazing fire of her dreams and the sad brown eyes of Croaks-with-the-frogs.

No such thing as started grief

After the chaos had subsided, No-point-shoe and Fire-in-his-hair took Sleeps-in-the-sun and Sniffs-the-wind back to the hive. The others stayed out digging. Now that the Eagle had fed, it was less likely to risk the spears and fires by returning. The tribe needed bracken and excessive sentimentality was a luxury they could not afford. In spite of this, the Eagle attack had reminded them all how precarious their existence was. The fear in the air was palpable. The hunters dug hurriedly and in silence, gathering as much as they could before, grief, fear and exhaustion drove them back to the hive.

That evening, there was no joyous singing or dancing. The tribes ate their stew with little conversation. Sleeps-in-the-sun toyed with her cake, dipping it into her stew and letting the sauce soak into the dough. Behind her blank expression, she was boiling with rage.

She felt like she was at the centre of a series of concentric circles. At the furthest edge were the children. They, of course were oblivious. For brief moments, when around the adults, they would mimic their somber tone but this would not last long. Soon they would wander off to play quietly amongst themselves. Their only nod to the grief was diminished noise. Sleeps-in-the-sun resented them, their innocence.

The Swamp people did not know Listen's-for-ducks very well. They only met him every other year at Wattle but a shared sense of doom led them all to know the death of one diminished them all. But it was a complex feeling, pity and dread, mixed with an effervescent tinge of joy because it was not them who was taken. They were still alive. Sleeps-in-the-sun hated them for that.

The Lake people were more wounded. They had grown up with Listens-for-ducks and hunted, laughed and sang with him. Everybody had a story about something he had done but their grief was at a distance. They were once her people and they felt her brother's loss, keenly. But they were not her people anymore. Time and distance had pulled them apart. And they had never been privy to the intimate bond only a brother and sister share. She knew she would never belong to them again and for reasons she couldn't explain this annoyed her.

Beside her, sat Sniffs-the-wind. She had not taken the bowl of stew No-point-shoe had offered her. The cake she had taken from Fire-in-his-hair was left lying in the dirt. Her face was blotched and her eyes were red but she had cried all her tears through the afternoon. There would be more tears to cry, of course, but not right now.

Sleeps-in-the-sun pitied her. She knew what losing a husband felt like, the awful hole in the pit of her soul that sucked all the joy out of life. Each new grief reminds you of all your previous griefs. But losing Listens-for-ducks was the worst grief Sniffs-the-wind had ever felt. It was so great, it did not summon any smaller ones. That would come later. For Sleeps-in-the-sun it was different. Losing Listens-for-ducks seared Sleeps-in-the-sun to her soul, but it also summoned the greater grief of Finder-of-snails' death in all its raw horror. As Sleeps-in-the-sun looked across at Sniffs-the-wind, the barrier between them was a solid mud wall. *There is no such thing as shared grief. We are always alone.*

Somewhere around the fire, a man started a low dirge.
Oh, Oh, Oh.
Oh, Oh, Oh.
Others took up the chant in close harmony and they began the litany of loss...
We come from the fire
 Come back to the fire
The fire burns within us
 Come back to the fire
Only the fire understands
 Come back to the fire
The fire is never extinguished
 Come back to the fire
And when our time is done, we
 Come back to the fire
Someday we all will be together when we
 Come back to the fire

Sleeps-in-the-sun felt her lip curl and she willed herself to straighten it. She looked around the fire again. No-point-shoe sang softly, staring into the flames. Fire-in-his-hair sat in silence, tears trickling down his face. He wasn't crying for Listens-for-ducks. Beside her Sniffs-the-wind sang through gritted teeth. Sleeps-in-the-sun understood that rage. When the dirge was finished, Sleeps-in-the-sun stood. No-point-shoe looked up at her with compassion in her eyes, but Sleeps-in-the-sun shook her head and walked off to her burrow.

Told you it works

In the pine forest, they took turns to nap and watch the fire throughout the night. With each change of shift, the awkwardness of the evening seemed to fall away more and more.

"Are you getting enough rest?" asked Croaks-with-the-frogs when he woke to watch the fire in the pre dawn chill.

"Yeah. I'm doing fine," she said, smiling. "I don't know how you do this on your own."

The boy shrugged. "I set the fire up big and take shorter naps. It's not as restful as when there's someone else watching the fire, because I'm always sort of partly awake."

The-tiny-one laughed. "Well, when you're watching the fire, I sleep like a log." She lay in the sleeping place between the tree trunk and the fire and closed her eyes.

Croaks-with-the-frogs watched her sleep for a while then collected some more wood. Pine burnt faster than gum so the fire burned brightly but not for very long. By the time the first hints of light were tinting the eastern sky he had collected a large pile of wood. This was now the dangerous part of the night, when the foxes and cats would hunt in the forest. The boy crouched by the fire, listening to the faint sounds beyond the ring of light.

The-tiny-one opened her eyes when the sky was a pale grey. Somewhere to the east, the sun was rising but it was hidden in a bank of cloud. She lay on her back and watched the faint tinge of pink spread across the clouds and listened to the crackle of the fire. It took a surprisingly long time for her to realise she was alone. Croaks-with-the-frogs was nowhere to be seen.

She leapt to her feet, her mind racing. Several competing thoughts and instincts were struggling for dominance. Fear of being abandoned, anger at him for disappearing, fear of the future out here alone, anger at her own stupidity, then the horror when she realised he might have been taken in the night. She grabbed her spear and looked around wildly. The fire was burning well, it hadn't been too long since wood had been added. A single pine cone had burned down to coals, it glowed crimson amidst the flames. The boy's spear was missing as was his back pack. These were certain signs he had not been taken by a fox or a cat. He had left the fire on his own accord, either temporarily or for good. She crushed down her panic. *He wouldn't leave me out here alone.*

In the distance she caught the faint flicker of fire and saw Croaks-with-the-frogs walking towards her from the direction of his traps with a dying brand in his hand. Dangling from his waist was a pair of dead mice, tied by their tails to his belt. He approached the fire with a satisfied grin on his face.

"Where have you been?" She failed to keep her annoyance out of her voice.

"Gotta collect the mice before they get scavenged." He threw the sputtering brand onto the fire and slung his pack down. In addition to the pair of mice at his waist, he had another mouse in his pack.

The-tiny-one stared in wonder. "A tall of mice! You've caught a tall of mice!"

Croaks-with-the-frogs grinned. "Yeah. I told you it works. They love that wattle seed goo. I dunno why."

"I thought you were crazy." Her voice seemed far away, lost in her amazement.

"Yeah. I had a feeling you thought that."

"But it works. This is how you catch those mice."

The boy laughed. He pulled out a shard of rock and began skinning the mouse from his pack. "We can eat this 'un for breakfast and take the others back to the hive for the pot." He gestured his head towards a stash of bracken root hidden beside the fallen tree. "You want some cake with it?"

While the mouse roasted over the fire, the young ones pounded the bracken into cakes. Croaks-with-the-frogs gathered some dandelion leaves from an open patch in the forest and added them to the dough. They made enough cakes for their breakfast, their lunch and to replenish the stashes they had eaten on the way here. By mid morning they were enjoying a hearty meal.

The-tiny-one watched him eat.

He looked up and caught her staring at him. "What?"

The-tiny-one shook her head in amazement. "You are a really amazing person, Croaks-with-the-frogs."

The boy flushed.

"I don't know anybody like you. You're like a whole fist in a single person. I can't believe you do all this!"

Croaks-with-the-frogs stared at the fire. Several responses bubbled away in his mind but again, something about this girl forced him into brutal honesty. "I can't explain this," he said softly. "Part of me thinks that I'm pretty good. I mean, I think you're right. I don't know anybody other than Fire-in-his-hair who could survive alone, the way I do. But at the same time..." His voice became heavy with feeling. "I absolutely loathe myself for doing this.... for being able to do this. You looking at me, now with that... in that way. Just makes me hate myself."

"Why?"

He bowed his head miserably. "I don't know."

She paused, staring at him. Then she reached out and rested her hand on his knee. "I think I understand the reason," she said gently.

He looked up into her eyes.

"You're crazy, Croaks-with-the-frogs," she said.

He stared at her in shock then saw the smile on her face.

They laughed until The-tiny-one nearly choked on her cake.

After breakfast Croaks-with-the-frogs climbed to his feet. "We'd better get that resin," he said.

They left the fire to burn while they set off into the forest to collect the resin. The-tiny-one followed him from tree to tree. In several trees Croaks-with-the-frogs had driven his axe into the wood, scarring the flesh. From each wound a thick trickle of resin had poured and hardened. The-tiny-one broke off pieces and stuffed them into her backpack. Croaks-with-the-frogs wandered from tree to tree, poking at various bits of resin, picking some but leaving others.

"What are you doing?" The-tiny-one asked.

Croaks-with-the-frogs didn't answer. He looked across sheepishly and began stuffing resin into his pack more hurriedly. The-tiny-one filled her pack and called, "Are you ready?"

Croaks-with-the-frogs seemed to jump, "No... um not yet. Nearly."

"What is taking you so long?!" She returned to the safety of the fire and watched the boy moving about the forest, choosing pieces of resin to stash in his pack.

At each tree, he examined the available lumps, pulled off some, wiped them clean, screwed up his nose in disapproval then moved on to the next.

The sun was higher in the mid morning sky now. The cloud cover was breaking up revealing large patches of blue behind the light grey. The sunlight sparkled in the water droplets on the trees. The-tiny-one rested her head against the trunk of the tree and closed her eyes. Even though the place was alien and disturbing, there was a beauty here.

Croaks-with-the-frogs called from further into the forest, "Why don't you pack up the camp while you're waiting? I won't be long."

By the time, Croaks-with-the-frogs returned, the camp was struck and the fire was merely smouldering. "I didn't set up a coal carrier," she said as he approached, "I'm not very good at it, so..."

Croaks-with-the-frogs approached her. His pack was full but he had a strange look on his face. He stood in front of her and chewed at his bottom lip.

"What?" she said.

Without answering, Croaks-with-the-frogs stretched out his hand. Nestled in his palm was a perfectly round piece of resin. "Would... Can I..." He took a deep breath. "For you," he said softly.

The-tiny-one stared at the resin then looked into his large brown eyes. Memories swirled within her. She remembered how she felt when she saw him give the resin to the children. The joy on their faces and the fire sparking through the amber. She remembered her dreams of the fire blazing in the middle of those sad brown eyes. As she took the ball and stared into its rich, golden interior, she felt a yearning she had never experienced before. Something in her was alive and bursting to escape. She had no idea what this thing was, but she was terrified to let it loose. It took all her will power to keep herself under control.

"Thank you, Croaks-with-the-frogs," she said bowing formally. But for reasons she could not fathom, tears ran down her cheeks.

~ 8 ~

GREEN WOOD BURNS

Return to The Hive

When Croaks-with-the-frogs and The-tiny-one returned
to the hive late on the following day, things seemed almost
normal. The day long return journey had been an enjoyable
one. Once they had reached the safety of the tea tree the
young ones laughed and joked as they walked the final *scout*.
The-tiny-one had tried to show Croaks-with-the-frogs how
to dance again as they walked. She sang out a simple beat and
swayed her hips to the music as she walked. Croaks-with-the-
frogs tried to copy her and they both laughed at his incompetence. By the time they reached the entrance to the hive,
the young ones were flushed with joy and triumph.

The sun had slipped behind the tea tree, casting the hive
into shadow. People were gathering around the communal
pots, preparing for the evening meal.

The children rushed to greet them shouting, "Oaks, Oaks-
wi-fogs."

Croaks-with-the-frogs laughed, throwing his arms wide
and called back, "Little oaks!" as if he was surprised to find
them there.

The children pulled at him and badgered him with questions, wanting to see if he'd caught something. "Oo catch mouse?" For the little ones, anything the boy caught was a mouse.

Croaks-with-the-frogs laughed. "Yes. A point of mice. They'll go well in the pot."

"Me 'kin, me 'kin?" asked the little boy.

"You can help."

The-tiny-one watched the banter with amusement.

She looked around the hive for Listens-for-ducks so she could deliver the resin. He was no-where to be seen. No-one from her fist was at the fire. Even Croaks-with-the-frogs' fist seemed to be missing.

"Where is everyone?" The-tiny-one said. "They can't all be sleeping."

Croaks-with-the-frogs paid no attention. He was engrossed in the antics of the children. "One day, when you are bigger, I will show you how to catch mice and then you can bring the mice to me."

The children stared at him with shining eyes.

The-tiny-one walked around the fire towards the burrow where the fist had been sleeping, looking for some clue to the absences. She could tell from the strained smiles and the tell-tale glances of the other tribespeople something was wrong. At the entrance to the burrow, she heard the sound of low voices. She slipped off her pack, rested her spear against the wall and crawled inside.

As her eyes slowly adjusted to the dim light, The-tiny-one took in the full implications of what she saw. In the centre of the burrow, curled in foetal position, Sniffs-the-wind lay on a pile of furs. Around her with their backs resting against the vertical poles, sat over a fist of people. She saw No-point-shoe sitting with her arm around Sleeps-in-the-sun, beside her was Fire-in-his-hair. Runs-like-a-rabbit and Hunter-of-flies were also sitting solemnly in the burrow. This was a ominous sign. They were the oldest members of her fist and tended to keep to themselves, rarely getting involved in the social activities of the younger members. Listens-for-ducks was nowhere to be seen.

Hunter-of-flies saw her enter and motioned for her to come and sit beside him. As she did so, the old hunter, spoke formally. His voice scarred the heavy silence of the burrow. "Listens-for-ducks has been taken by an eagle."

As the words were spoken Sniffs-the-wind whimpered and Sleeps-in-the-sun drew a sharp breath. The post was hard and solid at The-tiny-one's back. She did not cry. She should feel sad, but somehow it didn't seem real. She felt like she was listening to one of the stories told around the fire. The story had reached a sad part but she knew it wasn't real. Any moment now she expected Listens-for-ducks to crawl into the burrow and start berating her in his good natured way for leaving her spear out or not taking care of her tools. She had to force herself to realise he was gone and was never coming back. Only then, did the tears flow.

The fire burns but the wood is green

It was dark and Croaks-with-the-frogs had skinned and butchered the mice before he realised The-tiny-one had wandered off. The children were still following him around, keen to see what was going to happen to the mouse pelts they had helped create. "It's too late to go down to the swamp now," Croaks-with-the-frogs told them. "We'll ask Sleeps-in-the-sun if we can share her soaking pot." Sleeps-in-the-sun had a large pot in which she soaked small pelts before tanning.

The children stared at him with wide eyes. It was not at all clear how much they understood.

With his little entourage of children following, Croaks-with-the-frogs wandered off to find Sleeps-in-the-sun. Like The-tiny-one before him, he too found himself standing outside the burrow listening to the soft cries and the muffled voices within.

"Um, maybe we should look for Sleeps-in-the-sun later," he told the children. "You go and get some dinner now." As the kids wandered away, Croaks-with-the-frogs left his pelts outside and crawled in.

In the gloom of the burrow, The-tiny-one recognised the shape of Croaks-with-the-frogs' narrow head silhouetted in the entrance and something beyond words broke open within her. She clambered across the burrow, bumbling over Sniffs-the-wind and threw herself into his arms.

Behind her she was dimly aware of Sniffs-the-wind's yelp of pain and Hunter-of-flies' bark of disapproval but she didn't care. For reasons she could not explain, all she wanted at that moment was to be held by Croaks-with-the-frogs. It was as if the boy had become a place of safety and stability in a world suddenly in chaos.

Croaks-with-the-frogs was completely taken aback by the girl's response. His eyes had not adjusted to the light and he had not taken in the scene in the burrow. He only knew there were others there, and The-tiny-one was hugging him, clinging to him, her face wet with tears and snot.

On instinct, he held her tightly, marvelling at how small she was in his arms.

"Listens-for-ducks," she said. "They took him." Her words bundled out in short barely comprehensible sentences. "Taken by an eagle. He's dead. The *pargronts*! He's dead! We weren't there. I should have been there."

Croaks-with-the-frogs was beset by multiple conflicting thoughts and emotions as he held The-tiny-one in his arms. He was aware he had become the centre of attention in the burrow and he feared that would not end well. As The-tiny-one's words slowly sank in, he pieced together the story and the situation. He hardly knew Listens-for-ducks. They had barely exchanged a fist of words. He didn't really like the man very much and felt no loss in his death. But every death was a victory for the enemy and he shared the deep rage that burned within all of them. Hard on the heels of that feeling came another thought, *If she finds out you didn't like him, she'll stop hugging you.*

With that thought came an eruption of emotion that swept all other thoughts, fears and feelings aside. This little mousey girl was hugging him. The most magnificent human being he had ever met was small and weak and vulnerable. She needed him, and he would not let her down. He would stand alone against a fist of eagles to protect her. *I would burn down the whole world for this girl!*

* * * * *

G'pa stretched his back and yawned. "You ready for bed?" he asked.

There was no answer.

"Hey! You ready for bed?" he said louder.

Silence.

"Throwing-pine-cones, can you hear me?"

G'ma stared into the flames, her mouth hanging open, an alien, inanimate stare in her eyes. The empty nut of undiluted toddy stuck awkwardly in her nerveless hand. Her voice was small and high pitched. The old man had to strain to hear her words.

"It's happened too soon. They are not ready. The fire burns but the wood is green." Then, as if she were a small child lost in the dark, she said. "Something new is growing in the flames."

Never is a long time

The-tiny-one stayed in the burrow after the rest of her fist had left. Curled beside Croaks-with-the-frogs, she buried her head in his shoulder and drifted in and out of fevered dreams. Sleeps-in-the-sun slept between No-point-shoe and Fire-in-his-hair. Their warm bodies giving her some small comfort.

Croaks-with-the-frogs awoke early. He lay on his back, and stared at the ceiling. The air holes above let in a faint light that signalled the approach of dawn. He felt The-tiny-one's soft, warm breath on his neck, and her toes resting against his calf. The sensation was unlike anything he had ever felt before. He was swept up in a wave of joy. How can the close proximity of this single person make him feel so much? He lay, savouring the swirl of emotions within him as the faint light in the burrow slowly increased.

Like the gradually increasing light, realisation waxed within him. First came the deep conviction that he never wanted to be away from The-tiny-one again. Slowly, inexorably, another realisation dawned... Next year, the lake people would go to the coast, and she would marry there. He would be expected to marry a girl from the river folk. Once the lake people left at the end of this Wattle, he would never see her again.

The joy that buoyed him throughout the night disappeared, replaced by an inexpressible horror. He rolled over and grabbed her in a fierce embrace, burying is face in her hair. The girl responded and as the dawn broke outside, Croaks-with-the-frogs drifted back to sleep.

Fire-in-his-hair was the first to wake that morning. He stopped as he was crawling out of the burrow and stared at Croaks-with-the-frogs and The-tiny-one for a long time. Under the furs, the young ones were completely entangled in each other's arms and The-tiny-one had draped her leg over the boy's torso. The ease with which they lay disturbed him, but he couldn't put his finger on what it was. He left the burrow, got himself some stew and a cake and sat by the fire. After Sleeps-in-the-sun and No-point-shoe woke, they found him sitting and chewing, thoughtfully.

"What do you make of that?!" Sleeps-in-the-sun's eyes were wide.

Fire-in-his-hair looked up, hoping she was taking about something other than the youngsters.

No-point-shoe said, "Did you see how she flew into his arms when he came into the burrow?"

"Oh yeah... buried her face in his neck like they had been married for years."

"Are you taking about the kids?" asked Fire-in-his-hair.

No-point-shoe stared at him archly. "No! I'm taking about that pair of old coots, Runs-like-a-rabbit and Hunter-of-flies." She paused for effect, then, "Of course, I'm taking about the kids!"

"I think coots are always male," said Fire-in-his-hair flatly.

Sleeps-in-the-sun laughed shortly, then returned to the main topic. "So how do you explain this? Do you think they merged fires when they went to get the resin?"

Fire-in-his-hair recoiled in shock. "How could they? They're just kids."

No-point-shoe nodded. "They're definitely not fertile... they couldn't actually do anything but..."

"But!" said Sleeps-in-the-sun. "Something has definitely happened and I don't think the lake people will be too happy about it."

"Why not?" asked Fire-in-his-hair. "They're just kids. It's not like they can actually do anything."

No-point-shoe pulled off a chunk of Fire-in-his-hair's cake, dipped it in his stew and put it in her mouth. Sleeps-in-the-sun noticed the food for the first time and she did likewise. The man tried to frown at the women but his face suffused with a warm smile. Something about the thoughtless familiarity of their actions touched him.

They ate in silence for a while, then No-point-shoe said, "I think they've pair bonded early."

Sleeps-in-the-sun was still chewing. "Is that even possible?"

"I've heard of it happening before," said No-point-shoe. "Never seen it, but I've heard of it."

Inside the burrow, Croaks-with-the-frogs pushed himself into a sitting position and arched his back. The-tiny-one lay staring up at him, her eyes wide in an unreadable expression.

He stared at her for several moments, mesmerised by their blueness and the little clouds that flecked within them.

She smiled. "Hello," she said.

He stared at her intently. "I don't want you to go back after Wattle."

She laughed.

"No! I'm serious." His voice broke a little bit. "I cant... imagine life without you."

The laughter on her face dissolved into a compassionate, motherly stare. The-tiny-one reached out her hand and rested her palm against his face.

Croaks-with-the-frogs closed his eyes and leaned into it for a moment, then, "Next year, after you go back, you will go to the coast folk and marry there. I'll never see you again."

The-tiny-one shrugged. "Never is a long time. We don't know what's going to happen."

The boy was annoyed. His desperation was obviously not being matched. "What do you think happened last night?"

She scrunched her face. "What?"

His certainties evaporated. "Didn't you... Did you feel anything?"

She smiled. "We fitted nicely together, didn't we."

Encouraged, Croaks-with-the-frogs pushed on with more urgency. "I don't want to be apart from you. I don't want you to marry someone else. I want you to marry me!"

The-tiny-one's face burst into a radiant smile. "That would be nice, wouldn't it. We could go out to the pine forest whenever we wanted." Then her smile faded. "But we're too young. We can get married next year."

"But, you won't be here next year!"

She looked at him mildly.

"How can you not understand this!? Next year, you will marry someone from the coast, and I'll be expected to marry into the river folk! What is so hard to understand?"

"You're shouting at me."

"I'm not shouting!" he shouted. "Do you want to marry me or not?"

"We're too young. We can't marry until next year."

"Fuck! Fuck! Fuckety fuck!' muttered Croaks-with-the-frogs as he scrambled out of the furs, pulled on his clothes and crawled out of the burrow.

As he stood, Croaks-with-the-frogs saw Fire-in-his-hair, No-point-shoe and Sleeps-in-the-sun staring at him. It took only an instant for him to recognise their expressions. No-point-shoe was concerned, Sleeps-in-the-sun looked frightened and there was pity in Fire-in-his-hair's eyes. They knew. They had seen, and probably even heard the conversation between him and The-tiny-one. He stood, staring at them, torn between a desire to run to them and blurt out all his tortured feelings, but another part of him wanted to run away, to leave the hive and seek the lonely safety of the tea tree.

From across the other side of the fire, he caught glimpse of someone waving. He looked across and saw G'ma, staring across the fire with a vague smile on her face.

Croaks-with-the-frogs composed himself, straightened his back and walked over to the cauldron. He poured a couple of nuts of dandelion and took them across to where G'ma was sitting.

Fire-in-his-hair said, "Well, at least that solves the main problem."

No-point-shoe stared at him. "What?"

"You heard her. She doesn't want him. Poor kid."

Both women began talking at the same time leaving Fire-in-his-hair staring open mouthed as he tried to keep up.

"Why would you think that?"

"Ridiculous!"

"We all saw how she acted."

"She only said the truth."

"She wants him but maybe she just doesn't realise it yet."

"They're too young to marry."

"Doesn't mean she doesn't want him."

"We need to find out."

"I'll go." With that, No-point-shoe surged to her feet and went back to the burrow.

Fire-in-his-hair watched her leave and marvelled how the women were able to talk and listen at the same time. He shook his head, "People go crazy during Wattle season," he said. Then turning to Sleeps-in-the-sun he asked, "Can you please explain to me what just happened?"

G'ma's not good this morning

Croaks-with-the-frogs carried the nuts of dandelion to where G'ma sat by the fire. He held out a nut to her and she took it gratefully. Beside her G'pa sat scowling at the flames. On a whim, the boy handed the other nut to the old man. "Would you like a nut of dandy, G'pa?" he asked.

The old man looked up, the frown still on his face. He screwed up his face and began to shake his head, then he saw the uncertainty and doubt in the boy's eyes, and he stopped. "Um... Yes!" he said too loudly. "Yes, Thank you... um boy. That would be very nice."

G'ma twitched like a bird that had found a worm. "Then what about your drink dear?"

"I'll go and get another nut for me," said Croaks-with-the-frogs.

G'ma looked at him with sympathy. "No. Here, you have mine."

"No, G'ma. I'll just get myself another."

G'ma ignored him. Pushing her nut into his hand. The hot brew slopped and spilled over the edge of the nut.

"By the blazes, leave the boy alone!" snapped G'pa. "Let him go and get a nut for himself and then he can come back."

"He has nothing to drink."

"He will..." G'pa's face contorted in frustration. He calmed himself and turned to Croaks-with-the-frogs. "Just go and get a nut for yourself, I'll sort her out."

As Croaks-with-the-frogs walked back to the cauldron, he could hear G'ma and G'pa arguing about dandelion brew and toddy.

When he returned with his own nut, G'ma had slid to the edge of the log and was sitting, half turned away from G'pa. The boy sat between them.

G'pa looked at him sadly. "G'ma's not good this morning," he said.

Croaks-with-the-frogs stared at him. He wasn't sure what G'pa meant, but he sensed it was something bigger than a nut of dandy. The look on the old man's face hinted at agonies beyond the boy's understanding.

Croaks-with-the-frogs was absorbed with other things this morning so he pushed those thoughts aside. "G'pa, do people have to marry when they get to the age?"

The old man sat back a bit further in his seat. His mind shifted slowly to a new topic and it took a moment before he could reply. "They don't have to, but usually they want to." His old head wobbled even more than usual and he smiled. "I remember when I was your age, I thought the idea of marriage was... um... disgusting. But..." He laughed. "Things change when ah..."

G'pa hadn't understood. Croaks-with-the-frogs had an intuitive sense that conversations with G'pa don't last very long. If he let the old man talk much more, he would never get to the matter at hand. "G'pa, I want to marry The-tiny-one," he blurted.

G'pa hadn't heard him, "You what?"

Croaks-with-the-frogs took a deep breath. Tears welled in his eyes and blood rushed to his cheeks. "I don't understand... but I just don't think I can bear for her to leave at the end of this Wattle. I'll never see her again and I can't... I can't... but I..."

G'pa kept looking at him, a confused expression on his face. "Who?"

"The-tiny-one. I want to marry The-tiny-one."

The old man sat for quite awhile, stroking his chin and looking intently at the boy. Then he said, "It's too early. You're only a boy."

A tear trickled down Croaks-with-the-frogs' face. "I know, but... I don't understand."

Silence descended again. The old man sipped his dandelion. Flashes of memory passed across his mind like summer clouds blown on the wind.

On the other side of the log, G'ma had been listening, a distant smile on her face. "What a thing! Children getting married, people shouting. The wood is green, but the fire still burns. How lovely."

G'pa stared at her. He felt something shift under his feet and an unmistakable rise of fear in his chest, the dry lips and the urge to swallow. He sipped at his brew.

After a while, he said. "Does this girl feel the same way as you? If she is also young, she may not be ready."

Croaks-with-the-frogs shrugged. "I don't know. I thought she did."

The old man nodded and sipped at his dandelion. They sat together in silence.

After a little while, G'ma said, "It's cold this morning isn't it."

Croaks-with-the-frogs sat miserably on the log while G'ma twittered on about the weather, the fire and the need to keep it burning. When No-point-shoe led The-tiny-one out of the burrow, he sat straighter, every nerve taut. He watched in wide eyed trepidation as the older woman led the girl across the fire to where he, G'pa and G'ma were sitting.

"G'ma," she said, ignoring Croaks-with-the-frogs, "Can we please talk to you? We have a problem."

G'ma smiled at her but said nothing.

"G'ma is not too good today, dear," said G'pa.

No-point-shoe stared at them for a moment, an unreadable expression on her face.

The old man gestured to an empty place beside him.

No-point-shoe took a flattened log, and pulled it up for her and The-tiny-one to sit. "This is The-tiny-one. She's from the lake people."

G'pa nodded, a blank stare on his face. Then, slowly, like the sun rising in the summertime, he turned and looked questioningly at Croaks-with-the-frogs. Croaks-with-the-frogs was staring at the girl with undisguised longing. The old man laughed. "Ah! This is the one. Is this your girl?"

No-point-shoe looked across at the boy and shot him a reassuring wink. "We think that they may have pair bonded," she said. "They haven't merged their fires. They are too young for that, but from what they've said and the way they've acted, it seems that some sort of bonding has taken place."

G'ma smiled and wagged her head. "The wood is green," she said and laughed happily.

G'pa ignored her. He spoke to No-point-shoe and his head wobbled. "It has happened before that young ones bond early. It's rare, but I... you know... pair bond before they reach the age. I knew of a young couple many years ago. They were only a few years younger than me. One of our girls married a boy from the lake."

G'ma shook her head. "It didn't end well. They died."

"Yes, they died, but ah..."

"Drowned."

"Yes, they ... they drowned on the lake soon after..."

G'ma nodded and looked at No-point-shoe knowingly. "And everybody said it was because they bonded too young."

G'pa shook his head and raised his hands as if he were trying to brush away a swarm of insects. He turned to G'ma. "Yes, but that's all frog-shit! They drowned. These things happen."

G'ma was not deterred. "It's those... things they use over there... those..."

G'pa turned back to No-point-shoe and returned to the conversation, but G'ma kept speaking even though no one was listening to her. "They go right on the water with those... far out."

G'pa pressed his fingers against the sides of his head, massaging his temples. "We need to first establish if they are genuinely bonded," he said, and looked meaningfully at The-tiny-one.

G'ma was still talking, interjecting each time G'pa took a breath. "Nothing holding them up. Just a few bits of wood on the deep water."

"Then, what usually happens," said G'pa, "is they stay in the same tribe until they are ready to merge fires."

"The ... ah... thing... the whole thing tipped over and they fell in."

"But that will take some negotiation."

"That's why everybody said it was because they bonded too early."

"The elders will have to decide where they live. But both children have to be willing."

"Didn't even have one litter. Not like you, dear. You'll have many. The wood's green but the fire still burns."

G'pa speared The-tiny-one with his eyes and his head stopped wobbling. "Would you be willing to leave your tribe, your fist and your G'ma to live with us?"

The-tiny-one's eyes were wide. She bit her lip and looked across at Croaks-with-the-frogs with a nervous smile, then at No-point-shoe. Her eyes shining in hero worship. "Ye-es," she said.

G'pa frowned. "What if No-point-shoe wasn't here?"

The girl's head snapped back in shock. "Um... no... I want to be with Croaks-with-the-frogs."

G'ma laughed.

G'pa turned to the boy. Would you be willing to leave us at the end of this Wattle and live with her tribe for the rest of your life?"

Croaks-with-the-frogs' eyes welled with tears. "If I can be with her, yeah!"

The old man nodded, thoughtfully. "Yes... Well, that's what happened that last time, you see... This girl, went to live with the lake folk and they were married the following Wattle."

G'ma shook her head. "It didn't end well. They died."

"Yes.. yes but ah..."

"Drowned."

"Anyway... we'll talk to the Lake people and see what we can do."

G'ma cocked her head and looked at No-point-shoe again. "And everybody said it was because they bonded too young."

No-point-shoe nodded at G'ma, then looked questioningly at G'pa.

The old man closed his eyes and the sides of his mouth pulled down in sadness. "She'll be alright. It's just the toddy. She's bad in the morning but she'll be OK by afternoon."

G'ma's face was like a lost little girl. "I need it to *see*," she said. "It's happening now and I have to *see*."

Who are these young ones?

The morning's drama was too much for the youngsters. In silent mutual consent they acted as if the events of the last day and night hadn't happened. Croaks-with-the-frogs could think of little else but The-tiny-one seemed to slip back into her old ways with ease. The boy was not sure if she was pretending or not, but he sensed any attempt by him to talk about their possible marriage would not be welcomed. So he acted like it was all settled, but fretted and worried on the inside.

Sleeps-in-the-sun was glad of the distraction. She set about repairing The-tiny-one's spear but while she worked she demanded a full report from No-point-shoe and extracted a word for word account of the conversation with both The-tiny-one and G'pa. When No-point-shoe described G'ma's behaviour, both Sleeps-in-the-sun and Fire-in-his-hair became concerned.

"She's always been a bit scatty," said Fire-in-his-hair.

"But never like that…" No-point-shoe's voice was a fierce whisper. "I've never seen anything like that."

Sleeps-in-the-sun was melting resin on the fire. "What did G'pa say about it?"

"He said it was the toddy… that she'd be OK by this afternoon."

Fire-in-his-hair nodded but said nothing.

No-point-shoe shook her head in disbelief. "I can't believe we're relying on G'pa's word in all this. G'ma has always been the brains of that pair."

Fire-in-his-hair frowned. "Don't underestimate the old man," he said.

"What will happen to the tribe without G'ma?" asked Sleeps-in-the-sun.

They sat in silence, no one had any answer to that.

Late that morning, the sun poked it's way between clouds and cast a watery light over the land. The tribes went out again to hunt rabbits. This time they struck the other warren, to the south east.

The-tiny-one took the roll of lead flushfert again. Her new spear wasn't ready yet, so Croaks-with-the-frogs gave her his to use. There were the usual bruises and scratches and a hunter from the swamp folk broke a rib when a rabbit charged him. But apart from that, the hunt went off without incident. They brought a fist of rabbits back to the hive.

That afternoon, while the rabbits roasted and the hunters rested, the old ones gathered in the meeting burrow to discuss marriages. The atmosphere in the burrow was tense. The last discussions did not end well and the Lake tribe delegation was still smarting from G'ma's broadside. They sat with their backs straight and watched the swamp folk through narrowed eyes.

G'ma had returned to normality after last night's toddy had worn off and she remembered the morning's discussion with No-point-shoe and Croaks-with-the-frogs. She handed around a bark plate with a pile of bracken fiddles. The elders nibbled politely.

As they ate, G'pa started to talk. "Things seem to be going very well with our youngsters. They seem to have paired up nicely. "

The Lake folk said nothing.

"Our Me-not-talking and your Climbs-the-burrow seem strongly connected."

Silence.

"Climbs-the-burrow seems like a fine young hunter."

The lake folk's G'ma smiled thinly, acknowledging the compliment.

The old man from the Lake tribe nodded. "Yes, Rolls-in-the-berries and I were discussing just this morning how they both seem very happy with their partners."

G'pa was encouraged. "So it shouldn't be too difficult to sort them out." He looked across at G'ma hoping she would say something but she only sat and smiled at him. He pushed on, trying to emphasise more positives. "Also, I noticed that our young widower, Sings-at-dawn seems to have made a connection with your widow, Yabbies-in-winter. That is promising."

Rolls-in-the-berries twisted her mouth. "I do not believe they have merged fires yet. Your young man seems rather slow."

G'ma smiled at her. "Good things are worth waiting for, Rolls-in-the-berries," she said and laughed merrily.

Her laugh was infectious and even the other Lake people laughed.

Rolls-in-the-berries half smiled then forced her face to return to stony silence. "So now we have the problem of which pair goes where."

G'pa paused. G'ma stared at him and nodded. Her eyes were sharp and clear, but it annoyed the old man she was not taking any part in the negotiations. He shot her an annoyed look and started talking again. "We have another problem, my friends," he said and his head wobbled even more. He waited but there was no response from any of the lake tribe's elders.

With a sinking feeling, he realised The-tiny-one had not told anyone from her own tribe. They were going to be completely blindsided. The old man sat silently. Hoping to find a way to change the direction of the discussion. Now was not the time to drop this on the lake folk.

The silence stretched on uncomfortably then G'ma said, "A pair of our children have bonded. They are too young to merge fires or get married but the bond is real. We need to decide what to do with them."

G'pa wanted to scream. All through the negotiations, he had wanted her to get involved and now she does it just when he wanted her to keep quiet.

The lake folk were clearly rattled. Rolls-in-the-berries and Swims-like-a-fish spoke at the same time. "Who are these young ones?"

"Why have they not told us?"

G'pa said, "It has only just happened this morning. Perhaps the girl was a bit embarrassed."

Rolls-in-the-berries twisted her face. "She should be. Who has she supposedly bonded with?"

G'ma spoke calmly as if she was discussing the weather. "The-tiny-one has bonded with our Croaks-with-the-frogs. They are quite devoted to each other."

There was a series of audible gasps around the burrow as the Lake tribe digested this information.

Rolls-in-the-berries sputtered, "Our Tiny-one... with that... strange..." her words tailed off.

G'ma pushed on. "It actually makes things much simpler. Before this, we had a tall of couples and one tribe was going to take more than the other. Now we have an even number of couples. Which would you like?"

Rolls-in-the-berries opened her mouth but no words came out.

Swims-like-a-fish reached out his hand and rested it on her knee. "I think we'll need some time to consider this. I'm sure you understand this is all quite a shock. We'll need to discuss this with our young ones and ensure that your ... er... reading of the situation is accurate."

"Of course," said G'pa. "There's no need to rush. We have plenty of time."

Rolls-in-the-berries stared at G'ma savagely.

In response, G'ma replied mildly, "They are bonded. No amount of negotiation will change that, Rolls-in-the-berries. The wood is green, but the fire still burns."

Someone has designed us to fit together

That evening, while the tribes ate and danced to celebrate the successful hunt, G'ma and G'pa sat in their usual spots by the fire and fought with each other.

"You need help, you know," G'pa said savagely. "I don't know what's wrong with you, but whatever it is, it can't be fixed by anyone I know."

"You are what's wrong with me," G'ma retorted. "You're the one who makes my life a misery."

"Well no one's begging you to stay. Go home. Go back to your bloody river people."

"I will."

"They're so ashen caring and sensitive."

They paused, ruminating. Then G'ma said, "They wouldn't have you. Your too stupid to survive a single day on the river."

"I'm not frightened of those guys. They're all piss and wind."

"You'd drown." G'ma's eyes danced wickedly in the firelight as she thought of him drowning.

"Oh, well done! You've remembered the word now. Quick, drink some more toddy."

"I remembered the word!"

"You wouldn't want to accidentally regain any intelligence."

Once more the argument went into hiatus. G'pa was wondering if perhaps he had gone too far, but G'ma said in a low voice, "I'm so sick of you."

"I'm sick of you!" G'pa responded, instinctively.

"I don't know how much more of this I can take."

"Oh shut up!"

"Shut up yourself."

They lapsed into silence. Each scowling at the fire. After a while, G'pa started again.

"How many times did I look at you. Trying to get you to say something and all you did was nod. Like a bloody loose branch."

"I stupidly thought that you could handle it."

"I could! I was handling it!"

"Then why were you wobbling your head at me!?"

G'pa paused and took a breath to regain control. Then he tried to explain himself again. "I didn't want them to hear about the kids from us. I wanted them to hear it from their own people."

"It was too late. You had already blabbed!"

"I didn't blab. You blabbed!"

"You said we had another couple."

"I did not!"

"You did!"

"I never said that there was another couple."

"What did you say then?"

G'pa sputtered. "I ... I can't remember what I said, but... but..."

"Ah... Ha! See?"

"But I didn't say that there was another couple."

G'ma shook her head and forced a triumphant laugh. The old man scowled again and went silent.

On the other side of the fire, No-point-shoe and Fire-in-his-hair sat curled together with their backs resting against a large log. No-point-shoe rested her head against his chest and felt it rise and fall as he breathed. Fire-in-his-hair had his arm wrapped protectively around her as he watched the others dance.

Sleeps-in-the-sun didn't feel like dancing or singing. She had sat quietly by the fire while she ate her meal but as she was about to go to her burrow to sleep, The-tiny-one and Croaks-with-the-frogs had pulled her to her feet and insisted she dance with them. The-tiny-one claimed she wanted to show her how the boy's dancing had improved but in reality, she just wanted her to join in laughing at him. Before long they were soon joined by her litter. The little ones hung off Croaks-with-the-frogs and danced and laughed. "Oaks dance... Oaks dance," they squealed.

Sleeps-in-the-sun felt detached from the events as she danced. She smiled at the peculiar fist, twirling around the fire. She marvelled that the pair of toddlers had once been part of her. She pitied the pair of adolescents engrossed in their innocent romance and thought, *How is it possible these happy young people are connected to this sad and lonely woman?*

Off to the side, The-tiny-one's G'ma watched in disapproval as they danced.

The-tiny-one and Croaks-with-the-frogs danced until well into the night. Sleeps-in-the-sun and the babies had long crawled off to their burrows to sleep and the sounds of the wattle calls that had punctuated the evening had faded to soft snores. The young ones finally crawled into their burrow and found themselves a place between Sleeps-in-the-sun and Fire-in-his-hair.

The-tiny-one tangled herself in his body and snuggled under the furs. "We fit so well together," she said, sleepily. She lay on her side with her leg draped casually across his waist and her head resting on his shoulder.

He lay on his back, staring at the roof of the burrow in the darkness. "What do you mean," he asked.

She chuckled, slightly embarrassed. "My shoulder fits perfectly inside your arm pit. It's as if we were meant to be like this."

He looked at her in puzzlement.

"It's like we're a spear point and a shaft. Someone has designed us to fit together."

He laughed softly. "You're crazy, you know."

In response, she kissed his shoulder gently and closed her eyes in sleep.

9

THE END OF WATTLE

Rolls-in-the-berries knows what to do

Rolls-in-the-berries woke before dawn and crawled out of the burrow to sit and think by the fire. She was born and raised as a Lake woman. As a young spear she had married a coast man and after he died, a man from the swamp. She had borne several litters and her children had spread beyond her tribe and beyond her knowledge. But as she aged, her world-view expanded. She came to realise her small romances and the health and well being of various individuals were nothing more than component parts of a much greater purpose. She was now utterly focussed on what was best for her tribe.

Without the tribe, they were all nothing. Each member of her tribe was important, but they were only important be-cause they would enrich the tribe. Individuals come and go but the Lake people must remain.

Throughout her life she had seen the tribe's numbers rise and fall. Sometimes, it seemed there wouldn't be enough children born to keep the tribe viable. She vividly recalled, the dark years when she first became a G'ma, when the older ones, had considered merging the entire tribe with the

Swamp people because there were not enough marriagables to satisfy both the Swamp tribe and the coast people. She had fought hard within the councils of the Lake folk to keep the tribe functioning and had only just succeeded.

A few lucky breaks with children who survived to marriagable age, some good breeders who produced several healthy litters and tough negotiations with the neighbouring tribes were all that kept the tribe away from extinction. In her earliest days as lead negotiator, she had become known for her favourite slogan. *The survival of my people is at stake here.*

Swims-like-a-fish was not her husband. He was a few years older than her and his wife had died soon after they passed beyond fertility. For him the wattle season was a time of celebration and cooperation. If he had his way, the tribe would have been swallowed up long ago. He was far too agreeable to lead a negotiating team. It took only a couple of years for her to establish herself as the dominant one in their partnership. She knew he did not like her but she didn't care. He could frown and shake his head in disapproval as much as he liked, but the survival of the tribe demanded uncompromising negotiation.

Negotiation required Rolls-in-the-berries to deal with people both within and without the tribe. The most difficult person to deal with was Throwing-pine-cones from the Swamp people. The old Swamp witch had an uncanny knack of seeming so charming and agreeable on the surface but in every negotiation, the Swamp people walked away with a better breeding pair than the Lake folk.

Like all G'mas, Rolls-in-the-berries used the toddy at the start of every Wattle Season as a way of *seeing* the best path forward, but rarely did the drug give her more than vague hints or general directions. Somehow, Throwing-pine-cones was able to get specific information about significant individuals. And this had consistently given her an edge in the negotiations.

This year was different, however. The night before they left for the swamp, Rolls-in-the-berries had taken her usual dose and sat by the fire long into the night. She felt the swirling threads of destiny as they buffeted her, and though no images or words formed themselves in her mind, for the first time, she received a clear insight about an individual. The young *flushfert*, The-tiny-one was important. Her destiny was profoundly entangled in the future of the Lake people. She would be their salvation or their destruction and the future balanced on a knife's edge. Rolls-in-the-berries wondered why The-tiny-one would be so important when she wasn't even of marriagable age yet.

When Throwing-pine-cones mentioned the girl, Rolls-in-the-berries' heart skipped a beat. But when she realised that they wanted to marry her off to Croaks-with-the-frogs, her enthusiasm evaporated. There was little doubt in Rolls-in-the-berries' mind that Croaks-with-the-frogs was cursed. Both tribes knew it even though the elders of the Swamp folk refused to admit it publicly. The boy was not just peculiar, but he had a track record of destroying anyone who came too close to him. The old Swamp crone was trying to offload her cursed boy onto the Lake tribe and Rolls-in-the-berries was adamant she would not tolerate that.

The trouble was, there seemed very little wiggle room. After watching the girl closely last night, it was clear that somehow the accursed one had been able to bond with the girl. The intimacy was clear to see. But it was also clear how perverse and unhealthy the relationship was.

Croaks-with-the-frogs had her dancing with toddlers as if babies were fully human with names and spears. The boy had even given the toddlers names... "Little-Oaks." Rolls-in-the-berries wondered how the monstrosity was able to supplant the traditions of the tribe.

Clearly Throwing-pine-cones and Terror-of-magpies were losing their edge. They had been pandering to their young ones for so long now they couldn't exert control over this cursed boy to safeguard their traditions. They were desperate to get rid of him and Throwing-pine-cones must know how important The-tiny-one is to the Lake folk.

If she accepted that the pair had bonded prematurely, then Rolls-in-the-berries would face a terrible choice for the Lake tribe... either lose The-tiny-one or be saddled with Croaks-with-the-frogs. She knew what she had to do.

The sun had risen behind a bank of grey clouds and light had seeped into the world. Fire-in-his-hair and No-point-shoe were no longer in the burrow but Sleeps-in-the-sun and Croaks-with-the-frogs were still sleeping. The-tiny-one lay awake and listened to Croaks-with-the-frogs breathing heavily. She lay beside him for a while luxuriating in his closeness. She was tempted to wriggle around a bit in the hope of waking him but thought better of it. He would wake when he was ready. She slipped out from under the furs, pulled on her clothes, and crawled outside.

The hive was busy. People were moving around the fire, sharpening spears or repairing clothes. Some gathered in small groups, sharing food and talking. The-tiny-one walked over to where the stew was simmering, scooped some into a bowl and got herself a cake. As she looked around for a place to sit by the fire, she caught sight of her G'ma staring at her. The old woman waved her arm, beckoning. The-tiny-one smiled and went to her.

"Come and eat breakfast with me, Tiny-one," she said.

The girl handed her bowl and cake to her G'ma and went and got herself another serve. She then returned to a place beside the old woman and they sat, eating in silence for a few moments.

"So," Rolls-in-the-berries said, gently. "What sort of trouble have you gotten yourself into, dear?"

The-tiny-one laughed. "None, G'ma. I'm having a lovely Wattle season."

The old woman's frown lasted for only an instant. "They tell me you think you've bonded?" She allowed a faint chuckle to bubble beneath her words.

The-tiny-one suddenly felt a bit uncomfortable. "Um... I think so. No-point-shoe and the others think so too. It's wonderful."

Rolls-in-the-berries nodded thoughtfully and chewed her cake. "And have you merged fires with this boy?"

The-tiny-one recoiled in shock. "Oh no!" she laughed. "We're too young."

"Yes, of course. You are far too young." She let the silence hang for a moment then, "So what makes you think you have bonded?"

The-tiny-one's earlier confidence reduced even more. "Well... um... I really like him. And... he's such fun to be around. We laugh... and... um..."

Rolls-in-the-berries stopped eating and looked at her intently. Under that withering stare, the girl's words sputtered into an awkward silence. The old woman blinked a few times at her. "Do you find yourself getting wet around him, the way a woman does?"

The-tiny-one shifted on the log she was sitting on. "No."

"Does his penis stiffen in your presence as if the fire is blazing within him?"

"No, G'ma."

"And yet you've slept beside him in his burrow these last few nights?"

The-tiny-one nodded.

Rolls-in-the-berries looked at her for a long time then said, "I see."

The silence dragged on as they returned to eating their stew. The-tiny-one stared into her wooden bowl, her face colouring. She wanted to run away to hide in the burrow. She looked around for No-point-shoe. She would be able to answer G'ma's questions. Everything The-tiny-one was saying seemed to be wrong.

After a while, Rolls-in-the-berries sighed deeply, put down her bowl of stew and turned to face the young girl. "Oh, my dear, you have truly got yourself into a bit of a mess."

"Have I?"

Her G'ma's voice was kind. "Oh yes." She reached out and rested her hand on The-tiny-one's shoulder. "You haven't bonded, dear. You're too young. You just think you have."

The-tiny-one stared and her eyes began to water. "I... I thought..."

The old woman nodded sagely. "It has been known to happen in the past... for children to bond early, but this is very, very rare. It is much more common for a child to mistake simple friendship for something more."

"But... How do I know?"

Rolls-in-the-berries smiled without showing her teeth. "It's the moisture between the legs, dear."

The-tiny-one stared at her lap. "I am not moist."

"You are too young to bond."

The-tiny-one looked up pleadingly, her eyes shining. "But, No-point-shoe said..."

Rolls-in-the-berries shook her head sadly. "You have been misled, Tiny-one." She leaned in close and lowered voice to a fierce whisper. "Not everybody here can be trusted, dear. We are not at the lake. These people are dangerous."

"What do you mean?"

"They know that you are not bonded. They are attempting to steal you away from us."

The-tiny-one's stomach sank rapidly and tears welled in her eyes. "Who?"

"Not your boy," her G'ma said quickly. "He's just as innocent as you. He's just found a friend." She smiled comfortingly. "But the adults..." She shook her head and twisted her mouth. "They are the ones who are trying to steal you from us."

"But why?"

"My dear, you don't realise this because you are too young. But you are the best *flushfert* we have ever had in the Lake tribe. You are worth many rabbits. The Swamp tribe have seen you hunt. There is nobody in their tribe who can match you in the rabbit warrens. That's why they want you."

The-tiny-one frowned in confusion. "Nobody's told me this before. I know I'm good but..."

Rolls-in-the-berries laughed and waved her doubts away. "Of course, we're not going to make a big fuss of you. That's not our way. But make no mistake. You are in great demand."

"But... their G'pa said that Croaks-with-the-frogs might have to come and live with us."

The old woman frowned and her anger simmered just below the surface. "That would never work. He'd come and then next Wattle he'll want to marry you, but you will bond with someone else. He will be distraught and have to return to his own tribe in shame. Believe me. I know these things. By Summer, you will have forgotten all about this silly idea and next Wattle you'll be madly merging fires with some young spear from the Coast people."

"But I don't want..."

Rolls-in-the-berries twisted her head and raised her hand, threateningly. "Do not argue with me about this, Tiny-one.

You do not understand! You are not bonded to this boy and he is not bonded to you. At the end of the Wattle, you will come home with us."

The-tiny-one sat with her head bowed and cried softly. Her tears trickled down her face and her breath caught in short sobs.

What are you grinning about?

When Croaks-with-the-frogs crawled out of the burrow, he saw The-tiny-one sitting miserably beside her G'ma, but she didn't look up. He was a bit afraid of the old woman. She always seemed to look at him with undisguised malice, so he got himself some stew and went over to Fire-in-his-hair and No-point-shoe.

Sleeps-in-the-sun had replaced the soaking rabbit hides from the first hunt with the fresh hides caught yesterday. She had stretched out the soaked rabbit skins and left them to dry overnight.

Fire-in-his-hair and No-point-shoe were using the brains of yesterday's rabbits to tan the hides. It was smelly, unpleasant work and it was not a good place to eat breakfast but at least Croaks-with-the-frogs was among friendly faces. The boy pulled up a log and sat down to eat.

"Where's your lady?" asked Fire-in-his-hair.

Croaks-with-the-frogs shrugged. "She's with her G'ma. I think she's in trouble."

No-point-shoe lifted her head and looked around the fire for The-tiny-one.

As they watched, the older members of The-tiny-one's fist came over and spoke to the girl. They saw the G'ma say something to the Lake people and they lifted The-tiny-one by the arm and escorted her to their burrow. After a moment, they were joined by Sniffs-the-wind and the young *flushfert* The-tiny-one had rescued from the burrow. Croaks-with-the-frogs couldn't remember his name. They grabbed their spears and packs and headed out of the hive and into the surrounding tea tree.

Croaks-with-the-frogs stood. "Hey!" he called.

The-tiny-one either ignored him or didn't hear.

He made to go after her, but No-point-shoe grabbed his shirt with a sticky, brain stained hand. "Hang on, spark," she said. "We don't know the full story. Perhaps they've got to do something in memory of Listens-for-ducks."

Fire-in-his-hair nodded. "Ah... Yes. That's probably it. Best to give them some space, boy."

Croaks-with-the-frogs watched them leave, The-tiny-one's face was still red and blotchy from her tears. He wanted to believe what the older ones were saying but deep in his heart he felt a profound sense of foreboding. He took a deep breath, and decided to let things be.

"Come on," said Fire-in-his-hair. "Finish your breakfast and then you can help us tan these hides."

After lunch the elders gathered again in the meeting burrow. Terror-of-magpies could sense a palpable feeling of tension within the Lake folk delegation. Swims-like-a-fish' face was red and his eyes were stormy, while the younger members looked down as if they were ashamed. Throwing-pine-cones had recovered from the previous night's toddy induced fog but her mood was sombre. At first, Terror-of-magpies had wondered if she was still angry with him after their fight last night, but during lunch time, she had reached out and silently taken his hand. When he looked askance at her, she had smiled sadly and gently kissed the tips of his fingers. The old man found the experience more disconcerting than either her fogs, her visions or their fights.

He pushed those memories out of his mind. This had been a difficult Wattle season and it was clear to Terror-of-magpies that he would once more have to carry the burden of the negotiations. He hoped Throwing-pine-cones had been right, that with an even number of couples, the negotiations would work themselves out smoothly, but even as he felt this, something in the demeanour of the others in the meeting burrow seemed to warn against it.

They passed around the last of the avocado. Terror-of-magpies took his piece last, and while he was eating it, Rolls-in-the-berries began the negotiations.

"We have good news," She said around her full mouth. "I have been told your Sings-at-dawn has finally manned up and has merged fires with our Yabbies-in-winter." She smiled.

Terror-of-magpies forced down a strong feeling of revulsion. "That's very good. So it seems all the pairs are settled." He glanced across at Throwing-pine-cones but she was looking down, intent on her piece of fruit.

Rolls-in-the-berries tilted her head regally. "Yes, so there is no need for us to remain here for much longer. We would like to return to our own fire tomorrow."

Throwing-pine-cones looked up quickly. "That's very early. You are welcome to stay longer."

"We wish to return to our hive." Rolls-in-the-berries said sternly.

The old Swamp woman nodded silently.

Terror-of-magpies felt a surge of hope. "So how shall we divide up the couples?"

Rolls-in-the-berries speared him with her eyes. "The young ones are the most important. The older pair are unlikely to produce more than a litter or two before they age beyond fertility. You can have the older pair. I suggest we take a young couple each."

Swims-like-a-fish said, "We would be satisfied to only take Me-not-talking and Climbs-the-burrow to our hive, if that's OK with you."

Terror-of-magpies nodded. There was something he was missing but he couldn't put his finger on what it was. None of the Lake people seemed comfortable and they were being much more agreeable than usual.

Throwing-pine-cones looked up from her avocado. Her eyes were red rimmed. "And what about The-Tiny-One and Croaks-with-the-frogs?" she asked.

Rolls-in-the-berries laughed bitterly. "I have spoken to the girl at length and we do not believe she has bonded with your boy."

The other Lake people silently stared into their laps. The tension in the burrow increased.

"We do believe that she has bonded with Croaks-with-the-frogs," said Throwing-pine-cones.

There was a moment of silence, before Terror-of-magpies said, "Perhaps we should test this bond. Croaks-with-the-frogs can go with you, if the bond is not real..."

Rolls-in-the-berries voice was sharp. "No!"

Throwing-pine-cones said, "Very well, we'll take The-tiny-one. If the bond is not real, then we can return her to you before the next Wattle."

Rolls-in-the-berries pursed her lips and shook her head.

Throwing-pine-cones breathed, heavily. "You can take Me-not-talking," she said, "We will also offer you the other young couple and you can take Sings-at-dawn as well. All tall couples can be yours."

There was an audible gasp around the burrow. Terror-of-magpies looked at her in horror. It was unheard of for such an unbalanced offer to be made.

Throwing-pine-cones let the silence hang for only the briefest moment, then "But we want The-tiny-one to stay with us."

Rolls-in-the-berries pulled her lips back exposing her teeth.

Terror-of-magpies couldn't decide if it was a smile or a snarl.

"We are offering you all the marriagables in return for this," said Throwing-pine-cones.

Terror-of-magpies was horrified. They were rolling over and completely exposing their throats to the Lake people. Surely they will accept that deal. Throwing-pine-cones was sacrificing the future of the tribe for this. He stared at her, his mouth agape.

The muscle along Rolls-in-the-berries' jaw tensed as she shook her head.

Throwing-pine-cones raised her voice. "Then take Croaks-with-the-frogs too."

Rolls-in-the-berries spoke through gritted teeth. "You will not be unloading your cursed spear on us!"

Throwing-pine-cones and Terror-of-magpies stared at her dumbfounded.

Rolls-in-the-berries' eyes glinted in the dim light. "We will take The-tiny-one back with us and she will marry next year. You can have the point of couples. We will only take Me-not-talking."

Terror-of-magpies felt as if the floor was spinning. Both women were making bizarrely unbalanced offers to the advantage of the other but neither would accept it. He looked across at Swims-like-a-fish in puzzlement but the other man shook his head in resignation.

"Perhaps we can have a break, and discuss it some more amongst ourselves," said Terror-of-magpies. "We can meet again this evening to finalise the situation."

Rolls-in-the-berries shook her head decisively. "No," she said firmly. "The-tiny-one is too young to leave our hive. She is a girl and I am her G'ma so it is I who have the final say on the matter. We will not be leaving her with you. There will be a tall of marriages tomorrow morning and we will leave soon after. I have spoken."

Like a distant mourning dirge, Throwing-pine-cones' voice seemed to come from far away. "I'm so sorry, Rolls-in-the-berries," she said. "I tried. I really tried."

"I don't need your apology, Throwing-pine-cones."

Throwing-pine-cones shook her head sadly."Oh yes you do."

Runs-like-a-rabbit and Hunter-of-flies led their fist back to the hive late that evening. They had been gathering supplies for the journey home. The-tiny-one went through the motions of the hunt and gather as if she were in a dream. She barely heard anything the lead hunters said, acting on instinct as they carried out their tasks. She wished Listens-for-ducks was there with them. The new member of the fist, Twists-the-reeds, was a sweet boy but he was not the rock solid presence of her lost friend.

The way she missed Listens-for-ducks, however, was nothing compared to her yearning for Croaks-with-the-frogs. She had always been an obedient, hard working team player. That's why everybody liked her so much. The only time she had ever misbehaved as a child was when she left the fire with Croaks-with-the-frogs to see the cat tracks.

She was used to being good and it came naturally to her so when her G'ma told her she was mistaken and she had not bonded with the boy, she naturally believed her. She tried to tell herself the yawning hole in the pit of her soul was part of the mistake she had made, and G'ma was right. It will all wear off soon. Driven by obedience, she crushed down the small whisper that told her there was no mistake. She would never recover from this loss.

When she returned to the hive, she found Croaks-with-the-frogs waiting for her. His face was pale, and his eyes were edged in crimson.

"Have you heard?" he said.

When she looked at him The-tiny-one found herself smiling. "Yes," she said.

The boy was incensed. "What are you grinning about!?"

She forced the smile down. "I'm happy to see you."

"You... Haven't you heard? We can't marry. They're ending Wattle early. You're going home tomorrow!"

"I don't want to talk about this. Let's not ruin our last night."

Croaks-with-the-frogs face was stricken. He took a step backwards then turned and stalked off to his burrow.

My tribe is all I have

The following morning, soon after dawn, the marriages began. The fire had been banked high and the tribes sat in a large circle around it, rhythmically beating their log seats and stomping their feet.

The-tiny-one left her fist and found herself sitting beside Croaks-with-the-frogs. She told herself it was to get a better look at No-point-shoe as she married. Being close to Croaks-with-the-frogs was just a coincidence. The boy ignored her and stared blankly at the fire while the ceremony began. He had rarely been present at weddings and he didn't know the words or the harmonies, so he sat in stoney silence while the others sang. His emotions firmly locked down and held in check.

The tribes began by calling the oldest of the women.

"No-point-shoe, No-point-shoe. The fire calls you, come forward."

No-point-shoe got up from her seat and stood inside the circle facing the fire.

"I come to the fire," she sang boldly.

"What burns within you, No-point-shoe?" the tribes chanted.

"The fire burns. The fire burns deep and hot."

"Whose fire burns within you, No-point-shoe?"

"Fire-in-his-hair burns within me."

"Fire-in-his-hair, Fire-in-his-hair. The fire calls you, come forward."

The old hunter came and stood beside No-point-shoe. His battle scarred face was radiant with joy. He reached out and took her hand in his. His voice was low and breathy as if he were speaking to No-point-shoe and nobody else. "I come to the fire," he sang.

"*What burns within you, Fire-in-his-hair?*" the tribes chanted.

"The fire burns. The fire burns deep and hot."

"*Whose fire burns within you, Fire-in-his-hair?*"

"No-point-shoe burns within me."

"*Fire-in-his-hair, No-point-shoe. The fire calls you, forever forward.*"

And with that, the tribes burst into a joyous harmony.

No-point-shoe and Fire-in-his-hair stood in the centre of the circle, holding hands and looking at each other with shining eyes and singing together as if they were alone in the hive.

As The-tiny-one watched Fire-in-his-hair and No-point-shoe sing into each other's eyes, she felt a surge of emotion. She tried to tell herself it was because of the music and she was happy for No-point-shoe. But from deep within her a profound misery was welling up. She had been to many weddings. They were all joyful but they were also the last act before the tribes went their separate ways at the end of Wattle. She glanced across at Croaks-with-the-frogs and in spite of her best efforts, the realisation burst through her walls of obedience and propriety. *I will never see his face again.*

She began to cry. Softly at first but as the barriers broke, more tears poured through the gap. Her weeping broke into sobs and she fought to regain her breath. She was aware of Croaks-with-the-frogs sitting stony faced beside her and knew she too should keep silent, but the more she tried, the more she cried.

She sensed, more than saw, the disapproval from the others in her tribe. She knew that weeping like this at a wedding was very poor form and that everybody had heard about the false bond between her and Croaks-with-the-frogs. Her crying was just drawing more attention to herself and making the situation worse. But no matter how hard she tried, she couldn't stop. By the time Me-not-talking and Climbs-the-burrow were called to the fire, she was sitting bent over with her face in her lap to try to stifle her sobs.

Once the weddings were over, the Lake tribe collected their packs and prepared to leave. The G'mas and G'pas bid each other a stiff but polite farewell, then began leaving. The-tiny-one's chest was aching from her sobs. She was exhausted and barely able to stand. She threw her arms around Croaks-with-the-frogs and clung to him. In his embrace, she could feel the taut distance in the way he held himself.

"This is wrong," he whispered fiercely. "We belong together."

The-tiny-one started crying again. "What can I do? I have to go home."

"No you don't. Just stay here. Fuck 'em. We'll just stay here... or... we can run off to the pine forest. We don't need them."

Somewhere in her chest, hope erupted in a fiery burst but it was soon doused by fear. "I... we... can't. I can't disobey my G'ma. My tribe is all I have." She burst into tears again.

Croaks-with-the-frogs gently moved back, his face was set. "OK," he said sadly. "You go. Go with your tribe. Give your heart to them."

The-tiny-one threw herself back into his arms. "I can't! I've given it to you."

It was Runs-like-a-rabbit who came to get her. The older woman put her arm protectively around her and gently but firmly led her away. She shot Croaks-with-the-frogs a sour look and Croaks-with-the-frogs responded with a silent curl of his lip.

The-tiny-one was the last of the Lake folk to leave. Her legs were weak and her head was too heavy to hold up. She leaned on Runs-like-a-rabbit for support as they stepped through the exit of the hive. Just before they entered the tea tree, The-tiny-one turned and looked back at Croaks-with-the-frogs. He stood ramrod straight, his face set in silent rage.

10

HARVEST

This is your responsibility as G'ma

Swims-like-a-fish refused to speak to Rolls-in-the-berries on the journey back to the lake. He was still smarting over the way she had run roughshod over him in the negotiations. She was within her rights, of course. Strictly speaking, the young girls and marriageable women, were the responsibility of the G'ma while the young men were looked after by the G'pa. But in practice, decisions about marriages were made by all the elders.

This was not the first time Rolls-in-the-berries had run over the top of the other elders but never had there been such resistance and hostility. It was obvious The-tiny-one had bonded. Rolls-in-the-berries denied it, but she saw it too. Nobody wanted the strange, cursed boy from the swamp tribe. At least there was consensus there. But it was common sense to try to get an extra couple in exchange for the girl. When Throwing-pine-cones offered all tall couples in return for the girl, Swims-like-a-fish nearly jumped out of his skin. All the other lake delegates were appalled when Rolls-in-the-berries rejected the offer.

News of the negotiations spread through the tribe rapidly. Usually these things were kept secret but the rejection of an offer of this magnitude, and the over ruling of all the other elders made it impossible. Even before they left the swamp hive, the whole tribe knew Rolls-in-the-berries had given up a tall of solid breeding couples for a single unremarkable girl.

The journey back to the lake was a blur for The-tiny-one. She got her tears under control eventually but when the tribe reached the edge of the tea tree she started crying all over again. That night, the tribe camped in their usual place where a ring of stones had been left generations ago to form a fire pit. She nibbled at the cakes that were offered to her but did not feel hungry. When the time came to sleep, the rest of her fist huddled together for warmth and comfort but The-tiny-one wrapped herself in her fur and curled beside the root of a large tree. The night seemed to last forever. She woke with a headache and a sick feeling in her stomach.

The tribe packed quickly and set off again soon after the morning meal. As they walked, The-tiny-one found herself on the receiving end of a few sidelong glances. Nobody said anything to her but the looks were heavy with a meaning. Some looked on her with a touch of awe, G'ma's favourite. Others clearly resented her because she had put the tribe at risk by bonding with a cursed boy from the swamp. Some saw her continuing presence as a stark reminder of the tall of couples the lake people could have had. She walked a step away from the others and no-one came to speak with her.

Me-not-talking had never been so happy in her life. She walked proudly beside her new husband and it felt wonderful. Climbs-the-burrow was strong and clever. She could tell by the way he looked intently at her when she spoke, that he was taking in everything she said. He seemed to understand her in a way nobody else did. She was also thrilled to find the other lake folk treated her with great respect and appreciation. Throughout the journey, people were constantly coming up to her to ask her questions and tell her about what to expect when they got 'home.' Home! The word carried a sense of peace and belonging she had never felt before. *I'm going home.*

They returned to their hive by the lake as the night was falling. A few of the old ones had stayed behind with the point of nursing mothers and their husbands to mind the young children and keep the fire burning. The rest of the tribe had made the journey to the swamp for Wattle. The reunions were warm and heartfelt. There was muted grief at the loss of Listens-for-ducks and those who had joined the Swamp folk, but there was great excitement to welcome Me-not-talking. Only a finger of babies were born last Winter and the tribe sensed their fragility. Me-not-talking was a living embodiment of their hope for the future.

The tribe shared a meagre supper on their arrival and some singing and dancing began, but The-tiny-one didn't feel like staying by the fire. She nibbled at a cake dipped in a watery stew then took herself off to her burrow. The burrow smelt stale and cold as she crawled inside. She unrolled her sleeping pelt, pulled off her clothes, and curled into foetal position beneath her fur. She closed her eyes to sleep, but sleep wouldn't come. Her mind raced and her stomach churned as each memory stirred new emotions. She sat up and pulled her back pack towards her. She fumbled around in the darkness, feeling the small stash of things she had brought back from the swamp. Memories both sharp and sweet swirled as she explored the items. She ran her fingers across the pelt of a mouse which Croaks-with-the-frogs had caught and Sleeps-in-the-sun had tanned.

"I had planned to make a hat out of it," the young woman had said as she gave it to The-tiny-one on her last night at the swamp. "The colour matches your hair and I think it would look nice on you."

The-tiny-one had clutched at the pelt and fought back tears.

"Something to remember us by," said Sleeps-in-the-sun.

"You never know, I may come back." As she spoke the words, The-tiny-one really believed the future was uncertain, that perhaps she would return next wattle and marry Croaks-with-the-frogs, but the expression on Sleeps-in-the-sun's face showed, the older woman had no such hope.

No-point-shoe had not said anything. She sat on the other side of her, hugging her, and letting the girl rest her head against her chest.

On the other side of No-point-shoe, Fire-in-his-hair sat staring at the fire, a puzzled look on his face.

They sat like that late into the night. Every now and then, The-tiny-one would glance across to the burrow where

Croaks-with-the-frogs lay, hoping he would come out, but he did not.

She was still sitting with her head on No-point-shoe's chest and the mouse pelt clutched tightly in her hand, when the swamp tribe's G'ma shuffled towards them. It was very unusual for their G'ma to leave her usual place by the fire.

At her approach, Fire-in-his-hair immediately vacated his seat and sat on the ground at No-point-shoe's feet.

G'ma smiled at the old hunter. "No need to get up, dear," she said kindly. Then she tapped Sleeps-in-the-sun on the shoulder and tossed her head to the side.

The younger woman started. Climbed quickly to her feet and scrambled over to take Fire-in-his-hair's seat.

G'ma sat herself in Sleeps-in-the-sun's place.

The-tiny-one lifted herself from No-point-shoe's chest and sat upright, waiting for the old woman to speak.

G'ma held the girl's eyes for a long time, then she stretched out her hand. Nestled in her palm was a large piece of orange root. "You must take this with you, darling," the old lady had said. "Do not eat it or cook it. And tell nobody that you have it. Keep it safe and don't let it get too hot."

The-tiny-one stared at the root in the old lady's palm. It was just yellow root or turmeric. Most tribes had a patch growing nearby and the root was ground into powder and used to flavour stews and toddy. She wondered why the G'ma would give her such a strange gift. Not wanting to be impolite, she reached out and took the root. "Thank you, G'ma," she had said, bowing her head formally.

The G'ma did not smile. Her eyes burned into the girl's like a pair of black coals. "Keep this safe until you are carrying your litter in your womb. On that day, you will stand beneath a wattle tree and look across a creek. You will think to yourself, 'I never knew I could be so happy. I wish we could stay here forever.' When that happens, you will know." She raised her finger emphasising the certainty. "Then you must remember this root, clear a patch of dry ground and bury this. You will need to carry water from the creek to it each day through Fire and Smoke. This is your responsibility as G'ma." She wagged her finger at the girl, fiercely. "Do not forget this!"

With that, the old woman hauled herself, slowly to her feet and shuffled away.

The-tiny-one reached into her pack and felt the twisted hairy shape of the root. She pulled it out, wrapped it in the mouse pelt and hid it beneath a few pelts at the very edge of the burrow. The words of the swamp folk's G'ma echoed in her mind. *This is your responsibility as G'ma.*

The-tiny-one lay in the darkness for a long time, mulling over the old woman's words. Then she reached into her pack again and found the thing she had been looking for. The small, round ball of resin Croaks-with-the-frogs had given her in the pine forest. It was almost black in the darkened burrow but it's shape and smoothness was unmistakable. She clutched it in both hands and put it to her lips. Then lay back down, curled herself around the ball cried herself to sleep.

Harvest is the time for digging

It rained more often and the days got longer. The Wattle calls from the burrows became less frequent. The wind blew the dried blossoms from the wattles, leaving them with only a sprinkling of brownish gold. White flowers speckled the tea tree and the blackberries put out tentative new growth. Wattle Season faded to Harvest.

Fire-in-his-hair threw a large log on the fire and sat down to his morning meal. As he ate, he thought about the events of last season. He recalled No-point-shoe's wattle calls and marvelled at the desire she engendered in him. He found himself reminiscing about when they merged their fires but the memories were suffused with a hint of embarrassment. It didn't feel unpleasant, just unusual, like not turning away when another person urinated. He could hardly believe what they had done.

The hide covering the entrance to the burrow parted and No-point-shoe crawled out. She arched her back and stretched her arms towards the sky, pulling her head back to look vertically upward. Her breasts had gotten smaller in recent weeks but they still curved awkwardly from her chest.

Their enhanced shape, so intoxicating only a few fists of days ago, now seemed strange and misplaced. He watched her stretch out her leg and bend forward. Her bottom seemed too large and her waist too small. The soft curves that filled him with desire during the Wattle season, were now merely peculiar. *Women have such strange bodies.*

With this thought, came a surge of compassion. This strange looking creature cared for him, and he cared deeply about her. All his sexual desire had washed away with the wattle blossoms, but what remained was a deeper sense of companionship and gratitude. In a very short space of time, this woman had enriched his life profoundly. She had drawn him in from a lonely existence on the edge of the community to experience a warmth and belonging he never thought possible.

He thought of his first great bond. Would Eyes-are-dancing have liked No-point-shoe? He smiled. Of course she would have. No-point-shoe is an irresistible force. Everybody gets swept up in the power of her personality. When she is around, everyone walks taller. *And she is my wife!*

No-point-shoe walked over to him, her eyes scanning her surroundings. It had rained heavily overnight and there were still grey clouds scattered across the sky. She scrunched her face. "This rain is not going to last for ever," she said. "We should dig some more bracken today."

Harvest was the last season before the great dry of Fire and Smoke. The heat would gradually increase until the ground was baked hard. Even the water dumped by the mighty storms of Fire Season would just run off the adamant land. The ground would be too hard to dig for bracken roots, the heat would drive the rabbits further into their burrows, the swamp would shrink to a patchwork of puddles and the water birds would seek food elsewhere. Fire and Smoke were seasons of hunger.

As soon as the Wattle season faded, while the ground was still soft and the rain was still falling, the people would set themselves to harvest enough bracken root to tide them over the long, dry bake. Harvest was the time for digging.

Fire-in-his-hair handed her his bowl of stew. "Have something to eat first," he said. Then he walked over to the pot to get himself a new serving.

When he returned, he found Sleeps-in-the-sun sitting in his place. She was rubbing her fingers through her hair and staring blearily into space. Fire-in-his-hair silently handed her his bowl and cake then went off to get another serve.

They ate slowly, their conversation sparse and punctuated by long periods of comfortable silence. No-point-shoe said, "We need to go out and get bracken today."

Sleeps-in-the-sun nodded.

"Who will we take?" asked Fire-in-his-hair.

"It would be good to take the little spark out," said Sleeps-in-the-sun. "Do you think we'll see him today?"

Fire-in-his-hair shrugged. "I worry about that boy," he said. Croaks-with-the-frogs had been even worse than usual since the Lake tribe left. He hardly spent a night in the hive, and when he did, he would thrash and cry out in the burrow, depriving everybody of sleep.

No-point-shoe sopped the last of her stew with her cake. "We all worry about him," she said. "But he's not here and we can't stop living. He's got to find his own way thorough this." She paused then, "I think we should ask Sings-at-dawn and Yabbies-in-winter to come with us."

The others stared into the fire. Silence conveying their reluctance.

"Sings-at-dawn is a good worker and it would be nice to invite his new wife on a job... make her feel welcome."

Sleeps-in-the-sun put her bowl on the ground and popped the last of her cake into her mouth.

Fire-in-his-hair collected the bowls and made to move off towards the large pot of simmering water, which was used to wash their utensils.

No-point-shoe lost her temper. "I'm not suggesting we marry them! We need a point of spears to make a fist. We can't go out without a fist!"

Fire-in-his-hair paused, standing above her with the bowls in his hand. "OK," he said, softly. "You ask them." Then he turned and walked towards the washing pot.

Croaks-with-the-frogs left his camp in the pine forest soon after his morning meal. He reset his traps and slung the ring tailed possum he had caught the night before over his shoulder.

In the days since the Lake tribe's departure, the boy had made new traps further down the hill amongst the wattle and gum trees. The wattle seed goo was not as successful there as in the forest but little fruits and berries were sometimes able to lure a possum. A whole possum was too much for a single hunter to eat so he decided to bring the beast back to the hive today.

He tried not to think about why he was doing this. He simply didn't know. When The-tiny-one left, the boy had lost all interest in his traps and his camp in the pine forest. He was just going through the motions, like a stone rolling down hill. He built and set traps, caught game, and brought some of it back to the hive. *One foot in front of the other. Just one step at a time.*

His overwhelming emotion was pain. No matter what the weather was like, it always felt as if the sun was blanketed in a heavy layer of cloud. The light was dull and the colour was washed from the world. When he thought about those brief, brilliant days with The-tiny-one, his memory portrayed the scene in brilliant sunshine. If he closed his eyes, he could see her face, radiant with joy, returning from the swamp with a sprig of wattle in her hair. But then, hard on the heels of that memory would come the memory of her leaving the hive, barely able to stand and resting her head on that other woman's shoulder. Her hair falling disconsolately across her face. It was a painful memory but he knew he had to hold on to it. *That's my last memory of her.*

Sometimes, after he had lit his fire and he knew it was safe, he would scream. A heartfelt howl from the depth of his soul into an uncaring universe. A part of him imagined somewhere, someone would hear his cry and respond but the world was indifferent.

He walked slowly, in no hurry to get back. After a few steps, he stopped and looked down, expecting to see his chest torn open and blood seeping from an open wound. He was surprised to see his body, perfectly intact, because he could not imagine feeling this much pain without a physical wound.

Returning to the hive was a necessary discomfort. Fire-in-his-hair, Sleeps-in-the-sun and even No-point-shoe were kind to him. They spoke to him gently and tried to encourage him to get involved in their quests and tasks. But even their compassion felt like boiling water on his skin. He was miserable everywhere he went but at least when he was alone, he was free to think about The-tiny-one and grieve without having to deal with the sympathy of others. Sleeping in the burrow was agony. He knew he was keeping everybody awake with his fevered thrashing but he could no more stop the dreams than leap over a gum tree. Even the morning nut of dandy with G'ma was a chore.

He arrived at the hive late in the afternoon. Sleeps-in-the-sun's litter ran to meet him as usual, tugging at the possum and badgering him with questions. They got in his way as he skinned his prey and tried to play with the skin while he carried it to where the rest of his fist was cleaning the dirt from freshly dug bracken roots.

"Wow! Great catch!" Sleeps-in-the-sun said sincerely. "I'd really like to know how you can hunt so well on your own, Croaks-with-the-frogs."

"He's a champion hunter," said No-point-shoe. "Even better than Fire-in-his-hair."

The boy forced a smile and walked back to butcher the carcass, the little ones scrambling and chattering around him. One of them, the little girl, got tangled in his feet and the young man came crashing down on top of her. The child started howling. His knee had landed hard on her back and this had really hurt, but beneath the physical pain, Croaks-with-the-frogs sensed a deeper grief. She had interpreted the blow as a form of rejection. His tightly controlled emotions erupted. There was already too much pain in the world. He didn't want to add to it. He crawled to her and enveloped the little girl in his arms. "Oh, little Oaks... My little Oaks... I'm so sorry, little spark. I'm so, so sorry." And with that, his tears came in great heaving sobs.

The other child stood, staring in awe at first then he too started to cry and threw himself into the tangle of bodies before him.

Across the hive, conversation stopped as all eyes were fixed on the wailing trio. Croaks-with-the-frogs clung to the children and buried his face in their hair.

Fire-in-his-hair put down his bracken root, walked over to the possum and started butchering.

Keep your brand up!

Swims-like-a-fish sat in his place by the fire, sipping a nut of dandelion as he watched the fists go out to harvest. Unlike the rest of the tribe who shared gumnuts from a communal pile, Swims-like-a-fish had a gumnut only he would use. He had found it many years ago, before he was G'pa. It was by far the largest gumnut anyone had ever seen. The old man could wrap both of his hands around the nut and his fingers wouldn't touch. He kept it permanently beside his place and everyone knew not to move G'pa's gumnut.

The heat of the liquid coursed through him and eased the permanent, low level ache in his chest. Breathing was becoming increasingly difficult as he aged. As he sipped, he contemplated the future of the tribe. Me-not-talking had lost her appetite and was needing more sleep. The older women nodded sagely and declared she was carrying a litter. The death of Listens-for-ducks meant it was unlikely Sniffs-the wind was pregnant, so the tribe would only have a point of litters this winter.

Swims-like-a-fish was relieved to hear Me-not-talking was pregnant but it did not ease his concerns. A point of litters was not enough. Children wandered away from the fire and young spears were more likely to fall to the enemy than experienced ones. By the time this Winter's babies reached marriageable age, the tribe would be lucky to have a single spear still alive.

The tribe was in crisis. The trouble was, Swims-like-a-fish didn't know what to do about it. The sense of powerlessness and inevitability weighed heavily on him. He finished his drink, and pushed himself to his feet. The dandelion root went through him faster as he aged. He returned his nut gumnut to its place and went to relieve himself.

Twists-the-reeds walked in the midst of his fist as they headed out to harvest bracken root. He could feel the heat from the coal scalding his back. Hunter-of-flies had showed him how to wrap it before they left the hive that morning. The older hunter had tilted his head back and blinked rapidly. "The coal must warm but not burn you as you carry it."

Hunter-of-flies was the oldest active hunter in the tribe. He was approaching that mysterious age when men transition from hunter to G'pa. Twists-the-reeds didn't know how that transition occurred. Eventually hunters became too old to carry spears and they took their place as elders of the tribe. Hunter-of-flies had more white in his hair than black. His curls were thinning, flattening out at the top of his head and forming loose ringlets that framed his lined face.

The old man seemed to be unable to look at anybody when he talked to them. Sometimes, when they were making conversation, he would simply look into the distance, but when he was saying something Twists-the-reeds really needed to understand, he would affect this peculiar fluttering of his eyes. Unfortunately, it was that fluttering that would distract the boy so much he could never concentrate on what the hunter was saying.

Most young spears avoided Hunter-of-flies. Twists-the-reeds would avoid him too if he could but when he was invited to take Listens-for-ducks' place in the fist, he jumped at the chance. Ever since The-tiny-one had rescued him from being stuck in the rabbit warren, last Wattle, he had wanted to spend more time with her. She was everything Twists-the-reeds was not. She was the best *flushfert* in the tribe and everything she did was done with a smooth confidence. Despite her small size, she was strong, fast and she danced beautifully. *If I could be in her fist, maybe I could become like her one day.*

But since they had returned from the Swamp, The-tiny-one had seemed different, more reserved and less friendly. Twists-the-reeds wondered whether it had something to do with her new status as Rolls-in-the-berries' favourite. Even in that, she was the exact opposite of him.

Sometimes, he tried to be fierce or confident, but whenever he did, it backfired. If he ever talked himself up, it would usually lead to some sort of spectacular failure, like the disaster in the rabbit warren last Wattle.

She was walking a point of paces ahead of him, carrying her spear and digging stick lazily across her shoulders.

"Tiny-one," the boy whispered.

The girl grunted in answer.

Despite her grumpiness, The-tiny-one always had time for him. Twists-the-reeds said, "I think my coal is burning my back."

The boy saw her shoulders slump. "Is it!?" she said. "How can you think it's burning your back? Either it is, or it isn't."

Twists-the-reeds said nothing. His back was hot and it was hurting but this was the first time he had carried a coal. Maybe it was meant to be like that.

"Well!? Is it burning you or not?"

"I don't know," he whispered. "It hurts."

The-tiny-one turned around, an exasperated expression on her face. "We've got a problem here," she called.

The rest of the fist came to a stop and milled around the young boy. He removed his pack and unwrapped the coal.

Hunter-of-flies examined the wrapping. "You... haven't got enough grass padding here," he said without looking at him.

Twists-the-reeds frowned. It was Hunter-of-flies who wrapped the coal and yet somehow the old hunter had made the boy feel like it was his mistake. He glanced across at The-tiny-one. She was laughing.

"Yes," she said. "You didn't pack enough grass between your back and the coal, Twists-the-reeds. That's a really stupid thing to do."

Hunter-of-flies looked into the sky. His voice became even more self important. "Ah... it's an easy enough mistake to make."

The-tiny-one locked her eyes on Twists-the-reeds, her face glowing with a fierce joy. "Of course, you're right, Hunter-of-flies. It's an understandable mistake for a kid without coloured clothes. But by the time you're an experienced hunter, we'll all expect much better from you. We try not to keep bunnies in this fist."

Hunter-of-flies' face flushed and Runs-like-a-rabbit frowned in disapproval. The-tiny-one locked eyes on her and her smile disappeared. She stood with her arms folded across her chest, as if daring the older woman to challenge her.

Sniffs-the-wind knelt beside the still smouldering coal. "Let me wrap it for you, Twists-the-reeds," she said gently.

By the time the fist reached the bracken field, the other fists were already digging. Several small fires were burning in a scattered pattern to try to protect from predators. Hunter-of-flies led the fist to an area in the bracken equidistant from the other fists. "Set the fire here, boy," he said shortly, and moved off to to start digging. "Tiny-one, you can go sentry for the first shift."

Twists-the-reeds unwrapped his coal on a clear part of ground while The-tiny-one gathered some nearby dry grass and leaves. The young ones took it in turns blowing on the coal and gathering more fuel until the flames erupted from the little pile of kindling. Before long the small fire was crackling amongst the bracken.

Twists-the-reeds sat back on his heels and stared at The-tiny-one. "It wasn't me who wrapped the coal," he whispered.

The-tiny-one laughed. "I know that, fish head." She lowered her voice. "Why do you think I was making such a fuss about how stupid it was?"

Twists-the-reeds stared at her for a long moment. Several shimmering emotions played across her face, only a few were readable. There was laughter, of course, and compassion. She was not blaming him, and he felt a surge of warmth and gratitude but beneath the surface, her anger seethed. A powerful, implacable rage barely held in check crouched within her, waiting for an opportunity to erupt. *She is terrifying.*

The-tiny-one tossed him her digging stick. "Off ya' go, boy," she said smiling. "You dig, and I'll make sure an eagle doesn't shit on you."

Twists-the-reeds smiled back and set himself to his digging. The weather had been steadily warming since they returned from the swamp but there was still enough rain to keep the ground reasonably soft. The digging stick was well made and when the boy put his weight behind it, it slipped into the dirt efficiently. He didn't really enjoy physical activity. The others in the tribe thrived on digging, hunting or gathering wood. Their eyes would sparkle at the thought of it and once the task was completed, they would stagger back to camp, gasping for breath, but their faces would be filled with joy and satisfaction.

Twists-the-reeds felt no such satisfaction. For him, physical tasks were painful and uninteresting. He didn't like the sensation of sweat inside his rabbit furs and no matter how well made the digging stick, it always seemed uncomfortable in his hands. His favourite pastime was being down by the lake. He loved to watch the light play across the surface of the water. He would set traps for yabbies and sit in a shady spot where long grass spread from the bank into the lake itself.

He was only a boy when he discovered the long strands of the grass could be wound together to make a myriad of different shapes. He was often found by the lake, twisting the reeds into the shapes of animals or people. That's how he got his name. The gentle mockery behind it, was not lost on him. He was different from the others, less useful. They knew it, and so did he.

The-tiny-one sat cross legged on the ground and fed the fire as she scanned the horizon for threats. The sun was high in the trees now, burning off the early cloud cover. Patches of blue were clearly visible to the west. The-tiny-one knew the greatest threat would come from above. The memory of Listens-for-ducks was sharp in her mind as she scanned the sky that morning. That was why she saw it coming early. The streak of black and white.

"Enemy above!" she screamed, and threw herself towards where Twists-the-reeds was digging. She struck the boy in the small of his back with her full weight and sent him tumbling to the ground. She lay on top of him with her face to the sky and her spear pointed skywards. The magpie passed overhead with a terrifying swish of wind and a lightning crack of its beak.

The young ones clambered into a crouching position and watched as the magpie banked and returned to the branch of a large gum tree about a *sprint* away. The bird seemed to be looking at something to their right, but all the spears knew it was a feint.

"Magpie strike," called Hunter-of-flies. "Fall back."

The fists gathered the few bracken roots they had dug and retreated. The old hunter came and crouched beside The-tiny-one. "Get them out of here, girl," he said. "I'll cover you. That maggie won't stay up there for long." He grabbed a burning stick from The-tiny-one's fire and held it above his head as he moved around the retreating people.

"I haven't even got a single bracken," said Twists-the-reeds.

"Never mind, boy," said The-tiny-one. "Plenty of people will be going home empty handed today. Ashen maggies!"

The young ones collected their spears and digging stick and retreated to the denser bush at the edge of the bracken patch.

Hunter-of-flies waved the smouldering stick a few more times then turned to follow them to safety. He had taken only few steps, when he inexplicably let his arm drop. The smouldering stick was no longer pointing up.

For an instant, The-tiny-one wanted to shout out, "Keep your brand up!" but surely an experienced spear like Hunter-of-flies would know that. To call it out would shame the old man in front of the whole tribe. It was one thing to mock him within the fist, but a strange loyalty caused her to hold her tongue this time.

The magpie swooped. Several cries erupted from the safety of the trees. She heard Runs-like-a-rabbit scream but it was all too late. The magpie struck the old man high on the top of his head and he was thrown face first into the dirt.

The-tiny-one bolted from cover. "Come on!" she called as she ran.

Twists-the-reeds was terrified. His feet seemed frozen to the spot. He looked around desperately in case there was another magpie who may attack The-tiny-one. He had heard her call but surely she hadn't called *him* to run out with her!

The-tiny-one had already taken several paces into the bracken before Twists-the-reeds finally overcame his terror. Every instinct in his being told him to stay under cover, but he couldn't let her go out alone. He grabbed his digging stick and waved it desperately above his head as he ran out behind her.

Hunter-of-flies was still alive. Blood was streaming from a deep gash in the back of his head and the old man's eyes had rolled back in their sockets.

The-tiny-one rolled him over and slipped her arms beneath his armpits. "Cover us," she called as she began to haul the old hunter to safety. "Keep your stick in the air and point it at that *pargront* bird."

Twists-the-reeds stood between the prone body of Hunter-of-flies and the gum tree where the magpie sat, nonchalantly wiping its beak on the branch. He held his digging stick up and pointed its sharp end directly at the magpie. The-tiny-one strained and struggled to drag Hunter-of-flies away. After they had travelled a few *lengths*, other spears came out to help. A pair of older men got to them and carried the wounded man away swiftly.

The-tiny-one scowled at their retreating backs. She spoke softly so only Twists-the-reeds could hear but the bitterness in her voice was unmistakable. "They would have just left him out here if we hadn't shamed them into doing some-thing.... Pathetic cowards!"

Twists-the-reeds blinked at her and shame rose in his chest. He too would have left, Hunter-of-flies lying in the bracken patch if The-tiny-one hadn't been there.

We'll have to attack

Swims-like-a-fish knew from the sounds of the returning fists that there had been trouble on the dig. Voices were high and there was a hint of hysteria in them as the spears carried Hunter-of-flies back to the hive. He was laid on furs beside the fire and Rolls-in-the-berries studied his condition. After some hushed conversation, it was decided the ageing hunter, though wounded, had a reasonable chance of surviving, so they carried him to his burrow. The wound was bloody but not deep. The main damage was caused by the concussion. The elders put a salve of pine resin and eucalyptus oil on the wound to stop his fire from running out of control. Runs-like-a-rabbit remained in the burrow with him while he rested, a pot of fresh water beside her.

Outside, by the fire, the returning spears reported the events to Swims-like-a-fish. As they spoke, thoughts tumbled through his mind as he weighed up his options. They had returned with very few bracken roots. It was clear the magpies had nested in the nearby tree and would hinder the digging all season. There were other bracken patches further away from the nesting tree but they were small and over harvesting from them this season could destroy the food source for future years. Once magpies occupied a tree for nesting, they would return to it every year until they were driven out. There was no doubt about what had to be done. The question was how to do it.

Swims-like-a-fish looked around at the tense faces of the spears. Jumps-in-the-water was doing most of the talking. He was one of the oldest of the spears and the best hunter in the tribe. Whilst he was being careful to only report the events of the magpie attack, he too knew the magpies had to be driven from the tree.

The old man pushed himself to his feet with a soft groan. He walked over to where his spear was resting beside the entrance to his burrow and returned to the gathered hunters. "Take me to the bracken patch, Jumps-in-the-water," he said softly. "We need to plan."

Jumps-in-the-water's back stiffened with pride. His head rose a little bit higher as he motioned to his fist. They fell in behind him with a similar air of self assurance and moved silently into the bush.

Me-not-talking walked proudly beside Climbs-the-burrow. Ever since coming to the lake tribe, her life had been getting better and better. In addition to her status as the only new member, she and Climbs-the-burrow had been brought into the best fist in the tribe. Jumps-in-the-water was the best hunter and his fist was the most respected. Me-not-talking and Climbs-the-burrow were the youngest in the fist. All the other members were hardened, experienced spears.

The fist formed a ring around Swims-like-a-fish as they escorted the old man to where the magpie attack had occurred. Jumps-in-the-water led the group while the other experienced hunters covered the flanks. Climbs-the-burrow and Me-not-talking protected the rear. They didn't take long to reach the cluster of dense scrub at the edge of the bracken patch.

Crouching amongst the scrub, the hunters looked out across the open ground to where the nesting tree loomed a good sprint away. It was huge and its branches spread and twisted into the air. Somewhere in that tangle of foliage a pair of magpies lurked. The tree was old, in several places, mistletoe clustered and at one point, the mistletoe hung so low it brushed the tall grass below. Swims-like-a-fish had been involved in these sorts of campaigns before. As he surveyed the area, a plan formed.

"We're going to have to fight for this patch," he said. "We'll have to attack with everyone we have and the risk of casualties will be high."

Jumps-in-the-water nodded. "It can't be helped, G'pa," he said. "My fist can do it."

The old man looked across to where Me-not-talking crouched. "No," he said firmly. "We'll need to rearrange the fists to minimise the risks."

Swims-like-a-fish didn't wait for a response. He simply turned and headed back through the bush towards the hive.

Me-not-talking followed miserably. She had a sinking feeling she was going to miss out on the battle.

The battle for the bracken patch

The hive was bustling with activity for several days as preparations were made for the attack. Extra wood was gathered and the tribe's entire supply of pine resin was set aside for use. Dry sticks were made into brands by wrapping one end in gum leaves and coating them in pine resin. Once lit, a brand would burn brightly for several moments and give off pungent smoke. At night, Jumps-in-the-water would lead the most experienced hunters out to the nesting tree where the brands would be hidden and other preparations would be made without alarming the watchful magpies. It took several days but eventually everything was ready. All that was needed was to wait for the right weather conditions.

The day eventually dawned just as Swims-like-a-fish predicted it would. A calm dry day followed by a day of steady north winds. Me-not-talking need not have feared she would miss out on the battle. When the time came, every able bodied spear was sent out and everybody had a job. She was disappointed however in that she was no longer attached to Jumps-in-the-water's high status fist. Instead she and Climbs-the-burrow were teamed with The-tiny-one and Twists-the-reeds under the command of Sniffs-the-wind. The youngest and most fertile spears were not going to be risked.

The attack began at mid morning. Long experience had taught the tribe that magpies would only attack within a *good sprint* of the tree. Thus the hunters were free to move anywhere so long as they were outside that imaginary circle. While the rest of the spears hunkered down in the bush beyond the bracken ferns, a single fist of moderately experienced spears swept out to the north and set themselves in a line on the edge of the magpies territory. There they found a row of well laid sticks and branches with brands waiting for them. They set the fires and lit their brands and the attack began.

The northerly wind blew the smoke towards the tree and the magpies immediately reacted. They flew in great arcs to the north, assessing the danger then swinging back to their tree to guard their nest. Behind the smoke, they found the fist of spears with blazing brands in each hand moving slowly towards their tree.

As the humans advanced, they lit more fires. Grass burned smokily and every now and then, they came upon another strategically placed collection of wood and resin coated brands. They would set a new fire, replace their smouldering brands and push on. The magpies screamed and dove at them. But the people held their burning brands above their heads and the magpies could not strike.

While the enemy was distracted, the remaining hunters began to crawl through the bracken towards the tree. The noise of the magpies squawking was terrifying as they swooped and harried the northern fist but the distraction meant the main attack force was free to creep closer and closer to the tree. The attack was timed to perfection. The spears crawling through the bracken arrived at the eastern edge of the drip circle of the tree, just as the fist of fire bearers arrived at the north.

The screams were deafening now, as the pair of magpies hurled themselves more frantically at the hunters carrying brands. They did not see the spears cowering at the edge of the bracken only *a stones throw* from their mighty trunk. Twists-the-reeds lay on his stomach with his spear held tightly in his hands and watched Sniffs-the-wind closely. The ground ahead of him was flat and clear before the huge trunk sprung out of the ground. He tried to control his breathing but it came in ragged gasps. Beside him, was a pair of resin brands.

Sniffs-the-wind sprung into action. She unwrapped a coal from her back pack and set fire to a pile of twigs beside her. At that, Me-not-talking, Climbs-the-burrow and The-tiny-one leapt up and lit their brands. Twists-the-reeds began to shake. Once their brands were lit they would be noticed by the magpies and become a target for their attacks. It took all his courage to crawl over to the fire and plunge his brand into the flames. Then he dashed into open ground beneath the canopy.

Once exposed, the magpies turned their attention on this new threat. They screamed and swooped. Twists-the-reeds heard a deadly clattering as a magpie's beak snapped beside his head. He screamed in terror but he kept running. In strategic places around the drip line, small clusters of twigs, leaves and grass had been laid where the branches hung low above the ground. The young ones ran in a quarter circle from east to the south and set fire to every place they could.

Then they plunged their brands into the low hanging branches and set the canopy on fire. The driest gum leaves caught first but soon even the green leaves began to smoulder and smoke. The magpies dived again and again, but now the northern fist was also lighting the canopy and the magpies' attention was divided between a pair of fists, one at the north and one at the south-east. Acrid smoke filled Twists-the-reeds' nostrils. Me-not-talking and Climbs-the-burrow had lit their branches and run back to the relative safety of the long grass beyond the drip line.

Sniffs-the-wind stood between him and The-tiny-one covering them with her pair of brands. "Never mind the branches," she called. "Throw your brands into the tree and take cover."

Twists-the-reeds didn't hesitate. He threw his brand as high as he could into the canopy and without looking back, he dashed for the long grass. Once there, he turned and saw The-tiny-one and Sniffs-the-wind retreating slowly from the tree. Each of them were carrying one of Sniffs-the-wind's brands, their eyes following the diving magpies. Twists-the-reeds felt a surge of shame. *Why am I such a coward!?*

While the young ones were setting fire to the canopy, the remaining pair of fists dashed to the tree. Jumps-in-the-water was one of the oldest of the spears and the best hunter in the tribe. He lead his fist straight to the trunk while the other fist ran across to the western edge of the canopy where the largest low hanging branch loomed. Both groups began to climb the tree and approached the nest from different directions.

The magpies now abandoned their efforts against those lighting the fires and concentrated on the hunters climbing the tree. They screamed and swooped again and again, trying to knock the attackers from their precarious holds. Smoke swirled and billowed across the land, increasing the magpies' panic. The canopy was blazing in several places.

Jumps-in-the-water reached the first large branch and he propped himself against it with his spear pointed outward to protect himself while he caught his breath.

From where he lay in the long grass south of the tree, Twists-the-reeds could see the other fists as they scrambled up the trunk and across the outer branches, trying to make their way higher and closer in towards the centre of the tree. The nest was in the very highest branch, a dark cluster of twigs amongst the leaves. They were not going to be able reach it under this ferocious attack. The male magpie was larger and his back was a pure white. He swooped and snapped at the hunters in the canopy. Twists-the-reeds saw it strike one of the hunters on her hip and she lost her balance. The woman screamed and plummeted from the branch to the hard ground below.

Sniffs-the-wind saw her fall. Her brand had ceased to burn now so she ran out with her spear pointed upwards to drag the woman to safety. Climbs-the-burrow ran out with her and together they dragged her back into the long grass. She was bruised and bleeding but her wounds did not seem fatal.

The mother magpie was smaller with a hint of grey on her back. She was swooping the fist climbing the trunk. Jumps-in-the-water watched her swoop, and swing around for another pass. As she came on again, the veteran jumped. Instead of cowering against the tree as he had done previously, he threw himself with all his weight at the swooping magpie. The mother's momentum drove Jumps-in-the-water from his branch but his spear plunged deep into her breast. She screamed and pecked at Jumps-in-the-water's face as their bodies tangled. The hunter released his spear and grabbed onto a small branch to break his fall. The magpie tumbled out of the tree, squawking and scrabbling at the spear protruding from her chest.

The-tiny-one dashed from the grass and ran to where she had left her spear. "Come on!" she howled, her eyes blazing. Then she sprinted to the struggling magpie and thrust her spear into it. The bird screamed and pecked at her. Its vicious beak snapping a hairs breath from her throat.

Me-not-talking ran out and grabbed the spear which was still dangling from the magpie's chest. She pulled it clear and drove it with all her force at the weakened bird. The mother's claws grabbed her arm and tore though her rabbit fur. The-tiny-one roared and struck again, plunging her spear into the magpies neck. Sniffs-the-wind ran out as well and drove her spear into the beast. With a final piercing cry the magpie collapsed onto the ground and lay still.

The male saw his mate fall and broke off his attack on the hunters in the canopy. He swooped at the young women clustered around the magpie, snapping his beak.

"Fall back! Fall back!" called Sniffs-the-wind and they all scrambled to safety.

Twists-the-reeds watched as the male magpie, wheeled around the now blazing tree and swept down to land beside his fallen mate. For an instant all was quiet. The creature pushed at the mother's body with his head and pulled at her feathers with his beak but the mother was dead. Then the giant bird, raised its head, pointed it's beak to sky and gave off bizarre shriek. The sound was almost human, like a wail from the depth of the creature's soul. Twists-the-reeds felt something deep within him stir and his heart cracked.

The bird launched itself into the air circled the tree a few more times then with a series of howling cries, it flew off towards the east. Scattered around the blazing tree, the hunters erupted into triumphant cheers.

The-tiny-one and Me-not-talking lay in the grass and looked at each other. They were scratched and bloody but their eyes met and their faces shone. The-tiny-one reached out her hand, her fist clenched. Me-not-talking matched her, gently punching the young girls fist with her own.

With the swooping magpies no longer a factor, the hunters climbed the tree deftly, calling and joking.

"A point of eggs," they called excitedly.

Other hunters spitted the mother magpie on a spear and carried her back to the hive. Someone started a chant and the air pulsed with excitement.

As they carried their spoils back through the bracken field, and the joy of victory swirled around him, Twists-the-reeds did his best to push away the memory of the magpie's plaintive cry, but despite his efforts, he was swept by a feeling of profound sorrow.

~ 11 ~

FIRE AND SMOKE

The fist with an extra thumb

Throughout Harvest Croaks-with-the-frogs spent little time at the hive, preferring to hunt on his own on the other side of the swamp. His comings and goings got progressively more irregular, often arriving at the hive after dark or leaving again before dawn. Eventually the rains began to ease and the Harvest season gave way to Fire. The sun beat down on the land, drying out the leaves and grasses.

While the bush was still green and the ground still a little bit moist, the people would go out and burn a protective barrier around their hive. Even when Fire-in-his-hair was most obsessed with hunting the cat, he knew this was the most important season of the year. This was the season where the immediate safety of the tribe was decided. In the Fire season, both Fire-in-his-hair and Croaks-with-the-frogs would pull their weight.

When Croaks-with-the-frogs returned to the hive at the end of Harvest, Fire-in-his-hair pulled him aside. Each carrying their spears, they walked together through the tea tree beyond the hive.

"It's Fire season soon," the old hunter said. "We'll need you to help us."

Croaks-with-the-frogs looked at his mentor sadly. "Your fist is full."

"No it's not. We still need you. You belong with us."

The young man laughed bitterly. "Thank you, Fire-in-his-hair," he said bowing his head, formally. "But we both know that I don't belong anywhere."

The old hunter slapped his hand against his thigh. "That is not true, Boy!"

"I can't even sell my life to the enemy properly."

Fire-in-his-hair looked at him closely, a worried look on his face. "Are you serious?" he asked.

Croaks-with-the-frogs shrugged.

They walked on in silence following their usual path towards the other side of the swamp. After a little while Fire-in-his-hair turned off the path and sat on the ground with his back resting against a gnarled tea tree.

Croaks-with-the-frogs settled beside him, safe under the twisted canopy.

"Listen to me, Croaks-with-the-frogs," Fire-in-his-hair began. "I know how you are feeling. You have lost the one you have bonded to. The same thing happened to me, remember?"

Croaks-with-the-frogs twisted his mouth. "It was different, Fire-in-his-hair," he said softly.

"No. No it was not! We both thought our life was ruined. We both had no hope and we both wished for death. But..." The older man seemed to run out of words for a moment but he started again as the thoughts burst through. "... but life is not so simple. We can only see a thin sliver of our life. The part we are in now. The whole story has not yet been told. We can't judge our lives until the whole story is told. And there is still a lot more to your story that you don't understand."

The young man looked at his feet but said nothing.

"Your life matters, Croaks-with-the-frogs. You have to believe me! Your life matters. The fire doesn't burn for itself. It burns to keep the tribe warm. When you understand this, boy, you will become a man."

Croaks-with-the-frogs looked into the eyes of Fire-in-his-hair. Deep in his heart the young man felt a stirring, a flicker of hope but his doubts remained. "No-point-shoe has filled the fist," he said sadly. "You don't need me."

"You're still part of our fist, Croaks-with-the-frogs. It's just that our fist has an extra thumb."

The young man stared at him for a long moment then burst into laughter.

So it was that Croaks-with-the-frogs sat beside Fire-in-his-hair on the first morning of the Fire season. No-point-shoe's fist had an extra thumb and nobody made too much of a fuss about it.

The first burn

A chill wind blew from the south but there was no rain in it. After some discussion, it was decided to start the great burn. G'pa said little as the decision was made. He knew it was time to burn but he also knew the tribe needed to make that call for themselves. Various people spoke, each looking at him and G'ma for affirmation. He was careful to give none. G'ma smiled and encouraged everybody, but G'pa knew she wasn't following the conversation at all. Eventually, the majority of speakers approached agreement and G'pa decided it was time. He pushed himself to his feet and summed up the consensus. "So we'll burn to the north. Make sure we leave enough bracken and blackberry for next year. Are we all agreed?"

There were murmurs of assent, and with a nod, the old man sat back down.

G'ma smiled at the tribe as they prepared to head out.

Coals were wrapped and resin tipped brands which had been prepared beforehand were packed. There was much discussion about which fist would take which place in the line.

G'pa reached out and grabbed G'ma's hand. "They made that decision well," he said. "They need to get used to making decisions without us."

No-point-shoe led her fist into the tea tree. The desire to throw up had eased now. She had taken to getting Fire-in-his-hair to bring her a cake every morning before she left the burrow. If she ate something, before she got up, she usually felt better.

Behind her Fire-in-his-hair was complaining about her new habit. "It's not just the crumbs in the furs," he said, "There are ants in the burrow now."

No-point-shoe smiled. "Ah... a bit of fresh meat. I can eat them in the morning."

He didn't appreciate the joke. "They are eating me."

Most fertile women became pregnant after wattle, so the fact that No-point-shoe was expecting was not big news but Croaks-with-the-frogs was confused. He leaned forward to catch the conversation. "Why do you need to eat so early, No-point-shoe?"

The older woman turned and smiled. "I've been feeling a bit sick recently." As she said this, she placed her free hand on her stomach.

Fire-in-his-hair was still grumbling. "It's probably because you've been eating cakes before dawn."

The women laughed.

Sleeps-in-the-sun said, "I'll have to make an extra piece of hide for you soon, No-point-shoe."

"Yes. My trousers have been feeling a bit tight lately."

Croaks-with-the-frogs looked behind him at Sleeps-in-the-sun's laughing face. He frowned at her in confusion but said nothing.

The young woman laughed again. "Sometimes I forget what a weirdo you are, Croaks," she said.

"What do you mean?"

No-point-shoe called over her shoulder. "I'm having a litter, spark."

Croaks-with-the-frogs received the news with mixed feelings. A part of him was glad Fire-in-his-hair and No-point-shoe were having a litter but at the same time the news tapped into his sadness again and his heart cried out silently. *What is wrong with me!? Why does happy news make me sad!?*

The first burn of the season was always slow. The grass and scrub still had a lot of moisture and the fires smoked more than they burned. The fists gathered as much kindling as they could and fed the fire, driving it slowly away from the tea tree surrounding the hive. By the end of the day's burning they had burned a thin strip less than a *sprint* wide but nearly a *scout* long. They had at least formed some barrier between the hive and any fire from the north, but such a narrow strip would be no protection against a full blown bushfire. They would have to return many times during the season to build an effective break.

No-point-shoe threw her last brand into a patch of blackberry. She arched her back and pressed her hands against her hips. "Rightio," she said. "I'm calling it. Let's head back."

The rest of the fist followed her lead. Sleeps-in-the-sun, who was watching the sky for the enemy, didn't stop searching. She simply turned her body back towards the hive and started walking. The fist formed up around her and they began the sporadic sprints back. "It'll be nearly dusk before we get back to the tea tree," she said. "The enemy will be about."

Fire-in-his-hair laughed. "Good. Maybe we can catch something to eat. I'm hungry."

The others laughed.

No-point-shoe pointed towards a copse of bushes a short *sprint* away. "There," she said, "We can take cover there," and the fist raced through the smouldering land.

As they ran, Croaks-with-the-frogs watched the smoke rising in curling trails into the sky. He looked towards the south and wondered if the Lake tribe were also trying to burn today. Perhaps soon, he will be able to see their smoke trails. Maybe The-tiny-one was looking north and seeing the smoke from his fires. *Come back... Come back to me.*

Fish climbing trees

The heat built steadily, broken only by sporadic thunder-storms. The squalls sent water sweeping over the parched earth without soaking in. As the Fire season wore on, the storms carried less rain, until eventually, the great grey clouds that rolled across the sky, flashing lighting and res-onating thunder brought no rain at all. The season of Fire was becoming the season of Smoke.

Far away where the bush grew thick and dense, the dry storms hurled their lightening onto the desiccated earth. The trees burst into flame and the fires skipped and roared across the landscape. Animals scurried for whatever shelter they could find as the infernos wiped out everything their path and cast black billowing clouds of ash into the sky.

At the entrance to the Lake hive, Me-not-talking stood be-side Sniffs-the-wind and Climbs-the-burrow, waiting for the rest of her fist to gather. After the magpie attack at Har-vest, Hunter-of-flies and Runs-like-a-Rabbit had withdrawn from active hunting. The fists from the magpie attack then became permanent, leaving Climbs-the-burrow and Me-not-talking in the youngest fist in the tribe. No matter how often Rolls-in-the-berries tried to explain the reasons for putting her in this fist, the young woman couldn't help the feeling that this was a demotion. From being in the highest status fist in the tribe, she was now in the lowest. She wondered if it was something to do with Climbs-the-burrow. He was a decent, hardworking hunter, but he lacked personality. He rarely spoke and when he did, it was usually to repeat what someone else had just said.

"Here they come," said Climbs-the-burrow, pointing.

Me-not-talking watched the pair of youngsters approach from the other side of the fire. As usual, The-tiny-one led the way, her feet pointing outwards in her characteristic gait. Somehow, everything about the way the young girl walked oozed hostility. The only time the girl was happy was when she was killing something. Behind her loped Twists-the-reeds. He had grown taller and more gangly as the seasons went on, but he still remained vague and distracted. He followed The-tiny-one around like a toddler follows his mother and Me-not-talking considered it unhealthy. But this was the girl who had told everybody she wanted to marry Croaks-with-the-frogs last Wattle. Little wonder she'd get involved in another macabre relationship.

Sniffs-the-wind looked at her young fist as they stood in an irregular circle around her. "The wattle seeds are ready to drop," she said. "We need to gather as many as we can before the ants get them."

Me-not-talking pulled her face into a scowl. "I don't see why we need to go out just yet."

Sniffs-the-wind took a deep breath. She felt *the mood* stirring within her. "If we wait much longer, they'll fall and we'll lose too many to the ants."

"So?" Me-not-talking replied. "Then we get to eat the ants too. When I was at the swamp... "

The-tiny-one erupted. "For fuck's sake! Nobody gives a cockatoo's shit for what you did in the swamp." With that, the young girl hefted her spear and walked back to the burrow to get her pack.

Twists-the-reeds followed after her.

Sniffs-the-wind tried again. "Rolls-in-the-berries has asked us to go out and collect as many seeds as we can before they fall. We need those seeds to get us through the winter."

Climbs-the-burrow put his hand gently on Me-not-talking's shoulder. "We need those seeds, Me," he said softly.

Me-not-talking's knuckles went white where she clutched at her spear. "This has got nothing to do with the seeds," she said. "It's Rolls-in-the-berries stopping us from doing anything important."

"Well, maybe you should take it up with Rolls-in-the-berries later on," said Sniffs-the-wind sharply. "In the meantime, go get your pack. We're collecting wattle seeds."

Climbs-the-burrow and Me-not-talking walked back to their burrow to get their packs. The young woman grumbled as they walked. "We don't go out on the lake, we're not sent to scavenge roo, when we hunt rabbit, I have to tend the fire. It's just..."

Climbs-the-burrow spoke softly. "I think Rolls-in-the-berries is protecting you."

"What! Why?"

The young man rested his hand on her gently protruding stomach. "There are only a point of litters on the way. I think Rolls-in-the-berries is trying to make sure..."

Me-not-talking stopped walking and stared at him, doubtfully. "How do you know that?"

Climbs-the-burrow shrugged and giggled.

Me-not-talking closed her eyes in a slow blink. Looking at his chuckling face irritated her. He would often finish his comments with a high pitched, nervous laugh. Me-not-talking was surprised she had not noticed that mannerism before, but since their transfer from Jumps-in-the-water's fist to Sniffs-the-wind's it had annoyed her more and more.

When they arrived at the stand of wattles at the edge of the burnt hinterland, the fist moved into acton. Twists-the-reeds took his place beside the fire, scanning the area for threats. The others set about climbing the nearest tree to get the seed pods. Me-not-talking found the climbing hard. Even though she had loosened the laces of her pants as far as they could go, her midriff was still pressing at her trousers. She found the bending and twisting needed to climb the tree difficult. The G'mas had said she was big for this stage of pregnancy and raised their eyebrows appreciatively. They may be pleased with her girth, but Me-not-talking found it just another annoyance.

Sniffs-the-wind looked down from her branch and saw her struggling. "Me-not-talking, how about you stay down and we can drop the pods to you?"

Me-not-talking didn't look up. "No, thanks. I'll be alright."

Sniffs-the-wind felt the sky darken. *The mood* began hammering at the edge of her consciousness. She took another deep breath. Inwardly she kicked herself for her incompetence. When other leaders gave orders, people obeyed. It was clear who was in charge. No matter how many times, she told herself not to, she would always give orders as if they were suggestions.

The-tiny-one started to laugh. "You're not alright," she said bluntly. "You can't even reach the first branch. I've seen fish climb trees better than you."

Me-not-talking scowled at her.

"That's enough, Tiny-one," Sniffs-the-wind barked. "I'm sorry, Me-not-talking, it was not a suggestion. It was an order. Stay at the base of the tree and we'll throw the pods to you."

The-tiny-one's face reddened in shame. She had been too harsh. There was a time, when she was never harsh. She used be known as the most gentle and kind member of the tribe. People were often silly or proud or craven, but in the past she would make excuses for them, or at the least not humiliate them for their weaknesses. Now, bitter words regularly poured from her. They were often true but didn't alter their meanness. She felt a surge of self loathing.

Sniffs-the-wind, Climbs-the-burrow and The-tiny-one tugged on clusters of pods as they dangled from the branches. If they were ripe, they would come loose easily and they would drop them to the ground below. Me-not-talking collected the pods from where they fell and stuffed them into the back packs. Before long everyone's pack was full to bursting. The others climbed down, Twists-the-reeds put out the fire, they hoisted their packs and set off for home.

The-tiny-one lagged behind, her feet shuffling and her eyes downcast.

Twists-the-reeds dropped back to walk beside her.

She refused to look at him.

They walked in silence for a long time before the boy finally said, "It was really funny."

The-tiny-one's eyes widened in a mixture of fear and hostility.

"I know you got into trouble," he said softly. "And..." a smile threatened to break across his face. "I suppose it was a bit mean. But I nearly cracked my sides holding my laughter in."

She shook her head and suppressed her smile. Her face reddening.

Matching problems with solutions

Sniffs-the-wind left the burrow in the purple pre-dawn. The smoke hung thick and heavy across the sky. The birds who usually launched a cacophony of music at this time of day had fled. The bush was silent. She stood at the entrance to the burrow for a long time, her head bowed and hair hanging over her face. *The mood* was fully upon her now. No matter how hard she tried, she couldn't lift her head and face the world.

She couldn't return to the burrow. Behind her she could hear the faint snores of the rest of her fist. Even when they were asleep, she could feel the tension and hostility between them; elbows jostling, grunts in the darkness as they turned and repositioned themselves. After a long moment, she raised her head and looked around the fire. Only a handful of people were up.

She got a wooden bowl from the communal pile and went to the large pot of stew simmering by the fire. The stew was thin and watery. They would need to hunt soon to replenish the meat. She filled her bowl, took a fresh cake from a stone beside the fire and found a place in the circle.

She dipped her cake into the thin stew and touched it to her lips but she didn't eat. She stared into her bowl and watched as her cake slowly dissolved into the gruel. The silent darkness pressed around from all sides. Everywhere her mind went, there seemed to be a dead end. She felt trapped, like a *flushfert* lost in a warren. Part of her wanted to cry but even her sadness was trapped beneath a thick layer of helplessness.

She had no idea how long she sat there, staring into her bowl, but by the time her cake had completely dissolved, the morning sky was a greyish pink and there were several more people moving about near the fire. Her fist, mercifully, were still asleep. She looked across and saw Rolls-in-the-berries sitting in her usual place, eating her morning meal. The old woman was alone, Sniffs-the-wind watched her mouth as it chewed. For a moment it seemed like a giant beast and the cake was a burrow filled with sleeping people. In her mind's ear she thought she could hear them screaming as the gigantic teeth smashed through the burrow, crushing the life out of those within.

Without thought, the young woman got up, leaving her bowl of stew behind and walked around to fire to sit beside her G'ma.

"You're up early," Rolls-in-the-berries said.

Sniffs-the-wind said nothing.

"Have you had your breakfast?"

"G'ma," Sniffs-the-wind began. But the words wouldn't come. Instead she was swept up in a flood of tears.

Rolls-in-the-berries stopped eating and turned to her. "What's the matter, dear?"

Sniffs-the-wind wanted to talk, she wished she could just open her mouth and have all her feelings pour out, but all that would come were sobs.

G'ma put her hand gently on her shoulder and slipped it down to rub her back. "There, there, dear," she said kindly. "It can't be that bad. Tell me what's the matter."

Sniffs-the-wind shook her head. It was that bad and she simply couldn't find the words to explain what the problem was.

"Take you time, dear," said G'ma. "Talk when your ready."

The young woman sat sobbing for a long time. As more people roused themselves from their burrows, they saw the pair and made sure to sit as far from them as possible. Whatever was wrong with Sniffs-the-wind, G'ma would handle it.

But Rolls-in-the-berries felt completely unable to handle it. The young woman was crying ceaselessly and not explaining what the problem was. Countless possibilities ran through the old woman's mind, but with no clues as to what the problem was, she had no idea how to help her. Like small fish swimming beneath the surface of the lake, ideas and emotions rose to the surface briefly before diving into the depths as her mind rifled through the options. Should she start talking? Is this grief over Listen-for-ducks? Is she sick? Is she being silly? Should I get angry at her? Should I be kind? As the ideas whirled, Rolls-in-the-berries merely sat helplessly, her face arranged into a calm, compassionate expression and waited.

Finally, Sniffs-the-wind wiped her face with her shirt and looked up. "I can't do this," she said miserably.

Tears and snot were smeared across her cheek and they soiled the front of her shirt where she had wiped her face. Rolls-in-the-berries pushed down a desire to recoil in distaste and kept her facial expression set. "Can't do what, dear?"

Sniffs-the-wind tried to brush away a strand of hair from her face but the hair simply fell straight back to where it was. "Anything... I can't lead this fist... I can't keep going. I can't..." She broke down and returned to her sobbing.

Rolls-in-the-berries watched her dispassionately. The girl was clearly talented. She was strong, fit and clever. She was also kind and wherever she went, people warmed to her almost immediately. She had all the traits of an excellent leader. But now, as she sat sobbing beside her, Rolls-in-the-berries wondered. Perhaps Sniffs-the-wind was not leadership material after all.

All she had to do was take care of the youngest fist and ensure no one got hurt. Rolls-in-the-berries made sure to give them only low risk tasks, collecting wood, wattle seeds and the new gum nuts to replace last years. It should have been an easy fist for Sniffs-the-wind to lead.

The young woman regained control of herself again. "I... they hate me. They blame me. They think it's my fault we don't have any interesting jobs."

Rolls-in-the-berries leaned back and nodded, thoughtfully. Her instincts leant towards matching problems with solutions. Sniffs-the-wind had finally told her the problem and now the solution was obvious.

"Alright, dear." she said gently. We need to hunt today and of course we'll need the *flushferts*. But you, can set the rest of your fist around an open hole. Maybe you'll catch a rabbit for the tribe."

Sniffs-the-wind kept crying.

"Would that be good?" said G'ma.

Sniffs-the-wind nodded miserably.

"There... see?" said G'ma. "All fixed now. You go and get yourself some breakfast now."

Rolls-in-the-berries watched as Sniffs-the-wind walked back towards the communal bowls. *Why is this girl still crying? I've solved her problem.*

Rabbit hunt

By mid morning, the sun had broken through the smoke haze, creating a cap of blue surrounded by a rusty grey horizon. Sniffs-the-wind checked the net while Me-not-talking and Climbs-the-burrow sharpened their spears. Closer to the fire, The-tiny-one and Twists-the-reeds were preparing the brands and wrapping the coal. The fist worked efficiently and there seemed to be no hostility between them, but Sniffs-the-wind couldn't shake off her unease.

"I talked to G'ma about the missions we've been sent on, and she agreed to send us all out on the rabbit hunt today," Sniffs-the-wind had told the fist after they had breakfasted.

Me-not-talking nodded, a small smile playing at the edge of her mouth. It was not the enthusiastic response Sniffs-the-wind had been hopping for.

The young ones, of course were expecting to go on the rabbit hunt anyway. The-tiny-one was still the best *flushfert* in the tribe and under her tutelage Twists-the-reeds had also become pretty serviceable. The tribe only had a finger of spears small enough to fit down the rabbit runs so they were all needed for the hunt.

It was Climbs-the-burrow's reaction that caused Sniffs-the-wind to become more uncomfortable. He had smiled warmly and slapped her on the shoulder. "Well done, boss," he said breaking into a nervous giggle. "You got us a promotion."

There were half hearted smiles in response to the comment, but Sniffs-the-wind felt as if black clouds had suddenly covered the sky. *The mood* was threatening again. She hadn't got the fist a promotion. She had barely even spoken to G'ma. In fact, the more she thought about it, the more certain she was that G'ma had just offered the rabbit hunt to get rid of her.

She focussed on her net and pushed *the mood* away. It retreated to its lair, waiting for another opportunity to attack. Other fists were also preparing the hunt. At least she wouldn't be alone out there.

Nobody said anything or gave any signal, but somehow all the fists knew when it was time to move out. Each hunter finished their preparation and through some kind of subtle body language, they all knew when they were ready. Jumps-in-the-water led the way as they headed towards the rabbit warren in the grasslands. Once they arrived, a few spears set fires and watched the sky for the enemy while others blocked exit holes and placed the nets.

Sniffs-the-wind was overjoyed when she saw Jumps-in-the-water move into position beside her.

"Do you mind if I hunt at your exit?" he said easily.

"Not at all." She tried not to let her relief show.

"Sometimes, I like to have a break from my fist."

Sniffs-the-wind stared at him intently. Jumps-in-the-water seemed to be just making conversation but she wondered if perhaps the comment had more significance. Had he spoken to G'ma? Does he know I can't lead this fist? She said nothing but her mind continued to race as they crouched by the opening and waited for the *flushferts* to do their work.

The finger of *flushferts* stood up-wind of the entrance. The smoke from the fire blew across their faces and drifted into the warren. The-tiny-one looked at each of them in turn, holding their gaze. They were an experienced team now. There was little fear in any of their faces. They all knew what they had to do and they didn't need her to teach them how to ladle stew. They had hunted countless times together and no longer needed to remember to turn left then right, or right then left. They knew how big the runs had to be to accommodate them and The-tiny-one made sure she left the larger runs for the boys. Soon the boys would be too large to *flushfert* and they would need to be replaced by a pair of new spears from the children. But for now, the team was at its peak efficiency. She plunged her brand into the fire and with a joyful roar plunged into the darkness, knowing the others would follow.

Sniffs-the-wind heard the commotion within the warren as the *flushferts* worked their way through the runs. Beside her, Jumps-in-the-water shot her a glance and smiled. On the other side of the net, Me-not-talking and Climbs-the-burrow crouched amongst a thicket of grass. They didn't have to wait long. There was an explosion of tan fur and a large rabbit burst from the entrance and into the waiting net. They didn't want another rabbit to crash into them from behind so, Me-not-talking threw a brand down the open run while Climbs-the-burrow, Sniffs-the-wind and Jumps-in-the-water leapt at the rabbit struggling in the net.

The rabbit reared and howled as Jumps-in-the-water drove his spear into is right shoulder. Me-not-talking approached from behind.

"Keep clear of its back legs," called Sniffs-the-wind. "Attack with Climbs-the-burrow!"

The beast snapped and swung its bulk towards the pair of hunters on its right. The spear was ripped from Jumps-in-the-water's hands. Climbs-the-burrow saw an opening and hammered his spear through its rib cage on the left.

Sniffs-the-wind plunged her spear into its neck and blood spurted from the wound.

Me-not-talking drove her spear into its left haunch.

"Keep clear of the rear!" shouted Jumps-in-the-water.

Climbs-the-burrow threw his weight against the spear embedded in its ribs. At the same time the rabbit thrashed to the left adding to the force and the spear drove home into its heart.

The beast let out a blood curdling shriek and lashed out with its hind legs in its death throes. Its left leg struck Me-not-talking flush in the middle of her belly. She screamed as her body was hurled back towards the run.

For Sniffs-the-wind the whole world was immersed in deep water. Movements became slow, sounds became muffled and dull. The rabbit crashed to the ground twitching. Climbs-the-burrow kept pushing his spear deeper, while Jumps-in-the-water clambered over the dying rabbit to retrieve his weapon. Only Sniffs-the-wind saw Me-not-talking curling into a ball, clutching at her swollen belly, her mouth open in a silent howl.

I made you something

Rolls-in-the-berries was sitting with other elders by the fire. She was shelling wattle seeds. Others were roasting them, and another was grinding them between two heavy stones to make the powdery flour that could be stored for the winter. Swims-like-a-fish was nowhere to be seen. She cursed him, silently. That man was becoming more of a liability each day.

Movement at the entrance to the hive caught her attention. She sensed the disaster as soon as she saw the hunting party approach. Sniffs-the-wind and Jumps-in-the-water were carrying someone on a hastily made litter. Rolls-in-the-berries couldn't see who was on the litter but the person was groaning and the voice was clearly female. Beside the person Climbs-the-burrow was walking and making soothing noises. She pushed herself to her feet as the other G'mas burst into action. She didn't even notice the rest of the hunting party carrying the rabbits back to the camp. All her focus was on the litter. *No! Please not her. Not her!*

"What happened?" She barked.

"Kicked by a rabbit," said Jumps-in-the-water.

Rolls-in-the-berries pushed Climbs-the-burrow away and took his place beside Me-not-talking. "Where did it kick you, girl?"

Me-not-talking whimpered and closed her eyes.

Sniffs-the-wind said, "In the stomach, G'ma."

"She attacked the Rabbit from behind," said Jumps-in-the-water. "I told her not to."

Rolls-in-the-berries gritted her teeth. "I told you to keep her safe!" She said.

"I'm sorry, G'ma."

Rolls-in-the-berries wanted to get angrier at Jumps-in-the-water. She wanted to blame Me-not-talking or Sniffs-the-wind. She even silently cursed Swims-like-a-fish for not being in the hive, but she knew it was her decision to send that fist out hunting. The person she needed to be angry at, was herself. She regained control of her emotions. "Hold her still. You lot," she gestured at the young ones standing helplessly beside the litter, "go and get some furs from your burrow and lay them out by the fire."

Before long, Me-not-talking was lying on a makeshift bed of furs by the fire. Eucalyptus leaves were boiling and her head was been wiped with damp fur. Rolls-in-the-berries had her trousers removed and her shirt was raised exposing the deep purple bruise on her abdomen.

"Does it hurt?"

Me-not-talking blinked in fear. "Not now, G'ma," she said. "The pain comes in waves."

The older women exchanged concerned looks but said nothing.

Me-not-talking picked up on it. "Why?" she asked. "What does that mean? Am I going to die?"

Rolls-in-the-berries put her hand on her belly. It was still small. Too small to kill the girl. "I don't think you're going to die just yet, girl," she said brusquely. "But you might lose the litter if we are not careful. So rest, breathe deeply and do exactly as I tell you."

At these words, Me-not-talking began to cry. Someone brought her some blackberry tea and she sipped at it.

The returned hunters began skinning and butchering the rabbits. Sniffs-the-wind got herself a nut of dandelion root and sat by the fire, as far away from Me-not-talking as she could get. *The mood* danced at the edge of her awareness. Black clouds threatened to envelop her. She clutched the warn gumnut and tried to push them away. Twists-the-reeds appeared beside her, but she refused to look at him, staring instead at the steaming dark drink in her hand.

"I made you something," the boy said, softly.

Sniffs-the-wind didn't look up.

He sat beside her in silence for a moment, then gently placed a peculiar collection of reeds in her lap.

Almost without her volition, Sniffs-the-wind stared at them. The reeds were tangled and knotted into a fist of bunches, of varying lengths. There was a very short bunch, a pair of medium bunches and a pair of long bunches. It took several moments for her realise the collection of reeds looked exactly like a miniature person. She reached down and picked it up. The black clouds cleared a little and *the mood* scuttled back into its corner where it stared, warily.

"Thank you, Twists-the-reeds," she said with feeling. "How did you make this?"

The boy smiled at her and shrugged.

Sniffs-the-wind stared at the little creation for a long time, amazed at the way the reeds, whilst remaining reeds seemed to make a little human. She felt the fire burning within her as she stared at it.

The pair sat together in silence and watched the events play out across the other side of the fire. As the evening fell and the sun hung red in the purple smoke, Me-not-talking started to cry out and the area around her burst into activity. The G'mas were fussing and making soothing noises. She was raised to her feet. Someone got her another fur and draped it over her shoulders. The young ones watched helplessly as Me-not-talking walked around the fire, a hand on her belly and another holding the fur around her shoulders. She was favouring her left leg and weeping softly as she walked. Sniffs-the-wind had been there before. She too had once walked around the fire clutching her swollen belly. Me-not-talking was now in labour but this litter would be born too soon and be too small to survive.

Suddenly, The-tiny-one appeared on her left and Me-not-talking leaned into her, her dark hair covering her face as she looked down at her belly. The pair walked slowly around the fire, the younger girl supporting and looking up at the older. The-tiny-one's face was stricken with pain and tears streamed from her bright blue eyes.

Oh my darling girl

At the edge of the lake, Swims-like-a-fish splashed water onto his face and coughed. Even here, the air was not clear. When he was young, the Smoke season had no effect on his breathing at all, but his chest was getting worse as the days went on. Now he had no respite from his hacking cough. This morning, he had began coughing up small grey pellets from his lungs. Getting them up temporary eased his breathing but as the day the had worn on, it became harder and harder. When the last pellet came up, the old man had blacked out and fallen to his knees on the hard bank of the shrinking lake. Now he crawled to the water's edge searching for some relief.

He rested his knees on the bank and put his hands in the water, holding his face above the surface. The sun was sinking slowly into the purple smoke haze in the west and the heat was ferocious. He wondered if anyone at the hive had noticed he was gone. Faces and names ran through his mind, but as he knelt there, fighting for breath, a slow realisation dawned, there was no one amongst his tribe who really cared deeply for him. He was respected, of course, but over the years, he had kept himself aloof from their emotional issues. His deepest feelings were always shared with his wife, long dead. He remembered her now as he stared at his reflection in the still water. When he closed his eyes, he could picture her face, smiling at him in the soft Wattle glow.

Another coughing fit came upon him. His chest heaved as he fought to clear his lungs. His arms wobbled then gave way, plunging his face into the water. For a few, short moments he struggled to raise his head and fought to keep the water from his lungs, but the coughing was irresistible. His arms were too weak to lift him. The water was cool and soothing. He thought of his wife again, calling to him from across the blazing fire... *Oh my darling girl.*

12

BERRY

The fist with an extra thumb and point

After many days of baking heat, which threatened to suck all the life from the land, a reprieve was finally granted. The clouds built and became darker, shielding the worst of the sun's scorching heat. Then the rains came. Intermittently at first but gradually increasing in duration and regularity. The water hammered against the dry ground and flowed over the top of it without soaking in. Gradually, it refilled the swamp, which had shrunk to a few shallow puddles during the long Smoke season.

The rains became steadier and the weather cooled. The ground finally opened to receive the gift of water and became soft again. The warm rains enlivened the bracken, and blackberry and soon they burst into fruit. Berry season began.

Croaks-with-the-frogs returned to the hive early in Berry with his pack full of tart, barely ripe berries. They were the first of the season, just turned black but with no sweetness at all. He plonked himself next to G'ma and gave them to her.

"Here, G'ma," he said, softly. "I've found some berries on the other side of the swamp. They're nice and tart."

G'ma smiled at him. "Ooh... lovely." She popped one in her mouth and screwed her face up as the sour berry tingled in her gills. "I like tart berries," she said as if it was news. She handed a berry to G'pa who was sitting silently beside her, staring into the fire. "You?"

G'pa hadn't been listening. "What?"

"Nice berries," she said, cheerfully. "Croaks-with-the-frogs brought them."

"Ah!" said G'pa, as he smiled and put the berry into his mouth.

Croaks-with-the-frogs tried to stop him but he was too slow.

G'pa twisted his face and shook his head. "Arrgh!" He hacked and spat but still the sourness savaged his taste buds. "Blood and ash! This berry tastes like cat's piss." He turned savagely to G'ma. "How can you eat this!?"

G'ma laughed gaily, and that made the old man scowl even more.

Standing a respectful distance from the encounter Sleeps-in-the-sun's litter stared at them with wide, bright eyes.

Croaks-with-the-frogs caught sight of the pair and grinned, he left the old couple to their arguing and walked over to the children.

As the seasons had progressed and the year had aged, the toddlers had aged too. They were now children and their command of the language had increased. "Croaks-with-the-frogs, Croaks-with-the-frogs!" They chanted as the young man approached them. The little girl did a hand stand and stood with her arms outstretched, waiting for Croaks-with-the-frogs to compliment her.

"Wow! You really sizzle!" The young man said as he squatted before her.

Croaks-with-the-frogs had changed too over the long hot seasons of Fire and Smoke. He was taller. His ankles and the lower part of his hairy calves were now clearly visible beneath his ill fitting trousers. His thin gangly frame had filled out and the unmistakable cut of his muscles could be discerned beneath his tightly fitting shirt. His hair was still dark and tied back with a thong of hide. His beard, which had once been thin and straggly, was now thick, black and tightly curled. His face, was still narrow and his eyes were still large and brown, shining with the same luminous mixture of sadness and compassion but he was becoming a man.

"Did you bring berries, Croaks-with-the-frogs?" asked the boy.

The young man laughed, sadly. "Sorry, little-oaks," he said ruffling his hair. "These aren't ripe yet. They're only good for the stew. Soon they'll be plenty of ripe ones."

Even though the children had learned to say his name properly, Croaks-with-the-frogs still called them 'Little-oaks' and the names had stuck. Everybody else in the fist with the extra thumb called the pair little-oaks too. The children hung around the adult burrow even when Croaks-with-the-frogs was out hunting.

Sings-at-dawn and Yabbies-in-winter took a little while to get used to this unusual set up. Like most of the experienced spears in the tribe, Sings-at-dawn thought it unhealthy for children to get too attached to adults. He would respond gruffly when he found the children waiting outside the burrow when he awoke and whilst he didn't say anything to the others, he found it a bit unsettling when, Fire-in-his-hair and No-point-shoe would say good morning to them and call them "Little-oaks."

It was Yabbies-in-winter who adapted quicker. The pair were a nuisance but there was something about their faces that drew her in. Unlike other children, who avoided eye contact and tended to be surly or frightened, the little-oaks approached her with smiles on their faces as if they fully expected to be welcomed. When she dismissed them, as was the custom, they responded with a curious tilt of their heads, as if it was she who was the peculiar one and not them. She put the whole unusual situation down to the influence of the strange young man who was marked by the enemy and possibly even cursed.

Over time, the children's persistent enthusiasm wore her down and she too began greeting the children and calling them 'little-oaks.'

"Now you've started with this nonsense!" said Sings-at-dawn when he first heard her greet the children one morning.

Yabbies-in-winter shrugged her shoulders and laughed. "I don't know," she said. "They're hard to resist."

Her husband stared at her warily. "It's not... natural," he said.

Yabbies-in-winter smiled and walked over to the stew pot to get her breakfast. "In case you you haven't noticed, husband," she said formally, "there is a lot that is unnatural about this fist. The fact that we have an extra thumb? That we are not led by the eldest? That someone hunts on his own and comes and goes at odd times? Why shouldn't we also be the fist that has a point of juniors." She laughed and turned towards him, holding up her left fist and the thumb and pointing finger of her right. "We are the fist with an extra thumb and point."

By the end of Berry season, the extra point had become quite useful to No-point-shoe's fist. The children were keen to help with any tasks and their small fingers were adept at shelling wattle seeds or crushing blackberries. The other spears shook their heads disapprovingly at them but since the fist was accepted by G'ma and G'pa, nothing was said.

Fucking rabbits to get litters

The land recovered quickly once the Berry rains arrived, but for the people of the lake, the scars of the Smoke season took much longer to heal. Even by the end of Berry, the tribe was still reeling from the loss of Me-not-talking's litter and the death of Swims-like-a-fish. When Me-not-talking lost her litter, Rolls-in-the-berries' status as G'ma received a mortal wound. Now the tribe had only a point of older women carrying litters. Again and again it was whispered around the fire that she had traded a tall of healthy couples for The-tiny-one and rested the future of the tribe on one breeding pair. In hindsight, everyone claimed to have known what a catastrophic mistake it was going to be. Rolls-in-the-berries still received polite respect and was still the oldest G'ma, but her authority in the tribe was minimal. People would listen to her respectfully, but since that fatal day in the middle of the Smoke season, each fist would follow their own leader.

Had Swims-like-a-fish survived, he would have provided an alternate head of power, but the next oldest G'pa was not highly regarded. He was once a fearsome hunter and well regarded for his strength and courage, but as he aged and his physical prowess diminished, he had sunk into regretful old age. He was known to spend many evenings sitting by the fire, reminiscing about his past exploits with little interest in the concerns of others or the bigger issues of the tribe. As the Berry Season wore on, it became clear the tribe was effectively leaderless.

Sniffs-the-wind saw the consequences of this clearer than most. Whilst many people commented on the lack of leadership, only a few connected it to the greater problems facing the tribe. A point of litters each Winter was not enough to maintain the tribe. The death rate of children and young spears was high. There was no guarantee that enough of those babies would survive to marriage age. A tribe with a single marriagable cannot engage in the Wattle rites. A gnawing sense of doom hung over her and at times, it would spark a resurgence of *the mood*.

In the sleepless hours before dawn, Sniffs-the-wind would often try to unravel the complex tendrils of her thoughts and feelings. There was a difference between her sense of doom and what she called *the mood*. The sense of doom was rooted in a rational assessment of the state of the tribe. Everybody who could count, knew the numbers were not working. There were not enough babies being born and the casualty rates of fertile spears was too high. But even though everyone knew this, there was a dull refusal to face the logical consequences of it. The lake tribe was dying, but no one, not even the smartest of them, was to be able to respond.

Sniffs-the-wind had discussed it, several times around the fire and received sympathetic responses. But when she would ask, "What should we do?" her listeners would shrug or stare at her blankly. Nobody seemed able to face the question to which there was no easy answer. This often made her want to erupt in a cascade of powerful emotions. From frustration to anger to loneliness. She felt as if she was the only one who could see the eagle circling.

The mood was a very different feeling. It was like a heavy fur that covered her in the hot seasons, dulling all her senses

and feelings. She would sit staring out into the bush marvelling at how everything seemed so alive around her and yet
she felt so dead inside. *The doom* made her want to leap into
action, *the mood* made her want to curl up and sleep forever.

Interestingly, of all the people Sniffs-the-wind spoke to
about *the doom*, the one who seemed willing to face it with
her was the one she relied on the least. Twists-the-reeds was
always willing to listen to her when she spoke, and he would
often throw up ideas and suggestions of what to do. The boy
was completely open to any ideas, and was not afraid to make
the most outlandish suggestions.

"Maybe we should mate more often," he suggested one
day as they were collecting a fresh set of gumnuts.

The-tiny-one was watching the sky from the top of the
tree while the others clambered over the lower branches,
pulling off the largest, dry gumnuts they could find. Once
their packs were full, the fist would take them back to the
hive. The largest gum-nuts would be hollowed out and
turned into a fresh set of drinking cups, while the smaller
ones would be broken up and glued to straight sticks to serve
stew.

Twists-the-reeds and Sniffs-the-wind were high in the
tree, crawling amongst the fading red blossoms of this year,
and searching for the desiccated old nuts from the year before.

The young woman tried not to crush the boy's enthusiasm. He had not yet felt the fire, so he didn't understand
what he was suggesting. "I'm not sure that would work, boy,"
she said, suppressing her smile. "Mating is... You've got to ac-

tually want to do it. If you don't want to... it's... um... unpleasant."

Twists-the-reeds was not so easily put off. "Who cares if it's unpleasant," he said. "There are lots of things that are unpleasant. We just have to do it. We need babies!"

"It's more than unpleasant... It's impossible." She stopped her search and leaned across the branch to look at him closely. "Would you mate with The-tiny-one tonight if the tribe needed another litter?"

Twists-the-reeds recoiled in shock and horror. "Ew... No! We're both lake folk. And... I'm not old enough. Yuck!"

Sniffs-the-wind laughed. "That's how it feels for all of us when its not Wattle. I couldn't even have mated with Listens-for-ducks during Berry. It would be yuck! You see?"

The boy nodded sadly. At some level, he still thought more mating could help solve the problem but he had to admit the idea of it made his stomach roil.

From her perch, high above, The-tiny-one started laughing. "Burn me black! You guys talk about some seriously weird stuff!"

Twists-the-reeds had grown through the Fire and Smoke seasons. He still admired the The-tiny-one greatly but he now saw her limitations and was no longer frightened of her. "It may sound weird to you, Tiny, but we must do something. We're in serious trouble, and just doing what we did last year again and again, won't get us out of it."

Suddenly, from another part of the tree, a cluster of nuts and blossoms attached to a single branch was thrown to the ground. "Alright!" shouted Me-not-talking. "I get it! Alright!?

I've fucked up the whole tribe. I'm the liability and we all have to go fuck rabbits to get litters because I lost mine! You've made your ashen point, lets just stop going on about it, shall we?! Give us all a fucking break!"

Silence fell across the tree top. Twists-the-reeds looked down in shame, cursing himself for being so stupidly insensitive.

Sniffs-the-wind crawled across the canopy to where Me-not-talking clung to her branch, crying. "I'm so sorry, Me-not-talking," she said, softly.

The younger woman pressed her face against the rough bark and said nothing.

"This is not about you, anymore than its about me. We all lost your litter. Not just you. I should have kept closer to you and made sure you were at my side the whole time. I was the leader, and I failed you. You're not a liability, *broodha*. We really need you."

Me-not-talking leaned her head back and closed her eyes tightly. She wanted to believe Sniffs-the-wind. She wanted to belong and be needed, but beneath her needs, there lurked a hard stone of reality. She knew she was the one who had failed.

Craving cakeberry

By the middle of Berry season, No-point-shoe was heavily pregnant. She rarely went out on the hunts and spent most of her days sitting by the fire, roasting the last of the wattle seeds, pounding bracken roots, or replacing the spear points of the others in the fist. Berries were in full swing. The warm rains had caused the land to burst into fruitfulness and the swamp folk had burst into life as well. Blackberries were everywhere. Unripe berries were used to flavour the stew, giving it a tang. The ripe berries were eaten plain or mixed with the cakes to add flavour.

No-point-shoe lay in the burrow and stared at the faint light shining through the holes in the roof. Outside she could hear the sounds of the tribe as they moved around the fire. Voices engaged in easy conversation, mixed with the faint sounds of hammer stones striking quartz and the shuffle of feet as people moved around.

She could hear the shrill voices of the little-oaks as they played outside, pretending to hunt a rabbit and Croaks-with-the-frogs roaring.

"You can't catch me, little-oaks," he said in deep voice. "I'm a mighty rabbit and I will eat you!"

The children howled and No-point-shoe could hear the scuffles as they piled on top of him. "We will eat you, rabbit," they squealed.

"Oh no. Oh no!" shouted Croaks-with-the-frogs laughing. "I'm being eaten."

"Quieten, down you lot." Yabbies-in-winter scolded, "No-point-shoe is still sleeping."

Croaks-with-the-frogs whispered guiltily, "Oh sorry... Yes, yes."

No-point-shoe smiled and thought about cakeberry. Yabbies-in-winter made a special dish with ripe berries. She called it cakeberry. She would collect a large amount of the blackest, sweetest berries and mix them with bracken root paste. Unlike the normal cakes which had no more than one or two berries in each, cakeberry had so many berries it barely held together. She would pour the mixture into a specially made, small pot, cover it with a flat rock and bury it close to edge of the fire. After about a nap, the pot was removed and the sweet mixture could be scooped out and eaten. Soft and warm, No-point-shoe had never tasted anything so wonderful in her life.

The only people who loved cakeberry as much as No-point-shoe, were the little-oaks. When Yabbies-in-winter would make it, the children would stand by the fire, hopping from one foot to the other, waiting for the mixture to cook. No-point-shoe would smile as she watched the children as they stared at the pot with yearning eyes. It took all her will power to not stand beside them, hopping from foot to foot.

"I'm awake," she called from inside the burrow. "I was enjoying listening to the rabbit hunt."

Croaks-with-the-frogs poked his head inside. "I am sorry, No-point-shoe," he said bowing his head.

The older woman rolled herself out of the furs and onto her hands and knees.

Croaks-with-the-frogs retreated hurriedly as she crawled to the entrance of the burrow and stuck her head out. "Hey, Yabbies-in-winter," she called hopefully. "Are you going to make any cakeberry today?"

The little-oaks started jumping and squawking, "Yes, Yabbies-in-winter. Cakeberry? Please? Please."

Yabbies-in-winter laughed. "We'll need to get more berries," she said.

From her vantage point at the burrow's entrance, No-point-shoe scanned the hive until she saw Fire-in-his-hair sitting a little way off, working on a new spear point. She put a sweet, plaintive tone into her voice. "Fire-in-his-hair," she simpered.

The old hunter didn't hear her.

She called louder, the whine slightly more forced. "Fire-in-his-hair."

No response.

She exhaled roughly and her face took on a look of frustration. "Hey! Fire-in-his-hair!" She bellowed, all sweetness gone.

The old hunter looked up from his knapping.

Croaks-with-the-frogs suppressed his laugh.

Once she had his attention, No-point-shoe tried the sweet voice again. "Can you please get us some more berries?"

Fire-in-his-hair frowned at her and she smiled at him.

The children stared in silence as if their lives hung in the balance. A 'no' from Fire-in-his-hair would mean they might miss out on cakeberry and neither of them could think of a worse fate.

After a moment, Fire-in-his-hair's frown melted into a reluctant smile and he climbed to his feet.

The children squealed and jumped. "Cakeberry! Cakeberry!"

As Fire-in-his-hair walked to the burrow to get his equipment, he said to Croaks-with-the-frogs, "You wanna come?"

The young man smiled and gathered his pack and spear.

Croaks-with-the-frogs was elated to be leaving the hive with only Fire-in-his-hair at his side. It had been a long time since the two of them had gone out alone to hunt the cat and even though Fire-in-his-hair looked back on those days with some embarrassment, Croaks-with-the-frogs saw them through a rosy tint of nostalgia. Things were simple then. He was never alone and never lonely because he was with Fire-in-his-hair.

They skirted the fire and headed for the exit and the tea tree beyond the hive. Croaks-with-the-frogs saw the little-oaks standing beside the hive exit. They were staring at him with undisguised awe. He smiled. He was even younger than them when Fire-in-his-hair first took him out into the bush. His eyes switched from child to child and something within him stirred. He stopped short, staring at the children.

Fire-in-his-hair turned to him. "What?"

Croaks-with-the-frogs looked at the children, then looked at his mentor. The older man knew instantly what he was thinking.

Fire-in-his-hair shook his head, a bemused smile on his face.

Croaks-with-the-frogs kept staring. "We've got our winter hats in the burrow," he said. "They could carry them."

The pair stood staring at each other for a long moment as Fire-in-his-hair slowly processed what was happening. Many thoughts raced through his mind. They didn't really need the children, but Croaks-with-the-frogs wanted to take them as a favour to them. Slowly the implications of this crystallised in the old hunter's mind. Fire-in-his-hair was ashamed of what he did when he took Croaks-with-the-frogs out into the bush. Looking back on it now he saw it as taking advantage of the boy and using him for his pointless quest. But Croaks-with-the-frogs saw it as a gift. A gift he now wanted to share at least in part with the little-oaks.

Fire-in-his-hair puffed his cheeks as he blew the air slowly out of his lungs. Then with a smile and a cock of his head, he squatted in front of the children. "You wanna come?" he said.

The children's eyes widened. They looked to Croaks-with-the-frogs who was smiling encouragement. "I'll get you something to carry the berries in," he said. "But you have to do exactly what Fire-in-his-hair tells you to."

As Croaks-with-the-frogs headed back to the burrow to get the hats, the children started jumping but Fire-in-his-hair frowned and they immediately regained control. When the young man had returned to the hive's exit, they were standing beside Fire-in-his-hair in perfect mimicry of the of the old man's stance.

In the winter, everyone wore a hat. Many were made of the same rabbit hides that their clothes were made of, but some were made of mouse or possum. Like all clothes, they were worn with the fur facing inwards to keep the head warm. The outside of the hats were well tanned and they gave good protection from the rain. Once the adult sized hats were turned inside out, they made a pair of excellent child sized carry bags.

Once the children each had their bags, Fire-in-his-hair gave them their instructions. His face was very serious. "Follow me in single file," he said. "Stay between me and Croaks-with-the-frogs at all times and watch where you step. Look at the back of the person in front of you, then look down at your feet. Then back to the person in from of you." As he spoke, he pointed with his hands where they were to look and the rhythmic beat they needed to keep.

The children looked at him earnestly. They knew how dangerous it was beyond the hive and took their mission very seriously.

Croaks-with-the-frogs smiled, remembering when Fire-in-his-hair had given him similar instructions, "Look to the front, look to your feet." Of course, they were not doing anything particularly dangerous with the children, merely walking to the edge of the tea tree to collect berries but it was never too early to learn the patterns of survival.

The little party headed out of the hive in single file. Fire-in-his-hair led the way, instinctively watching the bush for dangers. Behind him came the pair of little-oaks, carrying their inverted caps. Bringing up the rear, scanning the sky for eagles, was Croaks-with-the-frogs. The children looked around in wonder as they walked. Every leaf and branch was new and magical to them. As Croaks-with-the-frogs watched them, he felt a swelling of the fire within him and for a brief moment, the agony caused by the loss of The-tiny-one was reduced to a dull ache.

Fire-in-his-hair led them to the blackberry thicket nearest the hive, it was only a few good *sprints* away and fully surrounded by tea tree. Even so, the children were tired by the time they had reached it. Their heads were drooping and their feet were dragging as they walked. However, once they saw the berries sparkling black and red in the morning sunlight, their tiredness evaporated. They made as if to dash at the bush, but Fire-in-his-hair pulled them up short with an admonishing hand.

"Steady on, sparks," he said. "The bush has thorns. It'll hurt you."

Croaks-with-the-frogs set himself beside the bush to watch for predators, while Fire-in-his-hair showed the little-oaks how to collect the berries. The children crawled amongst the thorns, picking the ripest berries, but they ate nearly as many as they put in their hats. Before long, Fire-in-his-hair had filled both packs and the hats of the two children.

The sun was high overhead when they returned to the hive. The children's cheeks were red with the juice and their eyes were radiant with excitement.

"Ah! The mighty hunters have returned," laughed Sleeps-in-the-sun. "It's good to see you making use of the hats I made you."

As soon as they crossed the threshold into the hive, the children dropped any semblance of self control. They squealed and ran to where Yabbies-in-winter sat, talking with the rest of the fist. "We got heaps of berries," the girl said.

"Heaps and heaps!" echoed the boy.

They dropped their hats on the ground and began running around them in circles, jumping and skipping.

"I think they've eaten too many berries," said Fire-in-his-hair flatly.

The others laughed as they watched.

"Cakeberry, cakeberry, I burn for cakeberry," chanted the girl.

The boy joined in, and soon they were singing in a tight harmony, hopping from one foot to another in an awkward dance.

No-point-shoe stood and raised her hand imperiously over the children as they danced. She affected the quavering voice of G'ma. "Well done, darlings. A lovely hunt."

Sleeps-in-the-sun stamped her feet and mimicked the deep chesty grunt young men made after a difficult but successful hunt.

Fire-in-his-hair laughed and joined in.

The children danced and sang in wild abandon.

Sitting a little bit away from the activity, Sings-at-dawn frowned.

"What's the matter?" asked Yabbies-in-winter.

The younger man's mouth tightened in disapproval. "I don't know. Children being the centre of attention... it all looks wrong to me."

Yabbies-in-winter reached across and squeezed his hand. "Yes," she said softly. "It looks wrong." She paused for moment, then, "but it feels right. The fire is burning here." With that, she got up and walked over to the flat rock where her cakeberry pot was waiting.

Dyeing clothes

The days turned over like falling gum leaves. The berries became scarce and the rain became colder. The season was ending. It was time to replace their clothes. Throughout the Berry season, hides had been tanned, smoked and trimmed in preparation for the great celebration. At the end of Berry, each person would cut and stitch a fresh pair of trousers and a shirt. The Lake tribe gathered the last of the blackberries and set up a fist-thumb of large pottery vats in a ring around the fire to boil their new clothes and dye the hides.

Twists-the-reeds had never dyed his clothes before and he was not very good at making them, so he stayed close to The-tiny-one as the preparations were made. They needed a fine, sharp cutter to make the clothes. But fine flakes of stone, whilst they made the sharpest blades, were also the most brittle. They would often break or become blunt before the cutting was finished. As a result, they needed their tools with them throughout the making process to repair or replace the cutters. The pair of youngsters were sharing The-tiny-one's hammer stone.

Hammer stones were rare and very valuable. Each hunter wanted one and once found they were kept in their tool kit for ever. Hammer stones were a deep reddish grey and they were the heaviest of all stones. Only hammer stones were hard enough to break the quartz into flakes for tool making and no other stone formed sharp edges like the sparkling hard rocks.

Like many young spears, Twists-the-reeds hadn't found a hammer stone yet and The-tiny-one was happy to share hers in exchange for his company. "What colours are you thinking of doing your clothes?" she asked as she stitched her trousers together.

Twists-the-reeds had broken his cutter and was striking a large lump of quartz with the hammer stone to create a new flake. "I don't know," he said. "I thought, I'd do the same colour as you."

The-tiny-one laughed. "What!? Like we're an old married couple?"

The boy blushed. "No! I mean... like... that fist from the swamp. They all had the same colour in their clothes."

The-tiny-one pressed her lips together tightly and stared at her stitching.

Twists-the-reeds put down the hammer stone and stared at her. "I'm sorry, Tiny-one," he said, formally. I forgot about... your loss."

Tears gathered in her eyes. "I miss him so much," she said softly. "I can't believe how much it hurts."

Twists-the-reeds asked, "Still?"

The-tiny-one nodded.

They sat together in silence. Twists-the-reeds could think of nothing to say but his heart ached for the girl. After a while, he said, "How about we put some green in our clothes?"

The-tiny-one turned and looked at him, emotions swirling within her. Part of her warned that wearing green would put her shame on full display and not help her to move on with her life, but another part knew there would be no moving on and she wanted everyone to know it.

After a moment's hesitation, she said, "Sure. Let's do it!"

Twists-the-reeds laughed. "We could be part of team green."

"It's the green team," The-tiny-one said as she put the finishing touches on her trousers. "Come on, hurry up. I'm going to keep my bottoms the same but I'll put my top in with your trousers."

"I was thinking of yellow for my top," he said. His face twisted in distaste at the stained, muddy trousers she was swearing. "Why do you want to keep your trousers the same colour?"

The-tiny-one smiled in embarrassment. "They don't look too good now. Nobody's clothes look good in Berry. They get old and stained." She lowered her voice to a conspiratorial whisper. "But if I just give them a short boil in the red, they end up almost exactly the same colour as my skin." she nodded proudly.

Twists-the-reeds gave his head a subtle shake, conveying his confusion. "So?"

She laughed and shrugged. "I dunno. I just thought it'd sizzle." She carried her trousers over to the vat with the blackberries boiling in it and dropped them in.

Twists-the-reeds went back to working on his clothes.

By the time he had finished, The-tiny-one's trousers were boiled and drying in the pale sun. It was true. The trousers were almost exactly the colour of her skin.

"You ready to do the green, boy?"

Twists-the-reeds gathered his trousers and together they walked to the vat of purple flowered leaves. They put their clothes in and waited. Twists-the-reeds wanted his trousers to be a dark green while The-tiny-one wanted her's to be a little bit brighter.

After a while, Hunter-of-flies approached the vat. He always dyed his trousers green. He had aged since the magpie attack last Harvest. He walked slowly and his shoulders were stooped. Everything he did seemed to require an enormous amount of effort. He peered over the rim of the vat and frowned.

"We won't be long, Hunter-of-flies," said Twists-the-reeds.

The old man sniffed the vat and shook his head. "No," he said slowly. "There's something not quite right here."

"This is the green vat," said The-tiny-one, pointing to the cluster of leaves beside it.

Hunter-of-flies looked inside the vat again. The steam hurt his eyes and made him squint. "It doesn't smell right, kids," he said. "And that colour seems too dark. I think it's been contaminated."

The young ones grabbed the thick sticks used to fish clothes out of the vat and pulled their clothes out. Once clear of the simmering liquid, it was obvious that Hunter-of-flies had been right. The colour was not green.

"There must have been an insect or something in the vat," the old man said. "We'll have to start a new one."

The-tiny-one stared at her shirt. The colour was dark, but she wouldn't be able to tell what colour it was going to be until until it dried.

With a sinking feeling, the pair squeezed the excess dye out of their clothes and laid them out in the sun.

While they were doing this, Me-not-talking and Climbs-the-burrow came over. They took the vat away from the fire and poured the liquid into the sand. The young ones heard the commotion and laughter immediately and went over see what was happening.

"We've found the contamination," laughed Climbs-the-burrow.

"Have you lost anything recently, Tiny?"

Twists-the-reeds stared at the ground where the vat had been emptied and his heart sank. There amidst the dark liquid, soaking into the dirt was The-tiny-one's hammer stone.

The girl turned on him. "You! I leant that hammer stone to you!"

"I'm sorry... it must have got tangled up in my trousers."

"Fuck! Fuck! Fuck!"

The next day, after their clothes had dried, the young ones found themselves wearing clothes of a unique colour. Twists-the-reeds' trousers and The-tiny-one's shirt were both a deep blue. The tribe marvelled at the new colour and many commented on the the way The-tiny-one's shirt seemed to match the colour of her eyes. She received so many compliments she had to apologise to Twists-the-reeds for her outburst.

"No need to apologise, girl," he said, seriously. "It was my mistake."

She looked at her feet in embarrassment. "Yeah, but... It was hardly worth my outburst. The hammer stone was unharmed." She tugged at her shirt and shot him a smug smile. "And our clothes are blazing."

Twists-the-reeds proudly smoothed his trousers with his hands. "Yeah. They really are, aren't they?"

13

WINTER

The hive's got pretty full all of a sudden

Hunger! Mice, birds and frogs were scarce. The cat prowled further and further afield in its endless search for food, its stomach constantly growling, gnawing at its insides, warning of imminent death. Hunger drove the cat all over the swamplands. It even dared to approach the human hive in its desperate quest to stave off starvation, but it would never approach too close or stay too long in the vicinity. With their sharp sticks and their agonising fire, humans were the cat's greatest source of terror. Sometimes at night, it would approach, drawn by the smell of fresh meat. It would crouch in the brush listening to their howls and grunts, not daring to get any closer, torn between its yearning and its fear. Any attempt to get their meat would cost its life. Eventually the fear would get too great and it would retreat to safety. Searching, always searching.

The shortage of meat changed the routine of the people of the swamp. They hunted less and spent more time around the fire, making wattle dumplings. Wattle seeds which had been roasted and stored over Smoke were ground into a powder and mixed with chewed bracken root to form small balls of heavy dough. They were then wrapped in large warrigal leaves and put into the stew. These replaced meat and kept the people well fed.

Croaks-with-the-frogs' traps in the pine forest were less productive in Winter. He built more, closer to the hive, on the other side of the swamp and tried to catch the water birds that frequented the swamp but he was not successful. The birds were reluctant to get too close and he couldn't find an effective bait. Every few days he would go out and try again but he rarely brought home any prey. He too spent most of his days around the fire, pounding wattles, making new spears or thinking about improvements to the traps.

Babies were born and the new mothers retired to their burrows to nurse and rest. To replace them, the oldest children received names and spears. Changes were made to many fists to accommodate the influx of new spears as they left the crowded children's burrows and moved into the shared burrows of the fists.

No-point-shoe gave birth to her litter and withdrew to her burrow. The usual pattern was for new mothers, their husbands and the litter to take over the burrow and for the other members of the fist to move out until the babies were weened, but there were several other births that winter and the hive was bursting with new life. Finding a new burrow was not easy.

Sings-at-dawn found a place for himself and Yabbies-in-winter with some of his former fist. But Sleeps-in-the-sun and Croaks-with-the-frogs were still crowded into the old burrow.

"It's a bit tight," said Fire-in-his-hair as they sat by the fire one morning, "but you don't have to leave."

Sleeps-in-the-sun laughed. "Its not the lack of space, *Bruhd*. It's your little squealers waking us up every nap."

He rubbed his hands through his hair, scratching at his ears. "Yeah. Fair enough."

From inside the burrow, they could hear No-point-shoe cooing to the babies as they nursed.

Sleeps-in-the-sun became serious. "I'm not leaving you." She paused, spearing him with her eyes. "You understand, don't you? I'll be in and out of that burrow until No-point-shoe has weaned and is ready to return to the fist. That woman has got me for life."

Fire-in-his-hair smiled and nodded.

On the other side of the fire, G'ma and G'pa were fighting.

"Why can't you just leave me alone?" G'ma said, bitterly.

"You! It's you who won't leave yourself alone."

"I never thought my old age would be like this."

"I never thought my wife would ashen kill herself right in front of me."

G'ma scoffed. "Rubbish."

"What rubbish!? You are killing yourself."

"Nonsense."

G'pa's head wobbled even more. "You must stop drinking toddy."

"I'm not drinking toddy."

"You drank it last night!"

G'ma tossed her head. "Yes, last night. But that was just once. I'm not drinking it." She placed her emphasis on the word, 'drinking.'

G'pa was incredulous. "What!? Are you crazy? If you drank it last night, you're drinking it!"

"No."

"You told me you would stop after last Wattle."

"I stopped."

The old man's lips tightened briefly and he slammed his fist into his open palm. "But you drank it last night!"

They sat in silence for a moment, then G'ma said quietly, "It was important."

"Rubbish!"

"I needed to *see*."

G'pa responded with a disgusted snort.

Croaks-with-the-frogs approached them, tentatively. He was carrying a steaming nut of dandelion. "Nut of dandy, G'ma?" he asked.

G'ma turned her shoulder away from G'pa. "Oh yes, thank you, darling. That would be lovely."

The young man hesitantly leaned across to catch G'pa's eye. "Dandy, G'pa?"

"No thanks, boy," the old man said gently.

"Yes. Yes," G'ma interrupted. "Get another nut for G'pa. We have something to talk to you about."

Croaks-with-the-frogs hesitated long enough to see G'pa start and squawk. "We!?"

The young man scurried back to the pot of simmering dandelion root to get a pair of nuts. He was keen to be out of earshot while the old couple sorted out their issues. By the time he had returned with a steaming brew for G'pa and himself, the old man was staring blankly into the fire with his mouth hanging open.

"Ah. Lovely, lovely," G'ma said as she took the nut and handed it to G'pa.

He took it, but his eyes were still unfocussed as if he was in a dream.

"Now dear," G'ma began, as Croaks-with-the-frogs took his seat beside her. "Where are you going to sleep now that No-point-shoe is nursing?"

"Oh... um... we're still in the burrow for now." The young man felt the colour rising in his face. "Sleeps-in-the-sun and I are looking but.... the hive's got pretty full all of a sudden."

G'pa turned to him, his expression serious. "Yes. Yes. It's quite full, so... um."

G'ma interrupted. "You must come and sleep in our burrow."

Croaks-with-the-frogs was stunned. G'ma and G'pa had a burrow to themselves for as long as he could remember. He stared at them blankly as he read their eyes.

G'pa was hesitant but willing, as if he was about to embark on a dangerous quest. G'ma's face was filled with a calm certainty. She would brook no resistance on the matter.

"There's plenty of room in our burrow," said G'pa. "There's just us. You and um..."

"Sleeps-in-the-sun."

"Yes. Sleeps-in-the-sun can share with us until the litters are weaned."

Croaks-with-the-frogs looked from face to face.

G'ma smiled. "That's settled then. Would you like us to tell Sleeps-in-the-sun or can you do it?"

The young man, sputtered. "I'll tell... I think I should talk to Sleeps-in-the-sun first."

"Yes, yes. Of course," said G'pa. "Tell her we've made the offer. She may have somewhere else to stay."

G'ma shot him a sharp look, then turned back to Croaks-with-the-frogs. "You tell Sleeps-in-the-sun and you can move into our burrow tonight." She turned back to the fire and sipped her dandelion brew.

Croaks-with-the-frogs' mind whirled as he tried to comprehend this development. They drank their brew in silence, punctuated only by the occasional smack of G'ma's lips. Once the drinks were finished, the young man, still reeling, collected the nuts, said his goodbyes and walked away.

G'pa watched his retreating back. "Do you think he realises that the other fists don't want him?" he asked softly.

G'ma's eyes brimmed. "It doesn't matter. We have to look after him."

You can't have it both ways

Cold rain fell in waves throughout the night. Squalls blew across the lake and swept into the hive. Sniffs-the-wind and Twists-the-reeds were awake when the rains came on so they set up the old kangaroo hide to shield the fire. They huddled between the pelt and the flames, and fed the fire through the small hours of the night.

"I'm getting sleepy," said Twists-the-reeds.

Sniffs-the-wind put out her arm and drew him close to her. "We can't sleep yet, boy," she said. "No one else is awake to protect the fire."

The pair sat in silence, staring at the flames.

After a while, the boy said, "This is just like everyday."

Sniffs-the-wind looked across at him, wondering if he had fallen asleep. In the flickering firelight, she could make out the dim shape of his face and gleam in his dark eyes. "What?"

He kept staring at the fire. His voice was soft. "Every day is just like this. You and me awake, trying to keep the fire burning, while everybody else is asleep."

Sniffs-the-wind looked at him in puzzlement. Her mind whirling as she tried to grasp what he was saying. She knew it was an important idea but it was just out of her reach.

Twists-the-reeds sighed. "Do you know I've heard people say how convenient it is that we don't need to rearrange the burrows this Winter."

"Idiots," muttered Sniffs-the-wind.

The point of pregnant women had successfully brought their litters to term and only a tall of children gained their spears and names. There was little need to change sleeping arrangements because the hive was not as crowded as it should be in Winter. The tribe was not growing.

Twists-the-reeds seemed to be speaking to himself. "Nobody seems to be able to understand what's going on. They're all asleep."

Sniffs-the-wind squeezed him tighter. Outside the darkness closed in but here beside the fire, she felt safe. At least they weren't alone. At least they had each other, the only people awake in the hive.

Gradually, the eastern sky brightened. The rain eased to a steady drizzle and others began to leave their burrows to face the day. Rolls-in-the-berries got herself some stew and sat beside them, sheltering under the kangaroo hide. "Not much meat in this stew," she said, absently.

"There are wattle rolls," said Twists-the-reeds.

Sniffs-the-wind shot him a quick look. Ordinarily, the boy wouldn't have dreamed of speaking to Rolls-in-the-berries. He would have remained silent and waited for her to speak and only speak when asked a question, but in the days since the Smoke season, he had become increasingly outspoken. It was as if facing the doom had made him fearless. He no longer had anything to lose.

Rolls-in-the-berries frowned. "I told Jumps-in-the-water to take his fist out fishing yesterday."

"Mmm," said Twists-the-reeds. "I don't think he went." With that, the boy pushed himself to his feet and walked over to the stew pot to get his breakfast.

Sniffs-the-wind felt sorry for Rolls-in-the-berries. The old woman was hard and demanding but at least she wanted the best for the tribe. She leaned across and looked into her stew. "Yes," she agreed. "It could do with some more meat. Would you like me to take my fist out today? We could get some yabbies."

Rolls-in-the-berries nodded. Her lips pressed tightly together.

A moment later, Twists-the-reeds returned with his bowl of stew and cake. "G'ma," he said as if he were speaking to an equal. "What are we going to do about the decline of the tribe?"

Rolls-in-the-berries looked at him sharply. Her eyes widened and Sniffs-the-wind glimpsed the rage simmering behind

the old woman's eyes.

The boy didn't notice. "We only had a point of litters this Winter. They will not all reach marriagable age. Only a tall of new spears were added to the tribe, we'd be lucky to have a point of them survive to their mating wattle. Something must be done."

Rolls-in-the-berries' nostrils flared. She took a deep breath and began to speak. "You have not seen many Winters, boy. There's no need to panic. This was a lean year, but next year will be good. It's always like this. Good times and bad times."

"Why would next year be better? There are only a point of spears who will marry this Wattle. We cant keep both of them."

Rolls-in-the-berries' annoyance was fully on display now. "You are not considering the older couples. Me-not-talking will breed again, and we'll marry off a few of the widows and widowers. We'll probably end up with a fist of litters next Winter. There's nothing to worry about." She spoke briskly in the way that usually ended conversations.

Twists-the-reeds pushed on. "Do we have that many widows and widowers?"

"Yes!" snapped Rolls-in-the-berries. "She's sitting right beside you, you foolish boy!"

Sniffs-the-wind squawked. "Me!?"

"Yes you, girl! You will be ready to marry again in Wattle."

Sniffs-the-wind couldn't breathe. Her heart raced and the dim morning light seemed to flicker. She stared at the old woman in horror but said nothing.

Rolls-in-the-berries stared at them reading the disapproval on their faces. Her lips curled into a bitter smile. "You can't have it both ways. You can't sit here, bemoaning the decline in the tribe but not be willing to do your part. We need to breed!"

Twists-the-reeds nodded thoughtfully.

Sniffs-the-wind blinked at her for a moment, then something clicked in her mind and she leapt to her feet. "Come one," she said, tapping the boy on the shoulder. "Let's get the others up and moving. I want some yabbies."

Strange rasping sounds

Croaks-with-the-frogs left the hive before dawn to check on his traps. The wattle dumplings hadn't worked as bait. Some insects had nibbled at them but nothing big enough to trigger the killing stick. He removed the bait stick and slung it over his shoulder as he headed back to the hive. He would have to try something else.

The winter sun was peeking through the tea tree in the east, casting long, tangled shadows across the swamp. He was a fair way from the hive when he heard the child crying. It was a wild, heart wrenching wail that reached deep into his soul. For an instant, Croaks-with-the-frogs froze, then slowly, recognition dawned. It was little oaks.

The young man lowered his head and sprinted through the tea tree. When he arrived at the hive, the boy was standing at the entrance, wailing into the bush. Sleeps-in-the-sun was holding him and trying to comfort the child, a terrible look of grief on her face.

"What happened!?" asked Croaks-with-the-frogs.

"The girl has left the fire," she said, and her voice broke.

"Where is Fire-in-his-hair?"

Sleeps-in-the-sun stared at him in confusion. "What?... Asleep... in burrow."

Croaks-with-the-frogs dropped his pack and bait stick. "Did you see which way she went?"

Sleeps-in-the-sun shock her head but little oaks pointed towards the north.

The young man tuned and dashed north, ignoring the screams of Sleeps-in-the-sun as she begged him to stay.

He followed the trail north calling desperately, "Little oaks! Little oaks!" Hysteria breaking through in his voice,

The cat had found her prey wandering aimlessly through the tea tree. It was a human pup, whimpering and looking around in all directions. She had leapt from her hiding place amongst the bushes and snapped her jaws around its neck. The prey screamed. With a flick of her head she had thrown the creature away into the brush, then bolted after it to ensure it wouldn't escape. The prey was still alive and clambering slowly to its feet. The cat swatted it with her fore paw sending it tumbling further into the scrub. She pounced again and grasped the pup in her jaws. The prey moved weakly and whimpered. She threw it high into the air and it landed in the bush. It pounced again, pining its legs with her paws. The pup's arm moved futilely, trying to waive her away. The cat breathed deeply, smelling the blood, sweat and fear. The fresh meat would taste good. After this long Winter, her hunger would finally be sated.

Croaks-with-the-frogs heard the tell tale crunch of movement amongst the tea tree. He knew what it would mean even before he burst through the bush to find the cat crouching over the prone child. He didn't hesitate. Little oaks was still moving but at some level, he knew she would not survive. It made no difference. Filled with rage, he screamed and threw himself at the animal thrusting with his spear.

The spear skidded off the creature's shoulder blade and tore through the skin above.

The cat whirled and lashed out. Driven by hunger, she refused to leave her prey. She sunk her teeth deep into Croaks-with-the-frogs' left shoulder and tried to throw him away. The young man stood his ground and the teeth tore through the muscle. He screamed and struck with his spear again, piercing through the skin of the cat's chest but not breaking through into the vital organs. The cat lashed out again, striking a powerful blow on the left side of his face.

The blow ripped through Croaks-with-the-frogs's skin and sent him staggering to his knees. The cat leapt at him. For an instant, he could feel hot breath on his neck and teeth scraping against the lower part of his skull. He twisted away and struck out with his spear again, this time, finding the soft underbelly of the beast. The monster wailed and blood poured from the wound. But as the cat leapt away, Croaks-with-the-frog's blood soaked hand lost its grip on his spear.

They faced each other now over the body of the child. Both bleeding, both wounded but neither willing to give up the child to the other. The spear, still embedded in the cat's abdomen, dragged on the ground and worked its way through sinew and intestines as the cat moved. Blood poured down the shaft, soaking into the damp, grey soil.

Croaks-with-the-frogs's left eye was closed and his cheek gaped open. He struggled to stand as blood streamed from the wound on his shoulder. His spear was out of reach and his fire was being quenched. He was not going to last much longer.

He had no energy left to scream. All his strength was channeled into a desperate lunge. He leapt at the cat with his bare hands and dug his fingers into her eyes. The cat swatted him with her paw and sent him tumbling to the ground. He tried to get up but he was dizzy and couldn't collect his thoughts.

The cat paused. She too was weak and the spear lodged in her abdomen was draining her life. For an instant, she was torn between a pair of desires. To either kill off the deadly threat of the adult, or to flee the battle with her prize. At that moment another human slammed into her from the side.

Fire-in-his-hair had been woken by the commotion around the fire and had poked his head out of the burrow without pulling on his clothes. He had seen Croaks-with-the-frogs running into the bush and heard the screams of Sleeps-in-the-sun and the remaining little oaks. It took a moment for him to realise what had happened. He didn't bother to get his shirt. Merely pulled on his pants and shoes, grabbed his spear, and ran.

He did not hesitate when he saw the cat poised over the prone body of Croaks-with-the-frogs. He threw himself at it and plunged his spear into its side. The head of the spear struck its ribs and the shaft broke. Both cat and man tumbled across the ground, scrabbling for purchase. They landed with the man on the bottom and the cat on top. Fire-in-his-hair had lost his spear and if he moved away from the cat, he would be pounded by its claws. To have any chance of victory, he needed to stay in close. He wrapped his legs around the cat's waist to stop the creature from pulling away. The cat tried to bite him but he drove his elbow into its mouth and pushed its head back. The cat's hind legs thrashed and flailed, its claws raking the naked flesh of his back but unable to dig in deeply as they struggled in the dirt.

Fire-in-his-hair held the cat's shoulders close with his free arm and pushed harder with the other, forcing the creature's head further back and stretching its neck. Teeth drove into his forearm and tore through muscle, tendon, and artery. Blood spurted into the cat's mouth in time with his racing heart. Its front claws hooked into his shoulders and tore at the veins in his neck. Fire-in-his-hair pushed his arm forward some more. The cat began to labour, emitting strange rasping sounds from its throat.

Croaks-with-the-frogs crawled to his knees and shook his head to clear the fog. Tangled in their death struggle, the pair had toppled onto their sides, Croaks-with-the-frogs' spear hanging limply from the cat's abdomen. The young man tried to stand but staggered back to his hands and knees. He crawled forward, his eyes focussed on the dancing spear.

Blood made the shaft slippery but Croaks-with-the-frogs grasped it with both hands. He rested the hilt against his chest and used his own weight to drive the spear up under the beast's ribs and into its vital organs.

The cat's scream was muffled by Fire-in-his-hair's elbow, wedged in its mouth. Blood bubbled from between its teeth and its hind legs thrashed again. Its front claws dug deeper into the veins at Fire-in-his-hair's neck. Blood spurted from both man and beast. The cat squirmed, twisted then collapsed onto the bloody ground.

Come back to the fire

Fire-in-his-hair rolled away from the dead cat. He tried to climb to his feet, but he was swept by a wave of dizziness and collapsed. Blood continued to pump from the arteries at his forearm and neck.

Croaks-with-the-frogs cradled him in his arms and wept. "Oh No... Oh Please. Oh No!"

Fire-in-his-hair's eyes rolled back in their sockets as the shock and loss of blood had their effect. He breathed deeply.

"No, no, no!" Croaks-with-the-frogs repeated as he buried his face in the bloody neck of his dying friend. "I'm sorry... I'm so, so sorry!" He sobbed and his tears mingled with the blood that smeared his face and matted his hair.

The old hunter's ruined elbow lay limp at his side, but he reached across with his other arm and gently tangled his fingers in Croaks-with-the-frogs' hair. "What are you sorry for, boy?" he whispered.

"I've done it again. I've... I shouldn't have... I no..."

Fire-in-his-hair took another deep breath. "You have nothing to be sorry for, boy," he said softly. The spurts of blood became slower and less forceful.

Croaks-with-the-frogs whimpered into his friend's shoulder and pawed at his face with his hands.

Fire-in-his-hair closed his eyes again, summoning his strength, his good hand still tangled in Croaks-with-the-frogs' hair. "I'm glad I ran after you. I'm glad you ran after her."

"I should have stayed in the hive! Little oaks... I didn't save her. I just... I'm cursed. Cursed!"

"No boy, no!" Fire-in-his-hair untangled his fingers from Croaks-with-the-frogs's hair and stroked his face. The surges of blood were were little more than trickles now. "You ran after little oaks for the same reason I ran after you. Because every life matters. You're not cursed. Your life matters. Every life matters."

Fire-in-his-hair's hand dropped away from his face and lay limp at his side. The blood faintly spurted only a few more times.

Sleeps-in-the-sun had gathered Yabbies-in-winter, Sings-at-dawn and a couple of other spears into a make-shift fist. When they arrived at the scene, they found Croaks-with-the-frogs the only one alive. He lay barely conscious in the dirt, covered in blood. They carried the young man back to the hive where the G'mas tended his wounds, then they returned to fetch the bodies of Little oaks and Fire-in-his-hair. The hive was swept with a surge of grief and anger.

The carcass of the cat was beheaded, skinned, butchered and thrown into the stew pots. The point of a spear was driven through its head and it was propped at the entrance of the hive, facing outwards as a sign of defiance to the enemy.

No-point-shoe wailed and howled as they brought Fire-in-his-hair back. She cursed and swore at Croaks-with-the-frogs and railed at the cat, the enemy and the even bush itself.

The others let her rage until she collapsed, sobbing at the entrance of the hive.

The other little oaks stood silently, staring at the body of his sister as if he were confronting a horror beyond his comprehension. Sleeps-in-the-sun drew the little boy into her arms and held him tightly. He was stiff and unresponsive. She began to cry and the tears increased until they erupted in profound upswelling of grief. Even as she clutched the boy and sobbed into his hair, a part of her marvelled at why she was so overwhelmed. She had no words for her loss.

Croaks-with-the-frogs lay beside the fire with his head resting on G'ma's lap. He felt his heart shrivel like a green leaf in the fire as he watched No-point-shoe storm and scream. He agreed completely with everything she said. "Yes... yes," he muttered as he cried.

"Shh now," said G'ma soothingly, stroking his head. "It's alright, darling."

Others cared for the wound in his shoulder and the gaping slashes on his face.

Sings-at-dawn and Yabbies-in-winter cleaned the bodies while others erected a frame of branches. The fist with the extra thumb and point was different to the others so nobody complained when Little oaks was given the same funeral rites as Fire-in-his-hair.

Eventually No-point-shoe picked herself up from the ground and fetched Fire-in-his-hair's shirt from the burrow. She dressed him, weeping softly as she did so.

The man and the child were laid on the frame of branches. The frame was manoeuvred over the fire and extra wood was added. The flames climbed the wood and licked the prone bodies.

Someone chanted the dirge and the tribe began the litany of loss...

Oh, Oh, Oh.

   Oh, Oh, Oh.

We come from the fire

   Come back to the fire

The fire burns within us

   Come back to the fire

Only the fire understands

   Come back to the fire

The fire is never extinguished

   Come back to the fire

And when our time is done, we

   Come back to the fire

Someday we all will be together when we

   Come back to the fire

A different purpose

The funeral pyre burned for several days. The swamp people, ate little and grieved much as Fire-in-his-hair and Little-oaks were slowly turned to ashes. Yabbies-in-winter and Sings-at-dawn returned to their old burrow so No-point-shoe wouldn't be alone at night. Sleeps-in-the-sun stayed in G'ma and G'pa's burrow and nursed Croaks-with-the-frogs. He slipped in and out of consciousness, bathed in tea tree and eucalyptus oil. The young man's body would carry the scars for the rest of his life but the damage done to his heart and mind, could not be estimated.

One morning as Sleeps-in-the-sun bathed Croaks-with-the-frogs' shoulder in tea tree oil, G'ma and G'pa made their way clumsily into the burrow. G'pa grunted and groaned as he squeezed his way in. G'ma said nothing, nimbly slipping past the rabbit pelt that covered the entrance. In her hand she carried a wooden bowl containing smashed fruit.

G'pa sat, resting his back against one of the uprights and gasped for breath as G'ma headed straight for Croaks-with-the-frogs, an intense look on her small face.

"What are you doing?" asked Sleeps-in-the-sun warily.

G'ma didn't look at her. "I need to give him this... um thing," she said and she squatted beside the young man and began feeding the pulp to him with her fingers.

Croaks-with-the-frogs groaned and twisted his face from her.

Sleeps-in-the-sun put her hand out to try to slow G'ma down. "He doesn't seem to, like it."

G'ma ignored her and continue to force the pulp into the young man's mouth.

"G'ma!" Sleeps-in-the-sun couldn't keep the alarm out of her voice.

G'pa roused himself from where he was sitting. "It's OK, girl," he said gently. "It's kangaroo apple. It's very good for rebuilding muscle. It will help his shoulder."

Sleeps-in-the-sun looked across at his face in the dim light of the burrow and the old man nodded towards G'ma and winked. "She can't tell you what happened yesterday, but she remembers everything she learned as a spear."

G'ma made Croaks-with-the-frogs lick the last of the kangaroo apple off her fingers, then sat back with a satisfied nod. "Very good," she said as if she were talking to a nursing baby. She smiled briefly, then turned to G'pa, a stern look on her face. "Now you need to go and find some more."

G'pa groaned. "I need to rest," he said.

G'ma nodded but kept staring at him, waiting for him to finish resting and carry out her instruction.

G'pa shook his head. "You've just given him a whole fruit. I'll get more for him tomorrow."

G'ma frowned.

G'pa's head wobbled in annoyance. "Just let me be for a moment. I need to talk to... this girl."

G'ma's mouth tightened. She tossed her head like a surly adolescent and crawled out of the burrow.

Once she was gone, G'pa rested his head against the upright at his back and breathed deeply.

Sleeps-in-the-sun awkwardly stared at him, waiting for him to speak. When he didn't, she went back to bathing Croaks-with-the-frogs' wounds. "These wounds are closing over nicely," she said. "I don't think his fire will run wild."

G'pa didn't respond. He sat silently with his head tilted back and his eyes closed.

Sleeps-in-the-sun finished bathing the wounds and made to leave the burrow.

"I think you should return to No-point-shoe and her litter," said the old man, suddenly.

Sleeps-in-the-sun stopped and stared at him. "I'm sorry?"

G'pa leaned forward, resting his elbows on his knees. He let out a small gasp as his joints ached. "No-point-shoe needs you," he said. "The... other pair are not the same as you. You're the one who must help her through her grief."

Sleeps-in-the-sun began to speak, but the old man raised his hand to forestall her.

"Your G'ma has seen this, girl. No-point-shoe is vital for the future of this tribe. You must make sure she is not destroyed by this. Croaks-with-the-frogs has a different purpose. G'ma and I will see him on his way."

Sleeps-in-the-sun stared at the old man in shock, her mind racing. "Does anybody have a purpose?" she asked sceptically.

G'pa's eyes were locked onto hers and she glimpsed the granite will masked by his ageing body. "Everybody has a purpose, girl. When you are a G'ma, you will understand more of this. But for now, you must think less and do more. Do this!"

With that, the old man rolled himself onto his hands and knees and with some intermittent grunts, crawled out of the burrow.

Sleeps-in-the-sun sat in the burrow while Croaks-with-the-frogs slept and her mind whirled. No-point-shoe was an extraordinary woman. She had never seen anybody with the ability to bind a fist together like No-point-shoe. She had a unique blend of compassion and hardness. She could instil confidence and demand greatness but at the same time she would show compassion for the failings of others because she wasn't ashamed of her own weakness. If anyone had an important purpose, it was No-point-shoe.

She looked down at Croaks-with-the-frogs, sleeping on the furs. The way G'pa spoke evoked a powerful image in Sleeps-in-the-sun's mind. It was if, Croaks-with-the-frogs was suddenly submerged beneath the brown waters of the swamp and utterly out of reach. *G'ma and I will see him on his way.*

As she replayed G'pa's words in her mind, Sleeps-in-the-sun's fears were soothed. G'ma and G'pa would take care of the boy. She had her own task, her own purpose. She had passed through the scourge of Finder-of-snails' death. She had seen her litter mate taken by an eagle and she had survived in no small part due to the love and support of No-point-shoe. Now it was time to test her strength. She had to carry No-point-shoe. The tribe needed her.

14

THE WATTLES BUD

Eating breakfast

As the days of Winter past, Croaks-with-the-frogs slowly recovered. Under G'ma's careful nursing, his shoulder regained most of its movement and some of its strength. The left side of his face carried a scar above his eye and another on the jawline. The scar tissue was raised, angry and red. The wounds gave him a fearsome appearance that contrasted sharply with his large, sad eyes.

Eventually Croaks-with-the-frogs was strong enough to leave the burrow. It was early morning before the dawn when he crawled out of the entrance and approached the fire. He sat on his own, away from the others, staring into the flames. There were few people moving around in the chilly darkness. The fresh, cold air with its strong hint of woodsmoke, summoned a myriad of feelings and memories. The memories danced beyond his conscious thought, teasing him with their presence but refusing to fit into a narrative. The feelings were not so reticent. They swept over him in waves. Croaks-with-the-frogs tasted them, savouring their sweetness and their bitterness.

He sat alone and silent as the faint predawn light grew. There was increased movement around the fire as more people left their burrows. Food was served and cakes cooked. People gathered in small groups talking quietly so as not to disturb those who still slept. When the children woke, the noise level increased as they played and ran around the fire.

Little-oaks crawled from the children's burrow and saw Croaks-with-the-frogs. The little boy's heart skipped a beat and he stood, frozen, staring at the young man with a mixture of fear and yearning on his face. After a moment, the child took a step towards him. Then another, and before long he was standing less than a *length* away, watching Croaks-with-the-frogs intently.

The young man finally noticed him and the pair locked eyes. They stared at each other in silence for a long time. Something in Croaks-with-the-frogs was trying to break out into a smile, but his face was numb and he felt somehow separated from the rest of the world, as if his soul were wrapped in a thick layer of furs.

Little-oaks was frightened of him. His fierce scars and silence were disconcerting. Croaks-with-the-frogs' eyes were still the same large brown orbs, but they had lost the joyous sparkle the child once knew. He looked into them for several moments. Then the child turned away and ran back to his burrow.

For an instant, Croaks-with-the-frogs wanted to call him back. He felt a terrible grief as he saw the child run away, but the furs nestled over him again and he savoured the hard ache of loss, luxuriating in the pain.

Little-oaks didn't stay away for long. He dashed into the burrow and a moment later, came out again. He ran back to where the young man sat and stood an arms length away, a solemn expression on his face. Croaks-with-the-frogs looked at the child curiously. The boy was carrying something in his hand and he hesitated as if unsure if he should proceed. Then as if a brief internal battle had been fought and won, Little-oaks thrust out his arm and opened his fist. Nestled in the palm of his hand was the small ball of resin Croaks-with-the-frogs had given him last Wattle. The child's face was stern and his eyes carried a deadly intensity. He stood with arm outstretched, offering the ball to Croaks-with-the-frogs.

It took a moment for Croaks-with-the-frogs to realise what was happening. The awareness of the action and its significance slowly seeped through the stifling furs of isolation and the thing that was struggling to get out burst free. He reached out and clutched the child to him, sobbing into his curly hair. The boy hugged back, burying his face into Croaks-with-the-frogs' shirt and revelling in the familiar smell of it. Then the child too began to cry, as the grief of the loss and the gratitude for the return swept over him. They sat there hugging long after the sobs subsided, while around them, the tribe went about their business.

After a while Little-oaks started wriggling so Croaks-with-the-frogs let him down. The child began running in a large circle around the fire, while the young man stood and looked around the hive. His eyes lingered on the old burrow he used to share with Fire-in-his-hair. Now No-point-shoe and her litter were there, grieving his loss. Little-oaks made a single lap of the fire and then ran around Croaks-with-the-frogs, laughing maniacally.

Croaks-with-the-frogs took a deep breath. "C'mon, little spark," he said. "We're going to visit someone."

Little-oaks followed close, eyes wide as the young man made his way across the hive and crawled into No-point-shoe's burrow.

When Croaks-with-the-frogs and little-oaks arrived, Sleeps-in-the-sun was overjoyed. She took little oaks onto her lap and fussed over Croaks-with-the-frogs' scars.

No-point-shoe tried to be polite. A part of her knew they too were grieving for Fire-in-his-hair and their visit was important for the whole fist. But every time she looked at Croaks-with-the-frogs, she couldn't help thinking about the chain of events that had led to this. His inclusion of the Little-oaks into the fist, the ridiculous decision to go running after the child when she wandered away from the fire, the strange hold he had over Fire-in-his-hair that led her husband to run naked into the bush to save him from his own madness. Now, he was alive and sitting in her burrow and Fire-in-his-hair was dead.

Throughout the short visit, she kept her face arranged impassively. She forced herself to smile when she had to, she made some vague attempts at polite conversation and accepted the grief and sympathy expressed by Croaks-with-the-frogs.

Finally, Sleeps-in-the-sun moved to lead the visitors out, the joy of the reunion still all over her face. At the entrance, she turned to No-point-shoe. "Shall I get you some break-fast?" she asked.

No-point-shoe exerted a last effort of will to keep her calm. "No, I'll just feed the bubs and then get my own."

Sleeps-in-the-sun's face burst into a radiant smile. "Yes. Of course, that's great. I'll see you out there."

After they had gone, No-point-shoe lay in her burrow while the babies fed. The morning light streamed through the small air holes into the gloom. She could finally let her face relax.

She held the babies tighter and turned her face to the side, immersing herself in their musky scent. Then she let her tears flow freely.

G'ma and G'pa sat in their usual places by the fire.

"They are all eating together," G'pa said.

G'ma smiled. "Who?"

"There." He nodded with his head to where Sleeps-in-the-sun and Croaks-with-the-frogs sat beside Sings-at-dawn and Yabbies-in-winter.

"Not where! Who?"

"This boy! You know..." G'pa's words sputtered to a halt.

G'ma didn't know. "Ah. Very good."

G'pa frowned. "Do you understand me?"

She looked at him mildly. "No."

G'pa spoke slowly, "Croaks-with-the-frogs is having breakfast with his fist."

"Ah?"

He took a deep breath. "It's going to be difficult."

"What is?"

"Oh by the blazes! To take the boy away!" said G'pa, his annoyance breaking through.

G'ma was shocked. "Why would we do that?"

"You told me we had to!"

"Who?"

"You!" G'pa's voice cracked in frustration.

"Me? What did I say?" said G'ma, mildly.

"You *saw* that we had to take the boy!"

"When?"

"At the start of Winter! You *saw* it!"

She smiled nervously. "No."

"Yes! You told me!"

G'ma stared into space, bemused.

"Do you not remember?"

"No," she said softly and her face crumpled.

G'pa reached out and held her hand tightly. "It's alright," he said soothingly, "Don't worry. I'll look after it."

I'll never let you go

In the early afternoon, Sniffs-the-wind sat on the bank of the lake and looked across at the faint dusting of yellow on the wattles of the south bank. The wattles on the southern bank of the lake were always the first to blossom. The sight of it had stirred the blood of the lake people and preparations had begun for the journey to the coast. There was more than the usual laughter and excitement in the hive. People collected the last of the avocados while others repaired nets and stored bracken roots. Sniffs-the-wind felt no enthusiasm for the coming wattle season. The thought of travelling sat like a heavy stone in the pit of her stomach. She did not want to go. Ever since G'ma had told her that the tribe expected her to join fires with someone from the coast, *the mood* had been building. She closed her eyes and tried to imagine merging fires with another man. From deep within, her grief surged. *Listens-for-ducks is my husband!*

She heard a footstep.

The-tiny-one and Twists-the-reeds were standing behind her, spears in hand and a puzzled look on her faces. "What are you doing here?" she asked.

Sniffs-the-wind closed her eyes slowly and turned back to the lake. "I dunno," she said lamely.

The-tiny-one frowned. "We were worried about you. You know you shouldn't leave the hive without a fist."

Sniffs-the-wind said nothing and continued to stare across the lake.

The-tiny-one crouched beside her and rested her hand on her shoulder. "Are you alright?"

Sniffs-the-wind sat for a moment longer, took a deep breath and said, "Yeah. We should be doing something. You wanna try and catch some fish?" She hauled herself to her feet and forced a smile.

The-tiny-one looked at her for a moment then nodded. "Sure, let's go get the others."

The weather was still cold, Winter hanging on for as long as it could, defying the faint sunlight sprinkled over the wattles. They assembled the fist and headed back to the lake, carrying the large circular net they had retrieved from the storage burrow. The net was made of lake reeds twisted into fine cord. Stitched into the perimeter were river stones which formed a weight around the edge. It took a fair bit of skill and two people to cast but if thrown accurately, it could bring in many fish.

Climbs-the-burrow and Me-not-talking carried the net while the others padded along carrying their spears and back packs. They had left their trousers behind, wearing only their shirts which formed a short skirt hanging down to the top of their thighs. Their skin puckered in the cold winter air.

"It's ashen cold!" complained Me-not-talking. "Where did they leave the raft?"

"Somewhere near the south bank, I think," said Twists-the-reeds.

The raft was made of bark and twigs lashed together with cord. It was long and wide and could carry an entire fist out onto the lake. A dead branch covered part of the raft to hide the hunters on board from predators. The raft had no means of steering so it was moored in a different place every time a fist used it.

They found the raft just as the boy had said. It was tied to a fallen branch by a long cord of tanned rabbit hide.

Climbs-the-burrow began to unwind the rabbit hide and move the raft into the shallows. "You gave us a bit of a fright this morning, Sniffs," he said, with a nervous laugh. "We thought we'd lost you."

"Yeah. I'm sorry guys," Sniffs-the-wind replied gently. "I ... um... just needed some time."

The-tiny-one scanned the surface of the lake looking for the tell tale ripples that signalled the presence of fish. "You want to be careful. You'll end up like Twists-the-reeds. Hanging around the lakeside making... stuff!"

The others laughed.

"There are worse things she could do," said Twists-the-reeds with feigned outrage.

"What's that over there?" asked Sniffs-the-wind, pointing further south. "Is that fish ripple?"

The-tiny-one scrambled across the shallows to the bank closest to the ripples. She waved her arms, and Twists-the-reeds untied the raft. He and Sniffs-the-wind dragged it through the shallows to where The-tiny-one stood. The water was above their knees as they pushed the raft a little further out.

The-tiny-one tied the cord to a young, blue wattle tree that had just come into flower, while the others clambered aboard the raft. They knelt with knees apart and hands splayed, spreading their weight. It rocked and wobbled, water running across its surface and wetting their legs and hands.

"Oh ash, I hate this," muttered Me-not-talking.

Sniffs-the-wind laughed. "It takes a while to get used to it, *brudha*," she said kindly. "I hated it when I first came here too. It takes a few years to learn to swim."

The-tiny-one rolled her eyes at Twists-the-reeds as she climbed aboard the raft.

The boy smiled briefly but his mind was elsewhere. "I want to come back to what Climbs-the-burrow was saying, Sniffs-the-wind," he said seriously. "He's right. You have to be careful. We need you."

The boy's words had an immediate effect. Climbs-the-burrow sniggered but his face betrayed his pride. He was not used to being given credit. The young man stared at Twists-the-reeds with shining eyes.

At the same time, Sniffs-the-wind snorted. "Yeah right!" She didn't make eye contact with any of them as she propped the butt of her spear against the bank and pushed the raft out onto the lake.

Twists-the-reeds looked at her intently. "I'm deadly serious here. We can't afford to lose you."

"That's true," said The-tiny-one as if she had only just realised it. "We'd be lost without you."

Sniffs-the-wind looked into the eyes of the rest of her fist. They were hardly a fist, just a motley group of youngsters who didn't even get along well with each other. But they were looking to her for guidance and support. She was swept by a wave compassion and responsibility. Then she said, "Well then, you're all fucked!" Their laughter echoed across the lake.

The raft drifted slowly. The lake was deep. Water lapped over the edge and ran across their knees. The fist perched beneath the camouflaging branch, waiting while the gap between the ripples and raft slowly decreased. Sometimes the ripples moved away or disappeared entirely only to reappear in a slightly different place. The raft drifted, the ripples moved, and the fist waited patiently.

The light began to fade. The winter sun sank into a bank of clouds in the west. Sniffs-the-wind was thinking about calling them back when the ripples finally got close enough for them to cast the net. She nodded at Climbs-the-burrow and together they threw it out towards where the ripples danced. Twists-the-reeds held Climbs-the-burrow's shirt and The-tiny-one did the same to Sniffs-the-wind so neither of them would fall. The raft recoiled and Me-not-talking let out a squeal of terror as she tumbled into the water.

Several things happened at once. The net spread out into a perfect circle, the stones sinking beneath the water to trap the school of fish. Me-not-talking screamed and scrabbled at the edge of the raft. Twists-the-reeds strained to reach her while The-tiny-one tried to keep the raft from tipping.

The struggling fish pulled on the net and the raft lurched. Me-not-talking's wet hands could not hold on and her head disappeared beneath the water.

It took a moment for Climbs-the-burrow to realise what had happened but once realisation dawned, he didn't hesitate. He threw the rope he was holding to The-tiny-one and dived into the lake.

Me-not-talking's hands flailed the surface. Climbs-the-burrow reached her in several fast strokes. She grabbed at him, dragging his head beneath the water as she pulled herself to the surface.

Climbs-the-burrow ducked beneath her and swam away. "Don't grab at me!" he shouted.

Me-not-talking thrashed, screamed and sank.

Climbs-the-burrow came at her again, this time from behind. Diving down, he grabbed her around the neck with his left arm, wedging her chin in his elbow. He slipped his hip beneath her and with a strong kick, brought both of them to the surface.

As soon as her face was free of the water, Me-not-talking began screaming again.

Climbs-the-burrow wrenched her chin with his arm. "Stop struggling!" he barked.

Her screams became a whimper but she was still teetering on the edge of panic.

Suddenly, Climbs-the-burrow switched modes. He spoke soothingly. "It's alright. I've got you. Just relax."

Me-not-talking gasped and sputtered. "Don't... let me ... go."

"Shh... shh... It's alright. I won't let you go." Then his voice broke a little. "I'll never let you go."

From her place on the raft, The-tiny-one heard the exchange and something threatened to break from within her. She crushed it down fiercely and hauled on the rabbit hide, trying to drag the raft back to shore. Sniffs-the-wind helped her haul while Twists-the-reeds held onto the net. The water bubbled and surged with trapped fish.

Climbs-the-burrow brought Me-not-talking back to the shore. Once in the shallows, they crawled out of the water. Climbs-the-burrow moved slowly, breathing deeply and Me-not-talking scrambling desperately, gasping and crying. Once on dry land she grabbed at Climbs-the-burrow, buried her face in his chest and sobbed. He held her gently, stroking her wet, tangled hair.

The others brought the raft to shore. They stood in silence, staring at the couple as the fish wiggled and thrashed in the shallows.

After a while, Me-not-talking regained control and sat up. She wiped the wet hair away from her face and began to steady her breathing. "Thank you, Climbs," she said softly.

He let out a nervous laugh, as he gently stroked her face.

The-tiny-one's mouth twisted and she turned towards the net full of fish. She dragged the catch onto the bank and began sorting the fish. Twists-the-reeds and Sniffs-the-wind started to help and soon, Me-not-talking and Climbs-the-burrow joined in. The trauma passed, their relief erupted into celebration. There was laughing and shouting. They had made a decent catch and would return home, with their packs full of fish.

Sniffs-the-wind made sure the raft was safely beached. "Now G'ma can stop complaining about there being no meat in the stew," she said.

Twists-the-reeds hoisted his pack and laughed. "Don't worry. She'll find something else to complain about."

Climbs-the-burrow and Me-not-talking wrapped the net carefully, Me-not-talking listening intently as he described the best way to fold it.

The-tiny-one tested the knot she had tied around the wattle tree. She gave the hide a solid tug with both hands. The knot held fast but the little tree shook with the force. Its first blossoms fluttered to the ground gently dusting her head and shoulders with yellow pollen dust. The smell of wattle assaulted her senses and she was overwhelmed by a profound yearning. Her soul ached with an excruciating sense of emptiness. She wanted Croaks-with-the-frogs. In that instant, nothing else mattered.

It's getting worse as time goes on, not better

The sun had slipped behind the tea tree. Croaks-with-the-frogs sat on his own, sipping a nut of dandelion and watching G'pa and Sleeps-in-sun as they sat by the fire. The old man was speaking and Sleeps-in-sun was nodding, tears flowing from her eyes. After a while, G'pa fell silent and the young woman reached out her hand and held his. They sat together, Sleeps-in-sun weeping and G'pa staring straight ahead, his face set like stone.

After a while the tribe began to sing. Croaks-with-the-frogs threw the last of his dandelion into the dirt and headed back to his burrow. His strength was slowly returning but there was still a way to go.

Croaks-with-the-frogs curled himself into a ball and released the emotions swirling within him. He was deeply grateful for G'ma's tenderness, but at some level, he knew he didn't deserve it. If G'ma understood how much damage he had caused the tribe, she wouldn't be so kind. Sleeps-in-the-sun and Little-oaks were genuinely happy to see him and the child's gesture of giving him his resin ball moved him deeply. But no sooner had he thought of this, than his mind leapt to the tight smile of No-point-shoe. She did her best to be polite, but it was clear she wanted nothing more to do with him.

His mind skipped to The-tiny-one. In the darkness, he could see her face, smiling, bathed in radiant sunlight. Recently the ache in his heart which had tormented him throughout the last year had increased. *It's getting worse as time goes on, not better.* The swirling emotions gave way to tears and he cried himself to sleep.

He woke the next morning feeling physically stronger but emotionally weaker. He was alone in the burrow and he could hear the sounds of people moving about the fire outside. He had slept for a long time. His body felt rested, strong enough to perhaps return to his traps on the other side of the swamp. Without thinking, he threw off the rabbit pelt and pulled on his clothes. Then the memory of No-point-shoe struck him. He froze. He didn't want to face the tribe. He wanted to stay safe here in the semi-darkness. He wished The-tiny-one was near.

In a strange fantasy, he thought if she were here, none of the bad things would have happened. Fire-in-his-hair and Little-oaks would still be alive, No-point-shoe would still care for him, and all would be well. He berated himself for his stupidity. He destroyed everyone who came close to him. He would destroy The-tiny-one too.

He crawled out of the burrow and grabbed his spear and pack. He crossed the area between his burrow and the rocks around the fire quickly, picked up a freshly baked cake and headed towards the exit of the hive.

"A nut of Dandy?" said a familiar voice.

He looked around. G'ma was waving to him and smiling broadly. He stood for a moment staring at her then his shoulders slumped. He put down his pack and spear and went to the pile of communal gum-nuts to make a brew.

"Ah lovely!" exclaimed G'ma as he handed her the nut.

"Would you like one too, G'pa?"

The old man smiled and nodded.

Croaks-with-the-frogs returned to the pile and fetched another point of nuts for G'pa and himself.

"Ah?" said G'pa in surprise when he presented the steaming drink to him. "You made one for me?"

"Did you not want one?"

"No, that's fine. I'll drink it." He bowed his head formally. "Thank you, Croaks-with-the-frogs."

They sat together, sipping their drinks and staring into the fire.

"Were you off to hunt the cat, dear?" asked G'ma.

Croaks-with-the-frogs cringed. "Um.. No, G'ma... I... um..."

G'pa interrupted him. "Listen, when you've come back from hunting, we need to talk. The blue wattles are nearly budding and we need to get moving."

G'ma turned to him. "Yes. We are going to the river folk this year. Find you a wife."

A cold hand grasped Croaks-with-the-frogs' chest.

G'pa looked at her intently. "We're not going to the river folk, remember?"

She looked at him blankly. "Why?"

The muscles on G'pa's jaw tensed. "We've discussed this! We are too old. The others will handle the negotiations. We must follow the fire, remember?"

She did not remember.

He shook his head in frustration, then stared intently at Croaks-with-the-frogs. "Be back tomorrow," he ordered.

Croaks-with-the-frogs stared into his eyes. In spite of his wobbling head, the granite will was irresistible. The young man nodded.

G'ma began discussing the change of the seasons.

Neither man listened, each absorbed in their own thoughts.

Why are we doing this

Croaks-with-the-frogs spent the day wandering through the tea tree beyond the swamp, checking his traps. They were empty, long cleared out by scavengers. It was hard to tell if they had successfully caught anything.

He set up camp in his usual place, where he and The-tiny-one had stopped on their way to the pine forest. As he lay by his fire watching the sky darken, he thought of her and his heart ached. This part of the bush held her presence in a special way. He half expected at any moment to turn and see her pushing her way through the scrub, her face lit in a blazing smile.

The morning's conversation with G'pa and G'ma kept replaying in his head. *Going to the river folk to find a wife.* He would be expected to marry and the new G'pa and G'ma who would handle the negotiations this year would be very keen to send him to the river folk. He thought of Little-oaks, and his heart broke. He would miss the little spark terribly, but at least the child would still have Sleeps-in-the-sun, who had drawn closer to him since his sister was lost.

G'pa had implied there was another alternative. Something they needed to do tomorrow. Faint as it was, G'pa's 'alternative' was the only hope he had now. As he closed his eyes and faded into sleep, he resolved to trust the old man, even though every rational thought screamed against it.

He rose as the eastern sky was tinting red, packed up his camp and headed back to the hive. He found G'pa sharpening his spear by the fire. G'ma was still in the burrow. The old man was concentrating intently as he worked the edges with a rabbit tooth. Small flakes of stone lay around him and his finger bled where it had been cut. His hands were no longer steady.

Croaks-with-the-frogs sat beside him and watched him work. "Are you OK there, G'pa?" he said hesitantly.

The old man didn't look up. "Good. Get G'ma's spear from by the burrow. You can work on that."

G'ma's spear had not been used for very long time. Spiders had made webs between it and the burrow wall. The shaft was rotten and the head was blunt.

"This spear's no good, G'pa," said Croaks-with-the-frogs as he brought it back to the fire. "It needs a new shaft."

G'pa reached out and felt the shaft. His face twisted in distaste. For a moment, he seemed confused, then the muscle in his jaw tensed.

Croaks-with-the-frogs felt a surge of pity. "I have a spare. I could cut that down for G'ma."

"No. You'll need both. Cut my spare down. It's over there somewhere." He gestured with his rabbit tooth.

The sun slowly rose above the tea tree and shone down on the young man and the old as they sat beside each other, working on the spears.

"Why are we doing this, G'pa?"

G'pa kept his eyes focussed on the spear point. "G'ma and I are too old to go to the wattle fires. It's time for us to sell our lives to the enemy. You're coming with us."

Croaks-with-the-frogs stared at him in horror as the slow realisation dawned. The old couple were already struggling to get around the hive. If they did not go soon, they would be unable to make the trip and they would be forced to die in the burrow. The horror gave way to resignation. The young man, pressed his lips together tightly. He would go with them and fight at their side. They would all go down to-gether.

The spears were sharpened and ready when G'ma crawled out of the burrow. "Ah... A nut of dandy?"

G'pa frowned at her. "No! No time for any dandy now. You slept in."

G'ma smiled. "Yes. A nice nut, and then we'll go."

"We don't have time for dandy!" scolded G'pa. "People are already up and moving around, they'll see us go, and make a fuss."

"No," said G'ma gently like she was soothing a small child.

G'pa's eyes widened. He took a deep breath and steadied his voice. "Fine! We'll go tomorrow. But I'm going to wake you up!"

"Don't forget to get a nut for G'pa too, darling," she said to Croaks-with-the-frogs. "He gets mad when we he misses out."

Croaks-with-the-frogs sat with the old couple and watched the tribe moving about the fire. People went about their business. cooking, baking, and preparing for the journey to the river. No one was paying any attention to G'ma and G'pa. As they had aged and their minds had collapsed, the tribe seemed to have already discounted them.

G'ma chatted about the coming wattle season, reminiscing about dancing around the fire when she was young. No one was listening to her.

G'pa scowled into the fire and sipped his brew. "We can use this afternoon to pack for the journey," he said. "Tomorrow, we leave before dawn."

Bracken roots and wattle seeds

The Sun was approaching its zenith when Croaks-with-the-frogs found Sleeps-in-the-sun pegging out a rabbit hide to tan. The blood and brain matter nestled in a pot beside her. Little-oaks followed her around, wiggling each stake. "I'm helping," he said proudly.

"Good on you, Little-oaks," Croaks-with-the-frogs smiled. "You're a good helper."

The child beamed.

Sleeps-in-the-sun looked up at him. "Are you gonna help or just stand there blocking the sun?"

Croaks-with-the-frogs laughed and brought the pot of brains closer to the hide. They knelt, dipped their hands into the mix and slopped it onto the hide. Little-oaks laughed with joy as the goo squelched between his fingers.

"How is No-point-shoe?"

Sleeps-in-the-sun hesitated for just a moment. "She's fine. You know, resting and feeding."

Croaks-with-the-frogs' voice was sad. "That's good. That's very good."

"I think I'm going to go to the wattle fires this year, Croaks," she said.

"Oh... um... that's good."

"I mean... I don't know if I'll feel anything but maybe I should try."

"I'm really glad." Croaks-with-the-frogs paused for a moment then, "I won't be going with you, Sleeps-in-the-sun."

Sleeps-in-the-sun stopped smearing. "Yeah," she said, sadly. "G'pa told me."

Croaks-with-the-frogs wasn't listening. "G'ma and G'pa are too old to go. They are going to sell their lives to the enemy, and they've asked me to go with them."

Sleeps-in-the-sun stared at the young man, her head cocked quizzically.

Little-oaks continued to daub the brains. "We smearing?"

Croaks-with-the-frogs looked at his bloody hands. "I just can't marry someone from the river tribe, Sleeps. I can't live without The-tiny-one." His voice broke and a tear trickled down his cheek.

Sleeps-in-the-sun nodded slowly and reached out to him. The brains sullied the side of his face, where her hand gently brushed his cheek. "Of course, little spark. I knew it would come to this eventually."

Croaks-with-the-frogs brushed away his tears and concentrated on plastering the brains over the hide.

She continued too. "We're all going to miss you."

He laughed bitterly and shook his head.

"Well... OK. Me and Little-oaks will miss you."

"No-point-shoe won't."

Sleeps-in-the-sun stopped and looked at him keenly. "She's mad at you now. But she'll get over it. You've made a big difference to our lives, Croaks-with-the-frogs. Don't forget us."

The young mad laughed sadly. "Not likely. But I'd like to be remembered."

"Of course," said Sleeps-in-sun, "We'll never forget you."

They finished covering the rabbit pelt with brains then went down to the swamp to wash their hands.

Little-oaks was excited to be taken on an adventure beyond the hive. "Girl here?" he asked hopefully as they knelt amongst the reeds.

"No, boy," said Sleeps-in-the-sun sadly. "She's not here."

The child began to cry. "Where's my girl?"

Croaks-with-the-frogs took him in his arms and held him close.

Sleeps-in-the-sun stroked the boy's face. "Losing Listens-for-ducks was nearly as bad as Finder-of-snails," she said.

They sat for a moment together silently sharing their individual griefs. Then Croaks-with-the-frogs pushed himself to his feet. "I need to show you something," His mouth formed a tight line. "It's important. You need to know about my traps."

The sun was was settling into the tea tree when Croaks-with-the-frogs, Sleeps-in-the-sun and Little-oaks returned to the hive. Sleeps-in-the-sun had been amazed at the traps the young man had scattered across the other side of the swamp and had promised to continue to work on perfecting them. "We should try insects," she said. "That would attract birds. Maybe ducks."

The young man felt a bitter-sweet tang. He was glad something of him would continue after he had returned to the fire.

As they entered the hive, Sleeps-in-the-sun put her arm around his shoulders and gave him a tight squeeze. "We will always remember you, boy," she said, then headed off to get No-point-shoe a bowl of stew.

Croaks-with-the-frogs was a bit disappointed. He had hoped Sleeps-in-the-sun would at least try to convince him that his life was worth living. She had accepted his decision with sadness but no resistance. He breathed deeply. "She knows," he thought. "There is no future for me."

G'ma and G'pa were packing. G'pa had collected his tools and a few cakes. G'ma had filled her back pack with bracken roots and wattle seeds. Croaks-with-the-frogs smiled inwardly. *Poor G'ma. She's probably already forgotten why we are going.*

"Pack your bag," ordered G'pa. "We leave before dawn."

Croaks-with-the-frogs would travel light. He packed his usual tools, and a few cakes. He laid out a coal carrier beside his pair of spears.

He wasn't sure how this was all going to play out but he wouldn't go into the fight without fire. He would take down as many of the enemy as he could before the end.

~ 15 ~

A LIFE TO MAKE US PROUD

Follow G'pa wherever he leads

It was still dark when G'pa shook him awake. "Come on, boy. Time to go."

G'ma was up and moving about the fire.

Croaks-with-the-frogs crawled outside and wrapped a coal in his carrier. G'pa hoisted his pack and watched him preparing the coal. The corners of the old man's mouth turned up slightly and he nodded his head in approval. Croaks-with-the-frogs smiled with pride. Beyond the ancient, worn out body, he could see the strength of the old man and understood why he was once a great leader.

The eastern sky glowed with a faint light as they set out. G'pa leading and Croaks-with-the-frogs at the rear. The old ones didn't look back but Croaks-with-the-frogs stopped at the entrance to take one last look at the hive. Sleeps-in-the-sun was standing by her burrow, silhouetted by the fire. She raised her hand and waved. He waved back then turned to the bush.

G'pa led them south along the trail that Croaks-with-the-frogs and The-tiny-one had taken on their journey to the pine forest. The going was slow because G'ma was struggling with her pack. "Let me carry it for you, G'ma," said Croaks-with-the-frogs.

"No, darling" she said with a soft groan. "I'll be fine."

"Let him carry your pack," G'pa barked. "You're slowing us down."

"Leave me alone," snapped G'ma. "I'm not slowing anybody down."

They followed the trail south and passed the turn off to the other side of the swamp. Croaks-with-the-frogs paused there, remembering The-tiny-one, *"This is the way to my hive," she had said.*

They pushed on until the sun was clear of the tea tree. Then G'ma finally relented and gave her pack to G'pa.

"I can take it, G'pa," said Croaks-with-the-frogs.

The old man hesitated, then with a sad smile, he handed over the pack and continued walking. He staggered a bit as he restarted but he soon regained his rhythm.

They reached the edge of the tea tree by the middle of the day. Pale clouds stretched over them and darkened as they spread into the west. G'pa called a halt and sank slowly to his knees, his head bowed.

G'ma looked at him like a bird hunting a worm. "What are you doing?"

"Just give me moment," he said softly. "I'll be alright."

She frowned. "I think you've overdone it."

G'pa ignored her and turned to Croaks-with-the-frogs. "Set a fire here, boy. We'll eat something and rest a bit."

Croaks-with-the-frogs collected some fuel and used his coal to start a small blaze.

G'ma unpacked a pair of cakes from G'pa's pack and lay them on pieces of bark near the fire to warm.

G'pa sat with his back resting against a tea tree and closed his eyes.

Croaks-with-the-frogs stoked the fire and looked around. Most of his scouting had been done around the swamp and the Pine forest. The rabbit warrens and the grasslands were east of the hive. He had never been south before. Looking out from the eaves of the tea tree, he could see to his right, Eucalypts, Wattles and smaller scrubby bush that formed a thick wall. Ahead of him, the bush gradually thinned, scarred and blackened by fire until it turned into the open grassy plains that stretched away to his left. *We tracked the dogs through there.*

G'ma sniffed at a cake. "They're not very warm."

"Never mind," said G'pa, gently. "They'll be ok, darling."

She chewed her lip, thoughtfully.

"Do you want me to build up the fire some more, G'ma?"

"No, no," she said quickly. "They'll warm up soon enough."

G'pa got up from where he was resting and came over to her. As he knelt beside her, he let out a soft groan. He stroked the top of her head gently, running his fingers through her thin, grey hair. "I don't need it warm, darling."

She looked at him and for a moment they stared into each other's eyes sharing an exclusive, silent communion.

After a little while, she took a cake, broke it into a few pieces and shared them out between herself, Croaks-with-the-frogs and G'pa. They ate in silence. Once they had finished, G'ma took the other cake and broke it into a pair. She gave the larger piece to Croaks-with-the-frogs and the smaller piece to G'pa.

"What about you, G'ma?"

"I've had enough, dear. You eat."

They rested until the fire began to die, then G'pa said, "Wrap another coal, boy. We need to make a start."

As Croaks-with-the-frogs wrapped the new coal, he wondered where they were going. G'pa seemed to have a very clear idea of his destination and he was keen to reach there before some deadline. Not fully knowing what the plan was, unsettled the young man, but G'ma was content to follow along. It reminded him how he used to blindly trust Fire-in-his-hair to lead him. He felt a pang of sadness as he remembered the days trusting his lost friend.

Croaks-with-the-frogs hoisted his pack and the coal onto his back. He took a deep breath and resolved to blindly trust once again. In this, his last journey, he would follow G'pa wherever he led and proudly stand at his side when the end came.

They walked on heading south, skirting the thicker bush with the grasslands stretching away to their left. G'pa was walking slower now, and every now and then, the old man would stagger a bit, as if he was losing his balance. Croaks-with-the-frogs tried not to notice. He scanned the sky for eagles, and the bush for cats and foxes. The enemy could come from anywhere.

Above them, the clouds darkened and light rain began to fall.

G'ma shivered. "I should have brought my hat," she muttered.

G'pa emitted an annoyed clucking sound. "Why didn't you bring your hat?"

"I forgot."

He stopped walking and fished in his back pack.

"Why have we stopped?" G'ma scolded.

G'pa ignored her and pulled his hat from his pack. "Here."

"No!"

"Take my hat."

"No! You wear it!"

The muscle along G'pa's jaw, tensed. "There's no point both of us getting wet. Take the ashen hat!"

"I don't want your hat!"

Their eyes locked. Rain began to soak into their hair. Croaks-with-the-frogs stared at a thin rivulets of water running down G'ma's neck.

"Fine!" G'pa threw the hat angrily onto the ground and set off walking again.

G'ma's eyes blazed at his retreating back. Then she picked up the hat and angrily squashed it down over her head.

"It doesn't fit," she grumbled.

The fire doesn't burn for itself

By late afternoon, the rain had eased. The sky had cleared and the bushland to their right cast long shadows across their path. Finally, G'pa slowed his pace. He took a few more steps, before turning right and heading into the bush, searching amongst the trees. Then he stopped and looked around. "Here," he said with a sly smile. "This is the place."

Croaks-with-the-frogs lay a fire using twigs and leaves that had been partially sheltered from the rain by the canopy. They were still damp and the fire took a long time to catch, but soon it was burning steadily.

G'ma collapsed onto the ground and lay with her head resting on her pack.

G'pa put a few twigs on the fire at first but eventually he too lay with his head resting on Croaks-with-the-frogs' pack. Soon, both of them were fast asleep.

Croaks-with-the-frogs gathered more wood and lay it close to the fire to dry. He then stripped some bark from nearby trees and lay a pair of cakes by the fire to warm. The sun disappeared into the trees and the forest descended into twilight.

By the time G'ma and G'ma woke, the fire was blazing well and the cakes were warm.

G'ma shared out the cakes, the same way she had done before. Croaks-with-the-frogs had also gathered some branches with wet leaves and they sucked the water from them to moisten their lips.

The night was overcast but not cold. G'pa sat by the fire with his back resting against his pack, staring into the flames. He looked across at G'ma as she sucked water from the last of the leaves. "Do you remember this place?" he said.

"No."

He laughed. "It's on the way to the lake hive."

"Where?"

"The lake hive. The hive where the Lake tribe live!"

"Ah yes." Mildly. She clearly wasn't following the significance.

G'pa laughed again and shook his head. "We've walked nearly a full day. But we're not at the night camp." He looked at her expectantly, his head wobbling. It was as if he was giving her clues.

G'ma squinted.

"The night camp is about a good sprint that way." He gestured towards the south.

"Ah!" G'ma started laughing. "A good sprint."

"A very good sprint."

They both started laughing, eyes only for each other.

Croaks-with-the-frogs had no idea what they were laughing about.

G'ma saw his confusion and smiled at him. "This is the place we first merged our fires," she said.

"Here!?"

"Yeah." She laughed and her eyes glinted in the fire light.

G'pa began the story. "We were all going to the Lake tribe for the wattle fires."

"The whole tribe." G'ma added in details as he went.

"There's a camp site a bit further on where the tribes can camp you know?"

"Camp overnight. There's a fireplace there and all."

"We were not married then so we were both supposed to marry into the Lake tribe."

"My husband had died a few years earlier."

G'pa laughed again. "But we had other ideas."

"I was from the River folk."

"We were collecting wood and wandered away from the rest of the fist."

"Ha!" G'ma mocked. "Wandered away! You lured me here!"

G'pa cocked his head smugly. "You weren't reluctant."

"So we lit a fire here and had a good time. A good sprint from the night camp."

G'pa laughed. "A very good sprint."

G'ma's voice carried a hint of embarrassment. "They all heard my wattle call too."

"That became the joke, then. The very good sprint."

She looked at his face and her eyes shone. For a moment they were the only ones at the fire. Croaks-with-the-frogs could almost see the young man and woman staring into each other's eyes. It made his heart yearn for The-tiny-one and he bit down on his feelings and stared into the flames.

G'ma lay down again with her head resting on G'pa's lap.

The old man stroked her hair. "Are you warm enough?" he asked.

"I'm cold."

He pulled his rabbit pelt from his pack and covered her in it.

She reached up and touched the side of his cheek with her hand.

"Sleep now, darling," he said, softly.

G'ma smiled gratefully and closed her eyes.

G'ma's gentle snoring and the fire crackling were the only sounds they could hear as they sat staring into the flames.

G'pa stroked the side of her head, running his fingers through her hair and staring down at her. "A good woman is a rare find, boy," he said softly. "There are not many men who are lucky enough to find a good one."

Croaks-with-the-frogs' insides heaved in agony.

G'pa kept talking, "You can marry many women and live reasonably happily with them, but sometimes you find the girl that was made for you. When that happens, you've got to take care of her." He paused for a moment, still staring at G'ma's face. Then his voice broke. "And never forget to be grateful for every day you share."

Croaks-with-the-frogs' tears flowed. The old man's rambling was tearing him apart.

He lapsed into silence again. Somewhere in the distance, a possum roared.

G'pa looked up from G'ma's face. "Tomorrow is the day, Croaks. Tomorrow you find out what sort of a man you are."

Croaks-with-the-frogs stared at him.

"The fire doesn't burn for itself. It burns to keep the tribe warm and safe. You must burn for your tribe." He paused for a moment and his head wobbled as he thought. "You will lose. We all eventually lose. Life is a long defeat, boy." He gestured towards the wood slowly being consumed in the flames. "But just like the wood sacrifices itself in the fire to keep us warm. You must sacrifice yourself in the fire for your tribe."

Croaks-with-the-frogs nodded. He was afraid of what tomorrow would bring, but he would stand beside these wonderful old people until the end. He would gladly lay down his life for them.

G'pa stared at him in silence for a long moment and said, "You're a fine young man, Croaks-with-the-frogs. I'm very proud of you." He flashed a confident smile. "You won't let us down."

"I promise you, G'pa," Croaks-with-the-frogs' voice cracked as his tears flowed. "I won't let you down."

The old man smiled, sadly and nodded. "Let's get some sleep, boy. Tomorrow will be a big day."

Were you not listening!?

Croaks-with-the-frogs slept fitfully. He woke often to add more wood to the fire and each time he did, it took longer to fall back asleep. Eventually he heard the morning birdsong and decided he would stay up to watch the sunrise.

In the pale morning light, G'ma stretched herself awake and looked around. Her face was filled with confusion. Her eyes fell upon G'pa sleeping at her side and she frowned. "What are we doing here?"

Croaks-with-the-frogs spoke softly. "Don't wake him, G'ma."

She didn't hear. She shook the old man by the shoulder. "Hey! Maggies, what have you done?"

The old man groaned and rolled over.

"G'ma," Croaks-with-the-frogs raised his voice. "We have come out here to sell our lives to the enemy."

G'ma stared at him. A puzzled expression on her face. "Are you sure?"

"Yes, G'ma. Let him sleep for now."

She frowned at Croaks-with-the-frogs then turned her attention to G'pa. "I don't think that's right," she said, but there was no confidence in her voice.

After a moment, she got up and laid another pair of cakes by the fire. Croaks-with-the-frogs took his spear and went into the bush to gather some more wood. By the time he had returned, G'pa was awake and the old couple were sitting close to each other in intimate conversation.

"I've brought some wet leaves too," said Croaks-with-the-frogs. "It's not dandy but...,"

"Ah lovely," said G'ma smiling.

After they had shared the bread and sucked on the leaves, G'ma said, "These leaves are lovely. I don't know why we bother with dandy."

G'pa ignored her. "Well, boy," he said with a resigned air. "It's time."

Croaks-with-the-frogs stared at him. He really didn't have any idea how this was going to play out. Would they walk out into the bush or wait until the wood ran out. He had heard of selling you life to the enemy, but nobody had ever talked about how to do it. He looked from face to face, uncertain. G'ma was smiling at him and G'pa was nodding.

"Are you ready?" asked G'pa.

"Um... I'm not sure what to do."

"It's time to go." G'pa said nodding his head.

"Without you?"

G'ma laughed.

G'pa frowned. "Yes. Of course."

Fear clutched at Croaks-with-the-frogs. He didn't want to sell his life to the enemy alone. "But I thought we were going to do it together."

"Do what?"

"Sell our lives to the enemy."

G'ma tilted her head to one side and let out a compassionate simper. "Oh isn't he sweet."

G'pa sputtered. "What!?"

Had the old couple forgotten? "We were going to sell our lives to the enemy."

"We!?" G'pa's face turned red. A vein pulsed at his temple and he tried to get to his feet. He lost his balance, and staggered back to the ground. "You!? ... Mad!?" The old man struggled for control, hands and knees on the ground.

G'ma reached out her hand and rested it on his back.

The action seemed to calm G'pa enough for him to start talking. "Have you not been listening to anything I've said!?" He pushed himself back and sat on his heels. "You're not going to sell your life to the enemy, you miserable old coot! You are going to go to the lake tribe and get your girl!"

Croaks-with-the-frogs stared at him in shock.

G'pa held his head in his hands. "Were you not listening to me!?"

"I think he may have been asleep," said G'ma gently.

G'pa took a deep breath. "G'ma and I are too old." He spoke slowly, articulating each word as if he were explaining things to someone who had trouble hearing. "We are staying here to sell our lives to the enemy. You..." he pointed his finger at him angrily. "...are going to the lake to get your girl and live a life that would make us proud."

Croaks-with-the-frogs could barely speak. "But they don't want me. The lake tribe hate me."

"So!?" G'pa voice was full of scorn. "You don't listen," he scolded. "Today is the day you fight for your life. Go get your girl." He paused and his teeth clenched in ferocity. "...And kill anything that tries to stop you!"

Croaks-with-the-frogs blinked.

G'pa turned to G'ma. He had regained enough control of his emotions to start giving orders, but his rage was still simmering below the surface. "Did you pack those bracken roots and wattle seeds?"

G'ma looked at him blankly.

G'pa's anger erupted again. "I told you to pack Wattle seeds and bracken roots for the boy!"

G'ma's eyes widened. "You never told me that!"

"I told you!"

"You did not!" G'ma raged.

Croaks-with-the-frogs waved his hands as if trying to put out a fire. "She packed them. She packed them." He gestured towards the back pack.

G'pa exhaled and his anger began to subside.

G'ma stared at the back pack in confusion but said nothing.

"Right," said the old man putting his emotions into order. "There's your pack. Here take my tools. I've got a good hammer stone in there and a few nice teeth. Take G'ma's pelt as well."

Croaks-with-the-frogs looked around helplessly. "But where will she sleep?"

G'ma tossed her head coquettishly. "We can share."

Croaks-with-the-frogs collected the things in a daze. He wrapped a coal, hoisted the pack bulging with roots and seeds and tied both pelts around his waist. His back was fully laden. He stood beside the fire and stared at the old couple who had also pushed themselves to their feet. "Will you be alright?" he asked.

"We'll be fine," said G'pa.

G'ma smiled and picked up her spear. She crouched as if ready to fight, forcing a ferocious expression on her face but her smile was still evident. "I'm ready for them," she said cheerfully.

"Mind that spear point," G'pa snapped. Then to Croaks-with-the-frogs, "Head south, you'll come to the night camp, the path is well worn and you'll find the lake tribe easy enough. Keep the lake on your left."

Emotions swirled in Croaks-with-the-frogs. He was leaving them and he'd never see them again. He was also frightened of what he would face at the Lake hive. Part of him wished he could stay and sell his life with G'ma and G'pa. That would certainly be the easier path. He hesitated.

G'pa locked his eyes in a commanding stare. "Go, boy," he said firmly. "Today you find out what sort of a man you are."

"I'll never forget you," said Croaks-with-the-frogs heavily and threw his arms around the old man.

G'ma embraced him too and they all shared a long hug. Croaks-with-the-frogs could feel the old man's breath catching in is chest and he heard G'ma's soft sniffles as she cried.

Eventually, G'pa pulled away, his face red and breathing ragged. "You've got to go," he said. "You need to get to the hive and then far away before dark."

Croaks-with-the-frogs brushed his tears away but more came.

"Go fast," G'pa said. "Go now!"

As the young man turned and disappeared into the bush, G'ma suddenly sucked in air between clenched teeth. "Oh

Ash! I forgot. I should have asked him to check for any berries along the way."

G'pa turned to her, an incredulous look on his face. "It's not Berry season."

"Yes, but just to check...."

A mad woman's quest

Croaks-with-the-frogs pushed his way through the scrub, his scouting instincts in command. He scanned the sky and nearby bush for threats, kept his spear pointed ahead and his body crouched. Behind him, G'ma and G'pa were preparing for their last battle but he would not be there for them. He wished he could have stayed with them. It was less frightening to face the enemy. At least he knew what to expect. A fight to the death with an implacable foe.

His path was leading him into the unknown and the uncertainty terrified him. What would he find when he arrived at the lake hive? Would The-tiny-one even remember him? Would she still want to be his wife? It had been nearly a year. What would the elders of that tribe say? Would they welcome him? Would they try to drive him away? Maybe, he was too late and they had already left the hive for their wattle fires.

The whole plan seemed crazy. He was racing south on the word of an old couple who had obviously lost their capacity to think clearly. It was a mad man's quest, but he didn't know who the mad man was. Was if G'pa or was it himself. Or perhaps it was a mad woman's quest, driven by some now forgotten *seeing* by G'ma.

He passed the night camp and saw the trail south. It was clear and easy to follow just as G'pa had told him. The reliability of G'pa's advice, gave him some hope. A day's journey for a fully laden tribe with children and old ones could be covered in a point of naps by a fit young spear in a hurry. He pushed his fears and doubts away, and raced on.

The lake hive was bustling. Bags were packed with pelts, food for the journey and avocados to give to the hosts. Extra wood, and bracken roots were gathered for those who were staying behind. The older members of the tribe were staying with the nursing mothers and their husbands. The older children were excited at the prospect of the great wattle journey and they squealed as they ran around the fire.

Twists-the-reeds found Sniffs-the-wind and The-tiny-one sitting together. Both women had drawn their knees up to their chests and wedged themselves into the tight space between their sleeping burrow and the burrow next door. They stared at their feet, staying nothing.

"Hey, guys," he said hesitantly. "You ready to go?"

Sniffs-the-wind didn't respond. Her hair fell forward, covering her face and her arms hugged her knees tightly.

The-tiny-one looked up, her eyes were red rimmed and bloodshot. Her face was pale. She breathed raggedly. She stared at Twists-the-reeds, her mouth open as if she were trying to find something to say, but no words came.

Twists-the-reeds didn't need her to speak. He knew she was feeling the loss of Croaks-with-the-frogs more keenly as the wattle season developed. Many of the early wattles were in flower now and The-tiny-one was in agony. He wished there was something he could say or do to help her, but he had nothing.

Sniffs-the-wind was a different case. Ever since G'ma told her she would be expected to marry this wattle, she had been beset by a slow sadness. Recently she had been the last one to leave the burrow each morning and often she would spend whole days sitting by the fire, staring into the flames. When supplies needed to be gathered or some preparations needed to be taken for the Wattle journey, Sniffs-the-wind often found herself paralysed by fear and indecision.

The-tiny-one wasn't much better. Twists-the-reeds often heard her whimpering in the night. The usual anger that simmered beneath the surface seemed to have evaporated as the wattle season drew closer. It left only a profound sadness. She was drawn to Sniffs-the-wind and the two women began spending more time together. They were making each other worse.

Now he stood staring at them, with absolutely no idea what to do. All of his attempts to distract or cheer had failed. His heart broke for them, but he could see no remedy for their wounds. He didn't even understand what their wounds were.

Twists-the-reeds heard a commotion behind him from the other side of the fire and turned. What he saw, caused his mouth to fall open in shock. At the entrance to the hive stood a young spear. He was clearly from another tribe, but Twists-the-reeds had no idea where he came from. The young man wore dark green trousers and a pale green shirt. His hair and beard were dark and curly. He was nearly fully grown, but not yet filled out to his full stature. An angry red scar snaked down the left side of his face. He stood with his spear planted in the ground and his feet apart as if in challenge. He oozed a simmering hostility and he looked into the hive like he was staring into the face of the enemy.

"I am Croaks-with-the-frogs!" The young man called. "I seek the shelter of your fire."

A life to make us proud

This was the traditional way a visiting spear would seek entrance to a hive but the young man's tone was challenging and defiant. Twists-the-reeds noticed he did not identify his tribe.

The lake tribe reacted to his tone rather than his request. Some of the younger ones grabbed for their spears and all eyes were trained on the visiting stranger.

Jumps-in-the-water waved the younger spears away. He walked to the entrance of the hive, carefully, like he was approaching a creature that might be dangerous. His face was calm and his hand was up palm facing outwards. "The fire protects us all," he intoned, but behind his words was a wariness. He stood, blocking the entrance to the hive. "You did not identify your tribe, stranger."

The young man spoke through gritted teeth. "I am Croaks-with-the-frogs. I have no tribe."

In a moment of clarity, Twists-the-reeds realised who the young man was. He had changed so much in the last year that Twists-the-reeds had not been able to connect the name.

The-tiny-one remained in her position, staring at her feet, oblivious to the exchange on the far side of the fire.

Twists-the-reeds turned and kicked her sharply. "Get up!" he whispered fiercely. "It's Croaks-with-the-frogs."

The girl scowled at him. "Yes! Alright?! I'm missing Croaks-with-the-frogs."

"No! It's Croaks-with-the-frogs... He's here!" Twists-the-reeds didn't wait for The-tiny-one to move, he whirled around and ran towards the entrance.

From her place beside the fire, Rolls-in-the-berries watched the exchange at the entrance to the hive. She pushed herself to her feet and walked over to stand beside Jumps-in-the-water. "We are preparing to leave for the wattle fires, young man," she said stiffly. "We leave in the morning."

Croaks-with-the-frogs' eyes locked onto the woman and his hostility was undisguised. "I am not interested in your Wattle journey. I have come for The-tiny-one!"

Rolls-in-the-berries's mouth tightened. "The-tiny-one is a woman of this tribe, under my protection. She is not a pelt to be taken by the likes of you." She shot a warning glance at Jumps-in-the-water and he moved quickly to get his spear.

When the rest of the tribe saw Jumps-in-the-water grabbing his spear they responded. The hive suddenly bristled with spears pointing at the stranger.

Croaks-with-the-frogs levelled his spear as well, and crouched into fighting position.

Twists-the-reeds was appalled. Generations of breeding had created an ingrained revulsion of human versus human conflict. All humans shared a common enemy. Any sort of violence between humans was abhorrent, but to use a spear against a fellow human was unthinkable.

Croaks-with-the-frogs' aggressive stance had shocked the Lake tribe's hunters. Their spears wavered as they looked at each other in confusion and looked to Jumps-in-the-water as the lead hunter for guidance.

Jumps-in-the-water put his hand up again. "Steady on, *brudha*," he said warily. "We only have one enemy."

Croaks-with-the-frogs ignored him. His eyes locked onto Rolls-in-the-berries.

Suddenly, The-tiny-one broke through the group of spears. Her face was red and tears filled her eyes. "Croaks-with-the-frogs!"

The young man looked at her. His voice broke. "Come with me," he said.

Rolls-in-the-berries inhaled sharply. "She's not going with you. She is a woman of our tribe."

The-tiny-one stood frozen to the spot. She couldn't believe he was actually standing there. Part of her wondered if this was some strange dream.

Rolls-in-the-berries saw the girl frozen in shock and smiled faintly. She turned to Jumps-in-the-water. "Take The-tiny-one back to her burrow," she ordered.

Jumps-in-the-water hesitantly reached out to take The-tiny-one's arm but the girl twitched violently, pulling away.

"No!" she screamed. "G'ma, please! It's Croaks-with-the-frogs. Let him stay!"

"He can visit at our fire, girl, but he is not taking you with him. Look at him! He's got no tribe, he looks like one of the enemy. He's cursed! He cannot stay here."

Croaks-with-the-frogs laughed savagely. "I have no interest in staying at your hive, old woman. I have come to get my wife, and then I will leave." He turned to The-tiny-one, his eyes pleading. "Come with me."

The-tiny-one turned and ran back to her burrow. As she ran she could hear her G'ma arguing and ordering her spears to protect the hive. No one moved. She hurriedly stuffed her tools into her pack. Then she remembered the little stash she had secreted beneath her pelt. She put the resin ball into her pack, rolled her pelt and lashed it to her waist. As she did so, her hand touched the yellow root the Swamp folk's G'ma had given her. A flash of memory erupted in her mind with such clarity that for an instant, The-tiny-one felt it was really happening.

Keep this safe until you are carrying your litter in your womb.

She shoved the root into her pack and crawled out of the burrow, grabbing her spear on the way out.

By now, Sniffs-the-wind had crawled out from her place between the burrows. She stood in stunned amazement. The-tiny-one put her hand on her friend's shoulder. "I've got to go, Sniffs," she said. "I can't live without him."

Sniffs-the-wind nodded dumbly.

The-tiny-one turned and headed towards the entrance. She saw Twists-the-reeds watching her. A sad smile on his face.

"Come with us," she said. She tossed her head over her shoulder towards Sniffs-the-wind "We can all go."

"I can't," he said sadly. The young man looked past her at Sniffs-the-wind standing forlornly beside the burrow. "My place is here," he said.

Rolls-in-the-berries saw what was happening and her heart raced. She was about to lose the whole future of the tribe. Everything she had strived for was turning to ash. She could not let The-tiny-one leave. "Stop her!" she commanded.

Once more, Jumps-in-the-water reached out to take The-tiny-one by the arm. But the girl suddenly crouched and hefted her spear. "Back off, bunny!" she snapped.

Twists-the-reeds smiled. Her old fire was back.

The others in the tribe were aghast. Violence against another human was taboo, but there was no coming back from threatening a member of your own tribe.

Croaks-with-the-frogs stared at her in awe. *What a woman!*

Rolls-in-the-berries couldn't keep the panic out of her voice. "Stop her! He's cursed and he's controlling her. Stop her!"

Croaks-with-the-frogs took a step into the hive. He pointed his spear at Rolls-in-the-berries' chest, and lowered his voice. The side of his mouth twisted into a wicked grin. "If anyone touches my wife... I'll. Kill. You."

Rolls-in-the-berries froze in terror. The spears hesitated, unsure of whether to defend their G'ma or obey her orders. Their ingrained conditioning against violence paralysed them.

The-tiny-one slipped through them easily and stood beside Croaks-with-the-frogs. She looked at him and grinned. "Where we going, boy?" she said softly.

Croaks-with-the-frogs hesitated. He hadn't thought beyond getting her out.

The-tiny-one laughed. "Come on," she said and ran into the bush.

She led him away from the lake and into the east. As they ran, Croaks-with-the-frogs looked behind him to see if they were being followed but there was no sign of pursuit. The tribe had backed off.

"Go and get your girl," G'pa had said "And live a life that would make us proud."

He felt a surge of gratitude towards the old man then he thought of G'ma, Little-Oaks, Fire-his-hair and all those he had loved and lost. *I will live a life to make you all proud.*

APPENDICES

Island Dwarfism

This story is set approximately 200,000 years in the future. The climate system has flipped and then re-stabilised at 4 degrees Celsius warmer than the Holocene average. In Australia, the central deserts have expanded and the sea level has risen, cutting the south east corner of the continent off from the rest of the world.

The disruption caused by the flipping has caused *Homo sapiens* and their domesticated animals to become extinct. Only those species that were able to survive in feral form have continued to reproduce. Humans, have undergone a process called Island dwarfism or Insular dwarfism. This is the process whereby a large animal reduces in size over many generations.

A reduction on habitable territory means a smaller food supply. As food supply and population declines, only smaller animals survive because they need fewer resources. Smaller size is also advantageous from a reproductive standpoint, as it leads to shorter gestation periods and generation times.

See: Foster J.B. 1964. The evolution of mammals on islands. *Nature.* **202**

The life cycle of *Homo angustus*

Like Homo sapiens, Homo angustus require about a third of their life to mature, a third of their life is fertile and third spent in old age.

Stage of life	Age in years	Comments	Examples
Baby	1		
Weaned	2	First few years are very similar to *sapiens*	
Childhood	From 3 to 9	*H.angustus* mature quicker than *sapiens*	
Young Spear	10	Early adolescence	Twists-the-reeds when he was stuck in the rabbit burrow
Coloured Clothes	11	Late adolescence (cultural construct)	Croaks-with-the-frogs and The-tiny-one in the pine forest
Marriage	12	Adulthood	Me-not-talking when she married Climbs-the-burrow
First Child	13		Fire-in-his-hair when he found the toddler, Croaks-with-frogs
Fertile Years	From 12 to 25	*H.angustus* are fertile for a third of their life	No-point-shoe was 20 when she married Fire-in-his-hair
Menopause	Between 24 & 26	The timing varies between individuals	Hunter-of-flies and Runs-like-a-rabbit are in this age group
Old Age	From 27 to 40	Old age enables cultural development	Rolls-in-the-berries is in her mid thirties. G'ma and G'pa are in their late thirties.

Seasons

The people do not have a strict calendar. The shift from season to season is vague.

Season	Description	Julian Calendar	Duration
Winter	Children born	June and July	8–10 weeks
Wattle	Adults become fertile	August and September	8–10 weeks
Harvest	Rainy, extra bracken roots dug	October and early November	6–8 weeks
Fire	Controlled burning around hives	Late November and December	6–8 weeks
Smoke	Very hot. Storms and bush fires	January, February, early March	8–10 weeks
Berry	Blackberries fruit	Late March, April and May	8–10 weeks

Distance measurement

The People's term	Description	Approximate metric equivalent
Fingertip	Length of an adult's distal phalange	1/3 of a cm
Span	A span of an adult's hand	5 cm
Pace	A pace of an adult	25 cm
Length	The height of an adult	50 cm
Stone's throw	The distance an adult can throw a stone accurately	6 metres
Good stone's throw	The furthest distance an adult can throw	12 metres
Sprint	The distance an adult can run in a short time	25 metres
A Good sprint	The distance an adult can sprint before stopping	50 metres
Scout	Half the distance an adult can walk during a sleep cycle (nap)	700 metres
Journey	The distance a tribe can walk during a day	3 km

Number system

The people count on their fingers. They have no number beyond a fist of fists

The people's numeral	Arabic numeral	The people's numeral	Arabic numeral
Thumb	1	Fist-point	7
Point	2	Fist-tall	8
Tall	3	Point of fists	10
Finger	4	Tall of fists	15
Fist	5	Finger of fists	20
Fist-thumb	6	Fist of fists	25

Terminology

Banksia syrup
A sweet drink made from the flowers of a banksia tree. *The people* would soak the flowers in water for a day, then remove the flower and boil the water to a concentrate.

Brudha
Literally "from *the same brood.*" A non-gendered term of companionship. Often shortened to *Brudh.*

Climate
H. angustus live in a world 4 degrees hotter than the Holocene. South Eastern Australia is in permanent El Nino. Due to their small size, *angustus* are sensitive to cold so even in the hottest time of the year, *the people* keep their furs on and their fires burning.

Dandy
The root of a dandelion plant can be roasted and ground. When mixed with boiling water, it becomes a hearty drink.

Fire
Without fire, *H. angustus* would have no protection from predators. Maintaining the fire in the centre of the hive is *the people's* primary concern. They have only one word for Fire, Love and God.

Fuck

Translated from *Sha'ark.* A strong expletive meaning to have sex with animals. Never sex between humans which is *Die-thum* (merging fires).

Nap

H. angustus sleep in cycles. A typical sleep cycle is 90 minutes. This is *the people's* primary unit of time measurement. They call it a "nap."

Pargront

A small piece of animal dung. Used as a slur.

The Windy trap

Croaks-with-the-frogs' windy trap is actually a Spanish windlass. This can be used to hunt small game.

Wattle Toddy

When the bark of a certain wattle tree is boiled with turmeric, the chemical DMT is produced. It is an hallucinogen in the same family as LSD. This is what *the people* call Wattle Toddy.

AUTHOR'S NOTE

I wrote the first words of the first draft of this story in Queenstown, New Zealand in the Winter of 2018. I began writing in optimism. I believed that the lives of my grandchildren would be broadly similar to mine; that Western Civilisation would change and grow but by and large remain viable. This story was merely a thought experiment. What if humans weren't the dominant species on the planet? Would the environmentalists of my generation be so sanguine about nature?

Now, as I have come to the end of my story, I have become convinced that the mighty edifice of Western Civilisation is on the brink of ruin and the world my generation is leaving to our grandchildren will be as hostile as the world of Fire-in-his-hair and No-point-shoe.

Many times, as I worked on this story, I felt like Sleeps-in-the-sun, hiding in her burrow with her litter, despairing of life and merely going through the motions. The sunny optimism I felt in the Queenstown public library seems like a distant memory for me now.

But writing a book is not a act of optimism. It is a act of hope. That is why I'm writing this for you, my grandchildren's grandchildren. I will never know you in this life, and you will only glimpse me through the dark glass of my written words. But I would like you to know that you have been on my mind constantly as I've written this story. Throwing my words forward into the dark tempest of the future, hoping that they give you some comfort. Consider it an apology for my failure to leave you a world as safe as the one that was left for me.

Don't despair. No matter what the future holds, as we fight the long defeat, there is always something bigger at play. Life, Love, The Earth itself; manifestations of a greater Thou that demands our allegiance and our trust.

We are not bearers of the Fire. The Fire carries us.

Darren Koch
Melbourne
Australia
December 2021

darrenk_au@yahoo.co.uk

www.ingramcontent.com/pod-product-compliance
Lightning Source LLC
Chambersburg PA
CBHW050103120726
47904CB00004B/1204